"A fascinating and exciting mystery that combines faith and historical fiction. Utilizing a riveting plot, the book shows the purposes of God throughout."

DR. GREGORY HACKETT
Senior Pastor, Bridge Community Church, Warrenton, VA

"Groux is a gifted writer with an amazing ability to balance unpredictability and imagination inside a purpose-filled dialogue. The questions that the characters raise about the meaning of life and the connection with a greater power are so crucial for our teens to contemplate."

BRYCE TAYLOR
Young Adult Pastor & Youth Speaker, Lancaster, PA

"Infused with Arthurian legend, grounded in faith, framed by the struggle between good and evil, the intricate plot, created by this talented young author, captures the reader in the adventures of Cassie, endowed with unique Brenwyd talents, and her three teenage friends, in their dedicated pursuit to rescue Cassie's captive parents. In the process, they interact with mysterious characters, careen back in time to meet King Arthur himself, and discover astonishing information about their own heritage. An imaginative and gripping tale!"

ELIZABETH DUNKMAN RIESZ, PH.D.
Education Consultant, Iowa City, Iowa

"*Brenwyd Legacy: Finding Secrets* grabs your attention from the very start. It is the perfect blend of mystery, fantasy, and adventure mixed with likable characters. This is the perfect read for any YA reader looking for a great book!"

GRACE PETRONZIO
Young reader, Warrenton, VA

Brenwyd Legacy

Book 2

Brenwyd Legacy

BOOK 2

FINDING SECRETS

Rosemary Groux

Illustrations by Margaret Syverud

BELIEVE BOOKS
Stories That Inspire
WASHINGTON, DC

All scripture quotations, unless otherwise indicated, are taken from the Holy Bible, New International Version®, NIV®. Copyright ©1973, 1978, 1984, 2011 by Biblica, Inc.™ Used by permission of Zondervan. All rights reserved worldwide. www.zondervan.com The "NIV" and "New International Version" are trademarks registered in the United States Patent and Trademark Office by Biblica, Inc.™

 Believe Books is a registered trade name of Believe Books, LLC of Washington, DC. www.BelieveBooks.com

Print ISBN: 978-0-9817061-4-6
E-book ISBN: 978-0-9817061-6-0

Cover design: *Jack Kotowicz, Washington, DC, VelocityDesignGroup.com*
Layout design: *Annie Kotowicz, AnnieKotowicz.com*
Illustrations: *Margaret Syverud*

First Edition

Printed in the United States of America

Publisher's Cataloging-In-Publication Data
(Prepared by The Donohue Group, Inc.)

Groux, Rosemary.
  Brenwyd legacy. Book 2, Finding secrets / Rosemary Groux ; illustrations by Margaret Syverud. ~ First edition.

    pages : illustrations ; cm

    Summary: Cassie and her friends journey to Glastonbury where they are suddenly thrust through a musical time slip that takes them to a kingdom ruled by the legendary King Arthur. Before they can return and finish the rescue mission they began in their own era, the four friends discover that they have a vital role to play in this one. But in order to preserve the legacy of this kingdom, they must first uncover several secrets and fight for their lives.
    Interest age level: 14 and up.
    Issued also as an ebook.
    ISBN: 978-0-9817061-4-6

    1. Gifted persons~Fiction. 2. Time travel~Fiction. 3. Arthur, King~Fiction. 4. Camelot (Legendary place)~Fiction. 5. Secrecy~Fiction. 6. Good and evil~Fiction. 7. Fantasy fiction. 8. Christian fiction, American. I. Syverud, Margaret. II. Title. III. Title: Finding secrets

PS3607.R689 B742 2014
813/.6

Once again I dedicate this book to God
and place it entirely in His hands
to do with as He will.

"FOR I KNOW THE PLANS
I HAVE FOR YOU, DECLARES THE LORD,
PLANS TO PROSPER YOU AND NOT TO HARM YOU,
PLANS TO GIVE YOU HOPE AND A FUTURE."

Jeremiah 29:11

Contents

Acknowledgments

My first thanks goes to God for helping me figure out the ideas and the storyline for this part of the trilogy, even though, much like Cassie, the central idea was one I had shied away from initially.

My next round of "thank-yous" goes to my family. All the support I've received from them has been great.

Annie, thank you for helping me iron out the inconsistencies in this story. You really made me stretch my brain at times, given the premise, but it all worked.

Mrs. Haskett, thanks for coordinating everything and working so hard to get the galley copies out for the Atlanta ICRS conference and all the other work you've done for these books.

Mr. Kotowicz, again the cover design is absolutely amazing.

Thank you to Dr. Celia King, our wonderful copy editor, for your professional touch in making sure the text is free from error and for your enthusiastic support of this project.

Thanks also to Meg Syverud for creating the fantastic illustrations and for always accepting our comments and suggestions with grace, especially when we kept asking for details that went above and beyond our original description.

Foreword

Brenwyd Legacy should be in every family's library of books. In *Finding Secrets*, the second in this trilogy, the story brings fresh new characters to life. You might think the plot would slow down in the second book and maybe even backpedal, but the plot keeps getting thicker and the adventure more intense! In reading through a chapter, I would find myself compelled to go back and read it over again because the adventure of it literally stole me away.

Rosemary Groux is a gifted writer with an amazing ability to balance unpredictability and imagination inside a purpose-filled dialogue. The questions that the characters raise about the meaning of life and the connection with a greater power are so crucial for our teens to contemplate. You will want to read along and discuss the character struggles that happen within this story with your young readers just because of the very real nature of these struggles.

I'm working with my own preteen son, in determining his ability to perceive what is real and what is imagined, and to help him contemplate that there is a spiritual realm, which we don't see but is very real. This book served as an opener to that discussion. Even in my thirties, I loved this book and look forward to reading the third and final portion of the trilogy.

As I have worked with teens through the years, I have always tried to refer excellent books to their parents, to help them in keeping their teen/preteen in good reading material. This book certainly fills the bill, especially if you are wanting a great primer to prepare your young readers for Tolkien or C.S. Lewis.

I hope and pray that this trilogy serves not only as entertainment but as a tool for individuals and families to discern, and learn to confront, the very real spiritual battles happening all around us every day.

Bryce Taylor
Young Adults Pastor and Youth Speaker
Lancaster, PA

PREVIOUSLY, IN BOOK 1:

FINDING TRUTH

*I*n ancient times, a special people known as the Brenwyds were blessed by God for their faithfulness, and marked with pointed ears to set them apart. They were given the ability to hear the silent songs emitted by every living thing, songs usually heard only by God. From the beginning of creation such songs were meant to rise in praise, but when a person is injured, their song suffers. A Brenwyd who listened to it could sing the right notes to mend its broken melodies, and thereby heal the person. What seemed to be a magical act was in fact a natural talent of the Brenwyd people, in addition to their keen senses, sharp reflexes, and exceptional beauty. They could also hear the thoughts of animals, and sometimes of other humans. Because of their strange abilities, the Brenwyds wrongly came to be feared as wizards and witches in medieval Europe. They were hunted nearly to extinction, forcing many to go into hiding. History nearly forgot them, except as the basis for stories of elves. In the modern day, Brenwyd blood continues to run through the veins of some families, but has become so diluted that for centuries Brenwyds have had neither pointed ears nor the remarkable abilities of their ancestors. Until Cassie.

Finding Truth, the first book of the *Brenwyd Legacy*, begins when a Brenwyd leader named Caelwyn dies in a fight against Mordred, the infamous knight of Arthurian lore – but not before whispering a prophecy that will haunt him for years to come. Fifteen hundred years later, in the present, a young girl named Cassandra Pennington wakes up one morning to discover that her ears have become pointed, literally overnight. Shocked, she informs her parents, who in turn inform her that she is descended from the Brenwyds. She has heard of them through stories told by her father Tyler, a history professor and archaeologist. Cassie is amazed to discover that those stories are actually true, though it does explain her lifelong ability to speak to animals.

For the next four years Cassie continues a relatively normal life on her family's horse farm in central Virginia, but always keeps her ears hidden under a headband, and begins to learn fighting techniques from her father. Although there is no sign of immediate danger, Cassie and her parents are aware of a hidden threat – an organization called the Reficul Brotherhood, begun in the sixth century by Mordred and now led by a mysterious Master, that will stop at nothing to wipe out all Brenwyd blood from the earth.

On Cassie's fourteenth birthday, she and her two best friends, twins David and Sarah Thompson, ride on horseback into the nearby Blue Ridge Mountains for a camping trip. But Cassie's mother's horse comes to them with devastating news: the Brotherhood has found the Penningtons, and Cassie's parents have been captured. Leaving a bewildered Sarah and David on the mountain, as they know nothing of her secret, Cassie races back home on her black mare Twi, with dogs Kai and Dassah following. She arrives just in time to save her father's horse, Chance, who was badly hurt during the Brotherhood's attack. Cassie heals the horse with song, using her special ability for the first time. She then sets out after her parents, whom the Brotherhood have taken far into the mountains, and phones her friends with a vague explanation that only leaves them more concerned.

David and Sarah hurry back to the valley after Cassie's call. Their parents know of the Penningtons' Brenwyd heritage and explain it to the twins, who sneak out later that night to go after Cassie. They and their dog Gracie catch up to their friend before she reaches the Brotherhood, and they all journey together to the enemy campsite. Unfortunately they are too late to rescue Cassie's parents, and watch hopelessly as the Brotherhood spirits the captives away on a plane to England. The three teens then decide to investigate the camp, not realizing that men have been left behind to capture Cassie. She and her friends fight for their lives, along with their animals, and end up killing all of the remaining Brotherhood members in self-defense – except for William, the fifteen-year-old son of the Commander who was leading the mission. William hides himself in a tent to see how things turn out, then makes it appear that he himself was a Brotherhood prisoner. Cassie and the twins have doubts, but decide to bring him home with them anyway.

Back in the Pennington's library, the group stumbles across a diary that once belonged to Caelwyn, whom Cassie knows was an early Brenwyd leader and a close associate of King Arthur. A prophecy in the diary states that one of Caelwyn's descendents, working with the heir of Arthur, will one day bring down the Brotherhood, and so start to heal the rift between humans and Brenwyds.

In other notes from the library, the teens learn that Mr. Pennington has been working to discover the location of King Arthur's treasure chamber, which is why the Brotherhood has kidnapped him instead of killing him. Cassie suspects that there is something very important and specific that the Brotherhood wants to find in the treasure hoard. Armed with notes that could help them find it, and desperately wanting to free her parents, Cassie proposes that they go to England, and the twins' father, Ben Thompson, agrees to take them.

The more time William spends in Cassie's company, the more uncertain he feels about his plan to betray her into Brotherhood hands. His organization teaches that Brenwyds are witches intent on enslaving humanity, but Cassie is kind, compassionate, and seemingly not very magical. William is thrown into further turmoil upon attending church with his new friends and hearing a message preached on the power of God's grace. As they all travel to England, he remains conflicted over whether to go through with his original mission, or help rescue Cassie's parents from the Brotherhood headquarters as he has promised.

Arriving in London with her friends and her two dogs, Cassie arranges to have lunch with Dr. Sadie Stone, a colleague of her father's who was helping him with the King Arthur project. Dr. Stone unfortunately has no useful information to offer Cassie, but reveals privately to William that she is a Brotherhood informant and the one responsible for the Pennington's capture. Swayed by her influence, he decides to betray Cassie after all.

The group then journeys to the hill known as Cadbury Castle, which Cassie's father believes to have been the site of the legendary Camelot and thus of the treasure hoard. There, William lures them into a Brotherhood ambush. Cassie and the others are captured and taken to the Brotherhood headquarters in Carlisle. On the way they stop for the night and William wanders off alone, full of remorse over what he's done. Realizing that he was wrong all along, he kneels to ask God for forgiveness and salvation. He then determines to do whatever it takes to get Cassie and the Thompsons out.

Before heading back inside, William makes a startling discovery: Twi, Fire, and Dreamer, the horses belonging to his three new friends from Virginia, have arrived in England. They reveal to William that they are descended from Brenwyd horses, and so can make their thoughts heard by humans (as can Kai, who is descended from Brenwyd dogs). Moreover, they can transfer almost instantly from place to place once they reach a high galloping speed, as long as they or their rider have been to the destination before.

The next day the whole party arrives at the Brotherhood head-quarters, an ancient castle built from dark stone. Cassie and the twins are thrown in a dungeon cell, while Mr. Thompson is locked up with Cassie's parents. William visits both sets of prisoners later that day, to apologize for his mistake and explain his plan to free them. The parents urge William to get their children out first, since they are locked up at the other end of the castle and it may not be possible to free both groups. When William goes to talk to Cassie and the twins, they are suspicious, but decide to trust him. He is their only chance.

That night, William succeeds in helping Cassie, David, and Sarah sneak out through secret tunnels underneath the castle, but they are forced to leave the parents behind. Once out, the teens escape south on their horses. At first they intend to ride to Cadbury before coming back for the parents, but Cassie ends up feeling that it would be better to go to Glastonbury, although she can't say exactly why. The others decide to follow her lead, and the journey begins.

PROLOGUE

England, Early October, 516 A.D.

A girl watched in silence as a group of people and animals gathered around a body in a forest clearing. Tears welled up in her eyes as she listened to the dogs' mournful howling. The girl yearned to approach the group and try to comfort them, but she had a job to do, the last command given to her by her mentor, and if she ran late, the consequences would be severe. Thanks to her mentor, there was a brief window of time to accomplish the task at hand, but if she didn't take quick advantage of it, the opportunity would slip away.

She felt a gentle tug on her pant leg. "I know, I know," the girl whispered to the black mare she was mounted on, who had bent her head around to pull on the piece of clothing. "We need to go." She turned her head to the other mare beside them, a dark bay. Her head drooped low in sorrow and, she suspected, guilt. "It's not your fault, you know," the girl told her soothingly, laying a hand on her neck. "Now come on, we've got to hurry. We can't miss the opening." She turned the mare and squeezed her into a walk, the other mare following behind. When the girl judged they were far enough away from the people that the hoofbeats would not cause alarm, she urged the horses into a fast gallop. Her mare picked up speed until their surroundings blurred and a city appeared in front of them. As they slowed, the girl looked around anxiously. She rested her right hand on the hilt of a long knife, one of two belted at her waist, but relaxed slightly as she sensed another equine in the area, then saw a horse and rider emerge from the trees.

"You're late," the rider said.

"Sorry. I... I just needed to stop for a moment," the girl said, her voice cracking. The rider nodded his understanding, his own eyes blinking hastily. "Any sign of them?" the girl inquired after a moment in a stronger voice.

"No, but that doesn't mean they haven't been and gone already." The two quickly pressed up close to the city's wall and rode along it. The gate was locked at this time of night, but there was another way to enter the city in times of need. They dismounted and the girl strode to several large boulders lying together. She examined each carefully, looking for the marking of a small cross. She spotted it faintly etched on a boulder that came to her waist and was easily as wide as her body was tall. Motioning to the boy to help her, they pushed against the rock with their combined strength. Fortunately, the inside latch was open, and the boulder slowly moved from its position, revealing a large hole that led down into the earth. There was a ladder which they descended, leaving the horses to wait and keep watch.

Once inside the tunnel, the boy used a crudely fashioned windlass to close the opening, leaving it open just a crack. The tunnel was dark, and made of packed earth and wooden support beams, but as the girl could see fairly well in the dark, she quickly found and lit a torch. She took the lead and within twenty minutes found a door through which the two entered a long stone hallway. The girl looked up and down the corridor as the boy closed the door. No one was to be seen, and they walked quickly and quietly until they reached another door. The girl knocked on it, hoping that no harm had come to the person inside. She heard footsteps and felt a huge wave of relief sweep through her as a woman opened the door. The woman's eyes widened slightly upon seeing them. "Is she... is she... dead?" the woman asked in a whisper, taking in their unusually solemn expressions.

The girl nodded, unable to speak. The woman's face displayed utter grief, and tears rose in her eyes and trailed down her cheeks as she raised a hand to her mouth. "It's time to go," the girl said after a pause. "She killed all the men Mordred had with him, but he might come back with more. And we have to be there at the spot when it opens."

The woman blinked, then closed her eyes and leaned against the door. She knew what the girl spoke of, but had dearly hoped it would not be necessary. "The girls?" she asked, worry and pain lacing her voice.

"We'll come back to check on them," the boy told her. "Right now, our main focus is making sure you get to where you need to go safely."

The woman sighed resignedly. "I prayed it wouldn't come to this, but it seems God has other plans. Very well," she said, opening her eyes again. "Give me... give me a moment to get ready." The girl looked into her deep blue eyes and nodded. The woman disappeared into the room, reappearing several minutes later in clothes more suitable for riding, with a bag at her side. The three hurried back through the door, down the tunnel, up the ladder, and out of the city. The horses were waiting for them.

"Let's go. We can't waste any time," the girl hissed to her companions as they mounted quickly, and her mare leaped into a gallop. Their surroundings once again blurred and an island appeared from the marshland in front of them, with a single small building at its peak. A bridge connected the island's inhabitants to those of the rest of the land. Thick mist rose off the water like tendrils of smoke, a heavier fog blanketing the landscape and reducing visibility. The girl reined in her horse and turned her as her companions emerged from the night behind her.

"A little warning next time would be nice," the boy told her.

Her lips twitched in what would have been a smile at any other time. "I'll try. We just took off a little more quickly than I was expecting." She looked at the woman. "Are you alright?" The woman nodded, a carefully composed expression on her face, sensing the double meaning in the question.

"Do I go now?" she inquired of the girl.

The girl shrugged. "Not sure. I have to listen to the slip first, and it's on the other side of the hill. Come on." The three riders quickly crossed the bridge, and sat in silence once they reached their destination over the hill. The girl closed her eyes, using her special ability to single out a particular melody from the many that she sensed. She found it quickly, as it was much louder than the others and was growing in strength and intensity with every second.

"Now?" the woman asked.

The girl hesitated, listening... listening... and heard the melody reach its full crescendo. The strength of it almost took her breath away. "Now!" she answered.

The woman's eyes reflected some fear and sorrow, but also determination and resignation. "Very well," she said. The girl tensed suddenly and scanned the countryside surrounding them. The horses went on the alert as well. "What is it?" The woman's voice held a tinge of alarm.

"I'm not entirely sure," the girl replied, lifting a bow from its resting place on her saddlebow and taking an arrow from the quiver on her back. "You have to go. It won't stay open for long."

The woman looked at the girl and boy. "You be careful. Please, tell my family that... that I..." She couldn't seem to get the words out, and tears threatened to spill from her eyes.

"I'll tell them," the girl said gently. "Don't worry." She paused for a moment. "One more thing: when you see us next, do *not* tell us anything. Just push us through the slip at about nine-thirty that night. You'll know what that means when the time comes." The woman narrowed her eyes, about to ask a question, but the boy stymied her.

"Really, you need to go." He slapped the bay mare's flank gently with the flat of his sword and the mare started forward into a trot, carrying the woman with her. She continued for several yards until she and her rider hit a certain point, and then vanished. The girl, listening, heard the melody begin to wane and then suddenly plummet in volume to almost nothing, and she knew they had gotten through. She heaved a sigh of relief, but didn't relax. Not yet. She warily replaced her bow and arrow as she and the boy headed back across the bridge.

Having crossed the bridge, they were about to urge their mounts to a faster speed on the flat plains when the girl saw movement in the mist and dug her heels into her mare's side, crying out to the boy to do the same. But before she had gone more than a few feet, she heard him cry out in pain. She reined her mare in severely, causing her to rear, and spun her around on her haunches. She ducked as an arrow streaked toward her, whistling only a few inches above her head. She reached the boy, and saw an arrow deeply embedded in his upper arm, blood flowing in a thin trickle from the wound. The arrowhead kept it from bleeding more, but his teeth were gritted in pain. She snatched up her bow and grabbed an arrow, setting it to the string and shooting in the direction of the attacker. She followed it with two more, and heard the dull thunk of a body striking the ground. No more arrows came from the trees and she assumed she'd hit the bowman.

"How bad is it?" she asked the boy, snapping off the end of the arrow to make it less of a hazard.

He let out a low groan as the movement jostled the arrowhead. "Bad. It's... my sword arm. Is... help coming?" he gasped out, grimacing in pain. "We need... to get out of here. We did it." She nodded, looking around. Were the men out there simply bandits, or were they Mordred's men? Five cloaked men on horses appeared from the fog. The teens turned their horses, but six more men rose up in front of them. They were surrounded.

One of the men stepped forward, and the girl shivered in recognition as he spoke. His words answered her unspoken question. "Well, well, who have we here? Caelwyn's wards? Perhaps you would be so kind as to tell us who it was that departed several minutes ago?"

"We'll be keeping that to ourselves, if you don't mind," the girl said.

"I do mind, as it happens. And your reluctance indicates that it may be the person my men and I are seeking." The man paused. His next words were directed to the boy. "If you tell us where she went, we shall let you and the girl go in peace. If not, we will take the girl with us and persuade her to tell us, and Mordred certainly will if we can't. You cannot defend her with a wounded arm. It will be much better for you and the girl if you answer my questions."

The boy scowled. "If you try to take her... you will regret it. She's quite capable of defending herself... I assure you."

"Is that so?" the man asked. "Well then, shall we test it?" The men began to close in around the boy and girl. The two exchanged glances, knowing they had no choice but to defend themselves. The girl whipped another arrow from her quiver and set it on the string – drawing, aiming, and releasing all at once. The speaker collapsed to the ground an instant later. The other men paused their advance for several heartbeats as they fully processed what had happened, allowing the girl to send off another arrow and the boy to painfully draw his sword from his scabbard before the men charged the two teenagers. Then everything became a blur of slashing, blocking, cutting, parrying, stabbing...

The Camelot House

Cassie Pennington jerked awake with a start, breathing hard, half expecting to see men with swords attacking her. She shook her head slowly as she sat up. What a dream! Never had she dreamed so vividly before! It had felt like she had actually been there participating in the events, as if taking part in a movie. She'd had some pretty weird dreams before, but nothing like this one. She looked out across the camp, hoping she hadn't woken anybody. Sarah still slept soundly beside her, swaddled in a blanket, a peaceful expression on her face. On the other side of the fire, Cassie saw two unmoving lumps in blankets, which she knew to be David and William.

She stood and stretched, wincing at the pain in her sore muscles. Riding for an hour or two at a time was all well and good, but riding almost nonstop for a week over hilly and sometimes mountainous English countryside was not something she had thought to prepare herself for. Fortunately, William had said that they'd reach Glastonbury today. Or tonight, rather, she thought, looking up at the sun. They'd done a lot of their traveling by night, trying to avoid people, towns, and roads, and they had traveled much faster than she thought was possible. Sometimes they had ridden all night and then gone for hours in the daylight as well. Both dogs and horses had shown incredible speed and stamina over the journey.

Seeing the sun low on the horizon, she calculated that they should head out in about an hour. Since they were close to their goal, they could afford to rest a little longer. She turned back to the campsite, noting that the dogs, Kai and Dassah, slept as heavily as the humans. She looked around for the horses and spotted them grazing a short distance away. She headed over to them. "Hey, guys. No alarms while we slept?"

Nope, her black mare, Twi, replied, lifting her Arabian-looking head. *Only a few birds and rabbits.*

"That's good, though I doubt they'd be able to follow us since we're keeping well outside the towns. I'm more worried about finding them at our destination."

They do not know where we are going, the mare assured her rider. Observing her frown, Twi added, *Are you upset about something?*

Cassie shook her head. "No. I just had a weird dream that woke me up."

What happened in it?

"Well... I'm still sorting that out. There was a boy and a girl, and they took a woman to some island where she galloped off and literally disappeared into thin air. Then they got surrounded by bad guys who started attacking them, and then it ended so I didn't see how it turned out."

Hmm. Sounds like one of those stories you like reading.

"Yes, it does, doesn't it? Maybe it's a result of not reading anything of that sort for the past week."

Perhaps. Twi sounded uninterested and went back to grazing. Cassie sat on the ground, leaning against Twi's legs. Normally this wasn't a safe thing to do, but Cassie knew Twi wouldn't move. It was one of the advantages of being able to talk to your horse. Her thoughts turned once again to her dream, this time wondering about the woman. Never once had she heard her name, but she had clearly been very important. And then there was the fact that she and the horse had just disappeared into nowhere. It didn't make sense, but not much in her life recently had made much sense, and then again, it was a dream. She raised a hand to her ear and fingered its shape, not rounded like a normal person's, but slightly pointed, a tell-tale sign of her Brenwyd ancestry. That ancestry was the reason she was currently sitting out in the middle of nowhere in the English countryside. She still had no idea how she would rescue her parents and Mr. Thompson from the Reficul Brotherhood, or what she would do next. There was the prophecy, which was somewhat reassuring, but she had no idea how to go about that either, and frankly, it freaked her out.

Her hand fell to the locket clasped at her neck and she opened it, gazing fondly at the images of her parents that were revealed. Could it really be only a day over two weeks since the camping trip that had turned her life upside-down? It seemed like so much longer. Fifteen days since her parents had been captured. Fourteen days since she'd met William. Eight days since leaving the States for England. Seven days since William's betrayal and six since his helping them escape, turning his back on the organization that raised him. He had gotten Cassie, David, and Sarah out of the Brotherhood prison, and now they were fleeing to Glastonbury on horseback. It would have been much easier to use the transfer ability that Brenwyd horses possessed, which allowed them to "tele-port" in a fashion from place to place when they hit a speed normal horses were incapable of achieving. But Phoenix, William's chest-nut gelding, was not a Brenwyd horse, and there was also the prob-lem of transporting the dogs, not to mention none of the teens had ever been to Glastonbury. It had come as a surprise to Cassie and the twins to learn that their horses were Brenwyd horses and had this unique ability, but Cassie privately thought it made sense be-cause all three had a large portion of Thoroughbred blood, and the modern Thoroughbred breed owed much of its origin to England, where the Brenwyds had made their home. It made her wonder about Phoenix, whom she could tell was a good chunk Thoroughbred, but the gelding had shied away from her questions and she figured he would have said if he was a Brenwyd horse.

Cassie looked down at her wrists and studied the faint, crisscross pattern of scars that now covered them, a souvenir from her time in devil's iron chains as a prisoner in the Brotherhood headquarters. Though the metal temporarily stripped Brenwyds of their vitality and special gifts, she had finally been able to heal what remained of her wounds, but the scars remained. Her thoughts returned to her dream. She was sure the girl had represented her, and both the boy and woman were familiar. However, though she could make a guess as to the boy's identity, she had no clue where the woman had come from. The events depicted matched no story Cassie ever remembered reading or hearing. Cassie tried to remember what exactly the woman had looked like, but the details were fading in her memory. She could picture long hair and blue eyes, but the image of her face was blurred. The details of the city she'd glimpsed were fading as well. Then there was the body in the clearing. Who had that been?

As Cassie continued to ponder the dream, she realized it seemed similar, in a way, to a dream she'd had back in the States, after translating her father's notes about the project for which the Brotherhood had kidnapped him. Cassie had thought the other dream was just random, even if it had given her an idea of what the Brotherhood might be after in Arthur's treasure trove, but now she wasn't so sure. That dream had referred to the King Arthur story, she knew, and hadn't one of the men in her recent dream mentioned Mordred? Perhaps it was just a sign she was thinking about her father's stories too much.

"Cassie!" a familiar British voice called. She looked up. Apparently, he hadn't noticed her sitting down next to Twi.

"I'm over here, William. Don't panic," she said, standing up. William wasn't that far off, but he was looking in the wrong direction.

He turned around, relief evident in his blue eyes as he caught sight of her. "I wasn't panicking. I was just concerned," he said.

She chuckled. "Yeah, right, and I'm the queen of England."

William looked at her askance, the strong breeze ruffling his black hair and blowing wisps of Cassie's own strawberry-blond hair into her face. "Well, you definitely are not, but you're still wrong."

"Am I?"

"Yeah."

She shrugged. "Okay, whatever. Learn to take a joke, why don't ya?" His only response was to roll his eyes, but she was pretty sure she detected a smile at the corners of his mouth.

They went back to where Sarah and David were getting out some of their dwindling food stores, namely granola bars. The twins looked up when they heard them coming. "Went for a stroll, Cass?" David asked. She nodded, and gazed at him intently, deciding that her guess was correct – the boy in the dream could have represented David. But why on earth would David have been in her dream? And he had been shot with an arrow. She had no idea why her subconscious would imagine that. "Cassie? Are you okay?" he asked.

"Fine. Why do you ask?" she queried.

He gave her a careful look. "You were looking at me funny."

"Sorry. I was just thinking."

"'Bout what?" Sarah asked. Her hazel eyes still looked sleepy, but she seemed alert enough. Her long, dark brown hair, the same shade as her brother's, was tied back in a ponytail, but Cassie could see it was much curlier than usual, likely because of the length of time since any of them had had access to a real bathroom and its niceties.

"Oh, just a dream I had this morning," Cassie said, sitting down.

Kai cocked his head at her. Neither he nor Dassah had deigned to move from their sleeping places just yet. The trek was hardest on them, having to keep up with the horses while on a lean diet, so they tried to conserve their energy whenever possible. *What kind of dream?* he asked.

"Just a dream. Nothing important," Cassie said, trying to dismiss his question.

If it was not important, you would not still be thinking about it.

Cassie shrugged. "If you're so interested, I'll tell you, but I don't really get it myself."

"Is anyone supposed to understand dreams?" William asked, raising an eyebrow skeptically.

"Eh, sometimes, maybe," Cassie said. She went on to narrate her dream as they ate their meager meal, describing all she had seen and felt. There was a thoughtful silence when she finished.

David spoke first, in a light, teasing tone. "So you dreamed I got hit by an arrow? Thanks. Now I know where I stand with you."

Cassie laughed. "It was your arm, not your heart, so I'd be grateful if I were you," she said. "And I don't think my thoughts had anything to do with it. I certainly wouldn't want you to get hit with an arrow. It just happened."

"But who was the dead woman in the clearing?" Sarah wondered. "Cassie, maybe it's not just a dream. Normally dreams aren't remembered that well."

"Do you have dreams that somehow turn out to be real, too?" William asked, sounding a little wary. Despite the fact he had realized the Brotherhood perceived Brenwyds all wrong, Cassie knew her abilities still made him feel a bit edgy.

Cassie chuckled. "Not that I know of," she said. She focused on Sarah. "But what else could it be? My brain can think really weird thoughts at times, ya know."

"I know that, but... I don't know... it just doesn't sound like something you would just think up randomly," Sarah said. "You've told me some weird dreams you've had before, and they were just weird dreams. But the way you describe this one... it sounds different, somehow."

The One often sends His people visions, Dassah said. *It is recorded in the Book. It sounds to me as if you saw something that is yet to happen.*

Cassie looked at the dog skeptically. "A vision? Why would God send me a vision? Not that some guidance wouldn't be helpful, but it looked like it happened a long..." Cassie's voice trailed off as something she'd missed hit her – everything had looked like it belonged in the Middle Ages, not the present day.

"A vision?" William asked. "Where'd that idea come from? You mean like what fortune tellers have in stories and stuff?"

"No," Cassie said. "Dassah just mentioned that in the Bible, lots of people had visions and dreams from God either giving a revelation about something or telling the future. But if the dream was supposed to be helpful, I sure don't get it. Besides, it can't be the future. As I was saying, it looked like it happened far in the past. So I don't think it could be a vision, but for some reason the woman seemed a bit familiar."

"Have you had visions before?" William asked.

"No." Cassie wasn't quite sure why they were all taking the dream so seriously, but figured it was preferable to talking and worrying about the Brotherhood. "Anyway, the impressions I got are confusing me more than the events. I felt like I – or the main person in the dream – had to hurry, that it was really important to get this woman to the hill in time, important for an urgent reason on a personal level. But if it was a vision and not just a dream, then it was of something that happened hundreds of years ago. It definitely couldn't have occurred recently. There is no logical way it could've been me, or David, but that's what I think I saw. Even the horses were the same. But that makes absolutely no sense." Everyone sat quietly, trying to figure it out. Cassie realized as soon as the words left her mouth just how impossible it all sounded, but enough strange things had happened lately to make her believe in almost anything. Except flying pigs. Maybe.

Describe the woman to us, Kai said. *Perhaps we can help you figure out why she looked familiar.*

"That's the thing. I don't remember exactly what her face looked like. She had blue eyes and long hair, but I couldn't tell the exact color," she said. "It looked brown, with maybe a hint of red." They all were silent in contemplation.

Cassie found her eyes resting on William, who returned her gaze steadily. "Don't look at me. Just because I have blue eyes doesn't mean I have a clue as to who she is," he said.

"Sorry." Her gaze moved to the surrounding countryside. Suddenly, something clicked in her brain as she thought of the foggy island. "That tower on the Tor was constructed around the fifteenth century as part of a church, right?"

"I think so," William said. "Why?"

"Because I think I just realized what the island is. Or was. I think it's the Glastonbury Tor."

In the wee hours of the morning, Cassie finally spotted their objective on the horizon. She had never seen it in person before, only in pictures, but it was unmistakable. She stopped Twi, and pointed to it. "There's the Tor. Not too far off now." Her voice was tired, and the others were all slumped on their horses.

David squinted, trying to see what Cassie was indicating. "Where?" he asked wearily.

"Right... oh, you guys may not be able to see it just yet. But we should reach it before long."

"As long as we get there, I'll be happy," Sarah said. "Do you think any hotels would take in four minors?"

Cassie groaned. "Don't mention the thought of a soft bed right now. I'll consider it when it's a reality." They moved off again.

"What exactly are we going to do when we get there?" David asked.

"Recuperate and figure out what to do next," Cassie replied.

"Any idea what that will be?"

"Not really. But we'll think of something."

David contented himself with that, too tired to inquire further. Cassie, on the other hand, felt her energy level rising with every step Twi took. Some sense told her that this was where they needed to go, echoing her initial feeling a week ago. Scrutinizing the distant hill, she decided that she was right in guessing that the island and the Tor were one and the same. She had once read that hundreds of years ago the area around Glastonbury had been swampy and marshy. Twi seemed to feed off her rider's energy and started stepping out more vigorously. "Anybody feel like a trot?" Cassie asked, strangely eager to reach the iconic hill as quickly as possible.

"Okay," William said, though without enthusiasm. "It'll help me keep awake, at any rate." The twins nodded assent and the teens urged their horses into the bouncy gait. They continued in a walk-trot pattern for a while, until they weren't far from the foot of the Tor. There they halted.

"Now what?" Sarah asked.

"I'd say make camp for what remains of the night, and find something more permanent in the... er, later this morning, rather," David said.

"Sounds good to me," Cassie said. They found a copse of dense trees with some soft ground to lie on, and everyone quickly fell into a deep sleep.

Gwen Smith sat up in bed and looked out the window letting in the first morning rays of sun. She didn't have to get up so early, but it was merely habit and she was too old to change now. Besides, the guests and children would be rising soon enough and they would need their breakfast. She headed to the kitchen to prepare it. Despite having lived here for nearly sixteen years, the ease with which she could do kitchen tasks that had once taken her kitchen staff enormous effort continually amazed her. If only she hadn't had to pay such a price... she shook her head of those thoughts and concentrated on making breakfast. Once that was done, she took some time to herself to read and pray, as was her custom, and then went to take care of her horse, Wynne. Usually by the time she was done with that, the first of the children were up and ready to eat, followed soon after by guests eager to start the day. Today was no exception.

It was as she was feeding the late risers at about nine that her day started to take an unusual turn. Katie, an eight-year-old foster child who had been with Gwen for about a year, rushed into the kitchen with news, exciting news to judge by the gleam in her light blue eyes. "Miss Gwen, Miss Gwen, there are four teenagers outside who would like breakfast. And they have two dogs! They're very dirty, but one of the girls says it's just because they haven't been able to take a bath in a while, not because they like being that way."

Gwen smiled at the little girl and patted her fair head gently. "Well then, why don't you invite them in? Everyone is welcome at my table." As Katie rushed off, Gwen moved to the window so she could see the teenagers in question before she met them. Her predecessor had started the inn years ago to give help to any who might need it, but to children especially as a foster home. The guests who frequented the place provided the revenue to cover its expenses, and many children had passed through the house as the years went by. But as charming as the children were, there were places in Gwen's heart that only a certain few people could fill, and she had lost them all long ago.

Looking out the window, she saw a group of the children clustered around four taller figures slowly making their way to the inn door. Gwen lived on the outskirts of Glastonbury, and the location appeared fairly isolated, though others actually did live close by. Her long driveway afforded her a good view of whoever might be coming up it. She saw now that most of the children's excitement was centered around the two dogs Katie had mentioned. The smaller one was medium-sized and looked like a Border collie. The bigger one was dark brown and resembled a wolf-hound, though not so big, and it reminded her strongly of dogs she once knew... *but that is behind me now,* she thought. She shifted her attention to the humans. There were two boys and two girls. One of the girls, with braided hair, bent down to one of the smaller children and seemed to whisper something that caused the child to giggle. The teenage girl smiled, and Gwen felt her heart warm toward her instantly, though a moment later her eyes narrowed as she continued to study her. She was close enough now for Gwen to see that her hair was strawberry-blond, her face was dirty, and her clothes were a little the worse for wear. The other girl had wavy, dark-brown hair in a ponytail, and resembled one of the boys so closely Gwen had a feeling they were brother and sister. The final boy had black hair, was the tallest, and his face... his face was achingly familiar.

Gwen felt her heart nearly stop, and she put a supporting hand on the windowsill, hardly daring to believe what her eyes were telling her. Yes, it had been sixteen long years, but was everything truly coming to pass at last? *Oh God, let it be so.*

❦

Cassie smiled at the little girl in her arms. "You're sure your mother won't mind us coming in?" she asked her.

The girl shook her head. "Nope!"

"She's not our mother," another voice piped up. Cassie looked at a fair-haired girl who seemed about seven or eight. "We don't have parents, but that's okay 'cause Miss Gwen takes care of us. She's the best mum anyone could have. And she sent me here herself to tell you to come in." The girl looked very pleased with herself for delivering this announcement.

Cassie smiled at her, and looked at William. "Trust my instincts now?" she asked, putting the girl down.

William returned the look. "I'll thank you when this woman gives us food and doesn't turn us out. You can't be sure. Although, please tell me if she gives you a Dr. Stone feeling."

"I will. But you have to admit, the sign was promising." They'd left the horses in the copse of trees and ventured out, hoping to get to Glastonbury, but they'd come across the sign for this inn and decided to try their luck. The sign had said:

The Camelot House
Everyone Welcome

They had been ambushed by the children halfway up the driveway as they ventured toward the large house. It looked like it had three stories, and the outward design was Tudor style, with white walls, a pitched roof, and decorative half-timbering. A woman came to the doorway and smiled at them, but Cassie thought she detected eagerness and something else in her eyes, something like... recognition? Or was it incredulity? The woman spoke to the children in a kind voice, scolding them good-naturedly. "Now, let them at least get in the door unhindered." The children backed away some, but they hung around Kai and Dassah.

"Can we play with the dogs?" a boy around twelve asked.

"If their owner says you can," the woman answered. The children all turned pleading eyes on Cassie and Sarah, and they both chuckled.

"Go ahead," Cassie said. Kai gave her an impression of horror, but she knew he didn't mind. He liked children.

"Please, come in. You look hungry," the woman said.

the
CAMELOT HOUSE
everyone welcome

They ventured toward the large house. The
outward design was Tudor style, with white walls,
a pitched roof, and decorative half-timbering.

"Yes, ma'am," they all chorused. They stepped in and Cassie looked around. The house was simply but elegantly decorated, and was neat and tidy, though some scattered toys made it obvious children lived there.

"I hope we're not imposing," Sarah said to the woman.

The woman smiled. "Not at all." Cassie turned her attention to her, and a slight frown formed on her face. The woman seemed familiar. She looked to be in her late forties to early fifties. Her facial features were strong and striking, though Cassie wouldn't necessarily have called the woman beautiful. Her eyes were blue, her hair a chestnut color with gray mixed in here and there. Cassie wondered where on earth she could have seen her before. Her voice sounded British enough, but Cassie detected a slight lilting quality behind her words that made her wonder if the woman was originally from Ireland. The woman's query jerked her from her ruminations. "What are your names?"

Cassie glanced at her companions, but they indicated that she was to be spokesperson. She gave them a look she hoped conveyed her feelings about that role. "I'm Cassie, and these are Sarah, David, and William." As the woman's gaze passed over all of them, Cassie got a strange feeling that she had known their names already. But how could that be? She noticed the woman's gaze lingered on William especially. *Uh-oh*, she thought. *I hope this woman isn't a Brotherhood informant.*

The woman blinked rapidly several times. "I'm Gwen, and I'm happy to meet you. Come on into the kitchen. There's some breakfast left." She turned quickly and went through a door, but the teens stayed behind, looking at each other.

"Anybody else pick up on how she focused on William?" David asked in a low voice. Cassie nodded, as did Sarah and William.

"Do you think she's like Dr. Stone?" Sarah asked.

William frowned thoughtfully. "I don't know, but we can't be too careful," he said, glancing at Cassie.

"I didn't get the Dr. Stone feeling, but that did come after we'd been with her for a bit." Cassie hesitated an instant before asking, "Did she look familiar to any of you?" They looked at her in surprise and shook their heads.

"Why?" David asked. "Does she look familiar to you?"

"I don't know. I thought so, but maybe I'm just imagining it."

William drew in breath to ask a question, but the woman – Gwen – looked out of the door before he could. "Is something wrong?" she asked.

"Oh, no," Cassie said. "We were just resting a minute." The woman's eyes reflected understanding, but Cassie thought she saw uncertainty as well.

"Been on the road awhile?" she asked. They all nodded. "Well, you can stay here as long as you need to," she told them as they headed through the door.

Cassie frowned. "Um, we really don't have much money–"

"Don't worry about it. I make it my business to help children in need," she said, looking them up and down with a slight smile on her lips, "and I think you qualify."

"I won't argue with that," William said as he sat down at the table. The others seated themselves as well. Cassie couldn't get the faint sense of familiarity out of her mind. Maybe if she figured it out, she'd have a valuable piece of information that could help her. But how? Surely if the woman knew them she would have said so. Cassie tried to dismiss such thoughts from her mind so she could focus on answering the questions Gwen would surely ask.

CONVERSATIONS

Hannah paced the floor, unable to sleep for the worries plaguing her mind. It had been nearly eight days since she had heard from any of the group in England. Ben had promised her that he would call every day, so a silence for this long could only mean one thing: they had been caught by the Brotherhood. She had been praying almost without ceasing, barely eating, and all her friends had noticed that something was on her mind. But she could not tell them what. Gracie thrust her head underneath her woman's hand, and Hannah patted the dog absently. She didn't know it, but the animals were just as worried as she was, and they were worried for her as well. They all tried to help and comfort her as best they could, but they couldn't talk to her, and she couldn't talk to them.

Hannah stopped pacing to kneel, asking God once again to send her family back safely. She had just stood up again when a thought came to her without warning: *Run.* It was as if she had heard the word in her mind, spoken lovingly, but with authority and urgency. She didn't hesitate, grabbing her purse and running to the car, not even stopping to replace her pajamas with jeans and a T-shirt. She started the car and sped down the driveway, deciding to go to the Shelbys'. They wouldn't ask too many questions. Her sudden departure put the animals on alert. Hannah had barely been gone fifteen minutes when a dark van drove up to the house, one that Smokey remembered well. This time, however, there were no horses and there were only three men. Gracie sneaked out of the house, but Smokey stayed, knowing well how to keep himself hidden. With no humans at home to protect, there was no need to attack these men. He watched them tear through the house looking for Hannah.

When it became apparent she was not there, one of the men cursed. "No sign of her. Where would she be at this time of night?" he asked.

"Seems to me like she was warned," another commented.

"Likely by that good-for-nothing traitor," the last agreed. Smokey's ears twitched. Traitor? He knew what the word meant. A traitor to these people meant someone was on the girl's side. Perhaps these people would be able to tell him about the girl, albeit indirectly.

"Aye," the first man growled. He looked around. "Pity she fled. We could have taken her to her husband." He laughed, but the sound grated on Smokey's nerves and sensitive ears.

"Do you know if they've made any progress in tracking the girl?" the second asked. He had what Smokey recognized as an American accent, while the other two spoke like the strange boy from the mountain camp.

"I don't think so. They took off riding across the country, so it will be hard to find them," the first man replied. Smokey crept cautiously from his hiding place so he could see the men and hear them better. This was getting interesting.

"How did they get away so quickly?"

"Through the tunnel system underneath headquarters. We thought only the Master knew how to navigate down there, but apparently William does, too. We were able to find their exit point, and there are a lot of hoofprints, but only William's horse is missing. We're waiting for them to pop up in a town. They have to eventually."

Smokey heard one of the men expel a loud gust of air in what he thought humans called a sigh. His girl did it frequently, especially when something was on her mind. *So the horses have gotten to England*, he thought. *Good.*

"What a blow it must have been to the Commander for his only son to betray us so," the American said. Smokey perked up. Had the strange boy proved a friend after all?

"All the more so for him to lead her to us, and then help her escape," the third man growled.

"Mmm, yes," the first agreed. "Although I've heard that the Commander has started to say that he's not..." They continued speaking, but Smokey heard nothing of interest to him in the rest of the conversation and so dismissed the men. He focused on what he had already heard. His girl had been captured, but she had escaped, with the strange boy's help. Gracie's woman needed to know, and she couldn't come home. He exited the house and told the other animals what he had learned. The men stayed in the house until it was almost dawn, then left, convinced Hannah would not be home anytime soon. They did, however, unknowingly transport two extra passengers in their van.

⁘ⷮⷦⷧⷦⷲ⁘

Cassie was sure breakfast had never tasted so good, though she had heard that "hunger makes the best spice." They certainly hadn't had anything this good on the trail. They hadn't even had anything hot, and she had decided she would never eat granola bars again. Or at least not for a while, at any rate. She ate everything as quickly as politely possible, and noticed the others doing the same. Gwen hadn't asked any questions, simply moving around the kitchen to clean up and refill plates when necessary. Looking out the window, Cassie saw the children romping with the dogs, and their laughter reached the kitchen through an open window. She sensed the dogs were happy to play with the kids, but they were tired and hungry as well. She turned to Gwen.

"I don't suppose you have any dog food," she said somewhat apologetically.

To her surprise, the woman nodded. "Actually, I do. I used to have a dog, and he died just a couple of months ago. I still have some from his last bag. Do you need some?"

Cassie nodded. "Sorry to hear about your dog. So this is a pet-friendly inn, then?" she asked, feeling relieved.

"Oh, yes. I enjoy animals as much as the children do. There's a stable out back where I keep my horse." She appeared to eye Cassie carefully as she said this, as if watching for her reaction.

"You have a horse?" Sarah asked.

The woman smiled. "She's not strictly mine, she belonged to a friend of mine for many years, but I... took the horse in when she died." Sadness crossed her face as she recalled the memory and she turned toward the window.

"What's the horse's name?" Sarah asked.

"Wynne. She's a lovely dark bay mare, but she does get a little lonesome in her stable." Cassie could understand that. Horses were herd animals by nature. Now that she was aware of the horse's existence and her hunger was sated, she did sense her, and sent the mare a polite query as to her welfare.

The mare reacted with surprise, not so much at the question as at the questioner. *When did you get here?* she asked Cassie. Cassie wasn't quite sure how to respond to that. Gwen had turned away from the window and had taken Sarah's plate. Sarah noticed the preoccupied look on Cassie's face and correctly guessed she was speaking to the horse, so she decided to make small talk with their hostess to keep her from questioning Cassie, who likely wouldn't hear the questions the first time. She was quite good at this and was able to keep up a lively dialogue while Cassie probed the mare.

I got here about fifteen minutes ago and have been having breakfast. Your woman is a good cook, Cassie said.

That is not what I meant, girl.

Then what did you mean?

Who are you talking to, girl? came Kai's voice.

I'm talking to the mare, Wynne.

Mare? Ah, I see. How are you, mare?

You, too? And the other one? What are you... Oh, I remember. You have not gone back yet, have you?

What? Cassie asked, extremely befuddled. The mare acted like she knew them... and they should know her. Abruptly she realized the table conversation had stopped and everyone was looking at her. She looked at them. "What?"

"That's what you just said," David answered. "What."

Cassie frowned, puzzled. "I know I just said what. I was asking you what."

"That's what we were wondering. What. What were you asking 'what' for?"

"Whaaat?" Cassie was feeling confused, and she wasn't the only one.

"That's way too many whats," William commented.

"I'd like to know what the original what was," Cassie said.

"That's what we were asking you about," Sarah said.

Cassie looked at her and was about to ask what again, but thought better of it and instead asked, "Why?"

"Because," Gwen supplemented, hiding a smile, "you said *what* a minute ago during a pause and we were wondering what, if I may use that word, prompted you to say it."

"Oh. Umm, I was just wondering what you'd just said. I wasn't listening. Sorry." She heard the dogs' and Wynne's amusement in her mind, so she sent a wave of irritation back at them, which only amused them more. She decided to save talking to them until she could see them and didn't have to worry about making up explanations.

"Quite alright, dear. We were merely discussing the countryside. Sarah tells me you've seen quite a lot of it recently," Gwen said.

That's one way to put it, Cassie thought. "Yeah, we have."

"And what brings you to the English countryside?" The four teens looked at each other. They had agreed on a cover story, but none were quite sure it would work.

"Well, Mrs. Smith..." William began.

Gwen waved a hand at him. "Oh, don't bother with that. You can call me Miss Gwen. All the children do."

"Um, okay then. You see, Miss Gwen, my friends here, as you've probably guessed, are from the States. Our parents have known each other for a while, so they came over to visit. We went out for a ride several days ago, but a big thunderstorm blew up and the horses bolted. We couldn't stop them, and by the time we got them under control and the storm ended we were hopelessly lost. So we've just been wandering around trying to get back to civilization, and your place is the first real stop we've found. We have cell phones, but they're dead, so we haven't been able to contact our parents." He finished and they all watched Gwen anxiously for her reaction. It was close enough to the truth, and they didn't want to bend the truth any more than they had to.

Gwen raised her eyebrows slightly, sensing there were pieces being left out, but she knew she wouldn't get anything more from them at the moment. "Goodness, no wonder you all look so bedraggled. Your parents must be worried sick. Feel free to use the telephone, but would you mind me asking a question first?"

"Not at all," William said.

"Where are your horses? You can't have just left them wandering the countryside."

William had been expecting this question. "We left them tied up a few miles away. We didn't want them getting into trouble."

"Bring them here, by all means. Wynne will be glad for the company, and there's plenty of room in the barn. I'll take you to go get them."

"Oh, we can fetch them ourselves," Cassie said hastily. "A car can't reach the place very easily."

Gwen gazed at her steadily for a few moments. Cassie couldn't read her expression. "Very well. But I need to take the children into town, so will you all be alright here by yourselves?" she asked with motherly concern.

"Oh, yes," Cassie assured.

"You can use the two rooms at the end of the hall on the second floor. No one's in them right now, and the showers are upstairs, too. Make yourselves at home."

Cassie looked gratefully at the woman, but felt she had to make some sort of protest. "We don't have any money–"

"As I said, don't worry about it. I don't need money and you all need somewhere to rest. Enjoy your stay, and welcome to the Camelot House." With that and a warm smile, she turned to go.

❦

Gwen hurried down the hall, grabbing her purse and car keys on her way out the door. Her thoughts were in a chaotic whirl. Yes, Wynne had explained everything to her, but it was different now that they were actually here. Gwen wondered what she should do now, praying for guidance. Should she reveal all that she knew? Would they even believe her? She went out the back door and called the children. They came, but reluctantly, not eager to leave the dogs. She smiled at them. "You don't want to wear them out now, do you?" she asked. They shook their heads. "So let them rest while we're in town, and they'll be ready to play with you again later." The children perked up at this, and the dogs assumed a grateful look.

As the older children helped the younger ones into the van, Gwen looked into the dogs' eyes. "You can go in, it's quite alright. The dog food is in the corner cupboard in the kitchen." The larger one, Kai, cocked his head at her. She had a feeling he was surprised at being directly addressed. The smaller one, Dassah, wagged her tail and entered the house, stopping over the threshold to wait for Kai. He went, but not before giving Gwen a long look.

Cassie listened for the van's engine to start before she let her friends start talking. That gave Kai and Dassah enough time to find them in the house. "Well, what do you think of her?"

"I like her," Sarah said. "I don't think she's like Dr. Stone at all."

David nodded agreement with his twin. "But I bet you she picked up just as much about us from what we didn't say as from what we did say."

"I'd agree with that," Cassie said. "Don't ask me why, but I got this strange feeling that she knows who we are, and is trying to act like she doesn't. But she doesn't feel dangerous. And then there's her horse."

"Would I be right in assuming the horse was the cause of that first 'what'?" William asked with humor in his eyes.

Cassie colored slightly. "Yeah. She was confusing me. I didn't realize I actually said that out loud."

She was confusing me as well, Kai said. *And I think we were confusing her.*

"What did she say?" Sarah asked.

"She asked when we got here, and then what we were doing here, and then asked if we'd gone back yet," Cassie answered.

"Gone back where?"

"I have no idea. That's why I asked 'what'!"

"So ask her what she meant," Sarah said sensibly.

Cassie reached for the mare. *Pardon me, but what did you mean by asking if we'd gone back yet or not? Gone back where?* she queried politely.

The mare hesitated. *I apologize. I thought... I spoke too hastily. You startled me. It is not just anyone who can talk to animals. You are part Brenwyd.*

Yes, I am, but you still haven't explained your comments. Do I know you?

Not yet, the mare replied mysteriously. *Go and get your horses. All will be made clear in* time. She put emphasis on the last word and seemed to find it amusing. Cassie sensed that was all the mare would say on the matter, and she knew better than to try to wrestle answers out of animals. They could be notoriously stubborn. The others were looking at her expectantly.

"Well?" Sarah asked.

Cassie shrugged. "The most definitive thing she said was, 'All will be made clear in time.'"

"You know," William said. "I had the impression that horses didn't talk in riddles."

"Usually, yes, but this horse is apparently an exception. It happens." She sighed. "And maybe it's impossible to talk in simple terms about something that isn't simple."

"Mysteries generally aren't," David pointed out. "That's why they're mysteries."

Dassah nudged Cassie's leg. *Girl, could you get the food? I am starving.*

Cassie started. "Oh, of course! Sorry, I forgot." She got up, but stopped abruptly. "She didn't say where it was."

In the corner cupboard, Kai supplied.

Cassie eyed him quizzically. "And you know that because?" she asked as she went to the cupboard.

The woman told us, Dassah said.

Cassie stared at them. "She told you?" she repeated in disbelief.

Yes, Kai said. *It was... odd. It was as if she knew we could tell you.*

Cassie frowned and put a hand to her headband to make sure it still covered the tips of her ears. "I wonder why."

"This woman seems as mysterious as her horse," William said. The others had caught the gist of the conversation, even though they could not hear Dassah.

"I still like her," Sarah said. "She seems very motherly."

"That doesn't necessarily make a person good, Sarah," David said. He looked over at William. "Why did she focus on you in particular when we were coming in? I don't get it."

William shrugged. "I don't know. I've never seen her before. Maybe I remind her of someone she knows."

Cassie looked up from where she was doling out the dog food. Kai and Dassah watched her like hawks, and it was easy to see that only their well-developed sense of self-discipline kept them from leaping on the bowls as Cassie was judging the correct amount for each of them. A slight whine emerged from Dassah's throat in anticipation. "Likely," she responded. "I never got the Dr. Stone feeling. And I actually listened to her song. It sounds fine, even Christian. I think we should take her up on her offer. It's not like we have a lot of options at the moment, anyway."

"True," William said. "We need somewhere to rest, and there's even a place for the horses."

David nodded. "And I'm not gonna argue with the chance for a shower and mattress." The others agreed emphatically.

"But we should keep an eye out and not stay too long," Cassie cautioned. "The Brotherhood likely won't be far behind us, and I don't want to put anyone in unnecessary danger."

William grimaced. "You're right, and staying in a town will make us more visible. That's just what they'd be looking for." They talked a little longer and decided that the boys would go get the horses and the girls would get the stalls ready. They left the kitchen and went about their separate tasks.

"You know, I don't know if I've ever looked forward to a shower so much," Sarah remarked as she and Cassie went outside.

Cassie laughed. "Yeah," she agreed, "not even when we came back from the mountain trip – Oh!"

"What?" Sarah asked, some alarm in her eyes.

"Your mom. We need to call her."

Sarah smacked her forehead. "I knew there was something we were forgetting. But isn't it, like, 4 or 5 in the morning over there?"

"She probably would want to hear from us anyway. Let's call her as soon as the boys get back." They continued toward the stable. The yard was bigger than they'd thought, and they could clearly see the Tor with the tower on top about a mile away. The barn was a little away from the house, and it looked similar with white walls and dark wood trim. It was a center-aisle barn and Cassie guessed it was made for a maximum of six horses, with an extra room for feed and tack, a grooming stall, and a hay loft. A horse pasture was located right behind it, and in the pasture stood Wynne, her head turned toward the house, ears pricked alertly. Cassie knew she was watching them, and sensed a great excitement from her. As soon as Wynne realized Cassie was examining her, she trotted out of sight, and Cassie saw that the pasture adjoined one side of the barn so Wynne could go in and out of her stall as she wished. She wondered if Wynne would mind sharing her pasture with other horses.

Sarah sneaked a glance at her friend. Her blue-gray eyes were distant, indicating she wasn't thinking about much in particular, or perhaps she was thinking about a lot of things at the same time. Sarah had noticed that vacant expression on Cassie's face more and more often lately, ever since that camping trip for her birthday when the Brotherhood had taken her parents. It worried her. Wanting to bring her back to reality, Sarah asked, "Does Miss Gwen really look familiar to you?"

Cassie looked at Sarah. "Sort of. It's a pretty vague feeling, like maybe I've seen someone who resembles her once in a crowd or something. But it's really bugging me, and I don't know why."

Sarah smiled. "It's bugging you because you can't figure it out. Whenever you can't figure something out, it bugs you, no matter what it is."

"True. It's pretty likely I'm just exaggerating things, considering everything we've been through recently. But the horse is confusing, too." Cassie shook her head. "I just don't know."

"That's okay sometimes, you know."

"Mmm," Cassie grunted noncommittally. Sarah suppressed a chuckle. She knew her friend well enough to know Cassie wasn't satisfied with just accepting that she couldn't know something. "I'll bet ya that when I figure all this out, I'll smack myself for not getting it sooner."

Sarah chuckled. "Cassie, you do that anytime you don't figure something out immediately."

"I do not. Only when I can't figure out something *obvious*."

"Well, who says the answer is obvious? I know most of the people you know, and she doesn't remind me of anyone in particular."

Cassie looked at her. "Have you really thought about it?"

"Well, no, but..."

"Then think about it," Cassie said. She looked at the stable. "And I want to question that mare. Horses are not mysterious without good reason." Sarah shrugged. She pictured Gwen's face in her mind, thinking about who she might resemble, if it was anyone at all. She frowned slightly. Now that Cassie pointedly asked her to think about it, Sarah did think the woman reminded her of someone. But who? Bother. Now it was going to bug *her*.

The two girls entered the stable. The mare thrust her dark head over the stall door as Cassie approached her. "You must be Wynne," she said.

The mare bobbed her head. *As there is no other horse in here, you must be correct.* Cassie grinned at the horse's droll tone. She held out her hand for Wynne to sniff. The mare was an elegant dark bay with no white markings, but she wasn't too big, maybe fifteen hands at the most. She looked sturdy enough for her size, though, and Cassie had already seen from her trot into the stable that she had good gaits. Cassie's grin slowly faded to a thoughtful frown as she studied the mare more thoroughly. She had seen this horse before somewhere, she was sure. But where? Definitely not at home, and she had never been around Glastonbury before. Perhaps Gwen had once lived in London and had kept Wynne in a stable there. Cassie had been around some of the London stables, or mews. Yet that just didn't seem right. Normally a horse would excitedly inform Cassie of where they had met before. And, more to the point, Cassie would remember it.

So where's the place that you were talking about where my friends and I are supposed to go? Cassie asked the horse.

You will find out soon enough, the mare replied.

How do you know we haven't been there yet?

If you had, you would know and would not be asking me. The mare blinked at her. *I believe your friend needs some help right now. I will tell you no more. You must discover the answers on your own.*

"Cassie, I know you want to hold an interrogation session, but I'm not doing this all by myself," Sarah's voice called.

"Okay, I'm coming," she called. "Just a minute." She looked back at the horse, her curiosity not at all satisfied with the cryptic answers. "One more question," she said aloud, thinking that a point-blank question might be worth a shot. "You look familiar to me. Where might I have seen you before?"

The mare looked at her with eyes that seemed very old, though Cassie didn't think the horse could be any older than fifteen or so. *That, I think, you know better than I. Perhaps you should pay more attention to the images in your sleep.* With that, the mare turned around and trotted back out of the stall and into the field, effectively dismissing Cassie.

Cassie stared at her for several seconds. *The images in my sleep? Is she talking about a dream?* she wondered. The dream that had wakened her that morning crossed her mind. There had been a dark bay mare in it. Could it be... ? Cassie shook her head, turning from the horse to go help Sarah. *There is no way,* she told herself. *I'm letting my imagination get away with me. After all, it was just a dream.* She frowned. *Wasn't it?*

❧✣❧

Morton glared at his subordinate, but did not allow his rising anger to affect his voice. "This is inexcusable, Commander," he said. "It has been nearly a week."

The Commander stiffened. "We are trying–"

"Don't try," the other man cut him off. "Succeed. You must find the girl and her companions as soon as possible. Understand?"

The Commander nodded. "But leave the boy to me," he said, his voice reflecting his rage. "He must have a traitor's death."

Morton knew who he meant. "Of course," he agreed. The men were interrupted by a quick knocking at the door. "Enter," Morton called.

A man entered briskly and made quick bows to his superiors. "Sir, we may have a lead on the kids." Morton raised his eyebrows. "They might be heading to the Glastonbury area."

"Really? Glastonbury? What makes you think so?"

"Dr. Stone sent a message suggesting that they might have an ultimate goal of getting to Cadbury, but they may pick a less obvious place close to it to stay in the meantime. She thinks Glastonbury is a good possibility because of its proximity and involvement in the legends. She plans to travel there and have a look around, and check some of the nearby towns as well."

"Hmm, yes, that does make sense. Brenwyds do like to be tricky, and they have been traveling for some time now. Thank you. Tell Sadie to make sure the children do not see her if they are there."

"Of course, sir." The man exited.

Morton looked at his Commander. "So... Glastonbury. Interesting. If Dr. Stone reports good news, Commander, you will take several men with you and travel there immediately. Take no chances. Kill the boy and girl who travel with the witch, and her dogs. Bring the witch and William back here. I will kill her myself," he said.

"Yes, sir."

The Commander turned to go, but Morton's voice stopped him. "One more thing, Commander." He turned back. "Bring the girl's father to me. I have a few questions for him about his daughter."

"As you wish," the Commander said. He left the room.

Morton went to one of his bookshelves and picked out a book. The fragile, parchment pages crackled as Morton carefully turned each one. Instead of words, the book contained hand-drawn pictures of people with names underneath them. Most were crossed out. Morton stopped at the drawing of a lovely young girl with pointed ears. Her name was not crossed out. Morton's gaze bore into the picture, scrutinizing every detail. He had examined it every day since seeing the Pennington girl. "Is it possible?" he murmured to himself. "Is it in any way possible?"

$\mathcal{A}$VALON

$\mathcal{W}$illiam stepped from the bathroom, thoroughly enjoying the feeling of cleanliness. He was sure a shower had never felt so good. Then again, he reflected, he'd never ridden for days on end through the countryside, either. He entered the room he and David had chosen, and saw David lying on the bed. Assuming his friend was sleeping, William tried to move about quietly. There had been spare clothes in the closet, along with a note that said anyone was welcome to them. It was nice to be able to change into clean clothes. William wasn't naturally fastidious about his appearance, but his father demanded he look respectable at all times, so he had developed the habit of always looking twice in the mirror. He lay down on the bed, thinking about taking a nap as David was doing, but he had too many thoughts swirling around in his mind to sleep. The sequence of events that had led him to this room was hard to believe, even for him, and he wondered what would happen next. He had no guilt over leaving the Brotherhood, seeing it now for what it really was: an evil organization that killed innocent people out of fear, shielding themselves by accusing those they hunted of the very things the members of the organization intended to do. He couldn't believe he'd once thought they were right and had followed them blindly.

Thankfully, that life was behind him now, though he knew he would have to confront the Brotherhood again... and his father. That idea made him uncomfortable. Though the man had certainly not been the best of fathers, rarely even speaking a kind word, William wasn't sure he wanted to go up against him in combat, for he was still his father. Perhaps if his mother were still alive, things would have been different, but he doubted that even that would have stopped his father from acting as he did. William didn't even really know what his mother had looked like, because his father had removed all her pictures from the house. One of the other men had told him she'd had blond hair and blue eyes, and though not especially beautiful, was not particularly plain, either. The man had gone on to say that, though she had never quite approved of the Brotherhood's methods, she had seen the necessity of their mission – ridding the earth of all Brenwyds. William gathered that something inside his father had died when she did, and it was part of the reason for his coldness. William wished fate had not taken her from him before he'd had the chance to know her.

He forced his mind off such topics, and focused instead on the woman who housed them. He had been telling the truth when he said he'd never seen her before but, like Cassie, he thought he sensed a vague familiarity about her. He didn't want to bring it up because he was pretty sure it was his imagination. Yet the sound of her voice wormed its way through his memories, as if it was trying to find where it belonged. He sighed. Everyone seemed to be familiar to him lately, and it baffled him. Lots of things had baffled him since meeting Cassie and the twins, though. He was beginning to grow quite tired of being baffled.

"Are you sleeping?" he heard David ask.

William turned his head to see him sitting up on the bed. "No, I thought you were."

"I was trying, but my brain's too engaged at the moment." David's lips were pressed together in a line. "I don't like how the

Brotherhood's going after my mom. What do they want from her?" The teens had called Mrs. Thompson right after the boys had returned from retrieving the horses and learned that she was hiding from the Brotherhood at the Shelbys'. The neighborhood they lived in was a less likely place for the Brotherhood to target, since the population there would add to their risk of being discovered. Hannah also told them that Smokey and Calico had disappeared, which worried Cassie. Hannah offered to come to England to join them, but collectively they had decided against it – at least, not yet.

William didn't have to think hard about the answer to David's question. "She could give them information as to our whereabouts."

David frowned. "That was a somewhat rhetorical question. I'm aware of what she could tell them. But I don't like it. And I don't like being all the way over here, either, with her in danger at home."

William grunted. "But if she booked a flight, they'd figure it out. You can bet they're watching the airlines."

"But how?" David asked. "How can one shadowy organization monitor all that?"

William shrugged. "They have methods, and not entirely legal ones. I know what you've seen of it looks medieval, and in some ways it is. But the Master keeps headquarters up-to-date with the latest technology, and makes sure to recruit people who know how to use it – hackers, to be blunt."

"Figures." David wondered if William had any knowledge in that field, but decided not to ask. It wasn't important at the moment. He lay back down and the two were silent for a while.

"David?" William asked after several minutes.

"Yeah?"

"Could I tell you something weird?" William heard David chuckle.

"Go ahead," he said. "It can't be any weirder than some of the things Cassie thinks up."

William smiled and propped himself up so he was facing David. "I don't know about that, but this seems pretty weird to me. It's about when we first met." William saw David's eyes narrow and his expression turn serious as he turned toward William. "I had this... really odd feeling when I saw you guys approaching the camp." He felt a little awkward confiding in David, as he'd never really confided anything in anyone before, but he knew he could trust David.

"Saw us approaching?" David asked.

"Yeah, I was looking through a pair of binoculars," William explained.

"So the other guys *didn't* tie you up?"

William shook his head. David looked confused. "Then how did you end up tied up? I thought it was part of a back-up plan you all concocted."

"I did it myself. I thought up the back-up plan when I realized that the other men wouldn't capture you. My... the Commander taught me how to do it. But that's not what I was going to say."

David felt his curiosity rise every minute William hesitated. "Okay then, spit it out," he said somewhat impatiently.

William took a breath, not quite sure how David would react to this piece of information. "You guys looked... familiar. I have no idea why. I know I had never seen you before that moment, but something inside me said I had... or I should at least know who you were," William said.

David's eyes widened. "That's weird, alright," he said. William nodded. He'd been expecting something like that. But he was not expecting what came next. "What makes it even weirder is that I had the same feeling about you."

William sat up straight. "What?"

"You heard me. I have no idea why." He paused. "Cassie, Sarah, and I have all been to England before. Maybe we saw each other in a crowded square or something."

William shook his head. "I don't think so. I would have remembered that by now," he said firmly.

"Do you think the girls had the same feeling?"

"Maybe. We could ask them."

David turned and looked out the window. He saw Cassie sitting in the yard reading a book on a garden bench. Gwen and the children had still not returned, and a peaceful quiet had settled over the house, all the guests having left for the day. David studied his friend as she sat. She had obviously taken a shower already, because her hair was several shades darker than usual, looking more red than blond. Instead of being back in braids, her hair was loose and obscured part of her face. Her posture was relaxed, making David guess that she was feeling at peace at the moment. "What are you looking at?" he heard William ask.

He looked away from the window. "Oh, nothing," he answered. "Just the yard. Cassie's out reading a book."

"She's actually relaxing?" William asked.

"She does do it occasionally." David lay back down on his bed, thumbing through a brochure he had found on the bedside table advertising some of Glastonbury's attractions. William went to look out the window, and focused on the Tor. The hill dominated the mostly-flat countryside for miles around, and the tower at its pinnacle was the only remnant of a medieval church destroyed long ago. It was a major tourist attraction for the town of Glastonbury, and was fabled to be the site of Avalon from the King Arthur legend. William studied the hill intently. He had never seen it before today, though he had been curious about it for several years after reading about it. He recalled Cassie's assertion that the island in her dream that morning had, in fact, been the Tor, and tried to imagine it as an island. Perhaps it could have been one long ago, but with all the modern houses it was hard for him to picture now.

"What is it?" David asked. William looked like he was a million miles away.

William blinked, jerked from his reverie. "Nothing," he said. "Just the Tor."

"Hey, do either of you know where Cassie is?" Sarah's voice came from the doorway. She had obviously just climbed out of the shower, as her hair was still pretty wet.

"She's down reading in the garden," her brother replied.

"Oh, I hope she hasn't been out there too long. I showered as quickly as I could." She started back down the hall, then looked over her shoulder. "You guys comin' or are you gonna take naps?" David and William gave each other do-you-have-any-idea-what-she's-talking-about looks. Sarah caught it and turned completely around. "Didn't Cassie tell you?"

"Tell us what?" David asked.

"That she's gonna go check out the Tor. She said she wanted to look for something or other. I'm going with her, so I just figured you two were comin' along."

"I haven't seen her since we came in after settling the horses," David said, frowning.

Sarah smiled teasingly. "Oh, don't take it personally, David. She probably meant to tell you but forgot."

"What did I forget?" They turned to see Cassie standing in the hall. "If you're talking about the trip to the Tor, I was just coming up to suggest that. I just wanted to take some time to read first. But since everyone seems ready, why don't we get going? I'll leave Miss Gwen a note."

⊷⧏⬥⧐⊷

"So what are we looking for?" David asked. They had arrived at the base of the hill and were looking up at the tower. It looked pretty impressive from their angle – and a ways up.

Cassie frowned as she studied the hill. "That's the thing. I'm not exactly sure," she said. She started climbing up the hill with the others following her.

There is much history here, Kai said as he sniffed the air. *Much has happened in this place.*

"Hmm," Cassie agreed. She paused in her climb and looked around. They were about a hundred feet up the Tor's side, where there was a level space for a few yards. There was something here, something she couldn't quite put a finger on – but something important. She thought she heard hoofbeats, shouts, the clash of weapons...

"Cass?" David asked. "You okay? Looked like you were spacing out a little."

"I'm fine," she said distractedly, and started walking to the left as if looking for something. The others glanced at each other with slightly concerned looks. Something was up. Cassie usually wasn't so spacey.

David went after her. "Cassie!" he called.

She paused, turning her head to look back at him. "What?" she asked.

"What are you doing?"

"Looking."

"For what?" he asked.

She gave him a puzzled look. "I'll know it when I find it," she said, as if it were the most natural thing in the world to not know what you were looking for. She continued walking around the hill. The others followed her. After several yards, she stopped. "Here," she murmured.

"What's here?" Sarah asked. Cassie met her eyes with such intensity that Sarah felt a chill go down her spine.

David reached out and put his hands on her shoulders, growing more concerned about her distracted state and wanting to bring her back to reality. "Cassie." She refocused.

"What?" Cassie asked him again, breaking his grip on her arms. "What's here?"

Cassie looked at him in confusion. "I don't know!" she could hear the frustration coloring her voice.

Are you feeling alright, girl? Dassah asked.

Fine. She looked around at the others and sighed. "Look, I'm sorry, I just... it feels like... there's something here. This hill, this spot,... it's *important.*" Silence descended. Cassie tried to figure out just what made this spot so important. She closed her eyes and rubbed her forehead, trying to think without giving herself a headache. Unbidden, the image of the woman riding and disappearing into the mist appeared in her mind's eye. Slowly, she realized what it was about this spot. "This is where she disappeared," she whispered.

"Where who disappeared?" William asked.

Cassie looked up at him. "The woman from my dream this morning. David hit the horse's rump with the flat of his sword–"

"Why did you imagine me doing *that?*" David exclaimed. Cassie ignored him.

"And the horse sprang into a gallop and disappeared with the woman... right here. I'm sure of it. The Tor *was* the island." She looked around. "But why is it so important?" she mused, more to herself than to anyone else.

William shrugged. "I have no idea," he said. "It's just a dream. Dreams aren't real."

"But what if it isn't just a dream?" Cassie speculated.

William frowned. What else did she think it could be?

Cassie recalled what Wynne had said about the images in her sleep. But if the dream really wasn't just a dream, how was it supposed to be helpful? And how would a horse she'd just met even know that? Cassie kept her gaze trained on William as she thought, not really aware of what she was doing. *You know,* she thought absently, *his eyes kind of remind me of* – she blinked as a thought occurred to her.

"Um... Cassie, why are you staring at me?" William asked. He felt a little uncomfortable with her gaze trained on him. Her eyes could be very penetrating.

"I was just thinking," Cassie answered, "that I might have found the answer to the Gwen mystery. Part of it, anyway," she mused. "Why didn't I see that sooner?"

"See what?" David asked.

Sarah looked between Cassie and William and remembered the conversation they'd had earlier. She narrowed her eyes and gasped. "Oh, my gosh. You're right, Cassie." Sarah grinned. "You have permission to smack yourself." Cassie laughed. The two boys looked at them in bewilderment.

"For Pete's sake, what *are* you two talking about?" William asked. The girls looked at each other.

"Gwen," Cassie said. "I told you she looked familiar to me, right?"

"Right," David and William said.

"Well, Sarah and I talked about it when you guys left to get the horses, and I said that maybe she looks familiar because she reminds me of somebody I know."

"Okay," William said. "That makes sense."

"That's what I thought. And just now, I think the reason she looks familiar to me is because she reminds me of you."

"Um... how, exactly?" William asked.

"Well, you both have blue eyes, but it's not just that." She cocked her head slightly as she studied William critically. "I think you have similar facial features, too."

Sarah nodded agreement. "Yeah. I can see it, too, so it's not just Cassie."

"Thank you for the reassurance, Sarah," Cassie said with a wry smile.

David looked at William. He didn't really see what the girls were talking about, beyond the fact that William and Gwen both had blue eyes, but if Cassie said she saw a resemblance, it was probably there. *I wonder what Cassie isn't saying about it*, he thought. He knew her well enough to suspect that she felt there was something significant about the resemblance.

William stared hard at Cassie for several seconds, then shrugged.

Even though he hadn't known her all that long, he knew she had various idiosyncrasies, and so he didn't really pay much heed to this new theory. Though with Cassie, it never hurt to ask. "Okay, so you solved the Gwen mystery. What's the big deal? There are a limited number of eye colors, you know."

"I don't know," Cassie said slowly. "But it feels important, somehow. And I haven't solved all of the Gwen mystery yet. I still have no clue how on earth she could have recognized us." She released a gusty sigh. "There's something else going on here. I can just feel it."

William raised his eyebrows. "Cassie, I'm not trying to doubt you – okay, maybe I am a little – but are you sure you should depend so much on just feelings and hunches? Yeah, you were right about Dr. Stone, and I understand that you've been right about other things based on feelings, but doesn't there come a point where you should rely more on what you know instead of going blindly off what you think or feel?"

Cassie looked at him thoughtfully. "There is, but I generally get to that point after going off feelings and hunches. These particular hunches I talk about... they're different from, like, an urge to have a certain sandwich, or watch a particular movie, or read a certain book, or ride at a particular time. They don't feel like just whims to me, they're more... substantial, I guess you could say. It's not so much going blindly, as it is trying to see what God might be wanting me to see. That's what faith is, after all – things we hope for but don't see. Paying attention to these hunches is, to me, part of faith, and I believe that I'll understand what they mean eventually. Do you also have enough faith to believe that?"

William wasn't quite sure how to answer that. Personally, he still didn't think she should depend so much on feelings, but she probably had a point about faith. He didn't know much about faith, and she did. But it did sound a little far-fetched to him. It wasn't very logical.

Cassie continued, "While you think about that, I'm going to try to figure out at least some of all this. Nobody disturb me for, like, ten minutes or so." She sat down, her head aching from trying to figure it all out. Dassah came over and lay down next to her, sticking her head into Cassie's lap for a scratch. The others walked away a little and started discussing whether to walk up to the top of the hill now or wait until their friend was done thinking.

Cassie stared at the side of the hill, trying to put all the pieces together. She had seen herself and David helping a woman in a dream. Then they'd met Gwen, who seemed to know who they were – her horse did, at any rate – despite the fact that none of the teens had met her before. Surprisingly, Phoenix had seemed to know Wynne. He had perked up on seeing Wynne and rubbed noses with her, but Cassie hadn't been able to get an explanation for the affection. And now she realized William looked a little like Gwen.

Wynne's words echoed in her mind: *You should pay more attention to the images in your sleep. Okay*, Cassie thought. *That clearly means dreams, and the only ones I've had lately are the one back home with the cup and the one this morning. There was a dark bay mare in the dream this morning, who had belonged to the dead woman. Then the live woman disappeared on the mare at this spot.* Brows furrowed, Cassie recalled one of the lasting images of the dream: horse and rider vanishing into the mist, the woman glancing back a little. The mare seemed the right height for Wynne. If only she could clearly recall what the woman looked like... *Well, Gwen does have blue eyes and long hair like the woman*, Cassie reasoned. *Seeing her in a dream would also help explain why she looks familiar. She seems familiar in a dreamy way, too. But why on earth would I have seen Gwen in a dream? Some premonition that I would meet her? And why were the people in the dream so determined to get her to this particular spot? And why on earth would I imagine everything in a medieval setting?*

If you think any harder, your brain might explode, Kai remarked, disturbing her train of thought.

She glanced at him. *I kind of wish it would. Then I wouldn't have to think anymore.*

Thinking is not a bad thing. It is when you think too hard that it becomes a bad thing, Kai said. *You cannot get a clear view of anything by looking at it too hard. To really see, you must step back.*

And how would you suggest I step back? Cassie asked him, a little tartly.

Focus on just one thing, Dassah put in, ignoring Cassie's tone. *It is like in hunting. One must block out all other scents except the one you hunt, yet if you get too close to the scent you cannot determine which way it goes, for it fills your nostrils and seems to lead in every direction. If you follow one scent from a little distance, it leads you to your prey.*

And which thing do you propose I focus on? Cassie asked.

This spot, Dassah replied. *You are here. Use your senses. You are a Brenwyd. You can sense things others cannot. Use your gifts to figure out how this place is different, how it is special, just as we dogs use our noses to investigate things we do not know.*

Cassie blinked at her. *What do you mean?*

Listen. Brenwyds can understand and read their surroundings. It is one of their gifts. They can sense things others cannot, just by listening. You can do this, too.

It is the same as how you listen and heal things, Kai added.

But there's nothing to heal here, Cassie pointed out. *Why should I listen?*

Because it can help you. Just try it. Your father was going to teach you this next. Just listen. Hard.

Okay, Cassie thought. *Why not?* She closed her eyes and listened with her Brenwyd sense. A faint melody entered her thoughts and as she focused on it, it grew stronger. She couldn't see anything unusual with her eyes, but she sensed the people and animals around her. The feeling of a powerful, ancient sentinel entered her thoughts, with a low, mysterious melody that she realized was coming from the Tor itself, with all its weight of history. She sensed

Dassah lying at her side, a quiet, simple melody, but with a quick crescendo every so often. There was a stronger, fiercer strain: Kai. Up the hill a little, she heard a light, fast, gentle melody with a feminine feel and underlying steadiness. Sarah. David she sensed as a similar melody, but deeper and with a more driving beat. William's melody was pleasant, but confusing and a little out of tune. As she listened, it kept straightening itself out at a slow, steady pace, perhaps because of his recent change of heart. Concentrating further, Cassie sensed all the people on the Tor. Some had such discordance and harsh melodies that she wanted to clap her hands over her ears.

Now listen harder, girl. Sense nature's song, Kai said. Obediently, she kept listening. There was a slight breeze, and in her mind it sounded like musical chimes that blended with the various bird songs rising from the trees and the slow, steady, repetitive notes of the trees themselves. Near her feet, she sensed the grass blades' tiny, simple, "do-re-mi" melodies, rising from all around her toward heaven, giving praise. Everything was in harmony. She felt awed by what she was hearing, all these melodies the master composer had created, sweeter than the best church choir. She felt she could hear the very air singing praise... but wait, there was something else, something that went against the flow. It wasn't a discordance, but it was different. She listened still harder, trying to isolate a certain melody from the others.

As she did so, she heard happy and sad strains, angry and melancholy ones, every emotion she could think of, packed into one spot. She concentrated all her attention on it. Her mind pictured a thin line of song that stretched from the ground to the sky till she could sense it no more, no wider than a strand of thread, yet the depth she sensed behind it seemed big enough to encompass all of history. There was a fluidity to the melody; it was inconsistent and constantly changing, flowing any direction it wished, and not following any pattern that Cassie could detect. Yet it did not disrupt the symphony around it and, behind all the wild harmonies, she could hear a constant, steady beating that sounded almost like a heartbeat. Probing deeper, she discovered rents in the strand, areas where it sounded almost like something had physically torn the melody from its measures, and other places she could only describe as having a mended sound to them, being weaker than the other parts of the melody. Still other places seemed to Cassie as if they were about to burst with the intensity and richness of the music. One place in particular seemed to have this sound, and she honed in on it. The melody there was definitely increasing in intensity, but slowly. Very slowly.

Cassie honed in to discern that all the melodies in that spot flowed around the steady, central one whose tempo exactly matched the beating. She also discovered that each of the wild melodies eventually ended, melding into the steady one. She opened her eyes, stood, and slowly walked to where she sensed the collection of melodies. The others watched her curiously from a distance, wondering what she was up to. She looked around and realized she was at the spot she had pointed out to them earlier, where the woman had disappeared. The tune at that spot sounded familiar to her, and she recognized it from her dream.

An image formed in her mind as she listened, and she watched, fascinated, as she saw the woman disappear again, but this time her mind's eye followed her. And some part of her knew that all this had occurred nearly sixteen years ago in early October. The woman passed into a dark place on horseback, and Cassie caught glimpses of images going by, too quickly for her to identify. After a moment the blackness shattered like glass, and the horse and woman emerged onto a green hill. The woman pulled back gently on the reins, and the horse stopped. The woman looked up and Cassie distantly knew she had come out in the same place she had left. But wait... something was different. There was no sign of the girl or boy, and no sound of battle. There was no mist rising off the water, and Cassie saw it was because there was no water. The woman looked up to the top of the hill. Cassie heard her gasp. Whereas Cassie remembered seeing a small building at the top of the Tor in her dream, now she saw the familiar tower sticking up into the night. The woman spoke, and though it was in a different language, Cassie somehow understood her. She also saw the woman's face clearly.

"Well, Wynne," she said, sounding a little scared. "It seems we have arrived." The mare nickered and the woman sighed, resting a hand on her belly. "But now what do we do?" Abruptly, the scene faded and Cassie blinked, refocusing, the melodies fading from her mind. She stumbled back a couple of steps, feeling a little dizzy. David caught her before she fell down, and steadied her. "What is it?" he asked, his dark brown eyes filled with concern.

"I'm not sure," she answered slowly. "But I think I should talk to Gwen. She has answers."

"To what?" William asked.

Cassie took a breath. "My dream this morning." She saw William frown and hurriedly went on to explain. "I just had another... um... vision, I guess, since I'm awake. So I was listening to this odd melody, trying to figure it out, when I saw the woman and horse from my dream this morning disappear again, but this time I saw where they went. There was this dark place with images flashing by, and then they came out right where they started. This hill. This spot." She gestured to the ground. "And the woman said something like, 'We've arrived.' And then... it ended." She drew in a breath to continue, but Sarah interrupted.

"You saw this just now?" Sarah asked. "And what melody? I don't hear any music."

"Yes I did, and... um... remember when I told you guys about my ability to hear the songs of living things?"

"Yeah."

"Well, the dogs told me to listen to the environment to figure out what's so odd about this place, and I did." Her eyes lit up in a way they hadn't for a long time as she remembered the glorious sound. "It was the most amazing thing I've ever heard. All different melodies, tempos, intensities, and they all blended together perfectly – better than any mass orchestra or choir. So I was listening, and I heard something that sounded kind of... off. Not discordant or anything, just going a little against the main rhythms. I investigated, and it's like this long, very thin strand of melody going up and down. It seemed to have... rips and tears in it, and places that sounded very... full, I guess you'd say. I was trying to listen better to one of the tears, and that's when I saw the vision. Does that make sense? I know it sounds kind of crazy." She looked at the others anxiously.

"How does music sound torn or mended?" Sarah asked.

Cassie thought for a moment. "Okay, think of a bunch of string hanging vertically. At the top, all the string is smooth and twisted in a slow circle around and around, and at the bottom all the strings are free to do whatever. But think of the free ones at the bottom as slowly becoming twisted into the smooth section, and think of some strings in the smooth section as snapped, but mended with thread. Does that help?"

They all still looked puzzled, but they nodded. Cassie had a feeling that no matter how she described it, they wouldn't totally understand it unless they heard it. Surprisingly, though, William looked like he had the best idea of what she was talking about. "In lots of the stories I've heard, Brenwyds could manipulate their surroundings through song," he said. "Song was supposedly how they worked witchcraft. That's why, if you want to know, they gagged you. They didn't want to risk you being able to sing yourself free."

Cassie snorted. "Fat chance of that. One, I have no clue how that would even work, and two, I only use it for healing. This is the first time I've even tried listening to something other than a person or animal," she said.

I told you, girl, did I not? Dassah said smugly.

Cassie smiled and scratched her black head. *That you did, but I'm still as confused as before.*

But now you know there is an irregularity at this spot. That may help you in the future, Kai said.

Maybe, Cassie said.

"So why does this vision thing make you think Gwen has the answers?" David asked. "We literally just met her."

"I know, but I caught a better glimpse of the woman's face. It was Gwen. Younger than now, but I'm sure it was her." The other three stared at her.

"How on earth did she end up in your dream?" Sarah asked. "Didn't you say it was set in the Middle Ages?"

"I thought it was, but maybe my brain just gave it that setting, imagining the clothes as Celtic tunics and breeches." She frowned.

"And maybe your brain just made the woman look like Gwen, now that you've met her," William pointed out.

"But it definitely felt like the same woman as in my dream," Cassie protested. "Besides, if it was David and me helping, I don't get why Gwen would have looked younger."

"Well," William said, "dreams often don't make sense."

"Yes," Cassie conceded, "but... there was just something different about this one."

"So just accept it," Sarah said. "You'll figure it out faster if you stop protesting about how things don't make sense." She was speaking to Cassie, but looking at William out of the corner of her eye.

She speaks truth, girl, Kai said so everyone could hear him. *Listen to her.*

Sarah smiled. "Thanks, Kai." She looked up the hill. "So are we gonna finish climbing it or not?"

"Let's," David said. "Then at least we can say we did one touristy thing in Glastonbury."

"Are you implying this is a vacation?" Cassie asked as they began walking upward.

"At the moment," David replied. He looked over at William. "Though I do have one more question. Are you sure Miss Gwen and William look like each other?" He was still having trouble seeing it.

William rolled his eyes. "I've never seen or even heard of her before. It probably means nothing. Sometimes people resemble each other because they just do. It's coincidence, plain and simple."

"I don't believe in coincidence," Cassie said flatly. "Everything happens for a reason, even seemingly small things." By this point the teens and dogs had reached the Tor's summit, and gazed out over the miles of picturesque, mostly flat landscape, along with the town of Glastonbury. It looked reassuringly calm and normal. Cassie continued thinking as she looked across the countryside toward the horizon. "You know," she said in a lower tone, as if speaking to herself, "her familiarity almost reminds me–" She stopped.

"Reminds you of what?" William asked.

"Of the first time I saw you, actually. I had the weirdest sensation that I should know who you were, even having never seen you before."

Sarah gasped. "You, too?"

William and David gave each other quick glances. "As a matter of fact," David said, "William and I were just discussing how we had that same feeling upon first seeing each other."

Cassie's eyes widened. "I thought it was just me... I didn't think anyone would take me seriously. It was part of the reason why I wasn't as... suspicious as I would have been otherwise. I wanted to figure out why." At the reminder of his recent betrayal, William looked down.

Sarah put a hand on his shoulder comfortingly. "Do you have any idea why now, since we all felt the same?"

Cassie shook her head. "Nope. Not a clue." She looked one last time out over the landscape. Her eye caught a small hill miles away and, focusing on it, she realized it was Cadbury. *We should go there tomorrow*, she thought. "Let's go back now. I'm hungry, and it's nearly lunchtime. I've discovered thinking generally goes better when you're not distracted by a growling stomach."

⁘⁘⁘

Sadie Stone strolled along the streets of Glastonbury, looking like just another ordinary person on the sidewalk running errands. And she was, indeed, running an errand, though not exactly a usual one. She scanned the people going past her, looking for the witch and her accomplices. She couldn't believe they had escaped, not after all the trouble the Brotherhood had gone through to get the girl. And for William to help them! When the Commander had delivered the news, she had sat there in shock, speechless, for a good five minutes. Her shock had given way to anger, and the anger was still there, burning in her chest. She should have known the boy's loyalties were in question. She'd seen the turmoil in his eyes in London. Yet he had seemed to rally well, and had even led the witch into the trap. But then he had freed them! Sadie pressed her lips into a thin line. The Commander should have listened to her all those years ago. Then this wouldn't be happening. But it was, so they had to deal with it. That didn't mean she had to like it, but she could give the Commander a very smug I-told-you-so.

She came to a park and left the sidewalk. She always enjoyed walking in parks. Besides, the witch liked nature – perhaps she would be here. A smile curved Sadie's lips as she imagined how she would get the girl. And if she did it before the Commander got here – ha! He would never live it down. She paused by a bench and surveyed the park's occupants, mostly children with their families. There were several dogs, but none like the witch had. Sadie watched a group of children playing tag, running and laughing. A gentler smile came to her lips. Children were so innocent and naïve, never dreaming anything bad could happen to them. As she watched, a woman called the children and they all ran over to her. *My goodness,* Sadie thought, *are they all siblings?* There were eight of them. She saw the woman whom she supposed was their mother across the park, her face obscured by the shadow of the trees. The main thing Sadie could make out was her hair, which was a brownish color. The woman and children left the trees, heading to a van parked on the side of the road. The woman looked around to call a child who was lagging behind, and Sadie got a good look at her face. She stiffened. *That's impossible,* she thought. *It can't be.* Yet there was no denying who the woman looked like. She was older, yes, but in every other way... Goose bumps appeared on Sadie's skin. *It is her,* she thought, *but how?* She continued staring at the woman. If she was here, alive, and they – more particularly, William – came here and met her... No, it would not do. She must report this to Morton immediately, but first she would find out where the woman lived, and whether she was a threat. Sadie turned abruptly and started back the way she had come. She had to have a serious talk with the Commander.

Secrets Mount

*T*wi looked at Phoenix from her stall across the aisle. Her ears faced in his direction, and she let out a short snort of disbelief. *You are sure this is all true?* she asked Wynne.

Yes, the mare replied. *If it were not, I would not be here, nor would Phoenix.*

You never told your boy about this, did you? Fire asked.

Phoenix looked at him, swishing his tail at a few flies. *No. It is not yet time. Soon, when we go back, then it will be time.*

I still do not understand this whole concept, Dreamer said. *It is... confusing. The girl would probably explain it better.*

But you cannot tell her, Wynne put in. *None of them can know until they get there. It is what she told me. Unfortunately, I was so surprised this morning that I almost let it slip. She is suspicious.*

Do you think she will figure out the connection? Fire asked. *There is that dream she had this morning.*

So she has been having dreams? Wynne asked. *Good. I thought so, but was not sure.*

She had a dream about the going forward, Phoenix supplied. *She did not understand it, and whether or not they connect it to the woman, I do not know.*

She may, Twi said. *But she likely does not realize exactly what it means and will try to think of some other explanation.* She swung her head toward the door. *Hush, she comes.*

The horses went back to munching hay as Cassie entered the barn. She went up to Twi and scratched around the bottom of her ears. "How're you doin', girl?"

Fine. It is nice to rest. The mare nuzzled her rider and blew out of her nostrils in contentment.

"Good." Cassie grabbed a stool from the feed room and dragged it to Twi's stall, where she sat down on it. She was still trying to figure out what that melody was at the Tor, turning over in her mind all the stories she knew that were connected to the hill. She knew that some people, in addition to connecting the Tor to the Avalon of the King Arthur legend, considered it an entrance to the Otherworld, the realm of faeries and the supernatural in Celtic lore, but she didn't believe that. Still, there had to be something strange at the Tor to spark those beliefs... but what? Could it be the strange melody?

Twi nudged her back. *What is it, girl?*

Cassie sighed. "That's just it, you see. I'm not sure."

What are you not sure of?

"Oh... everything, I suppose."

That is a lot of things, Twi mused. *Well, water is wet, summer is hot, winter is cold, carrots are good, and humans walk on two legs.*

Cassie laughed. "Thanks, Twi, but that wasn't exactly what I meant. I know that."

Then you are sure of some things; do not say you are unsure of everything. Everyone is unsure about some things, but it would be very hard to be unsure of everything.

"Hmm... You're right, I suppose."

Of course I am, Twi said without a hint of modesty. *Where are Kai and Dassah?*

"They played with the kids a bit, but they're so tired they're taking naps now. The trip was pretty hard on them, you know."

I know. Where are the little two-legs?

"Well, some of them are taking naps. The others are playing quiet games or reading. Sarah's with them, and I'm pretty sure David and William are sleeping. Gwen's in the kitchen with an ear out for any problems."

I think you should take a nap.

"I could probably use one, but I've got too much on my mind."

Then tell me so you can get it off your mind and take a nap.

Cassie smiled. "Who made you the boss of my life?"

I did. Now tell me what is bothering you, girl. And so Cassie told the horses what had occurred on the Tor. They were quiet for several minutes afterward.

I wondered when you would learn how to do that, Twi said.

"Dad never told me about it."

He may not have known, Wynne spoke up. *It was a jealously guarded secret, and I am not surprised it would be lost throughout the centuries.*

Cassie eyed her thoughtfully. "You talk like someone who knows." She paused, but Wynne made no response. "You know," Cassie continued. "I took your advice about paying more attention to dreams and realized that I saw a horse that looked surprisingly like you in a dream this morning. The rider looked a lot like Gwen, too. You wouldn't happen to know anything about it, would you?" Cassie sensed the mare's wariness.

It is not for me to tell you, Wynne answered.

"Then who can tell me? Gwen?" The mare remained silent. Cassie sighed inwardly and addressed her next words to Twi. "And there's another thing I realized at the Tor. Gwen and William resemble each other a bit. Normally I wouldn't think too much about it, but I feel like it's important."

Really? Twi said, swishing her tail back and forth at flies. *Interesting.*

Cassie looked at her. "Is that all you've got to say?"

What should I say? Many two-legs look alike. If it was not for the fact there are different mane colors and you all smell differently, it would be very hard to tell you apart. Cassie knew that was true. Horses didn't rely much on facial features to tell humans apart. She shrugged and retreated back into her thoughts. After several minutes she turned toward Phoenix abruptly as she remembered a question she'd been meaning to ask for several days.

"Hey, Phoenix, who's William's mom? He's never mentioned her. I keep meaning to ask him, but whenever I think of it, he's generally asleep. All I know is that she died somehow." She could tell the question took the gelding by surprise. She waited. Unbeknownst to Cassie, Phoenix was facing a dilemma. After thinking for a minute, he decided on what to say.

Well, he began, *William told me that his mother died giving birth to him. He never knew her. He was always sorry about it, and felt it most when the Commander was being particularly cold. He is not a loving parent, even though he did show gruff affection on occasion. Even before he met you, William was never really happy in the Brotherhood.*

"Couldn't imagine why," Cassie muttered. "Hey, does the Commander have a name?"

I have never heard it.

"Died in childbirth... but how? Isn't that really rare nowadays?"

I would not know. But Silent, the Commander's old horse, said that the birth was early and fast. He said it was her death that caused the Commander to become as he is.

"His horse is named Silent?" Cassie asked.

It was what we horses called him. He did not talk much.

Cassie thought about the information. "Well, that's too bad for William. Everyone needs a mom." She paused for a moment. "William must look like his mother," she mused, mostly to herself. "He and his father don't share any looks."

Phoenix chewed a mouthful of hay thoughtfully. *Perhaps.*

Cassie raised her eyebrows at the horse's skepticism. She hadn't been expecting him to comment on her musing. "Why just perhaps?"

Phoenix swallowed the hay and grabbed another mouthful, choosing his next words carefully. *I heard a rumor once in the stable that William may not actually be the Commander's son.*

Cassie cocked her head slightly. "Really? You mean his mom might have had an affair?"

I do not know what that means. But... Silent said that there was a pregnant woman prisoner at the castle the night William was born. She gave birth there.

"You mean that woman was William's mother?" Cassie was starting to feel confused. She hadn't meant for her comment to open up a vein of gossip concerning William's birth.

Phoenix paused and Wynne whickered softly, shaking her head. Cassie glanced toward her curiously, wondering what had stirred her up. Phoenix got the message, but added, *I just thought you might want to know. According to Silent, the child did not live.* He then dropped his head to the stall floor and concentrated on his hay.

✺✺✺

Gwen moved restlessly around the kitchen, her thoughts in turmoil. So far, none of the teens had asked her any hard questions, but she sensed they had a clue as to her identity. At least, she had seen some faint recognition in Cassie's eyes. But if they knew who she was, why weren't they talking! She decided she should go talk to Wynne. The horse had a greater understanding of things than most horses, and even some humans – not surprising, considering who her original owner had been. Gwen sighed. And then there was William. She'd known for sure the moment she'd laid eyes on him – how her heart sang! But how would she explain it? And did she need to wait any longer?

Gwen pondered what to do next. The main thing she was sure about was that the teens had to go back. Otherwise history would not run its course correctly, and God only knew how that would end up. She heard the back door open and looked up to see Cassie come into the kitchen, looking thoughtful. Gwen guessed she'd been in the barn. She wondered what the horses had told her. "Are you going to take a nap?" Gwen asked. "Sarah just went up to get some sleep. It would probably be a good idea."

Cassie smiled. "That's what my... I mean, yes, I'm going to." She stifled a yawn. "Just trying to calm my thoughts down, if ya know what I mean." Her cheeks were slightly pink. Gwen guessed she'd been going to say, "That's what my horse told me," but caught herself before she made the slip.

Gwen smiled at her. "I know exactly what you mean." She turned to the stove. "I've found that tea is most helpful in calming the mind down. Would you care for some?"

"Umm... I guess. I've never had tea before." She sounded dubious.

Gwen chuckled. "Thought it was only for the British, did you now?"

"Not exactly. I've just never really had the urge. And, uh, having a cup of tea, to me sounds very... umm, proper, you know?"

"I understand. What part of the States are you from?"

"Virginia, in the Appalachian Mountains west of Charlottesville. My dad's a history professor at UVA."

"UVA?"

"University of Virginia."

"Ah, I see." Gwen turned back around to face her and sat down at the table, indicating for the girl to sit next to her. "What's Virginia like? I've never traveled to the States."

"It's hot and humid right now, so the weather here's nice. The mountains aren't really tall, but they're covered in trees and perfect for trail rides. Sarah, David, and I all live in the same valley, so we go out on the trails a lot."

"Is it close to a city?"

"Not too close, but not especially far, either. We're about thirty minutes from Charlottesville, and there are some smaller towns nearby where we go to school and church. But there really aren't too many people out there. It's very beautiful." Cassie sounded wistful.

"What kind of history does your father teach?" Gwen asked.

"He teaches European history for the school, but his particular specialty is the early Middle Ages." The tea kettle whistled and Gwen rose to get it.

She was about to ask Cassie another question when they heard footsteps and William entered the room, still looking a little sleepy. "Was that a tea kettle I heard?" he asked.

"Indeed it was," Gwen told him as she gathered the tea bags. "Your friend here wants to sleep, but her mind is too active."

William sat. "I didn't know you liked tea, Cassie."

"I don't know if I do. I've never had it before."

"What? Isn't there tea in the States?" He sounded shocked, but an undercurrent of amusement ran in his voice.

"Of course, but we threw it all overboard in the Boston Tea Party. Didn't you hear about it?" She grinned mischievously at him. He let out a short laugh. Gwen wasn't well versed in modern history, so she decided to look up this "Boston Tea Party" soon.

"Another example of why Americans are a little odd," William replied, smiling slightly.

"Thank you. We take great pride in it," Cassie said saucily.

Gwen set the cups on the table, amused by their banter. "How long have you two known each other?" she asked.

Cassie and William exchanged glances. "We've known *of* each other for a while, but we only actually met recently," William said at last. It was close enough. Cassie took a sip of tea.

"Well?" Gwen asked.

"It tastes like tea, I suppose," she replied with no great enthusiasm. She took another sip. "The warmth is comforting. It's way stronger than I thought, though." Gwen and William smiled. "David and Sarah still sleeping?"

"Yeah," William said, glancing at Gwen. After discreetly studying her all through lunch and really thinking about it, he conceded
that yes, Cassie was right in claiming there was a resemblance between them. However, the fact that it was subtle made him certain
that it didn't mean anything, particularly as Gwen was a woman
and much older than he was. He wondered how he could convince
Cassie of it. Maybe he just shouldn't say anything and the subject
would drop from her mind naturally. "How long have you lived in
Glastonbury, Miss Gwen?" he asked.

"Sixteen years come October," Gwen answered readily.

"And before that?" William inquired.

She sighed, looking wistful. "A long time ago I lived near Cadbury. I moved here after... my husband died."

"Oh. I'm sorry," William said.

Gwen smiled a little, but sadly. "It's alright. You didn't know."

"Where did all the children come from?" Cassie asked.

"The foster system... there are, unfortunately, many orphans and
homeless children in the world. I try to help them as best I can. A
friend of mine started the house, and I continued it after her death."

"Do you... Are any of the children yours?" Cassie asked, but immediately regretted it as she saw the pain that came over Gwen's
features.

"No, but... I had three once. Two girls and a boy." She turned
from the table and busied herself with clearing the teacups and
saucers. Cassie and William looked at each other, both wondering
at the hesitation.

"What happened to them?" Cassie blurted out, cringing as she
heard the words. Why had she asked that? Clearly they had all died
in some horrible accident.

The woman sighed. "I lost them. It's, ah... it's a long story."

"I'm sorry," Cassie said.

Gwen turned back around and smiled wanly at her. "It's alright.
It was a long time ago. In fact, it's part of why I enjoy working with

the children so much. They help fill the hole." Her smile grew more real, though still sad.

Cassie decided to change the subject. "What do you think of all the legends surrounding the Tor?" Gwen was surprised at the abrupt change, but grateful. The previous questions had been wading into dangerous territory.

"That depends on which legends you mean," she said, sitting down at the table again. "If you're talking about those people who think it's a faery kingdom, definitely not."

"What about those who claim it as the site of Avalon from the King Arthur legends?" Cassie asked idly.

Gwen narrowed her eyes. This girl was clever. "First, I think there's a great misconception about Avalon. Many legends have it as the home of faeries and where Arthur went to die, but it was actually just a church – one of Britain's first churches, in fact."

"Then you think the legends are wrong?" Cassie asked. Now she was genuinely curious.

Gwen shrugged. "I certainly don't think it was ever the home of faery women, but... Arthur may have been buried there, which would explain that part of the legend."

"There were those monks in the late 1100s who claimed to find the bodies of Arthur and Guinevere near Glastonbury Abbey," William put in, "but the bodies disappeared in the sixteenth century. Do you think it really was them?"

Gwen almost laughed at the question. *Arthur and Guinevere indeed!* "There's a chance it may have been Arthur, but I doubt the lady was really Guinevere."

"Why?" Cassie asked. This conversation was getting more and more interesting. Actually, anything relating to King Arthur attracted her interest, but this woman sounded like she'd made a full study of the legend.

"Because it makes no sense. Guinevere didn't die at the same time as Arthur, and the legends say she lived in a convent the rest of her life. They probably weren't buried together." Cassie noticed an odd inflection in Gwen's voice, almost a wistfulness, when she said Arthur's name. Why would this woman feel so strongly about a man who lived and died over a thousand years ago?

"So you believe in the King Arthur legend," Cassie noted.

"Yes, of course," she replied, with a hint of restrained laughter. "Do you?"

The corner of Cassie's lip twitched up in a half-smile. "Oh, yes. My father always says most legends and myths are based on some truth, and the King Arthur legend is one of the biggest ones out there. He's always wanted to prove Arthur's existence beyond a shadow of a doubt."

Cassie caught sight of an unusual pin on Gwen's shirt collar that was shaped like a dragon and looked like pure gold, with emeralds for eyes. It looked like a Celtic design, as the dragon's body was a Celtic knot, and something about it seemed familiar. Perhaps Cassie had seen a picture similar to the pin at some point in the past. Opening her mouth to ask about it, she let out a long, involuntary yawn, and decided the question could wait until later. "I think I'll head upstairs for my nap now. It's been nice talking to you, Miss Gwen."

"Likewise, Cassie."

Cassie turned and left the kitchen, lingering for a few minutes by the door to hear what Gwen and William would talk about. They continued discussing King Arthur, and Gwen began sharing a story that sounded remarkably similar to one Cassie's father had told her, about how Arthur and Guinevere had met. She frowned thoughtfully and began to climb the wide, wooden staircase. Reaching the bedroom, she saw Sarah passed out on one of the beds with the blinds closed. Cassie lay down on the other bed, certain she wouldn't be able to sleep right away, but her body had other ideas and by the time Dassah slunk into the room five minutes later, wild horses couldn't have woken her.

The woman turned her horse from the tower to the right. Whereas before there had been no habitation save the monastery for miles, now she saw lights dotting the land around her like flowers in a springtime field, even though it was full dark. She wondered at it. Seeing some lights not too far off, she squeezed the mare into a walk and headed toward them, making sure she could easily reach the dagger she had concealed in her clothing. She had been told a little of the strange place she was going and had learned a few words of the language, but there was no telling what danger could be lurking. Old habits die hard, especially ones formed in a world of shifting loyalties and alliances.

Soon enough she reached the lights, and stared in fascination at the strange building in front of her. It was much larger than the typical village dwelling. Perhaps it belonged to the leader of the village. The light seemed to come from several round objects made of a clear material she didn't recognize. "What is this, Wynne?" the woman murmured. The horse shifted uneasily. She picked up strange smells that she didn't recognize and therefore wasn't sure if they were dangerous or not. The woman took a breath. "Well, God willing, the people who dwell here will permit me to sleep by the fire, at least." She dismounted and left Wynne several yards from the door, knowing the horse wouldn't go anywhere.

The woman went up to the house and knocked hesitantly on the large wooden door. After waiting several minutes with no answer, she knocked again, more boldly this time, and was rewarded by the sound of movement from within. A gray-haired woman opened the door and looked curiously, but kindly, at the young woman on her doorstep. "What are you doing out at this time of night?" she asked. The woman heard the words and tried frantically to place them in her scant vocabulary of the language. She got the gist of the query, if not the exact meaning, and tried to answer as best she could.

"I fled ... bad man ... need place... to stay. I... stay here... until morning? I go... first light." The old woman's features softened as she heard the young woman's broken English. The visitor had striking features and looked to be in her mid-thirties, so the older woman took a guess as to what she meant by running from a "bad man."

"Of course you can, dearie. Don't let anyone ever say Eleanor Smith turned away a soul in need. I couldn't face my Maker if I turned you out. Come on... oh, my. Is that horse yours?" She gestured to Wynne. The young woman nodded, correctly guessing the meaning of her question. Eleanor frowned thoughtfully. "Well, there's the old barn in the back, but there's not much in it. There haven't been any horses here for many a year, but we can make do." The woman listened to this, catching a word here and there, but not really sure what the old woman was talking about.

Eleanor stepped out from the house and started walking around the side. "Come follow me, dear, and we'll get your horse taken care of." She beckoned to the woman, who grabbed Wynne's reins and followed her. Eleanor wondered why the woman would be dragging a horse around, but decided to wait on that. "Now then, what's your name?" she asked her. The woman looked at her blankly, not comprehending. "What is your name?" Eleanor asked again, using her hands to demonstrate. The woman nodded her understanding.

"Gwen," she said after a brief pause.

"And your horse's name?" she asked, pointing to Wynne.

"Wynne," Gwen replied. The woman nodded again and fell silent. They reached the stable and went inside. Eleanor found the light switch and turned on the lights.

"That's better. Now we can see what we're doing." The woman looked shocked, and said something in an odd language. "What

FINDING SECRETS

was that?" Eleanor asked, cocking her head. The woman frowned in concentration.

"How... do that?" she asked.

Eleanor raised her eyebrows. "What, turn on the lights? Just like this," she said, flipping the switch. The woman stared at it in awe and said something else in her strange language. Eleanor was starting to think there was something very odd about her guest. She spoke and understood some English, but spoke it with a very thick, lilting accent. She seemed to never have seen a light switch before. And her clothes were very odd-looking – a tunic-like shirt extending to just above the knee, belted at the waist with an odd, loose pant underneath. Both garments looked finely woven. She wore a plaid sash diagonally across her body, and what looked like a solid gold brooch shaped like a dragon pinned on the sash at her shoulder. It looked medieval to Eleanor. She opened a stall door and surveyed the inside. There was no bedding, but the floor was smooth earth with no holes, so the horse should be fine for the night. "Alright, you can put your horse in here. There isn't any bedding, but I can get some tomorrow."

"Thank you," the young woman said, and went about untacking the horse. Now that the horse was in the light, Eleanor saw that the saddle was oddly built. It had a high cantle, no stirrups, and in front there were two knobby protrusions from the leather that looked like places you could hook bags onto. The seat looked uncomfortable, but the thin saddle pad had intricate Celtic designs on it and appeared handmade. The bridle was more normal, but it had no bit. The young woman – Gwen, she'd said her name was – quickly finished caring for the horse and put her in the stall, whispering to her like the horse was actually listening.

Eleanor felt a rush of compassion for the woman. Her face looked like it had endured more than its fair share of suffering, but Eleanor also saw laugh lines. Her eyes were a startling, deep blue, and her bearing was proud. *No wonder she's run into trouble with men*, Eleanor mused. *Nice young thing like her.*

The woman turned to her. "We... to house... yes?" she asked. She looked plenty tired, poor thing, but just then Eleanor caught sight of something by the woman's side that made her stiffen.

"What's that?" she asked, pointing.

The woman drew a dagger from her side. "Way to... protect me... if danger." Eleanor stared at it in shock, and Gwen frowned. "Women, too... must protect selves... when men gone." Her blue eyes flashed as she challenged the old woman about her right to carry a dagger, and her expression indicated that she was a person not used to being questioned.

"Oh, I wasn't worried so much about your right to carry it, dearie. It makes no difference to me, but normally people don't walk around with weapons casually on their hips, except for bobbies. How did you get it?" Wynne understood more than Gwen and advised her how to answer, though both wondered what "bobbies" meant.

"Husband gave me... on wedding. Said... I must be... protect self."

Eleanor's eyes opened wide. "Are you married, child?" Gwen nodded. "Then what's this trouble you've had with a man? And where is your husband?" Gwen frowned in concentration. Wynne translated and gave her the words to answer.

"Men... enemies of husband... wish to... capture me. I had to... come save... my child." She enunciated the words carefully.

Eleanor stared at the woman. "You have a child, lass?" she exclaimed. "Where is he or she then?"

"Not... not born yet."

"Ah, so you're pregnant," Eleanor realized, studying her. She must be only in her first trimester, as she showed no visible signs of pregnancy. The young woman nodded. Eleanor was bursting with more questions, but could see now was no time to ask. The woman looked tired and if she was with child, she needed rest. "Come up with me to the house, dearie, and we'll have a nice cup of tea and then off to bed." The women left the barn. The older kept stealing glances at the younger. She'd had a strange feeling tonight would be different; it was why she was still up. During her prayers the Lord had prompted her to expect a guest and to treat the person well. She supposed this young woman was the guest, but what was so important about her? At least the children were all asleep. The woman held herself with poise and pride, despite her halting English. Eleanor wondered who her enemies were, and why they disliked her husband, and who he was. She opened the back door for the woman and held it for her. She waited outside a few minutes after the woman went in, looking up at the sky. "Alright then, Lord, I'll do my best to care for this woman. She seems like a kind soul, even if she is mysterious. But then, so are You." Eleanor went inside.

⚜

Cassie opened her eyes. She stared at the ceiling, hardly believing what she'd just seen. It was a continuation of her previous dream and the vision she'd had earlier. But why? Why was she having these dreams? At least this one had actually had names, though they didn't necessarily make sense. The young woman *was* Gwen, and she had been pregnant when she arrived here. But what had happened to the child? And what was all that about running from her husband's enemies? They were probably the men in Cassie's earlier dream, but why had they been after Gwen? Had her husband worked in some secret branch of the government? And why on earth hadn't she spoken English, especially since she had said she lived in Cadbury before Glastonbury? Where had she come from, and why had this dream clearly been in the present day, while the previous one seemed to have been hundreds of years ago? Cassie groaned. How was she going to figure all this out?

Dassah lifted her head from the floor. *What is it, girl?*

"I don't know... nothing makes sense."

Then stop trying so hard to figure it out. Accept what you know, and leave what you do not to the One. He knows all, and He alone can grant you understanding. It will come.

"Good point." She closed her eyes. "God, I know You know already, but I am seriously confused down here. These clearly aren't just random dreams, but I have no clue what to make of them. I'm giving myself a headache trying to figure them out. Please help me. Please be with Mom and Dad and Mr. Thompson while they're with the Brotherhood and keep them safe. Be with Mrs. Thompson and protect her and give her comfort. And be with us God, as we try to rescue our parents from the Brotherhood, and help William progress on his journey with You. And Lord, it would be really nice if You could prompt him toward being a bit more open-minded. Thank You for weaving together all those melodies in Creation. They are truly awesome. And God, please help me figure out this woman we're staying with and that weird tune I heard on the Tor. Amen." She opened her eyes and looked over at Sarah's bed. It was empty. "Is everyone up?"

Yes. I waited until you woke. It is late afternoon. Cassie looked at the clock. It read 4:30. She'd slept for about three hours. She heard shrieks of delight coming from outside and pulled up the shade. The children were playing in the garden with Kai, and the others were down there as well. William was standing to the side, looking a little uncomfortable. Cassie guessed he hadn't been around children much. Sarah and David were fully ensconced in the game, and Cassie realized they were playing Blind Man's Bluff. She remembered playing that game the day her ears had become pointed. That was four years ago, close to the very day. Who could have guessed that four years later it would be played again with full knowledge of who lurked in the shadows?

Dassah nudged her hand. *The One knew. And I think, somewhere, you may already know the answers to your questions.*

Cassie grunted. "Well, if I do, I hope that somewhere becomes the front of my mind very soon." She rubbed her temples, then decided to read a little in her Bible. That should help. She took it out and placed it on her bed. "Okay, God," she said, looking upward. "It would be very helpful if I could open my Bible to a verse that would help me figure things out. Please." Closing her eyes, she opened the Bible. She could tell from the thickness of the pages between her fingers that it had landed somewhere in the New Testament. She opened her eyes to see Matthew 19, the story of a rich young man who had asked Jesus how he could gain eternal life. Cassie knew the story, but her eye was drawn toward the twenty-sixth verse, one she had both highlighted and underlined in the past: *With man this is impossible, but with God all things are possible.* She let the words slowly sink in. *All things are possible,* she thought. *Okay, how does that apply?* With that phrase in mind, she slowly began reshuffling through all the information that had been whirling around her brain like a runaway train on a circular track. In the middle of comparisons, musings, and conjectures, an idea came to her. Normally she would have dismissed it immediately as being absolutely preposterous, but with the verse in mind, it dawned on her that it could explain almost everything. Even though she still had no clue how such a thing could ever be possible.

Dassah could tell that she had found a potential explanation. *What is it?* she asked.

It's something, Cassie answered. *And that's good enough for me right now.* She stood and continued aloud, "But I think I'll keep it to myself for now. Even with the verse, I can't really believe it's possible at the moment. But who knows, by the time this all is over, I might even believe pigs can fly."

5

GOING BACK

Ty stared boldly into Morton's gray eyes. "I told you, I have
no idea what you're talking about," he said tersely.

Morton gazed back at him. "Are you sure?" he asked.

"Yes! What would I gain by lying to you?" The tension in the
room was palpable, like a faint crackling noise or goose bumps
on your arms. The air separating the two men nearly seemed to
shimmer, like heat waves off a highway in the middle of summer. If
looks could kill, both men would be long dead. Tyler Pennington,
though not nearly as strong a Brenwyd as his daughter, was still a
force to be reckoned with. Any lesser man would have stopped arguing upon seeing the intense, smoldering anger in his green eyes.
But Morton was equally formidable and paid no heed.

Without taking his eyes from his prisoner's, he opened a draw-
er and drew out a slim, leather-bound book. "Then explain this."
His voice was soft, but as sinister as a snake's hiss. He was testing
the man, not entirely sure of his own theory, but determined to get
to the bottom of the mystery. Ty took the notebook from Morton
and leafed through the parchment pages carefully. It was full of
portraits, and Ty's professional mind noted that it was likely from
the fifth or sixth century. All the portraits had names underneath,

and most of the names were crossed through. Ty came to one page and stopped. The page on the left showed a woman's face. She was beautiful, and Ty could clearly see pointed ears. Her name was almost unreadable because the cross out was so thorough, but Ty could still make it out: Caelwyn. He looked back up at Morton, fury crossing his features, but the Brotherhood master simply waved him to continue. Ty looked at the right page. It also showed a woman, but she was not a Brenwyd. Her name was also crossed out and Ty couldn't quite make it out. It hadn't been written very well, and the only thing he could tell about it was that it started with a G. "Keep going," Morton said. "I'm sure you'll find the next page quite interesting."

Ty turned the page – and froze. His daughter's portrait stared up at him. His eyes dropped to the name, which had not been crossed out, and read: *Caelwyn's student*. His brow furrowed in confusion. He could tell it had been drawn a long time ago, because it had the same look as the others, so it couldn't be his Cassie. He shifted his gaze to the next page and recognized William, the Commander's son, the one who had gotten Cassie and the twins out. Studying the pictures carefully, he saw the drawings weren't perfectly accurate, as if drawn from verbal descriptions, yet there was no denying the resemblance. Turning the page, he saw portraits that resembled David and Sarah. Those also had inconsistencies, and upon close inspection he decided that they were just people who looked like the teens. But still, it was disconcerting. He looked up at Morton, who was watching him carefully. "Where did you get these?" Ty asked him, curious.

"I drew them. A personal record of all who annoyed me and had to be silenced."

"You've never seen Cassie."

"Actually, I glimpsed her on the day she arrived and was reminded of this picture."

"Then why have you waited until now to ask me about it?"

"You have been busy, Professor. I did not want to interrupt your work."

Ty turned back to the page and tapped the portrait. "At first glance, I admit, it looks like her, but further inspection reveals certain discrepancies that show it's merely someone who has similar features. It's not her. I know."

"I don't doubt you, Professor." Ty thought Morton looked disappointed and a little wary. "But the resemblance is there, don't you think?"

"Yes. And with the others as well." Ty examined the book more closely. "But given the apparent age of this book and the differences I see, it's not them."

Morton nodded. "What if I told you I drew them after only several brief glimpses of the subjects?" He seemed to be asking Ty's general opinion as an archaeologist, not as his prisoner. Ty wondered what stake he had in the portraits.

"I would say it greatly increases the probability it's not them. The mind can remember things wrongly, and the eye can be deceived, especially when you have only had a few encounters with the subject."

Morton sighed. "Yes, I know." He appeared greatly puzzled. Ty flipped through more of the book, curious, despite himself, about the people portrayed. There were various men and women, almost all with pointed ears, but there were a few who looked like regular humans. Ty wondered what they had done to earn Morton's hate. He handed the book back, and Morton spoke again. "I hear you are very nearly to the end of your research. So close, in fact, that you could start dig work in a few days." His tone was more relaxed.

Ty narrowed his eyes. "And who told you that?" he asked.

"You did." At Ty's show of surprise, Morton smiled lazily, his good humor apparently regained. "Since our recent... security lapse, we have outfitted your quarters with a camera and microphone.

We hear every word you say. I am pleased to inform you that we will be moving to the dig site within the next few days, as soon as I get the final few snares worked out." Ty glared at him. "Come, come, Professor, get excited. It will be your largest discovery and one men have fantasized about for hundreds of years."

"It should go to a museum where the people can see it. It's their history," Ty said. He lowered his voice. "And don't think I don't know what you're really after."

Morton gave him a piercing look. "I thought you might. Then you should be grateful to me. Museums can be robbed. If kept quiet, it and the treasure will be secure for all time."

"Grateful? Are you out of your mind? Once you find that treasure, I'm of no further use to you. Don't think I don't know what happens then, especially given my Brenwyd blood."

"Oh, no? You are a professional archaeologist with many projects in mind that I'm sure would be beneficial to the Brotherhood. I won't be getting rid of you so quickly, Professor."

Ty tensed. "And my wife?" he asked.

"She will stay, to give incentive. Your friend, unfortunately for him, is expendable. He knows too much. We will leave his wife alone, however, as long as you cooperate."

Ty stared, anger once again filling his eyes, along with pain. He didn't want to ask the next question, knowing the answer, but he couldn't help it. "And Cassie?"

Morton met his gaze with undisguised malice. He was enjoying this. "I think you know the answer to that, Professor. You know the prophecy. She is a threat, and a threat cannot be tolerated."

"She's only fourteen!"

"And filled to the brim with Brenwyd blood!"

"Then you will kill a fourteen-year-old out of fear," Ty charged. He knew it was dangerous to cross Morton, but he didn't care.

Morton's eyes darkened and became as ice. "Security reasons, Professor. And because of that, her friends will have to go, too, and those brutes that guard her. Perhaps you should have considered that before you decided to have a child." Ty glowered at Morton, but inwardly his heart plummeted to his toes. Morton's words only confirmed a guilt that had become all too common in his mind over the past week. "Thank you for your opinion, Professor. You have set my mind greatly at ease. Get ready to move." With that, Morton summoned guards from the hall to escort Ty back to his cell.

⁓⑤⊗⑤⁓

"If we wait for the Brotherhood to come to Cadbury, we probably have a better chance, right?" David asked William. "Then there wouldn't be so many men around guarding the parents." The teens were out in the stable discussing how to rescue their parents from the Brotherhood, and though no one had brought it up point blank yet, the prophecy was on everyone's minds.

"Probably," William said. "But they may also be expecting us to do something like that."

"So are you saying the best thing would be to go straight back to the castle and get them out through the tunnels? 'Cause if that's the case, we should have just hid somewhere around Carlisle instead of riding all the way here," Cassie said.

"You were the one who had the feeling we should go to Glastonbury," William pointed out.

"But we had decided to go to Cadbury anyway, and this was on the way," Sarah countered. "Anyway, if we decide going back to the castle is the best idea, we could use the transfer thing because we've been there."

"Good point," Cassie conceded.

"But weren't we going to find the treasure first?" David said. "Cassie, you mentioned several times last week that you think there's something specific in there that your dad doesn't want the Brotherhood to get their hands on, but you never said what it was. Shouldn't we go look for that as soon as possible? We have no idea what the Brotherhood is doing at the moment, so we should take advantage of whatever time we have."

"And what *is* this mystery object?" Sarah put in.

Cassie opened her mouth to reply, deciding she might as well tell them her idea, crazy as it sounded, but the faint approach of footsteps checked her. "Someone's coming!" she hissed. "Act normal."

"I would like someone to define normal after the last two weeks," William muttered under his breath.

Sarah fortunately got the message. "So I was reading this brochure today about the Chalice Gardens in town, and I think we should visit there tomorrow, too, along with the Abbey. The legend surrounding them is all about Joseph of Arimathea with a King Arthur connection, so it's probably worth checking out."

"Oh, yeah, that sounds fine," David agreed hastily, as if they had been talking about the gardens all along.

Gwen entered the stable at that moment and looked around at the four of them. "I hope I'm not interrupting anything, but I have a favor to ask you," she said with an apologetic tone.

"Oh, no, we weren't talking about anything too important," Cassie said, trying to sound assuring. "What is it?"

"Well, some of my guests are starting to filter back in, so I was wondering if you could occupy the children while I start working on supper."

"Oh, I'd love to," Sarah said, smiling. She enjoyed playing with little kids. Cassie nodded, too.

"Thank you." Gwen turned to go, but hesitated and turned back. "This may sound a little odd, but I've got a feeling that you have some questions for me. Why don't you come to the kitchen at quarter past nine? All the children and guests will be mostly taken care of by then." She retreated from the barn, and the teens stared after her.

"She knows something about us," Cassie said.

"But how? Are you sure?" William asked.

Cassie shrugged, feeling reluctant to share her most recent dream and her subsequent ponderings at that moment. "I don't know, but I really get the feeling that there's way more to this woman than meets the eye," she said.

They returned to the house and time went by quickly. Dinner came and went, and the teens met a few of the guests staying at the Camelot House, an older couple and a younger couple. Gwen mentioned that there was also a family, but they had gone out for dinner. The teens finished dinner quickly and made themselves scarce, not wanting to answer too many questions from guests. At last, the time Gwen had mentioned arrived and they went to the kitchen – but she was not there. They sat down to wait. When Gwen entered a few minutes later, she did not sit, but gestured for them to follow her as she went out the back door. The foursome looked at each other.

"What is she up to?" David wondered.

Cassie stood. "I don't know, but come on. We won't find out by staying in the kitchen." A strange excitement was growing in her chest. They found Gwen waiting outside. Wordlessly, she led them to the stable. The horses looked over their stall doors alertly, as if expecting their riders.

Cassie went up to Twi and rubbed her nose. *Have you been able to figure out what this is about?* the mare asked.

Sort of. Maybe, Cassie answered, thinking of her theory. Gwen was studying them closely, and Cassie was reminded intensely of the woman from her dreams, especially now that it was dark.

However, Gwen didn't speak, instead disappearing into the tack room and reappearing with a saddle. "Tack up. I need to take you somewhere," she ordered, going to Wynne with the saddle.

"Where?" Sarah asked, feeling a little nervous.

"To where you need to go, and must go."

"And where might that be, exactly?" William asked suspiciously, half-wishing he had his sword. He had enjoyed talking with her and listening to her King Arthur stories, but it never hurt to be too careful.

Gwen didn't pause in her task as she answered him. "You'll find out."

"How do you know we need to go there?" he pressed.

"Because you've already been there. Now make haste, we don't have all night. Time is precious." Cassie, David, William, and Sarah all exchanged glances. What had come over the woman?

Kai butted Cassie's hand. *Do what she says, girl. She is on our side,* he assured her.

How do you know that?

Because I do not sense evil about her. She does not wish you harm. You could sense it if you listened. Cassie did as Kai suggested. As before, she didn't find anything wrong with the woman's song, and so decided to trust her.

Dassah came to Twi's stall as Cassie was cinching up Twi's girth. She had Cassie's emergency bag in her jaws. *Thanks,* Cassie told the dog.

You are welcome, Dassah said, dropping it at her feet.

Once everyone was tacked up, Gwen led Wynne into the yard and mounted. The others followed suit. They walked until the house was hidden by trees, then Gwen urged Wynne into a trot. Cassie knew where they were going now. The Tor was the only possibility. Gwen led them around the hill, stopped, and dismounted by a clump of trees at its base. She let Wynne loose and entered the deep shadow of the trees, vanishing from sight. The teens stayed mounted, feeling uneasy. Gwen reappeared soon, carrying a long bundle. Cassie tried to make out what was in it, but saw only vague bulges. Gwen knelt and laid the package on the ground.

"Come," she said. She waited until they had all dismounted and gathered around her before speaking again. "You will need these." She unwrapped the bundle and the teens gaped as their weapons were revealed.

"How did you get those?" William demanded, his disquiet growing.

"From your rooms. I had a feeling they'd be in there. I brought them here earlier so I wouldn't have to deal with transporting them now."

"How did you know we had them?" David asked, eyeing the woman suspiciously.

"You need not fear me, David Thompson. I knew because... well, I cannot say just yet. But you shall find out. I am not your enemy." Her gaze rested on William for a brief second. "You all have a long journey ahead of you, and it is a journey you must take. I dare not even consider what will happen if you do not." She closed her eyes and Cassie saw her shudder slightly. Cassie was starting to feel a little weirded out. What exactly was going on? "Now remount, all of you. The slip will not stay open long."

"What slip?" Cassie asked.

Gwen locked eyes with her. "I think you may have an idea." Cassie narrowed her eyes, frowning as she racked her brain to fig-ure out what the woman meant. Gwen studied her for a moment. "Mount!" she commanded sternly. They didn't dare to disobey her. Wynne went to Gwen's side and they backed away slightly. Gwen glanced up the hill. Cassie followed her gaze. It seemed to rest on the level area where she had discovered the strange melody. She listened to it again, and one part of it in particular seemed to impose itself on her mind. It was full and rich, with a clear Celtic influence, and Cassie thought that if it were a piece of cloth it would burst from its fullness. As she listened, it hit what she sensed was the highest point of its crescendo, and she couldn't help gasping at the intensity. "Cassie," Gwen said then. Cassie looked at her. "I cannot hear the slip's melodies, but are you hearing an opening?"

Cassie stared at her. How did she know about her gift? "What... how... ?"

Gwen smiled mysteriously. "You're not the first Brenwyd I've known. Is there an opening?" Cassie heard the others gasp. Stunned, she stared at Gwen. How did she know about Brenwyds?

"What?" she asked "How do you-?"

Does it sound like something coming to the fullest volume it can, to the point where it can do nothing but decrease? Wynne demanded. *I can sense you do, from your reaction. Go. Now!* Cassie still stared at Gwen, but Twi took things into her own hooves at that moment and started forward up the hill. Cassie lurched backward slightly, but quickly regained her balance and decided to trust her horse. The others looked on in confusion, not aware of what was happening. Their horses had a good idea, however, and pawed the ground impatiently, straining at the bit. Phoenix went so far as to rear up slightly to evade William's tight rein. That earned him a sharp reprimand from his rider, but it worked.

"Go!" Gwen said again as Phoenix came down. "Follow her! Quickly!" The riders may not have been sure, but their horses were and promptly ignored all attempts to stop them. Cassie and Twi quickly achieved a slow canter, reached the place of the melody, and disappeared with Kai and Dassah on their heels. David stopped fighting Fire and urged him after her. No way was he about to let Cassie get stranded somewhere on her own. He also disappeared, and Sarah and William weren't far behind. Within a minute, the only sign the four teens had ever been there was the set of hoofprints dug into the earth. Gwen watched where they had disappeared, remembering another similar night.

Wynne lipped her hair. *They are alright. Do not worry.*

"I know. I just can't help it," Gwen murmured. She remounted and started for home, but something told her she was not alone. She stopped and looked to the top of the hill. Silhouetted against the backdrop of the night stood a figure. She did not appear to have seen Gwen, but Gwen felt her blood run cold. It was an enemy, she was sure. Gwen and Wynne retreated into the trees, out of sight but hopefully not out of earshot. The figure started to move down the Tor and Gwen saw that it was a short, blond woman.

"So close," she heard the woman say as she stopped at the place the teens had disappeared. "So close. But where did they go?" The woman looked keenly at everything around her. Gwen prayed she would remain unnoticed and her prayer was answered as the woman turned around abruptly. "Bah. Brenwyd tricks. At least I know who I can question. She's bound to know something." The woman went back the way she had come. Gwen waited until she was quite gone before leaving the shelter of the trees.

That woman has evil in her, Wynne said.

"I won't argue with you," Gwen said. "And I think she's looking for me."

⁘⁘⁘

Cassie could see nothing but darkness and flashes of images that flew by too quickly for her to identify. She felt like she was actually inside the melody, and it wrapped around her, taking her... taking her somewhere. The steady beat behind the music she had noted earlier seemed to grow louder and louder. The only way she knew the others were with her was because she could sense their horses. The darkness was so absolute she couldn't see her hand in front of her face. Her stomach felt slightly nauseous. She prayed.

Suddenly she saw a thin strip of lighter darkness, which seemed almost like day in that dark place, and she and Twi burst out into the night. Cassie sank her weight down in the saddle, pulling on the reins gently to get Twi's attention. The mare obliged by slowing. Cassie turned her around and saw David, Sarah, and William appear seemingly from nowhere, as if they'd just completed a transfer, though she had thought Phoenix couldn't transfer. Kai and Dassah had made it as well, and they definitely couldn't transfer.

William slowed Phoenix while looking around, trying to figure out what had just happened and more importantly, where they

Cassie felt like she was actually inside
the melody, and it wrapped around her,
taking her... taking her somewhere.

were now. The night had suddenly become quite foggy. His brow furrowed and he drew in a sharp breath. "We're still at the Tor! We haven't moved more than a few meters."

"What?" Sarah asked, incredulous. She couldn't possibly believe they had stayed in the same place, not after that ride, but she saw William was right. "How? And what on earth was that... place?"

"I'm not sure," Cassie said, looking to the top of the hill. "But something's up. Look! There's no tower." And indeed there wasn't. There was some sort of low building, but no one could tell exactly what it was. The she looked the other way and gasped. "Maybe we're not at the Tor after all." The others followed her gaze and gasped as well. The area that had previously been flatlands, full of houses and trees, was now covered in water. A lot of water, only several yards away from them.

"This makes no sense," William said. "If we had transferred, it would only have been you three, and the dogs wouldn't be here."

"So you're saying that the water just appeared and the tower just disappeared without us going anywhere?" David asked.

"That seems to be what happened," Cassie said, her brow wrinkled in puzzlement. Kai and Dassah had been sniffing the air and communicating non-verbally, trying to sort out what they were sensing.

We are in the same place, yet we are not at the same time, Kai said slowly. *The air smells different. I do not sense many humans here, or the scent of any nearby town. And it is later in the night than it was. But we are in the same place.*

"What?" Cassie asked. She looked at her watch. It still read the same time, but when she looked up at the sky she realized Kai was right. The stars were in different positions, and she guessed it was into the early morning hours. "How? Did we cross time zones or something? Was that a transfer after all?"

No, Fire said. *Not the kind you are thinking of.*

"This makes no sense at all," William repeated, his eyes darting all around. "Where are Gwen and Wynne? She had better explain this." His voice had an angry edge to it.

"Relax, William. We'll figure it out," Sarah said, though sounding a little nervous.

"But where could they have gone? They were *right there*," David said. "And how does she know about Brenwyds, anyway? What the heck is going on? Water does not just appear out of nowhere. Especially not that much water."

"I don't know," Cassie said, a hint of desperation tingeing her voice. "I just don't know."

"Gwen mentioned something about a slip not staying open long, and then she mentioned an opening. Maybe that's what we went through," Sarah suggested.

"So what's a slip?" William asked.

Sarah shrugged. "How would I know?"

"It felt like we traveled through... something, but I don't know what," Cassie mused aloud. "She said we needed to go on a long journey and if we didn't there would be severe consequences. I don't get why she thought going through whatever-that-was would help us understand. I feel more confused than a penguin at the equator."

Phoenix stamped his foot and nickered. William patted his neck reassuringly. "It's okay, boy," he murmured.

Phoenix stretched his head toward Cassie. *Go up the hill, girl. This is where we start*, he said, sounding completely calm.

"Start what?"

You will see. I cannot tell you everything yet.

"You know what's going on?" He was silent. Cassie caught a guilty feeling from all the horses. She looked around at them sharply. "Do you all know what's going on?"

Twi shook her mane. *In a manner of speaking. We do not fully understand all the details – we do not have all of them. But the woman does not mean you harm, and we had to come back. It is the only way,* she said, as if that explained everything.

"What?" Cassie couldn't recall Twi ever being so mysterious. Horses were generally very straightforward. Well, except for Wynne. Maybe she'd rubbed off on Twi. "Come back... where?"

Not where.

"Huh?"

You will find out. It is very likely in your mind already. You just need to remember you know it. Now Twi sounded amused.

"Thanks, that's *so* helpful. I'm not going to get anything else out of you, am I?"

Nope. The mare sounded entirely too smug.

Cassie sighed and rolled her eyes. As she did, she caught sight of a light at the top of the hill. "Look! Someone's up there," she said, pointing.

"Maybe it's Gwen," Sarah suggested.

"I don't think so, Sarah. Gwen didn't have a light."

"Maybe we just didn't see it," Sarah persisted. Cassie started to dismount. "Cassie, what are you doing?"

"I'm going to find out what that light is. It doesn't look like a flashlight. It's flickering too much. And we should find *someone* who has an idea of what's going on," Cassie reached the ground and almost fell. "Whoa!"

"Are you okay?" David asked, dismounting from his own saddle. Upon touching the ground he felt extremely dizzy, and his head started to pound. As quickly as the sensation came, it left, leaving him leaning against Fire for balance. The bay gelding bent his head back and nuzzled his rider worriedly. "I'm okay," he murmured. "Guys, I'd take your time on the dismount if I were you," he said in a louder voice.

Cassie chuckled ruefully. "Yeah. Serious balance issues."

"Are you guys alright?" William asked, staying firmly in his saddle.

"Yeah. Just got really dizzy for a sec. It was weird," Cassie said.

"Maybe it's an after-effect of that black place," David suggested, shaking his head slightly to clear the lingering pounding. The pounding left, but he had a dull headache.

"Maybe," Cassie agreed, keeping a hand on Twi's neck as she recovered her equilibrium.

Sarah looked a little pensive. "If you guys don't mind, I think I'll stay here while you investigate. Yell if you need help," she said. The time she'd spent in the black place had jarred her. She hated the dark, and usually slept with her bedroom door cracked open so the nightlight in the hall could shine into her room.

"I'll stay with you," William offered. "It may be a good thing to have a couple of people in reserve in case something goes wrong." Cassie nodded. Too many weird things had happened that night to not be careful. She took her knife-belt from her bag and strapped it around her waist, but pulled her shirt down over it some and shifted the sheathed knives so they rested against her back and weren't too obvious. David followed her lead and kept his sword close, repositioning the belt so it was strapped diagonally across his back instead of hanging at his side. They crept up the hill toward the light with Kai and Dassah following them. The light moved back and forth at a slow, steady pace.

David wondered what was going on in Cassie's mind. He was feeling unsettled and wondered if they'd been wrong to trust Gwen, though he didn't want to think ill of the woman. She seemed too nice for anything like subterfuge, but he'd been through too much recently not to be suspicious of her, even with Cassie's reassurances. They were now much closer to the top of the hill, and David saw that the building was low but long, built of rough-cut stone, with a thatched roof. A thatched roof? Who had a thatched roof nowadays? And where had the tower gone? David remembered Cassie saying that the tower hadn't been built until the fifteenth century, and that it hadn't been there in her dreams. Come to think of it, she had also said that the Tor had been an island in her dream.

Had they somehow traveled into Cassie's dream world? Now that was a scary thought.

"There's the light," Cassie breathed into his ear, disturbing his thoughts. "It looks like an old- fashioned wooden lantern with a candle. A man is carrying it. He looks like a monk, and he has a cross hanging from his neck." David wondered how she could possibly see that well, even with her super-senses. It was fully dark, and foggy.

"Why not just use a flashlight?" he mused. "And what's a monk doing here at this time of night?"

"Let's ask." Before David could voice any objection, she called out, "Hello! Who's there?" The light stopped moving and turned toward them. Now David could see the man for himself. He was, indeed, dressed in what appeared to be a monk's habit. The man brought the lantern up to his eyes and they narrowed. He said something, but neither David nor Cassie could understand it. "What'd he say?" Cassie asked.

"No idea. Must be foreign," David assumed. The man approached and stared at them curiously, while they did likewise. He spoke again, more slowly this time, but the two teens couldn't make heads or tails out of it.

Any ideas, guys? Cassie asked Kai and Dassah, who were standing a little behind them out of the man's immediate line of sight.

No, Dassah replied. *But I do not think he means us harm.*

"I'm sorry, but we don't understand you," Cassie said, shaking her head. The man looked her over very carefully, and gestured to her clothes, sounding disapproving. Cassie looked down, but saw nothing out of place. She put a hand to her headband, making sure it hadn't slipped somehow and exposed her ears. Kai stepped in front of Cassie, his tail wagging slowly, sniffing at the stranger curiously. The man stopped talking to look at him.

"Now what?" David asked in a low voice. Cassie shrugged. The man turned to David.

"Brenwyd?" he asked slowly, with a thick accent that, oddly enough, reminded Cassie of Gwen's, though hers was not nearly as strong.

"How'd he know that?" Cassie whispered.

"No idea." David stepped a little in front of Cassie. The man held up his hands to show he had no weapons, correctly interpreting the move as protection, and held up his crucifix.

"I don't think he's going to hurt us," Cassie said. "Monks don't generally hurt people." She used her ability to listen to his song, and relaxed a little. "His song sounds fine."

"Whoever and whatever he is, it doesn't mean much if we can't communicate."

"What's going on?" William's voice asked. David, Cassie, and the monk jumped. Focused as they were on each other, no one had noticed William and Sarah approaching. They had been wondering what was going on and worrying as time went by, so they'd decided to investigate.

"We're trying to figure that out," Cassie said in answer to William's question. She nodded toward the monk. "He speaks a different language and we can't understand each other, but he looked at Kai and figured out he's a Brenwyd dog."

"Really?" William asked, looking at the man. The monk raised his lantern to get a better look at the newcomers and his expression became one of shock. He spoke rapidly in his language, gesturing with his hands toward William. William's eyebrows shot up in surprise. "Well that's... weird."

"What? Do you understand this language?" David asked.

William nodded, but he looked utterly flummoxed. "It's the original language of the Brotherhood, the same Caelwyn's diary is written in – an ancient Celtic dialect called Brythonic."

"What's he saying?" Sarah asked. "And why would he be using that language, anyway? Does it still exist somewhere in Wales or something?"

"It's supposed to be dead, so I have no clue why he's using it. He's saying something about a king and asking what we're doing here." William answered the man in his language, but haltingly. He didn't speak the language much, but could read it fluently. He and the man exchanged several phrases before William started to translate. "He says his name is Joseph and that this is the Church of Rest. He wants to know why we have a Brenwyd dog, because we don't look like Brenwyds." Cassie looked at the man, debated with herself for a few seconds, and took her headband from her ears, turning her head so the man could see the points. The monk and William had another exchange. William's cheeks turned a little red and he made a choking sound. "He wants to know if we're lost."

Cassie thought there was something else. "That all?" she probed.

William looked at her, an acutely uncomfortable expression on his face. "Um, well, this is going to sound strange, but he asked if any of us were... married. Or engaged." They all stared at him.

"What?" David said. The monk looked at them in confusion and said something else. William stammered back a response, and the monk looked slightly abashed.

"What'd he say that time?" Sarah asked warily, not sure if she wanted to know.

William stumbled over the words. "He said... he said that if we weren't all siblings or... um, married, we should have a chaperone around. I told him that people do *not* get married this young where we're from. He apologized."

Cassie wondered what on earth would prompt a monk, of all people, to ask such a question of a group of teenagers. The days of young teenagers marrying had ended a very long time ago... Cassie snapped to attention as she realized what had happened. Why hadn't she realized it before? It was crazy, but that didn't mean it wasn't true. She'd considered the theory earlier and had dismissed it, but that had been in the comfort of Gwen's twenty-first century inn. Twi had been right. "William, ask him what year it is," she requested with some urgency.

William looked at her in astonishment. "Ask him what year it is? What kind of question is that?"

"Please, just ask," Cassie said, serious.

"Okay." William didn't look or sound convinced, but he put the question to the monk. When he got the answer, his eyes narrowed. He asked the monk again and got the same answer, with a little extra information. This time his eyes widened in shock as he realized what Cassie had already guessed. He drew in a ragged breath, trying to accept the answer. *You have got to be kidding me,* he thought. The monk noticed his apparent distress and asked if he was ill. William responded by saying no, he was fine. Sarah put a hand on William's arm. He had gone a little pale, and his expression concerned her. Cassie knew from his reaction that her guess had been correct, and just stared straight in front of her in shock.

"William, what did he say?" Sarah asked, looking up at him with worry in her eyes. The possibility had also grown in her mind, and she had an idea as to the source of his distress.

"He says..." William broke off, trying to wrap his brain around the answer's implications. It was way outside the boundaries of what he considered sane. "He says it is the year 516 A.D." The other three gasped, and the dogs showed signs of surprise. Cassie felt the horses in her mind, and they were not so much surprised as relieved. Cassie made a note to question them later. Sarah opened her mouth to ask a question, but William held up a hand to stop her. "There's more." He locked eyes with Cassie. "He also says it is the twenty-first year... in the reign of King Arthur."

INTRODUCTIONS

Caelwyn felt a dog's head nudge her side, so she rolled onto her other side and snuggled closer to her husband to avoid it. She needed her sleep. She'd gone without it too often lately, trying to get to the bottom of the disturbing rumors that were circulating. The nudging continued and grew in intensity.

Caelwyn, wake up. Joseph needs you. I know you are awake, a familiar canine voice chided. Caelwyn sighed and sat up. She'd sleep more later. She crept out of bed, hoping not to wake her husband. He, too, needed sleep, even more than she did.

What is it? she asked the dog. He was a large, handsome dog, his back level with Caelwyn's waist and his coat a dark gray color. One spot of lighter color on his ear reminded Caelwyn of a dragon's wing, which is how he'd gotten his name: Dragon. He'd been with her for many years, since he was a puppy, and they knew each other very well.

I do not know. The hawk has come with word that Joseph needs you, Dragon informed her.

Caelwyn pinned her hair up and quickly pulled on her tunic, breeches, and shoes. *Something important?* she queried.

Aye. I cannot tell you what, though. He did not say.

"Well, I suppose I shall have to find out, then." She went out to the low stable in the yard. Her mare looked at her as she entered. "Something has occurred at the Church, Wynne. Joseph has requested that I go to help him."

Very well, the mare said.

Caelwyn quickly grabbed her tack and saddled the mare. "Do you wish to come, Dragon?"

I will stay here in case anyone inquires after you, the dog decided.

Caelwyn nodded and mounted. "Let's do a transfer, Wynne. The sooner I discover what it is that has Joseph concerned, the sooner I can return to sleep." The mare walked from the yard and quickly accelerated into a gallop, gaining speed until their surroundings blurred, and the large island that Joseph's church was built upon appeared. A bridge crossed over the water from the flatlands to the island. Caelwyn slowed Wynne, thanking God as she often did for blessing the Brenwyd horses with that particular talent. It came in handy more times than she could count.

They trotted across the bridge and up the path to the church, halting several yards from the door. Caelwyn was surprised to sense four other horses in the church's stable. Joseph and his two fellow monks did not keep horses, though the stable was open to any who needed it. She led Wynne into the stable, curious. Wynne pricked her ears forward and nickered a greeting, which the other horses reciprocated. Caelwyn extended a greeting, too, but was confused that the horses apparently did not understand her. She got Wynne settled quickly and went to examine these horses. Joseph must have foreign guests. She felt them trying to communicate with her, but didn't understand exactly what they said, only got the impression. That was odd. She knew most of the languages surrounding Britain, but had never heard this tongue before.

The horses were finely bred. Two were mares and the others were geldings. One mare was black with a white star on her forehead and white sock on her right hind leg. The other was a blue roan. The horse next to Wynne was a bright bay with no markings, and the last one was a chestnut with a blaze and socks on both hind legs. He was quite tall. Before she left the stable, the shine of metal caught her eye. She turned to see very odd-looking saddles in the storage room. They had long leather strips down the side with metal rings attached, low pommels, cantles that were nearly on the level of the seat, and a curiously designed flap. Her interest fully aroused, she headed indoors to meet the owners of the horses.

Joseph greeted her at the door. He seemed either distressed or excited. "Ah, Caelwyn, I'm glad you could come. I give my deepest apologies for summoning you from your bed so late, but..." He stopped and shook his head. "I have no idea what to do!"

Caelwyn smiled reassuringly at him. "Do not concern yourself overmuch on my account, Joseph. What has happened?"

"Well, I was outside taking a late-night walk because I felt curiously restless. As I was about to return to the church, a voice hailed me. I headed toward it, wondering what someone would be doing here at such an hour. I discovered it was a young man and young woman, both of them perhaps fifteen years of age. I tried to ask them what they were doing, but they speak a language I do not understand, and they cannot speak ours. Upon closer examination, I realized they were dressed most oddly. The young woman was wearing something very similar to what the young man had on, and I have never seen such clothes before. Then a dog came into my view, and it was a Brenwyd dog." Caelwyn's eyes narrowed. How could that happen? Brenwyds rarely, if ever, gave their dogs to normal humans. "I asked if they were Brenwyd, and it seemed to alarm the young woman. I found it most strange, Caelwyn. She wore a strip of cloth around her head, and after I assured them I meant them no harm and asked about Brenwyds, she removed it to reveal that she is, in fact, Brenwyd. She was hiding her ears under the cloth." Joseph looked at Caelwyn. "I have heard rumors accusing Brenwyds of witchcraft, but are they so bad as to force a Brenwyd to hide her identity?"

Caelwyn frowned, disturbed by the news. "I did not believe so, nor have I heard of such a thing. Please, go on. There must be more."

"Yes. Well, after I queried about the dog, another young man and woman appeared, wearing the same clothes and speaking the same language. Fortunately, this young man can also speak our language. I've established that they come from a land very far from here, one with strange customs. I asked if they were married or siblings and, if not, where their chaperone was, and it seemed to cause them great embarrassment." He was distressed, Caelwyn could see, and also a little disapproving. She suppressed a smile. Joseph had very firm views on modesty and proper decorum for unmarried, non-related young people of a certain age.

"That does sound odd," she said. Joseph nodded, looking behind him. Caelwyn could tell there was more on his mind. "Is there anything else I should know before I meet them?"

He hesitated a minute. "Well... there... there is one thing. The second young man. It means nothing, I am sure, but he, ah..." He leaned in closer to whisper in her ear, as if afraid someone would overhear.

Caelwyn raised her eyebrows. "Does he? He must be of Roman descent. Common enough."

"Yes, but... well, you shall see. Come." He turned and Caelwyn followed. He led her to the small kitchen at the back of the building, where the monks made their meals.

There, seated around a table, were the four young people. They all looked at the door as the adults entered. Two dogs on the floor raised their heads. Caelwyn examined the foreigners. Two of them, a boy and girl both with dark brown hair, appeared to be siblings. The other girl was the Brenwyd. She and Caelwyn studied each other thoroughly and frankly, the girl's eyes wide in what seemed to be something like awe. One of the dogs – Caelwyn could tell he was the Brenwyd one – moved closer to the girl. Caelwyn extended greetings to him, and felt his surprise. She also saw the girl's gaze sharpen. *So she's an animal speaker as well*, Caelwyn mused. She turned to the last boy, and caught her breath. His hair was black and his eyes deep blue. His features were Romanesque, and Caelwyn fully understood Joseph's disquiet. The boy looked at her curiously. Taking in the group as a whole, Caelwyn felt a thrill rush through her. These were the ones, she was sure. She had seen them in her dreams.

Joseph spoke. "This is my friend who I told you about. Her name is Caelwyn, and she serves in the king's court." The blue-eyed boy started, his mouth coming partway open in surprise. Caelwyn wondered at the reaction. She did not consider herself so well-known, though stories had indeed spread about her role in the kingdom. The boy quickly translated for the others, who showed similar signs of surprise and shock.

"It is a pleasure to make your acquaintance," Caelwyn said. "What are you called?"

"My name is William," said the boy who understood her. He gestured to the others as he named them. The other boy was named "Dafyd," his sister was Sarah, and the Brenwyd was named Cassie. An odd name. The dogs were Kai and Dassah, more odd names.

"Where do you hail from?" Caelwyn asked, sitting at the table. Joseph left, assured no harm would occur. William hesitated and consulted with his friends. Caelwyn listened carefully to their language, trying to gain an understanding of it. She watched, interested, as she deduced the Brenwyd girl was the leader. She also kept trying to figure out their clothing. The breeches were made of a smooth, dark blue material that didn't look like wool or linen. Their tunics were unbelted and short, not coming far past the waistline of their breeches. The girls' breeches, instead of being loose, looked tight. The tunics were bright colors, and she could not guess what dye had colored them.

"We are from a very... um, faraway place," William said carefully. He spoke the language well enough, but did not appear to have had much practice. "It's called America."

"Armorica? That is not very far." Caelwyn said. It was just across the channel in Gaul. Where did they think they were? The Brenwyd girl shook her head and said something Caelwyn guessed was "no" in her language. William appeared to ask her a question, and her response seemed to startle them. The other boy, Dafyd, looked at Caelwyn uneasily. Cassie stood and beckoned for Caelwyn to follow her. Caelwyn saw the others stand as well. She met Cassie's eyes, and the strangest feeling came over her. She half-fancied she saw shadows of her own features in the girl's face. She dismissed it quickly and followed the young people out the door.

Cassie hoped she wasn't about to make a huge mistake, but she saw no other way at the moment. They wouldn't be able to get far in this time if at least one person didn't know where, or when, they were from. She knew they could trust Caelwyn. She'd sensed it the moment the woman had walked into the room. And she felt she needed to tell this woman where they were really from. Cassie could hardly believe they'd landed in Arthurian England, and had just met Caelwyn, no less. Dad would needle her with endless questions when they got back to their own time... if they did. That worry had been growing on her mind: Would they be able to get back? And if they did, how much time would have passed? Part of her wondered if this was just some fantastic and vivid dream, but it felt very different from her dreams. She had a certainty in the pit of her stomach that this was completely real.

"Do you think she'll believe us?" Sarah whispered into Cassie's ear.

"Hopefully," Cassie whispered back.

I think she will, Kai said.

"Why?" Cassie asked.

Because I have heard tales of these... time gateways. They have worked their way into animal lore. Being a Brenwyd, she may know of them already.

Cassie looked at him. "You've never mentioned them to me."

I never really believed they existed. It is hard to believe.

"And yet it just became our reality," David muttered. Cassie saw Caelwyn looking at them curiously. It was extremely odd for her to be in the presence of this woman, who was supposed to be her ancestor, and to see another person with pointed ears. She'd grown so used to hiding them, but in this time period it didn't seem necessary. Caelwyn was also the most beautiful woman she'd ever seen. Sure, she knew all the stories about the beauty of the "Fair Folk," but hadn't really appreciated it until now. Caelwyn's hair was light blond; her facial features were delicate, youthful-looking, and perfectly proportioned. Her eyes were green-gray. Cassie felt slightly awed and a little intimidated by her beauty. She wondered if that was the reaction people had when they looked at her. It was an unsettling feeling. Though perhaps she just felt that way about Caelwyn because it was, well, Caelwyn. While other kids had enjoyed comic book heroes and such, Cassie had always admired the characters from her dad's King Arthur stories, Caelwyn in particular. Actually meeting her in the flesh... well, she now understood a little better how people could go nuts in the presence of their favorite celebrity.

She was so absorbed in her thoughts she almost didn't register when they reached the slip spot. She stopped abruptly. Caelwyn was looking at her, and Cassie thought a wary look had appeared in her eyes. "William, explain to her what happened as best you can."

He gave her a dubious look. "If you say so," he said, and started speaking in the other language. Cassie watched Caelwyn carefully. The woman's eyes narrowed, then widened. Then they seemed to go unfocused, as if her mind had traveled a million miles away. Abruptly they snapped back into focus, and she held up a hand for

William to stop. She started speaking, and Cassie caught the Latin words "lapsus tempi."

"A slip of time?" Cassie interrupted. "Time slip! That's what Gwen meant. And she knew because... oh, good grief. I am *so* dumb."

"What?" Sarah asked.

"That dream I had. It *was* David and me, and we *were* helping Gwen. That's why she sent us back here. We'd already been, but not yet in our time, if that makes any sense."

William frowned, thinking through the scenario, then nodded. "That makes a lot of sense, actually, considering our current situation. That's how she knew who we were, and what Brenwyds are. She'd met us already, in this time... but then, who is she?"

"We could ask Caelwyn," David suggested. "What was she saying?"

"You mean before Cassie interrupted?" William asked innocently. Cassie gave him a look. "She was saying how she'd heard of such things, and was aware of the one here, but hadn't realized it could really be used." He paused a moment. "Um, Cassie, would you happen to know what Ynis Witrin means? I know the literal translation, but I think she's talking about the Tor..."

"Ynis Witrin is the old Celtic name for the Tor," Cassie explained. She continued speaking thoughtfully. "A time slip... maybe that's why the beat sounded sort of like a heartbeat, like it was keeping time." Caelwyn asked something, and William answered her. He continued speaking, probably explaining how they'd gotten through it. Cassie could see Caelwyn's eyes reflecting intense interest. She was quiet for a while after William finished. When she spoke again, her voice was soft.

William nodded and turned to the others. "She says she believes us. I asked her about Gwen, and she said she has an idea."

"How much did you tell her?" David asked.

"Not too much. Just that we'd met a woman in Glastonbury who'd taken us to the time slip. I didn't mention... all the other stuff." Looking at Cassie, he added, "She also said that she's been having dreams about something like this happening. She's invited us to her house."

"Sounds good to me," Sarah said. "It's not like we have lots of options."

Cassie nodded, remembering the similar reasoning that had led them to Gwen's house. *I guess if God knows the plans He has for us*, she thought with a grin, *and if He's only providing one option, then it must be the right one.*

⚜

Caelwyn's mind was racing. It was happening, just as Merlin had predicted. How she wished he were here to see it! These young people had come from a distant future, and if she was right about the identity of the woman who'd helped them... the stage was being set. Only a crisis would compel the woman to do something as drastic as traveling to the future, though, so Caelwyn couldn't help but wonder what was about to unfold. They entered the stable, and Wynne nickered to her rider. Caelwyn scratched her behind the ears. "Ready your horses," she told William.

He nodded, but his attention was riveted on Wynne. "She's... is she your horse?" He sounded like he was straining to keep his voice nonchalant. Caelwyn nodded, wondering at his reaction. She noticed the others staring out of the corners of their eyes. The smaller dog, Dassah, came up to Wynne and started a conversation. Kai contributed something and Dassah turned quickly, looking guilty.

What did they say? Caelwyn asked Wynne.

I am not sure. The mare sounded confused. *The small dog was saying something, but then the large dog cut her off.*

Hmm, Caelwyn thought. *I wonder what that's about.* She watched as the teens tacked up. Their saddles were very different from her own, and no wonder. But how could they stay in the saddle during a battle with such low cantles and nothing on the pommel to keep them centered in the seat?

"Do you not ride into battle in your time?" she asked William.

He shook his head. "No," he said. "Unless..." His voice trailed off and he busied himself with fastening his tack to his gelding. Caelwyn sensed it was a touchy subject. She wondered why. She studied his horse. He was well-built, with clean lines and long legs. He looked fast but sturdy, reminding her somewhat of a Brenwyd horse.

"What's his name?" she asked.

"Phoenix." Caelwyn wondered where they got such names.

"Have you had him long?"

"About seven years. He wandered onto the... place where I live and I took care of him."

"Is he a Brenwyd horse?" The horse swung his head toward her and looked slightly alarmed, pinning his ears back slightly.

"No. At least, I don't think so. He's never talked to me," William said, not catching the horse's expression. Caelwyn smiled. The ability of Brenwyd animals to talk to whomever they chose was a fable far and wide, but few people realized it was actually true. Animals were fairly selective about whom they chose to talk to.

Caelwyn heard Cassie's voice from across the aisle, and saw that she appeared to be arguing with her black mare. "What is she saying?" Caelwyn asked William, who was smiling slightly.

"Nothing much. Twi can be pretty... um, uncooperative about the... tacking up process."

"Twi? The mare?"

"Yes. It's short for Twilight." That made sense.

"And the other two?"

"David's gelding is Fire, and Sarah's mare is Dreamer. They're all Brenwyd horses."

"Dafyd and Sarah are not Brenwyd, are they?"

"No."

"Then how do they have Brenwyd horses?"

"From what I understand, they all came from the same place and they all had the same dam, and she was descended from

Brenwyd horses. Sarah and David didn't find out until recently that they were Brenwyd horses, nor did Cassie, for that matter." The more the boy spoke this language, the easier it seemed to be for him.

"Why not? Would she not have known?" Caelwyn wondered just what their full story was. She knew William hadn't told her everything.

"Umm..." He sounded hesitant, and not because he was looking for words. "It's... it's a bit of a long story. In our time... most people don't know about Brenwyds."

Caelwyn guessed correctly at what he meant, and sighed. "I had hoped nothing would come of it," she murmured to herself.

William looked at her curiously. "What do you mean?"

Her expression tightened. "I'll explain later." Soon enough, they were all ready. Sarah asked a question.

"She wants to know how far away your house is," William translated.

"A couple of hours. Normally I would transfer, but seeing as–"

Then we should do that, Phoenix interrupted. *They are more tired than they realize and should rest as soon as possible.* The kids all gasped at the double shock of hearing Phoenix speak in the ancient language, and hearing him speak at all. Caelwyn examined the horse more closely.

You are *a Brenwyd horse,* she said.

Yes.

And you never told your rider.

I had to wait. I will explain why when the time is right. William stared at his mount as if a horn had suddenly sprouted from his forehead. Phoenix swung his head around to look at his rider quizzically. *What?* he asked, shifting back into English. William answered in kind. The others seemed to get over their shock more quickly and were grinning. Cassie said something that caused laughter to break out.

William looked back at Caelwyn, still in shock. "I think we can use the transfer ability thing," he said.

Caelwyn smiled. "Your horse has never talked to you, eh?" William gave her a careful look and muttered something she didn't understand, but she caught Cassie's name.

Are you going to spend all night thinking, or are we going to get going? Wynne asked, stamping a forefoot.

We're going. Caelwyn nodded to William. "Follow me. Wynne will tell your horses where to go."

"What about the dogs?" he asked.

"What about them?"

"Well, we can't leave them, and they can't transfer. Unless there are more things I don't know about our animals?"

Caelwyn chuckled. "We can place them on the horses, in the front of the saddle."

William frowned. "Put the dogs on the horses? Aren't they a bit big?" He looked at Kai while he spoke.

"It will not be the first time I have done so." Caelwyn cast an eye over the dogs, who had their ears cocked alertly. "It is fine. Brenwyd horses, and Briton horses in general, are sturdy for their size." She reached for the dogs and presented them with an image of what they would have to do. Kai growled slightly, not cheered by the prospect, and she could hear him talking with Cassie. Cassie looked at Caelwyn, eyebrows raised, and shrugged. She beckoned to Dassah, and the dog came to her willingly. Cassie turned to her mare and spoke with her for a few seconds. Twi snorted and pinned her ears briefly, then lowered her head and chewed in submission. Cassie then bent, picked Dassah up, and with a grunt, positioned her to lie across Twi's withers like a saddlebag. Twi snorted again, shifting at the unfamiliar weight, and Dassah squirmed a little to reposition herself. The two settled, and Dassah looked at Cassie, wagging her tail slightly. Cassie smiled, then turned to Caelwyn with a questioning expression. Caelwyn nodded, smiling in return to indicate she had done it correctly.

Caelwyn still sensed grumbling from Kai. She understood it. Lying on a horse in a rather helpless position was not very dignified. Dragon wasn't fond of it either. *Come, Kai,* Caelwyn called, crouching slightly as she held a hand out to him. *It will not be for long.* She made sure to impress upon him her meaning since he might not understand all her words. After a moment's hesitation, and a brief command from Cassie, the dog walked over and allowed Caelwyn to put him on Wynne, with William's help. After Kai was positioned, Caelwyn beckoned to the four and led Wynne out of the stable. They mounted outside, careful not to crush the dogs.

Caelwyn then led them in single file down the path, across the bridge, and onto the plain. She urged Wynne into a trot, then a canter, then a gallop, keeping a hand on Kai to keep him balanced as the horse accelerated. As Wynne increased her speed for the transfer, Caelwyn decided to send a message to her cousin when she got home. These young people were important, and she needed him to meet them. She hoped he wouldn't be too busy this morning. At the very least, she would be able to see his wife, who could get the information to him. But you never knew how long you'd have to wait to meet with the king, particularly if that king was as busy as Arthur.

⁂

Cassie looked around curiously after they arrived at Caelwyn's house. It was bigger and more finely crafted than historians in the twenty-first century thought sixth-century British houses had been. Of course, as Caelwyn had been an important person, it made sense for her house to be more elaborate than usual for the time period. The walls were made of close-fitting dark gray stone with wooden support posts at certain intervals, and it even looked like the house had a second story. The roof was made of dark wood. The front door was framed by wooden beams, and the house as a whole looked elegant. A little away from the house, constructed in the same fashion, was a smaller building that Cassie took to be the stable. The sun was just peeking over the horizon, and the scene looked very picturesque with trees surrounding the yard.

A dog came to meet them, his tail wagging in welcome. He resembled Kai in build, but was gray and taller. Caelwyn dismounted and scratched his head, then turned to get Kai down from Wynne, which he was very happy about. *I am not doing that again unless absolutely necessary,* he grumbled. Cassie smiled, but didn't reply. Kai and the larger dog sniffed each other courteously.

Caelwyn said something and William translated: "She says the dog's name is Dragon."

Thank God one of us knows this language, Cassie thought.

Caelwyn said something else with a gentle laugh, and William looked puzzled, but translated dutifully. "She also says we should prepare ourselves for the descent of a barbarian horde, whatever that means." No sooner had the words left his mouth than two fair-haired children, a boy and a girl, flew out the front door and into Caelwyn's arms, followed closely by a red-haired boy a few years older. He waited patiently while the younger ones chattered excitedly to their mother.

"Oh my gosh, they're adorable," Sarah said. Cassie nodded, smiling, and dismounted. This must be the "barbarian horde" Caelwyn had warned them of. She'd never really thought about Caelwyn having kids, but she must have, for Cassie to be descended from her. Which meant one of the kids in the doorway was her who-knew-how-many-times-removed-ancestor, which meant Caelwyn was her who-knew-how-many-greats-grandmother. Cassie shied away from that thought. It was just too weird. She concentrated on getting Dassah down instead. Once she was down, Twi shook herself. *That felt strange,* she declared. *Dogs were not meant to ride horses.*

But it is fun, Dassah said, panting happily. She hadn't minded the ride as much as Kai had. More people headed out from the house. One, a man Cassie supposed was Caelwyn's husband, looked at them with a friendly but curious gaze. He had blond hair and brown eyes. Two girls who looked about fifteen stayed close to the door. One had dark blond hair and green-blue eyes, while the other had brown hair and eyes. They also stared at the foursome curiously. Cassie realized abruptly just how strange they must look to these people, as she took in their tunics and breeches and dresses.

The brown-haired girl met Cassie's eyes with a slight smile and then turned eyes to William, who stood nearby. Cassie saw her stiffen as surprise entered her eyes. She jabbed the girl next to her, whispering something. The second girl also looked at William. Cassie wondered what on earth it was about William that seemed to surprise these people so much. First the monk, then Caelwyn, and now these girls. Cassie also noted that everyone had slightly pointed ears like her own, except for the brown-haired girl. She appeared to be a regular human.

The light-haired girl turned from William to examine Cassie, holding eye contact. Her gaze was piercing and the twain colors in her eyes melded until they were no longer distinguishable from each other. Cassie felt an odd sensation, almost like a bee was buzzing in her ear, except it seemed deeper. She felt a presence, wary but curious and definitely not animal, almost as if the girl was reading her mind. She instinctively imagined a wall concealing her thoughts, and the presence retreated.

Caelwyn extricated herself from the smaller children and embraced her husband, giving him a quick kiss on the cheek. She whispered to him quickly, and Cassie guessed she was explaining them to him. The man nodded several times and said something to her. Caelwyn smiled and turned back to William, beckoning the rest of her family forward. She spoke to William while pointing to each person, and he translated the introductions for Cassie, David, and Sarah. "Okay, let's see if I can pronounce these names right. The man is her husband, Siarl. The little kids are Aeddan and Addiena and the redhead is Selyf. The girl standing next to him is Telyn, and the brown-haired girl is Ganieda. She's not Caelwyn's daughter, but she lives with them because she has no parents. Caelwyn has another son, Bleddyn, but he's married and lives nearby with his wife."

Cassie nodded and smiled at them. "I think you got all the names right, William," she said.

"I tried," William replied. Caelwyn's husband, Siarl, said something to them, motioning to the horses and the stable, then the house.

"He says we can put the horses in the stable," William translated. "And then we can come to the house for breakfast."

"Good." David said. "Time-traveling makes me hungry. But what's for breakfast?"

"Probably porridge or something like that," Cassie said. Caelwyn said something to the children, then went inside with Siarl following, probably wanting a little more information about their guests. Dragon sat by Dassah and Kai and began a conversation with them. Telyn grabbed Wynne's reins and started leading her toward the stable. The little girl, Addiena, went up to Sarah and tugged on her stirrup, asking a question.

Sarah looked at her. "William, what's she saying?" she asked.

"She wants to know what it is. The stirrup doesn't really exist in this century, if I remember correctly."

"Oh yeah, I think I remember that history lesson." She looked back down at Addiena. "You put your foot in it," she told her, demonstrating. Addiena smiled and clapped her hands. She went up to William, having deduced he could understand her, and told him something. He smiled a bit and said something back. Telyn called from the stable, probably asking what the holdup was. William answered her, and she nodded. They went into the stable with the others following. It didn't have stalls per se, but two low walls ran parallel almost the full length of the stable, making an aisle that separated two sections. Several horses were in the sections and they left their munching as the kids entered the stable. There were also some goats and a cow. Cassie sensed much non-verbal conversation going on between all the horses – Wynne being welcomed back, everyone being introduced. The cow simply listened placidly while chewing her cud, and the goats constantly butted into the conversation with questions. Cassie couldn't make out all the animals talking at once, so she tuned them out and paid more attention to the people.

Telyn said something to William, and he nodded. "She says that after we untack, the geldings go on the right, and the mares on the left."

The teens untacked their horses, with Aeddan, Addiena, and Selyf helping, asking questions the whole time. The saddles looked very strange to them, and William was hard put to answer some of their questions. He didn't want to reveal the fact that they came from the future just yet. Telyn and Ganieda didn't ask questions, but conversed in low tones, sneaking glances at them occasionally. Cassie noted most of their glances were directed at William.

She studied her friend critically, trying to figure out just why he seemed to unsettle so many people. She just saw his normal features, strong but well-proportioned. He was taller than her by several inches, and his arms were muscular because of all the sword work he did. She compared him to David, wondering if it had something to do with his looks. David's features weren't as strong, but good-natured and friendly, though Cassie knew those features could turn hard as steel when he was upset about something. His resemblance to Sarah was obvious, but his brown eyes weren't as wide or trusting as his sister's, and he was about an inch shorter than William. His muscles also showed the effects of swordplay and sports.

In fact, Cassie thought while comparing the two, *they're both good-looking, just different.* The realization surprised her somewhat, because she'd never really thought about David in that light before. David caught her looking at him and raised his eyebrows inquiringly. Cassie shook her head and mouthed *nothing*, turning back to Twi. She wondered if he'd guessed at what she was thinking, and a slight blush came to her cheeks. *Oh relax, girl,* she told herself. *Why would David suspect you of thinking that? Besides, it's not like it matters much overall.*

Twi looked at her rider in amusement, but kept her feelings to herself. Some things humans just had to figure out on their own, though in some matters they seemed particularly dense. Cassie put her in the loose box and Twi busied herself with some hay, leaving human emotions to humans. They were too complicated for her.

Cassie watched the horses for several minutes, letting her mind take in the peaceful scene and relax a bit before joining the others. William and Telyn were having a conversation. She watched them, trying to glean any information she could as to what they were talking about. Dragon entered the stable, and Cassie could tell he was saying something about a message needing to be sent to an important person. In this language, it was easier for her to understand animals than people, because she could sense some of their meaning even without understanding every word. William's eyes widened, and his lips parted slightly as if to ask a question, but Telyn beat him to it. Through the dog, Cassie understood she was asking if he was sure. Dragon replied affirmatively. Aeddan asked a question that seemed to be why, but Dragon didn't answer him.

"William, what are they saying?" Sarah whispered.

"Dragon says that they need to send a message, and wants to know where the hawk is," he whispered back.

"Who to? Do you think it's about us?"

"Yeah." He fell silent.

Sarah gazed at him. "You still haven't answered the who question."

"Umm... let me get my brain around it first."

Her gaze turned more inquisitive, but she nodded acceptance. "Okay. Let me know as soon as you do."

Selyf went out and after a few minutes came back in with a large hawk on his shoulder. Telyn disappeared into a room at the end of the stable and came out several minutes later with a slip of parchment. She attached it to the hawk's legs, and Selyf went back out. Cassie felt the hawk being released and asked him his destination. He gave her the image of a town on a hill ringed by a wall, with a large building at its peak. Cassie slowly recognized the place as the hill-fort from her dream. Reflecting on it, she realized the location itself, if not the city, was familiar to her. She pondered it as Telyn led them to the house.

Caelwyn looked at Siarl expectantly. She had shared with him what William had told her. Siarl sat with his hands on his chin, his gaze distant as he thought. At last he spoke. "You believe they are the ones you have been waiting for?"

"Yes. It all fits with what I've Seen and what Merlin said. It is beginning," she said.

He "hmm"ed thoughtfully. "And you're telling Arthur."

"Not exactly. I am not going to tell him where – or when, rather – they're from. But he needs to know about them and what they mean, and knowing him, he will also wish to meet them, so I might as well bring them."

"I do not doubt your instincts, Caelwyn. But why tell him immediately? Our culture is unknown to them, and only one speaks the language."

"And it's partly because of that one that I wish to tell him as soon as possible. Do not tell me the resemblance escaped you."

Siarl sighed. "Yes, I saw, but it most likely means nothing, Caelwyn. You know he would never betray his vows."

"I am not saying he would or did, Siarl, but it may mean something, and he should still know, in any event. Someone helped them get here, to this time, and based on his description, I believe I know who it was. But we must start making preparations. The rumors and suspicions are spreading. Arthur's doing his best, but it may not be the best idea for him to support us so much. There's enough grumbling with no male heir to succeed him, and no sign of one in the near future. I must talk to Guinevere at least." Siarl nodded.

"And you need a respite. You've been pushing yourself too hard. We can handle chasing rumors without you for a day," he said.

"It wouldn't be the whole day," she protested.

Siarl smiled lovingly at her. "Wife, take as much time as you need. If it doesn't take too long, come back here and get some sleep. You have gotten too little of that lately. Consider that an order." She smiled back at him, and he kissed her tenderly. They heard the door open as the kids entered. Siarl stood. "I must go. I told Bran I'd go with him today, and I don't wish to be late."

"Very well. Be safe and careful."

"I will." He picked up his sword from where it was lying against the table, buckled it on, and went out of the kitchen area as the children were coming in.

Strangers in Camelot

William cautiously ate the breakfast porridge that Caelwyn had set before him. It wasn't that bad and actually reminded him of oatmeal, but it had an odd taste that would take some getting used to. The added scrutiny of Caelwyn's four children and ward, Ganieda, made him feel uncomfortable. The two littlest ones, who couldn't be more than eight, stared at him and the others openly, occasionally asking a question. For such young children, they asked very penetrating questions. The two older girls studied them more discreetly, and Selyf tried to follow their example. William judged the redhead to be about eleven and the girls around his own age. He noted the looks that passed between Telyn and Ganieda from time to time, especially after he answered one of Aeddan or Addiena's questions, and got the sense that they were having some sort of conversation, even though they remained silent. He wasn't quite sure what to make of them all. They seemed to regard him with a kind of wide-eyed incredulity different from the curious stares directed at the others, like he was a ghost or something.

He glanced over at Cassie. She looked like she was thinking hard about something, not really tuned in to what was going on around the table. William thought it was a little ironic that out of all of them, for once Cassie was the one attracting the least attention. In their own time, though he wasn't sure if she was aware of it, he'd noticed her looks attracted many admiring stares and much attention. Here, though, surrounded by this Brenwyd family, she seemed to fit in perfectly – and he, David, and Sarah were the oddballs.

Caelwyn had left the room soon after serving them, saying something about expecting a message. The thought reminded William that he still hadn't answered Sarah's query about the recipient of the hawk's message. He was still in shock about having traveled back in time fifteen centuries and having come out right in the reign of King Arthur. If he thought about it too hard, his brain froze up on him. *At least we can confirm to the world that yes, he did exist*, he thought. How long had that monk said Arthur had been king? Twenty-one years? William almost choked as he considered the implications of that number. Hadn't Arthur's entire reign been about twenty-one years? Had they come back to the time of Camlann? Of all the events in Arthur's reign to travel back to, Camlann was hands-down the least desirable. *Is Cassie aware?* he wondered. *Most likely. She probably figured it out soon after that monk told us.*

Addiena interrupted his thoughts abruptly by asking another question. "Are you... of Roman descent?"

William blinked. Was it normal in this era to ask about the ethnicity of complete strangers? She sounded completely serious. "Me? Um, I don't think so. Why?"

Addiena looked puzzled, but slightly relieved. "Oh... merely curious." Telyn frowned at her slightly and Addiena's head dropped a few inches. William got the feeling that look had contained an entire non-verbal lecture. He wondered if Brenwyds could communicate with their minds. It wouldn't surprise him.

"Have you ever seen the king before?" Ganieda asked.

William looked at her in surprise. "King Arthur?" She nodded. "Of course not. Why would I have seen him?" He realized right after he asked the question that it was probably not an uncommon occurrence for someone to see King Arthur in this time, but the idea just sounded ludicrous to him.

Ganieda raised her eyebrows. "Well, he was in Armorica recently for the campaign against the Goths and traveled through many villages, so you might have."

"Oh. Right. Um, well, my village is pretty far out of the way so... no, I did not see him."

"What are they saying?" David asked. He'd been trying hard to follow the conversation, but wasn't having much luck.

"She asked me if I'd ever seen Arthur," William answered.

"Huh. That would be a feat. Wonder why she asked."

"Same here."

"What did Addiena ask? It seemed like it was a question she shouldn't have asked." Cassie interjected.

"She asked if I was descended from the Romans," William said.

Cassie raised an eyebrow. "Hmm. Interesting question. I can see why she'd think so, but any idea why she asked?"

"No, she said she was just wondering. Why do you suppose she'd think so?"

"Well, you look a lot more Roman than Celtic. You've got the dark hair and the features. But it must be more than that. I doubt that's a question she'd ask every Roman-looking person." She paused. "I've noticed that you cause people in this century to do a double-take. Maybe there's something more to you than even you know."

"Like what?" William asked, feeling very puzzled. There was nothing particularly special about him that he could think of. In a sense, he was the least special of the four, since he could actually speak the local language.

They were interrupted by Caelwyn re-entering the room. She looked at William and the others expectantly. "I would like to take you to meet... a good friend of mine."

"Who would that be?" William asked.

Caelwyn smiled mysteriously. "You'll find out." She turned to Telyn. "I need you and Ganieda to take the little ones to Bleddyn's today. I don't know how long I'll be gone, and your father's gone to meet with Bran."

Telyn nodded. "You're going up to the city?" she asked her mother.

"Yes."

"Do Ganieda and I have to stay at Bleddyn's all day?"

"Don't you like your brother?" Caelwyn asked with a gentle laugh.

"Of course, but we would like to come and visit with Gwendolyn. We have not seen her since Arthur returned from the campaign in Gaul."

"Ah, I see. You may go after dropping your siblings off and making sure Eira doesn't need your help with anything."

Telyn smiled. "Thank you, Mother." She and Ganieda said farewell and ushered the children out of the room.

"Behave yourselves for Eira," Caelwyn called after them.

"We will," three voices chorused. William guessed that Eira must be the wife of Caelwyn's son.

Once the door closed, Caelwyn returned her attention to the teens, scrutinizing them carefully. "You'll have to change clothes," she said finally. "Those will raise too many questions, and we don't want that. I have some clothes that I think will fit."

"Okay," William said. He translated for the others.

Cassie looked a little apprehensive. "If we're riding, I hope Sarah and I don't have to wear dresses. That would be pretty awkward and I don't think sidesaddles have been invented yet, not to mention I would have no idea how to ride in one," she said, frowning.

"Caelwyn's not wearing a dress," Sarah pointed out.

"I know, but the other girls were, and if we're going somewhere important she might put one on and we would have to wear them, too."

"Good point. Maybe we'll be walking."

William and David looked at each other with the same thought going through their minds: *Girls and clothes and complications.*

"What is it?" Caelwyn asked.

"Cassie and Sarah are concerned about riding in dresses," William answered her. "In our time, we're taught that women in this time always wore dresses."

Caelwyn nodded understandingly, the hint of a smile playing at the corners of her mouth. "Human women do, but in Brenwyd culture women do most of the same things as men and are taught to fight, so our women often dress in very practical gear, what some might perceive as men's clothing. Since you will be with me, no one will think too much of it. They know and respect our culture, even if they think it is a bit peculiar."

William translated. Cassie and Sarah looked relieved.

"Did she say where we're going?" David asked. William shook his head and repeated David's question for Caelwyn, though he already had a pretty good guess. Caelwyn's response confirmed it. He looked at the others with excitement smoldering in his eyes.

"Where else would we be going in this time period? She says we're going to Camelot!"

ৼৡৢৢৡৢ

Cassie stared at the city-fort that covered the hill and expanded onto the immediately surrounding plains. It wasn't big at all when compared to the sprawl of cities in the twenty-first century, but it was rather impressive nonetheless. A large, dry stone wall circled the city about half a mile from the base of the hill, topped with wooden breastworks and several square towers that reminded Cassie of Roman milecastles. The only way into the city itself appeared to be through a gate at the bottom of a particularly large tower. The gate doors were made of wood and reinforced with iron. Before the wall were several deep ditches that she guessed were used for defense in times of war. She could see the pitched roofs of houses beyond the wall.

As the group stopped on a high spot in the road, Cassie could see over the wall a bit, and noticed many of the houses were Celtic-looking round huts, with low walls and thatched roofs. Despite the rude craftsmanship, they looked neat and tidy. Interspersed among the huts were slightly larger houses made of wood and even of stone. At the hill's base there was another wall that Cassie could tell was older than the outer wall, and she guessed that it had encircled the original settlement on the hill.

At the hill's top stood a large hall that looked to be made of stone, with a wooden roof and another, smaller wall enclosing it. She assumed it was the "castle," even though the classic medieval castle design wouldn't be around for another few hundred years. The wind was blowing toward her, and it carried with it the sounds and smells of the city. The sight of the city on the hill seemed almost alien to Cassie, who was so used to seeing the hill in her own time with no city, and yet the city fit with its surroundings. The area was much more wooded than it was in her time, and there were, of course, no asphalt roads or cars. Her gaze dropped from the hall to an area slightly to the left, still inside the outer wall, where the Brotherhood had grabbed them. For the hill she was looking at was none other than Cadbury Castle, though the people of this century knew it as Camelot, King Arthur's main residence.

"Now that's something I sure never thought I'd see with my own eyes," David breathed out from beside Cassie. "That's Cadbury, isn't it?"

"Sure is," Cassie confirmed. "Dad was right, as usual."

"It certainly doesn't look like the modern perception of Camelot," Sarah observed.

"Actually, it does," Cassie said.

Sarah looked at her quizzically. "How? That's certainly no medieval castle sitting up there."

"The modern world as we know it doesn't exist yet. We ourselves won't technically exist until about 1500 years from now. This time now, *is* modern for these people, so this *is* the modern perception of Camelot, and the right one, because it actually is *the* Camelot."

Sarah rolled her eyes. "You know what I meant, Cassie," she said in a slightly exasperated tone.

Cassie grinned. "I know. Just thought I'd point that out."

Caelwyn observed the group's reactions. She wondered what people in their time thought of Camelot, or if they even knew of it at all. "Is it what you expected?" she asked William.

He was staring at the city intently. "Yes and no, if that makes any sense," he answered.

"It does. Many feel that way upon first viewing the city. They imagine Arthur living in a grand palace to match his many great deeds, and they are surprised to see that his main residence is rather basic and not a magnificent city of legend. And yet, they see it fits him perfectly. Arthur wishes to keep himself humble, close to his people. Living here is one of the ways he does that and he's a lot more comfortable here than in his court at Caer Lial in the north, which is more the typical king's court. Camelot is also a recently built city," Caelwyn explained.

"You sound like you know him well," William noticed.

Caelwyn chuckled. "Oh, yes. We have known each other a very long time." She had stopped the group a little way off the road to let the four young ones get a good look at the city. It was a fairly easy ride from her house to the city. Caelwyn had explained to them that using the transfer ability too much drained the horses, and that it was generally only used in emergencies or on long-distance trips.

Cassie looked upward as she felt raindrops spatter across her skin. The sky had been overcast when they'd left Caelwyn's and she'd given them cloaks in case it did start to rain – which, from what Cassie could gather, was an event that happened in sixth-century Britain with the same regularity as in the twenty-first century United Kingdom. She drew her hood up over her head, but not so much that it would obstruct her vision. She glanced down again at the clothes she was wearing. They were Telyn's and fit pretty well, but it was just odd to see herself wearing them. Instead of jeans she had on lightweight wool breeches, and in place of her T-shirt she wore a simple tunic that was belted at the waist and extended to her knees, creating a dress-like effect. The clothes weren't plaid, as Caelwyn had explained plaids were more often used by human tribes, but the tunic had an intricate, Celtic design embroidered around the neckline. It was a tannish color, while the breeches were brown. They were actually pretty comfy. William, David, and Sarah wore essentially the same thing; the main differences were the colors. The boys' tunics didn't have the embroidered neckline, though, and were a little shorter.

They'd left their weapons at Caelwyn's house, and the dogs had stayed as well. They were utterly exhausted, having traveled hard and long without enough food, and the respite at Gwen's hadn't fully recharged them. Cassie knew Kai had had mixed feelings about letting them travel without him, but Cassie had encouraged him to rest. His acquiescence had let her know just how tired he really was, and also that he trusted her to take care of herself. Coming from Kai, that was pretty flattering.

Twi bent her head around to nudge her rider's leg. *He thought that there were enough people going who could keep you out of trouble. You still need some work before you can handle trouble by yourself.*

Hey now, I think I've handled myself pretty well when it comes to getting out of trouble lately.

But you still get into it.

It's not my fault.

I never said it was. But hopefully you can learn to fend for yourself soon enough so we will not have to keep dragging you out of whatever trouble you find.

I don't find trouble, trouble finds me!

You still get into trouble. Cassie could tell that this conversation was going nowhere. Caelwyn said something to William and started walking on with Wynne.

"She says that we should canter the rest of the way so we don't get too wet," William said before urging Phoenix after her. Fortunately, the road was cobblestone so Cassie, who found herself at the end of the line, didn't get mud thrown up in her face. The horses' easy canter soon brought them to the gate, where they slowed to enter. Before they reached the gate proper, Caelwyn halted in front of William and spoke to him. A puzzled expression crossed his face. Cassie wondered what they were talking about. After several minutes he nodded and drew his hood up, concealing his face. Cassie did the same, as hers had fallen and the sprinkling was becoming a drizzle. It also gave her an extra sense of security, because she was not wearing her headband in public for the first time since she was ten. It wasn't necessary in this time period, but leaving her ears uncovered still felt odd to her and made her feel vulnerable, despite the many times she had wished she didn't have to wear the headband back home.

Caelwyn led them through the streets at a brisk walk. Looking around, Cassie saw that even the peasant areas were relatively neat and tidy, though there was inevitable mud from the rain. People went around with cheerful expressions despite the weather, calling out greetings to each other as they went about their business, haggling in the marketplace and hawking their wares. Children ran hither and thither through the streets, nimbly avoiding people and horses. Beggars dressed in ragged clothes sat with hands stretched out. The group paused several times and Caelwyn handed them some coins. Based on the small stone houses interspersed throughout the huts, Cassie got the impression that the city was slowly becoming more permanent than the military outpost it had likely started as. She suspected that some of the stone had come from Roman buildings, but the houses were built in a clearly Briton style. As they journeyed from the outer gate deeper into the city, Cassie could see the progression from the poorer outskirts to the wealthier center of the town. The small huts completely disappeared, and the wood and stone houses became more common.

At last they approached the wall surrounding the great hall that Cassie had seen from outside the city. Caelwyn rode up to the gate and called out. A voice from above answered her, and Cassie saw a man looking over the gate. She assumed a walkway existed on top of the wall. Caelwyn answered him, smiling, and Cassie guessed the man was a friend of hers. He laughed, and then disappeared. A few minutes later the gate opened and they rode through. A large, dirt courtyard met Cassie's eyes and she saw that the hall was large, but not huge. The walls were made of stone like the city walls, but there was some sort of adhesive agent, and wooden beams at regular intervals for support. The roof was made entirely of wood, as were the massive doors leading into the hall. Cassie stared up at them. They were only a few feet shorter than the wall itself and quite wide. Intricate iron work decorated the doors. A tree was on each door near the hinges, with branches spreading out to the outermost edges. Vines came off of the trees, forming various designs such as animals or flowers. Cassie suspected that in addition to its aesthetic appeal, the ironwork also served to reinforce the door in case the city was attacked. All in all, it was a very impressive hall. The buildings attached to the hall were made in the same style.

The man who'd opened the gate was walking toward them. Before he reached them, Caelwyn turned to William, who'd started to put down his hood. She spoke to him urgently. He narrowed his eyes and replaced the hood. Cassie could've sworn a look of relief briefly crossed the woman's face as she turned to greet the gatekeeper.

Phoenix, what was that about? Cassie asked the chestnut.

She wants William to keep his hood up until we meet the king, he answered.

Well that's... hang on, meet the king? King Arthur?! That's who we're meeting?

Who else, girl? The horse sounded amused.

Cassie didn't answer as she tried to take that in. She supposed it was the obvious answer, as they were in Camelot and dismounting in the "castle" courtyard, but the idea had never crossed her mind, being so far from what she considered normal. *There must be a limit as to how much a person can be shocked in a day,* she thought, *but I clearly haven't reached it yet. Why would Caelwyn want us to meet Arthur?*

Why not? Twi asked. *This is his time period.*

Well, yeah, but... William knows already, doesn't he?

Yes, Phoenix said. *His reaction was very much like yours.*

I'll bet. Hey, Fire, Dreamer, tell your riders who we're meeting, would ya?

Of course, they replied. Cassie watched David and Sarah's faces as their horses told them. Surprise and shock registered, and David looked at Cassie with wide eyes, trying to convey a question. He leaned over Fire's mane and seemed to whisper something to the horse, as the gelding's ears flicked backward.

He wants to know if you have any idea why you are meeting him, Fire relayed. Cassie met David's eyes and shrugged.

Sarah wants to know if William has gotten his brain around this yet, Dreamer requested. William had been concentrating on the conversation between Caelwyn and the gatekeeper. He swung his gaze to Sarah and shook his head with a slight, rueful smile.

He says he would have told her if the right opportunity arose, Phoenix said. Sarah cast a skeptical glance at William, clearly not thinking that was a good enough excuse. William chose that moment to return his attention to the conversation between Caelwyn and the gatekeeper.

Very handy this communication system we have going, Cassie observed. *But anyway, Phoenix, did Caelwyn give William a reason as to why he needs to keep his hood up?*

No.

Hmm. Maybe it's to keep him from freaking out the people here like he's done to everyone else we've met in this century so far. Cassie didn't realize the horse conveyed this last thought to his rider until William turned and gave her a sour look. She rolled her eyes. *And do you have any better ideas, Mr. William Douglas?* She asked tartly through Phoenix. He frowned, but he shook his head reluctantly. *I thought not.* Cassie looked at Caelwyn and the gatekeeper. *Phoenix, who is that?*

I think he said his name was Glue-wyd.

What?

That is what it sounded like.

Gluewyd... Glewlwyd?

Yes, that was it.

Huh. So he did exist. Or does, rather. Interesting.

Is he in the story? Dreamer asked.

Yes, in one of them, anyway, as the gatekeeper. Must have done something pretty important to be remembered for so long. What are they talking about?

I think they are just catching up, Phoenix said. At that moment, Glewlwyd called across the yard and several boys of about eleven or twelve ran up from where Cassie had seen them lurking at the corner of a building that seemed to be a stable. Caelwyn indicated for the teens to dismount, so they did. The boys went to take the horses' heads, confirming Cassie's guess that they were stable boys. A man came from the stable, calling something. The whole place was really a cacophony of noise now that Cassie wasn't focused on mental conversations. She winced slightly. Horses were banging their stalls, nickering and neighing, and people were talking as well.

She even heard the clash of weapons and guessed a practice area must be somewhere nearby.

Twi looked dubiously at the stable boy who had her reins. He seemed equally wary of her, noting her bright eye and high spirits.

Be nice, Cassie told her sternly.

Twi tossed her head. *Do I have to? What if they hurt me?* the mare asked fretfully.

They won't, and if they do it's because they're trying to help you. Be nice.

I will try. Just as long as that boy does not jerk me around.

Twi. Just deal with it.

Okay, she caved. But Cassie could sense she was still nervous as the horses were led away.

Cassie prayed that the boy was gentle and knew his way around horses. Twi had never forgotten her previous home, where she had been abused horribly, and she was always nervous around new humans. *Fire, Dreamer, keep an eye on her, please.* Both horses assured Cassie they would, which made her feel a bit better.

Caelwyn beckoned to the four and they followed her toward the hall. Instead of entering it, she took them through a smaller door to the right of the hall. They followed a corridor to a garden that was open to the sky, reminding Cassie of the gardens in Roman villas. Here Caelwyn motioned to them to wait, saying a few words to William. Then she headed off down another hallway that Cassie guessed would lead to the main hall.

"Where's she going?" Sarah asked.

"She said she's going to get her friend, a.k.a. the King," William said, pushing his hood back. The others did the same, since the rain was now no more than a faint sprinkle.

"Sure you're s'posed to do that, William? Caelwyn seemed pretty insistent you keep it on," Cassie said.

"I know, but it's wet and I don't think it matters now, anyway."

"What?" David asked.

"Caelwyn wanted me to keep the hood up while we were around

other people. Don't ask me why," William explained.

"Weird. Maybe she thinks you're a criminal or something," David deadpanned.

"David!" His sister frowned at him. "I'm sure she thinks nothing of the sort."

"Maybe he just looks like a criminal that would cause an angry mob and she wants the king to officially say no, he's okay to be around," David persisted, still keeping a serious expression.

William snorted. "Funny, David. Really funny. I think she would have told me about anything like that," he said.

"All joking aside," Cassie said. "We've seriously got to get a handle on why you unsettle these people, William. It's very strange."

"Mmm." He looked up at the gray sky. "How long do you think we'll be in this time period?"

Cassie hesitated, hating to admit the truth. "Honestly... I have no clue. I never took any class in school that discussed time travel." He nodded. He'd been expecting an answer like that.

Sarah turned worried eyes to Cassie. "Cassie, how do you think time passing here corresponds to time passing in our own time?"

Cassie sighed, half-wondering why they all thought she had answers. "I don't know. I've only ever read about this sort of thing in fictional stories. And all the books about time travel differ. There's Narnia, which isn't time travel exactly, but time speeds by in Narnia while it creeps in our world. Then there are books where people spend time in a different era but go back to their own time right when they left. And in some stories, time passage in the past is the same as in the present. It will be impossible to tell how it really works until we get back ourselves."

"Do you think we can?" David asked.

Cassie nodded violently. "Yes. We must. But I don't know exactly how. Gwen knew we'd come out in the right time, but we don't have that certainty going back home."

"That's another thing. How'd she know?" David wondered.

"Because we already had been, in a sense," Cassie said. "We had gone back and made her go forward, but she needed to help us make the initial jump back so we can find her and help her go forward. It's the same as how we know that when we do send her forward, she'll end up in the right time, because she was already there." David had to think about that for a minute. "Actually," Cassie continued thoughtfully, "this may even explain why we all seemed familiar to each other when we met. We already knew each other fifteen hundred years ago in the past, before we technically existed."

"Okay. That makes sense in an extremely convoluted way," David conceded, though a little dubiously.

"But we sent – or will send, whatever – Gwen into a time almost sixteen years before we meet her. That's how long she said she'd lived in Glastonbury," William pointed out.

Cassie frowned, thinking. "I wonder why. Maybe that's just when she popped out."

"All this still doesn't help us figure out how time's passing in our time or how long we'll be here," Sarah said. "And there's another thing. If we are stuck here for a long time, like a year or something, but come out at the same time we left, will we have aged in our own time? Or will we do a Narnia thing and come out in our time the same age as when we left?"

"Sarah, let's hope we don't stay here long enough for that to become an issue. I can just see explaining that one to my parents, or anyone else we know for that matter. That would be supremely awkward," Cassie said, shuddering at the thought. "I'll think about it if it becomes a reality."

"Well, we do know one thing about this whole time issue," William said.

"What?" the other three asked.

"We can't be stuck here permanently if Cassie is the one in the prophecy. She needs to get back to make it happen."

"Good point," Cassie said, surprised he was the one to bring it up. "But maybe I'm not."

William smiled wryly. "No pun intended, but only time will tell."

Caelwyn hurried through the passageways. She had a good idea of where he'd be at this time of day, and she didn't want to risk anyone walking in on the young people in the garden, particularly William. She could just imagine the gossip that would start circulating. Thank God there had been an excuse for him to wear the hood. It wouldn't be good to attract any undue attention.

"Well, well, if it isn't Caelwyn. What brings you to Camelot today?" a voice said from behind her.

Caelwyn felt herself stiffen as she recognized it as belonging to her least favorite knight, but she turned with what she hoped was a pleasant enough smile. "Good morning, Mordred. I hope you are well. As for my business, it is my own and no one else's."

"I hope nothing worrisome has occurred," he said.

"No, but I must speak with Arthur about it all the same."

"Some Brenwyd matters you need solved? Can't you and your people govern yourselves without coming to Arthur with all your problems?" He narrowed his cool gray eyes at her.

"That's not it at all, Mordred. I must be going. Good day." Caelwyn wished Mordred would at least attempt to be civil. Everyone knew he had no great love for Brenwyds, but as a knight he should exercise better manners. Still, he kept himself just polite enough for Arthur to keep him in service, and he was loyal, always a valuable trait.

She turned to go, but he followed her. "If you want to see the king, you're going the wrong way."

"Am I? Perhaps you could tell me the right one, then."

"I might be persuaded to, if you tell me what you are going to tell him."

She looked at him hard. "No."

"Not even a hint?"

"No. Where is Arthur?"

"I'm sure you can figure it out. You Brenwyds always claim to be smarter than us mere mortals."

Caelwyn gritted her teeth, but fortunately another knight entered the conversation, one she liked far better. "What are you still doing here, Mordred? I thought you were headed north." That voice belonged to Kay, who was Arthur's foster brother, steward, and one of his oldest friends.

Mordred bowed his head in greeting. "I was doing just that, but I ran into Caelwyn here and we've been having a nice chat."

"I see. I'm afraid I must end it, as Arthur just sent me to look for her. He's expecting her."

"Oh, then go on, by all means. You should not keep a king waiting." Mordred turned on his heel and went down the passageway.

Caelwyn let out a breath. "Thank you, Kay," she said gratefully.

He smiled at her. "Don't bother yourself about him, Caelwyn. He's just overly inquisitive."

"Humph. Where is my cousin? Sir Overly Inquisitive did not deign to tell me."

"He's in the round room. He's most curious to hear what you have to say." Kay looked at her with an eyebrow raised. "Can you tell me what's going on?"

She shook her head. "My apologies, Kay, but it's not something I can go around telling."

He nodded. "I understand." He looked up and down the hall and lowered his voice. "You should tell your people to watch themselves. We've been hearing more grumblings from the north and they're becoming more worrisome."

"We've also been hearing things. Siarl is meeting with Bran today to discuss it."

"I don't think anything will come of it, but be on your guard. Arthur has sent Lancelot to investigate."

"Good. I should go to him now. Mordred was right about one thing, you shouldn't keep a king waiting too long. Good day, Kay. Tell your dear wife I said hello."

"I will, and good day to you as well. Has Eira had the babe yet?"

"Not yet, but soon."

Kay smiled. "How the years have flown." He began to walk on, but turned back as if remembering someone. "Arthur was actually going to summon you soon to advise him on something, so he'll likely mention it. Officially I don't know anything, but," Kay paused, a secretive gleam entering his eyes, "Gwendolyn is reaching an age."

Caelwyn raised her eyebrows and a smile curved her lips. "Is that so? Well then, I'll have to talk to Guinevere as well. Farewell." She walked up the corridor, making turns as she needed them. Yes, Arthur would want to consult her about that, considering the political implications. But speaking of which... she quickened her pace. She hoped Mordred wouldn't go anywhere near the garden on his way out. The last thing she needed was him, of all people, spreading rumors.

Meeting a King

Caelwyn headed to the round room, stopping at the door to knock. "Come in," a familiar masculine voice said.

She pushed the door open and entered. The round room was called round for a reason. The walls curved in a circular shape, since this room was supposed to have been the base of a new sort of round tower, but Arthur had decided a tower would be of better use on the city wall and stopped the construction. This room was the result. It was fairly large, with a round table in the center that could seat all the knights and sub-kings. It was where the king held his most important meetings and councils, and where he met monthly with his knights.

Arthur was standing with his back to Caelwyn, gazing fixedly out of the narrow window at his city. He wore his everyday court attire, not the fancy clothes people might expect kings to wear at all times, but still several cuts above the everyday attire of the common people. Caelwyn walked up behind him and asked quietly, "What do you see?"

"I see people going about their daily business in contentment and peace, with no worry about invading Saxons, Irish, or Picts. It is good to see," he said without turning. "Especially after seeing all the suffering the Goths have been causing in Gaul."

"You certainly worked hard enough for this. And I doubt the Goths will make trouble again anytime soon, now that they know how fully you support Ban."

"I pray it is so. I have no wish to fight another campaign anytime soon." He turned to her, his green eyes keen and curious. "Your message was intriguing, but vague. I couldn't make out much of it."

"That was the intention. If somehow it got misdirected, I didn't want others understanding it. You can never be too careful."

"True." He went to the table and sat, indicating the chair next to him. "So tell me about this information you've found, Caelwyn, and then tell me how your family fares. I have not talked with you in too long, and for that I am sorry."

She sat, smiling. "No need to apologize. We have all been recovering after arriving back from the campaign. Your second question is the easier one to answer. All the children are well. Eira is getting close to her time."

Arthur smiled. "You will tell me when she gives birth, will you not?"

"Of course. Oh, and I believe Telyn and Ganieda will likely be over later to visit Gwendolyn."

"She'll like that. How is Ganieda doing?"

"She seems to be doing well enough. She is less sorrowful as time goes on, thank the Lord." Caelwyn sighed inwardly at the thought of the girl. She would likely never again be quite the same as before her father's disappearance.

Arthur nodded. "That is good to hear. And Siarl?"

"Fine, but he and Bran are meeting today with several others to discuss the rumors. They are spreading. Some villages I visit to treat illness and injuries no longer welcome me like they used to. I've even seen some cross themselves when they think I'm not looking, as if to ward off evil." Her expression had turned serious. "I have been told that stories are spreading of dark magic, saying that Brenwyds practice it and are merely biding our time for a chance to enslave humanity."

Arthur scowled. "Preposterous. I, too, have heard such rumors, but I haven't been able to track down their source. Stories of black magic come from somewhere, and I have no wish for the events of ten years ago to be repeated." Caelwyn nodded agreement. "I have also heard stories of Brenwyds disappearing in a strange manner in the north. Almost as if they vanish into thin air. Have you heard those?"

"Yes," Caelwyn said. "We are trying to discover the truth of them, but they disturb me greatly. I feel it is only the beginning of something, I know not what, but we should all of us be on our guard. Evil is starting to stir against us, trying to find a toehold. I have felt this since Merlin disappeared, but it has started to grow of late." She paused and lowered her voice. "Do you know if... *she* is moving?"

Arthur shook his head. "No. I have asked Mordred about it, and he says she is still in her exile in the Orkneys. He assured me that he will keep a closer eye on her for a time. Pray she stays there." He considered the rest of Caelwyn's words and sighed. "I will send a message to Lancelot with your warning. He will know what to look for." He paused. "Perhaps I should send someone in secret to the Orkneys. Mordred has never given me cause to doubt his loyalty, but it never hurts to be too careful."

Caelwyn frowned. "I dislike his opinion of Brenwyds. Considering who his mother is, I cannot altogether blame him, but it troubles me."

"I know," Arthur said. "But you must admit, he has improved." Caelwyn grunted. "But enough of that for now. It's good you came today. I wish to talk to you about Gwendolyn."

"Oh?"

"She is of an age to be married, and several of the kings with sons are starting to pressure me, especially after the close calls in Armorica."

"That's not surprising. Does Gwendolyn have a preference?"

"Not that I know of, but it's not just that I'm concerned about. Whoever marries her will, at this point, inherit the kingdom. I want her to wed someone she likes, but it needs to be someone steady, a good warrior but a lover of peace."

Caelwyn nodded agreement. "But many of the king's sons I know itch for battle. They believe they must fight to prove their worth, having missed the Saxon wars."

"Yes, I know. That is what concerns me. We fought for peace too long and too hard to have it destroyed by a young hot-blood."

Caelwyn nodded again. "But do not give up hope for an heir yet, Arthur. Guinevere is still able to conceive." She paused. "I have something important to tell you, Arthur, and I need to do so quickly. You remember Merlin's last prophecy before he disappeared, correct?"

He gazed at her for several moments, his features inscrutable as he replied. "Of course."

"Well, last night Dragon woke me with a summons from Joseph. I went to Ynis Witrin and found four young people, two boys and two girls, in the church kitchen. They had wandered onto the isle after dark. I took them to my house, as Joseph is not really equipped to deal with visitors late at night." She paused. Arthur waited. "The reason I bring up Merlin's last prophecy was because it told of two boys and two girls who would appear to help the kingdom at its weakest hour and help continue its legacy."

Arthur's gaze sharpened. "Yes, I remember the words. You believe they are the ones?"

"I firmly believe so. I have had several dream visions with their faces. One of the girls is a Brenwyd."

"From where do they come?"

"I'm not at liberty to say. Only one speaks our language. It's a very foreign place, I'll tell you that."

"Hmm." He paused. "I suppose that means the time Merlin spoke of is drawing close. Perhaps this is why you sense evil stirring, why we are receiving these strange reports and rumors." His features turned grave and weary. "And after we have just returned from Gaul..."

"It may not be for a while yet. Prophecies don't necessarily follow a timeline. It could be merely a warning," Caelwyn tried to encourage him.

"Warnings are given for a reason and only fools discount them," he said. "You must bring these visitors here so I can meet them. What are their names?"

"Cassie, William, Dafyd, and Sarah. They're about Gwendolyn's age. And they are here already. I thought you would like to meet them, so I left them in the west garden."

Arthur smiled. "You know me too well. Are they siblings?"

"Sarah and Dafyd are, but otherwise they are unrelated. Not married or betrothed either, and unchaperoned. Joseph was in hearty disapproval."

Arthur laughed. "He would be. Come, take me to them."

He started toward the door and Caelwyn stood. "There is one last thing," she said.

He turned. "What?"

"I'd like you to take a good look at the tallest boy. He has black hair and blue eyes."

Arthur looked at her quizzically. "And?"

"Please, just do it. You shall see why."

He gazed at her, trying to divine the reason. "Very well," he said at last, having learned long ago not to question Caelwyn when she wished to be mysterious about something. "I will do as you ask." She led him from the room to where the teens were waiting.

Sarah looked up as she heard the light pattering of rain on the roof and in the garden slow and then cease. "That didn't last too long."

"It might start up again in a bit. That would be classic English weather for you," William commented, looking up at the gray clouds that still loomed threateningly.

"But is it still the same in this century?" Sarah wondered.

"Pretty much," Cassie answered, inspecting things in her emergency bag like she was taking an inventory.

Sarah did a double-take. "Where'd that come from?"

"I hid it under my cloak so as not to attract attention. I'm just checking what I've got in here," Cassie answered.

"Oh. I wondered what that lump was. Clever," Sarah said.

"How long till Caelwyn gets back, do you think?" David asked.

"No clue. I don't have many answers today, if you hadn't noticed. This isn't exactly a well-documented period of history," Cassie said. "Oh, good, there's the duct tape."

"But what happens when she does get back?" William wondered.

"That I might actually have an answer to. I think there are two likely choices. A, she'll come back and take us to wherever the king is, or B, she'll bring the king back with her. I'm going with B. I don't think she wants to risk us running into too many people," Cassie reasoned. William nodded.

"Does anyone know the proper etiquette for greeting a legendary king?" David asked. "Because I did not learn that in school."

"I'd say just be extra polite and respectful. Beyond that, we hopefully won't get in too much trouble for not knowing the precise etiquette, since it's not exactly something we do every day," his sister said.

"Sounds like a plan," Cassie said. "Man, my dad is *so* not going to believe me when I tell him I actually met King Arthur – that sounds really weird – and then he's going to be so jealous and question us about every little detail we can remember so he can write it down." She smiled at the thought till she recalled the perilous situation her father was in. A moment later she cocked her head. "Someone's coming. Two someones, and one's walking with a heavier step than the other. I think I was right."

"Wow. Never would have guessed that," David said, straight-faced.

Cassie rolled her eyes and re-zipped her bag. "It does happen upon occasion," she said drolly. They all stood and turned expectantly toward the hallway Caelwyn had disappeared down earlier.

Soon enough the footsteps became audible to the other three and Caelwyn appeared, followed by a man wearing a fine tunic and a gold torc around his throat. Cassie examined him curiously, assessing this man of so many legends. He was of average height, not particularly tall, but not too short either. His hair was black, his eyes a piercing green, his expression sharp and alert, and the lower half of his face covered by a beard. His facial features spoke of Roman ancestry, but Cassie could detect hints of a Briton heritage as well, having learned the differences from her father. She was struck by the air of regality and command that hung about him like a cloak. It was in his face and the way he walked, and even the way he held himself with assurance and confidence. This, more than anything, told her that this was a king, and not a weak one. Here was someone indeed capable of being the basis of legends that had persisted for fifteen hundred years. There were faint worry lines on his forehead, but Cassie also saw laugh lines spreading from his eyes and mouth, which she took as a sign that he enjoyed merriment and simple pleasures as much as anyone. This king was no tyrant. She could well imagine why he had been remembered in so many stories when history had forgotten others. Her initial thoughts were confirmed by a quick listen to his song, which was strong, clear, and firm, yet had a gentle edge. He was also younger than she had imagined, looking to be at most in his early forties.

He met her searching eyes and a welcoming smile crossed his features. She dropped her eyes, feeling a little embarrassed and disconcerted. It wasn't just that she wasn't sure of the rules about looking kings in the eye, but she had seen a sudden and striking familiarity in his features that unsettled and startled her. She heard

Caelwyn saying something, probably giving introductions, and thought that bowing was probably appropriate. She did so, bending at about a forty-five degree angle from her waist, and saw from the corner of her eye that the others were following her example. She straightened and returned her gaze to the king in time to see surprise, and then absolute shock, enter his eyes, although the rest of his face didn't change.

She had a pretty good idea of what – or rather, who – was causing the reaction. She heard Sarah stifle what was likely a gasp and looked from the corner of her eye as William straightened and flicked his eyes to the king's face, trying to look at him as politely as possible. Cassie saw similar surprise and shock cross William's features, though he doused the expression as soon as it came over his face. Caelwyn spoke again, and Cassie thought it was more to break up the atmosphere, which had suddenly become tense, than because she had anything that needed saying. Cassie had no idea what she was saying and could tell William wasn't paying much attention. She took a small step toward him and elbowed him as discreetly as possible. "Hey, pay attention. You're the only person who can understand her," she hissed under her breath.

"Right. Sorry." He turned his attention to Caelwyn with what Cassie thought was relief. He answered what was apparently a question, though maybe it was just confirming whatever Caelwyn was saying. *I have got to get a handle on this language, quick,* Cassie thought. The king spoke, and even his voice seemed vaguely familiar, like she'd heard it in a whisper or a dream. He turned his head toward Caelwyn, and the odd sense of recognition struck Cassie anew. Particularly with his profile outlined against the gray sky, King Arthur looked strikingly like William.

Caelwyn watched what was unfolding before her with no small apprehension. She had seen shock and confusion cross the faces of

Particularly with his profile outlined
against the gray sky, King Arthur
looked strikingly like William.

the visitors, though they tried valiantly to disguise it. Arthur's facial expression had never changed, but she knew him well enough to tell he had realized. And by seeing him with them, her suspicions had been very nearly confirmed, though she wouldn't know for sure until she did one final test, and that might have to be another day. She wasn't going to tell anyone, not yet. She knew that, in order to really believe it, the young ones had to figure it out on their own without any help from her. The best thing to do now was to get them out of Camelot without notice and wait until the time Merlin had spoken of came. But in the meantime, she had no intention of being idle. She needed to know how well they could fight and how much the girl knew about Brenwyd abilities. Because if Caelwyn was right, that knowledge could mean the difference between life and death for them and for others.

After all the proper formal pleasantries had been exchanged, she asked for herself and Arthur to be excused and drew the king to the other side of the garden, well out of William's hearing and perhaps Cassie's, though even if the girl did overhear them she wouldn't be able to understand them. "Well, what do you think?" she asked Arthur. His gaze was firmly attached to the other side of the garden, where Caelwyn knew the young people would be having a conversation mirroring the one she was about to have with Arthur. The king looked agitated and didn't seem to hear her. "Arthur? Don't you dare ignore me." She infused a light teasing into her tone, recalling the times they had spent together as children, before either of them were aware of his birthright and parentage. He tore his gaze from the other side with visible effort.

"Who is he?" Arthur demanded, but trying to ask it in a casual tone. He was tense, but Caelwyn also saw a certain longing in his eyes for something ever hoped for but never granted.

She sighed, trying to figure out how best to answer him without giving away the children's secret. "Someone who is here to help, though none of them are aware of it yet."

"What of his lineage? Do you know it?"

"No. But you see what I meant."

"Yes. He must come from a Romano-Celt family. Such a thing is common enough." He seemed to be talking more to himself than to her. Caelwyn didn't mind. It happened often, as she was one of the few people Arthur could completely relax around. "Has anyone else seen him – them?" he asked after a minute, correcting himself.

"People saw them ride in with me, but it was raining so I had an excuse to ask him to keep his hood up. They never saw his face. I know to be careful," Caelwyn assured him.

"I know, but I don't need any more heir talk and rumors going around..."

"I know." She put a hand on his shoulder comfortingly. "That's why I wanted you to meet them first. I can't control the kingdom's gossips, but I can give you a warning. Don't worry so. The people know your character."

He grunted. "It's not the people I'm particularly concerned about."

Caelwyn smiled. "She knows you better than anyone else, Arthur. She will not doubt you." She looked up at the overcast sky. Several minutes passed before she spoke again, her tone serious as her eyes sought the group across the garden. A certain knowing expression came over her face. Arthur could tell by the expression that her next words would be a prophecy, and mentally steeled himself. Caelwyn spoke slowly. "Darkness starts to fall, yet God has given us the tools and hope with which to fight it. He will prevail, though the struggle will cost us much." She looked straight into Arthur's eyes. "Yes, perhaps even your very life."

"I sure hope someone besides me noticed that," David said as soon as Caelwyn and Arthur were out of hearing, his brown eyes darting around to look at everyone else.

"If you're talking about what I think you're talking about, I did, but have no idea what to make of it," Cassie said, brow furrowed in thought.

"The king looking like William? That's exactly what I'm talking about." David glanced to the other side of the garden where Caelwyn and the king were standing. William was also looking in that direction and Sarah gazed at him curiously.

"William? You okay?" she asked cautiously, not quite sure of the answer.

"Hmm? Oh, yeah. It's just... I was not exactly expecting *that*." He sounded startled and a little unsettled, but he leaned against one of the columns and crossed his arms in a relaxed manner.

"Neither was I," David said. "There goes my criminal resemblance idea."

"You sound almost disappointed," Sarah said, frowning at her brother.

"Hey, I thought it was a pretty good idea." At that, William made a noise Cassie took as suppressed amusement. She also fought back a grin. It just didn't seem entirely appropriate.

"Then I hope you'll forgive me for thinking that *this* is a better scenario than that," William told David.

"Well, it could or it couldn't be," Cassie put in. "Now we know why people have been reacting to you funny, and I can imagine very well what one of their first thoughts was after seeing you. You can probably bet Arthur is thinking about that very thing at the moment." She nodded in the direction of Caelwyn and the king.

William looked at her inquisitively, with a vague idea of what she was implying. "Cassie, could you forgive me for asking a potentially dumb question and say what that thought would be?"

The look she gave him indicated that she'd thought the answer was totally obvious. "Well, if I'm the average British citizen who lives in Camelot, knows what the king looks like, and suddenly sees a fifteen-year-old boy appear who resembles the king greatly, I would probably think something along the lines of, *Good gracious! Could that be a, pardon me, bastard son of the king?*" She frowned. "Well, maybe they would use some British euphemism, but..."

"I get the picture," William assured her.

"So you think the king is thinking something like that?" Sarah asked, feeling a bit confused.

"Of course not, but he knows that his people will think that, and that might cause him some issues, since I don't think he actually has any children and therefore no heir. But it might not. The Arthur in my dad's stories was totally faithful to Guinevere, so the idea of an illegitimate child would be completely out of the question. True, those were just stories, but they were closer to the truth than most of the Arthur stories in our time. Either way, it makes sense as to why Caelwyn wanted us to meet the king so soon after getting here. She needed him to know about William, probably kind of as a heads-up thing."

William scowled at her. He disliked being talked about in the third person, particularly as a show-and-tell item and possible cause of trouble, but Cassie started talking again before he could voice an objection. "I think Caelwyn brought us here on our first day for another, bigger reason than William, though. Unfortunately, I don't know what that would be. I don't ever recall finding anything about four mysterious teenagers showing up late in Arthur's reign in the stories I've read and heard. Of course, that could just mean we didn't do anything special. Or won't do anything special. This whole time travel thing is confusing. Do we have to follow what we know as history, or can we do anything we want because we know how it will all turn out anyway? Since we're here now, that means what we've done so far has already affected our time." She blinked. "That is one big convoluted loop of logic." There was a brief silence as the others wound their way through her logic and the way her mind jumped topics.

"I agree with you about the convoluted logic," David said, "and

I have no clue as to how the whole space-time continuum works. But don't worry about not knowing Caelwyn's reasoning, Cass. We don't expect you to read minds. We just expect you to know everything in recorded history, that's all."

"Thanks," she said, chuckling a little. "I'll do my best on that score. But speaking of reading minds, I think Telyn can do it."

William raised an eyebrow, both at the sudden change of subject and her proposed idea. Mind reading? "Reading minds only happens in books and movies," he said.

Cassie snorted. "Uh-huh, William, remind me again, what century are we in?" she asked, a little sarcastically.

William rolled his eyes. "Point taken, but seriously–"

"Wait a minute," Sarah cut in. "Dad mentioned something about mind-reading that night Calico explained Brenwyds to us – when you had gone after your parents, Cassie. That's a Brenwyd trait, right? Please don't say you've had it all along and never told us."

"I don't, thankfully enough, but it is a Brenwyd trait."

William blinked. He had heard rumors of such in the Brotherhood, but hadn't put too much stock in them. Actually, many of the Brotherhood stories of Brenwyd abilities had turned out to be largely true, but the purpose of the abilities had been twisted. The amount of actual truth in the Brotherhood accounts of Brenwyds was likely a factor in their believability.

Cassie stopped talking and pondered for a moment. Now she definitely understood why Caelwyn had wanted William to keep his hood up. But why would William, born nearly fifteen hundred years after Arthur's death, look so much like him? Even if William was a descendent of Arthur, it was highly unlikely that he would have so much resemblance to an ancestor. At that idea, her thoughts slowed. If William was Arthur's heir, maybe he was the one Caelwyn's prophecy had referred to. It would certainly make sense.

"So what do you think of the king, Cass?" David asked her, interrupting her thoughts.

She shook herself from her contemplations to answer him. "Well, he certainly appears to be a very real man," she said. "He seems very practical, going off looks. He looks like a king and a commander."

"A lot of people going around the city as we rode in looked happy and content, indicating they have a good ruler," Sarah put in thoughtfully. "The city was fairly clean, and the people seemed friendly, though there were the beggars. But I guess every city has them."

"He's not pure Briton," Cassie added musingly. "With that dark hair and those features, he has to have some Roman blood. It would be common enough not to be much of a rarity in this time period, I think. The last of the legions pulled out a little over a hundred years ago, in about 410, though many Romans stayed, and the empire fell in 476. This is 516, and that monk said it was the twenty-first year of his–" She stopped as she realized the possible implications. "Ooooh."

"This is around when Camlann happened, then?" William asked, his expression serious.

"Well, maybe. It depends on when Arthur was officially crowned. He drew the sword from the stone when he was fifteen, but I don't think he was actually crowned as king until later. He looks older than he would be if he was crowned at fifteen. The twenty-one year mark is the length of time between Badon Hill and Camlann. Dad thinks that Arthur was officially crowned and recognized as king after Badon, because by that time he would have proven himself to all the other sub-kings, or chieftain kings, of Britain and they would have been more willing to recognize him as High King. I – or actually, you – will have to question Caelwyn. But if the latter is the case... then we might very well be on the edge of Camlann. Which would seriously stink."

Before anyone could respond to that worrying idea, Caelwyn called over from the other side of the garden. Both her expression and the king's looked troubled. Cassie wondered what they had been talking about. She suspected it had been more than William's resemblance to the king.

William nodded to Caelwyn and called out a reply, then picked up his cloak. "We're leaving," he announced. "Let's talk more later." They all walked to the other end of the garden, where they stood for a few minutes as Arthur asked William some questions about their families and where they were from. William answered each one after a little hesitation, trying to formulate answers without revealing the fact the teens were from the twenty-first century. Eventually Arthur nodded in satisfaction, smiled briefly at the teens as a farewell, spoke a few words to Caelwyn, and left. He walked down the hallway from which he'd entered, his stride purposeful and quick. Cassie wondered what he was going to do. See Guinevere, perhaps? Guinevere... the one the legends had made the cause of Arthur's downfall, along with Lancelot. She wondered what Guinevere looked like, and why she would be faithless to Arthur. Caelwyn led them back along the passageway by which they had entered the garden, but when they were almost to the end of it Cassie realized that her bag was still in the garden.

She turned on her heel and almost rammed into Sarah, who was right behind her. Sarah took a step back. "What is it?" she asked.

"I left my bag in the garden. That is one item I do *not* want anyone finding," Cassie said. William quickly translated for Caelwyn, and Cassie glimpsed an anxious look on her face for a fleeting moment as she answered him.

"She says to go, but make it quick," William said.

Cassie nodded. "I will." She ran back up the passageway and across the garden. The bag was lying where she'd left it by one of the columns, but it was unzipped. She frowned and looked around, but saw no one. She did a quick check to make sure everything was still there. First aid kit, extra change of clothes, small flashlight, a granola bar (the only one left after their cross-country trip), a water bottle, duct tape, her Bible... the extra book she had wasn't there. She looked around for it. It was a new book she'd gotten for her birthday from her friend Livvie which she hadn't had time to finish reading yet. She didn't see it anywhere. *That's weird,* she thought. *Who would take the book?* She looked around again, and realized she wasn't alone. She felt curious eyes on her back, and heard a slight movement of air and rustle of breath as the person breathed in and out. She turned and saw a quick movement behind one of the columns. "Hello? Who's there?" she asked, knowing the person wouldn't be able to understand her, but hoping her friendly tone would encourage them to abandon their hiding place.

A head poked around the side of the column, then the rest of the body of a girl who looked about ten. She was rather petite, a full head and a half shorter than Cassie. She had brown hair, and her eyes were a deep green with a lively look to them. In her hand she held Cassie's book. "Can I have that?" Cassie asked her gently, bending down to be on a level with the girl and pointing toward the book. The girl's brow furrowed as she held up the book and said something in her language, pointing from the book to Cassie. Cassie guessed she was asking if it was hers, so she nodded and smiled. The girl handed it to her, looking at her curiously with those big green eyes all the while. She seemed slightly familiar to Cassie, and she realized the little girl's eyes were like Arthur's. Her dress was finely woven, and she wore a necklace made of gold with precious stones. *Arthur's daughter?* Cassie wondered. She'd never heard of Arthur having a daughter, but it wasn't impossible. He was married, after all.

Cassie placed the book back in her bag, the girl looking on. She had obviously realized Cassie did not speak her language, and she pointed to Cassie's ears. "Brenwyd?" she asked. Cassie nodded. The girl pointed to Cassie, then at the passageway where the others were waiting. "Caelwyn?" Cassie nodded again.

"I need to leave now," she told the girl, making signs with her hands so the girl would understand. The girl's face fell a little. She put a hand on Cassie's bag and touched the book, which was still visible because Cassie hadn't zipped the bag yet. She drew the book back out and opened it, looking at the printed words with wide eyes. She said something, but Cassie shook her head, indicating she did not understand.

The girl repeated herself more slowly, and Cassie realized she could understand her. The girl was speaking in Latin. "Est liber?" she asked. *Is it a book?*

"Ita vero," Cassie replied. *Yes.* The girl's face lit up. She started jabbering quickly in Latin. Apparently, the language was not dead in this time period. Cassie held up a hand to stop the flow. "Desine!" *Stop!* "Ego bene Latine non loquor. Tarde loquere." *I do not speak good Latin. Slow down.* The girl nodded, but before she could speak, a voice called from the hallway leading into the house, sounding impatient. The girl turned toward the voice, answering it. Cassie started moving toward the passageway to grab Caelwyn and/or William, but the girl grabbed her hand and started pulling her toward the other passageway, the one the voice had called from.

"Veni mecum. Volo te congredi meam matrem." *Come with me. I want you to meet my mother.*

Oh, dear, Cassie thought. *I'm not supposed to be noticed.*

Twi!

Yes?

Please tell William that some help would be appreciated.

Are you in trouble?

Not really, but I need a translator and some backup. This girl is dragging me to meet her mother.

And that is a bad thing? Twi sounded amused.

When you don't want to be noticed, yes!

Very well. I will tell them.

Thank you. Cassie and the girl were almost to the hallway's entrance. Cassie could hear footsteps approaching from the passageway, but the clouds were breaking up and the sun coming out, and the dimness of the passageway against the brightness of the sun prevented Cassie from being able to clearly see who was coming. The girl was talking to her mother quickly and excitedly. Her mother replied, her tone sounding gentler than she had before, no doubt because by now her daughter had told her there was a guest. She stepped out of the passageway and into the light. The sun was now shining down in Cassie's eyes, blinding her momentarily, and she blinked. The woman came into focus, and she blinked again. *No way*, she thought, staring at the woman but trying to make it look like she wasn't. She inclined her head respectfully. The woman wore fine clothes, and a delicate gold torc around her neck with the ends carved in a loopy, Celtic design, as well as some gold bracelets.

Apparently the girl had told her mother that Cassie understood Latin, for she spoke it. "Salve, amica. Unde es?" *Hello, friend. Where are you from?*

As Cassie tried to formulate an answer, she heard the others come up behind her. *Thank God,* she thought. *Caelwyn can take it from here.* She turned toward them with relief. Caelwyn and the woman exchanged greetings, looking happy to see each other. Cassie saw the others' faces radiate shock, and she understood the expressions full well, but she was not prepared for what came next.

The girl tugged on Cassie's hand and Cassie looked down at her. "Est mea mater. Nomen ei est Guinevere. Meus pater est Artos. Sunt rex et regina Britanniae. Sum Jenifer."

Cassie stared at the girl, incredulous. *This day has just taken on a whole other layer of shock,* she thought. She looked at the woman again. Long chestnut hair. Deep blue eyes. Mid thirties. The girl had said, *She is my mother. Her name is Guinevere. My father is Arthur. They are king and queen of Britain. I am Jenifer.* Cassie looked at her friends, knowing they were thinking the exact same thing she was: They had found Gwen.

WEAPONS PRACTICE

He knelt by the window, eyes closed but seeing far beyond natural sight. He watched them as they made their way to the gate and out of the city, neatly avoiding pedestrians. His Sight jumped forward to them at her house, and he surmised he was viewing the past, recent as it may be. It zoomed in on their faces, young, confused, and troubled. He pitied them, being thrust into such an extraordinary situation. They had much to learn before they could fulfill the role God had planned for them, but they knew much already, more than they realized, and Caelwyn would see that they learned the rest. They dismounted, and all but the Brenwyd girl led their horses to the stable. She lingered, gazing up at the sky as if sensing she was being watched. It wouldn't surprise him if she did. She was powerful, even more than she knew, as she had to be if she and her friends were to succeed in their as yet unknown mission. His heart went out to her. Her features were filled with beauty, as all Brenwyds' were, but a deep sadness lingered in those gray-blue eyes, the outward trace of a great grief locked inside. He wondered what it was. His sympathy increased as he watched her, knowing that there would be more grief ahead ere her journey was over. But it was a journey that must be taken if evil was to be cleansed from the land.

The other girl came out of the stable and went to her, speaking to her, but the man could not understand their tongue. The two friends hugged for a brief moment after they finished speaking, then headed for the stable with the horse following behind. The man could see his pupil in the doorway watching them, and he knew they were in good hands. His Sight zoomed out and he found himself back in his prison, looking out at the vista he had memorized over the past year. They would be coming for him soon – the mistress was in residence. They were becoming less patient and more frustrated as he endured their tortures without breaking. He knew they would kill him before many more months passed. He was not frightened of death. He knew the glory of the next world would erase all memory of pain suffered in this one. His only regrets were that he would not see his dearest daughter and only child happily married and settled, that he could not be there for his king at this time of trial, and that he could not be there to help guide these children along their path. There was one thing, however, that he could do for them. He closed his eyes once more and bowed his head in prayer.

⋈⋇⋈

William watched Cassie pace up and down the room. Caelwyn had left to collect her twins and Selyf from her daughter-in-law, leaving the teens to their own devices. They'd convened in the house's common room to discuss matters. The ground floor of the house was divided into two sections, a small area that functioned as a kitchen, and a large area that appeared to be a combined dining and living space. Cassie was trying, as they all were, to assimilate all the information they had gathered in the last twenty-four hours and make sense of it all. All four were having a hard time even just accepting the information, let alone figuring out how it all fit together. It was, William mused, like trying to put together a puzzle with half the pieces missing.

"I don't get why she'd need to go into the future anyway," Cassie was saying, speaking of Guinevere.

William thought that finding out Gwen's real identity as Guinevere was the biggest shock of all. He would never have guessed from talking with her that she had once been the queen of Britain, though it did explain her views and knowledge of the King Arthur story. *And to think I suggested to her that her dead body had been found by twelfth-century monks*, he thought with embarrassment.

"I mean, I know that the atmosphere at the end of Arthur's reign wasn't exactly great for her, with the whole Lancelot business going on and whatnot, but one thing that stays consistent in all the legends is that she retired to a convent, and some say she died soon after Camlann," Cassie continued.

"But maybe people just said that because she disappeared mysteriously and so they assumed she died," David said. "It's a logical conclusion."

Cassie nodded acceptance. "True, but still..." She shook her head. "I need more time to think about this. My brain is on serious overload."

"Seconded," William said. "I didn't even know it was possible to be shocked so often in a day."

"You're telling me," Cassie replied fervently. She stopped pacing and stared out of a small window. "I remember the astonishment of finding out I was part-Brenwyd. That pales in comparison to this. I guess this is why I felt we should go to Glastonbury, though why God would want us to come into the sixth century is way beyond me."

"Which is why you're not God," David said. "By the way, do you know why Caelwyn keeps calling me Dafyd?"

"It's the Celtic version of David," Cassie answered. "That I know, at least."

William was looking at Cassie curiously. "You think God is the one who wanted us in this century? Not just Gwen?" he asked.

Cassie nodded. "For sure. Gwen was His earthly means of getting us here, but He definitely had this planned. Now we need to figure out what it is He brought us back for, even if only to push Guinevere forward and... oh. That complicates things a little." Cassie's frown returned.

"What does?" Sarah asked.

"The fact that she was pregnant when she went forward - er, will be pregnant, that is."

The other three all stared at her. "Um, what?" Sarah said.

"Oh, right, I didn't tell you," Cassie said, looking a little sheepish. "Well, when I took that nap at Gwen's, I had another dream that continued the one I had that morning. It seemed to pick up right when the last one left off, but from the woman's - Gwen's, Guinevere's, whatever - point of view. Didn't see what happened to us, but we'll find that out, I guess. Anyway, she arrived in our time, with the tower on the Tor, and went toward the inn because she saw the lights. She knocked on the door and this old lady - Eleanor Smith, her name was - came out. I guess it was the lady she got the place from. They talked, and the lady agreed to let her stay. During the conversation, Gwen said she was pregnant. She can't have been too far along, though. She wasn't showing at all."

Who was pregnant? Kai's voice asked as he and Dassah ambled into the kitchen.

"Gwen, when she goes forward to our time. Kai, we found out that Gwen is Guinevere!" Cassie told him.

The king's wife? he asked, sounding surprised.

"Yes."

But why would she go forward? Dassah asked.

Don't know, Cassie answered her. *We're trying to figure that out.*

David shook his head and said, "Well, that certainly puts a new spin on things. How does that little factoid fit in with all the other stuff?"

Cassie shrugged, her brow deeply furrowed. *How, indeed?*

"So does that mean that there's a child of Arthur wandering around in our time?" Sarah asked. "But I don't remember meeting any kid who was Gwen's child. He or she would be what, fifteen?"

"I guess so, but the kid didn't live," William piped up. "Cassie and I talked with Gwen while you and David were sleeping, and she mentioned that she'd had three children, two girls and a boy. The girls are obviously that girl Jenifer, and the one Telyn mentioned, Gwendolyn. That means she'll be pregnant with the boy, and she said she lost all of them, so he must have died somehow."

"Or maybe she had a miscarriage," Cassie suggested, frowning thoughtfully.

"That's so sad," Sarah said sympathetically.

What are you thinking, girl? Kai asked Cassie privately so no one else could hear.

Quite a lot of things, Cassie answered. *I need time to sort everything out before I say anything to anyone.* Aloud, she said, "Yes, it is, especially since if the boy had been born alive in this time, he would have been Arthur's heir." She released a gusty sigh. "I don't know about the rest of y'all, but I need at least a night to sleep on all this before I can start making sense of things, I think."

"I think that goes for the rest of us as well," David said, nodding agreement. "Or for me, at any rate." Cassie nodded distractedly. William didn't blame her for being overwhelmed. He felt overwhelmed himself, and no matter how much Brenwyd blood Cassie had, she was still part-human.

Silence descended on the room. After several minutes Cassie straightened and turned her gaze toward the window, head cocked slightly in her listening position. "I hear horses. Caelwyn's back," she announced. William strained his own hearing but could hear nothing resembling hoofbeats and, not for the first time, he marveled at her keen hearing.

Cassie went to the window, apparently watching for them to arrive, and sounds of chatter finally reached William's ears. Soon enough, Selyf and the twins entered, talking excitedly. From what William could gather, their sister-in-law Eira was extremely close to delivering her first child and Caelwyn had left her messenger hawk with her so he could come get Caelwyn at the first sign of labor.

When they reached the kitchen and saw its occupants, they reined in their enthusiasm and plied William with questions about his meeting with the king. William had never really been around children much and felt a little uncomfortable, which was made more acute by his friends' obvious amusement as he struggled to keep up with the questions. He had just replied negatively to Aeddan's question about whether he'd seen Telyn and Ganieda in Camelot when Caelwyn entered the house, sparing him further queries. He noted she had a double-knife belt like Cassie's strapped around her waist.

"Would you be willing to practice a round of swordplay?" she asked. "I'd like to see how well you can use your weapons. It is a vital skill here."

"Maybe," William said. He felt himself perk up at the suggestion. He liked to practice his swordplay, and it was just what he needed at the moment. It would help clear his head. It was something familiar.

He relayed her words to the others, and saw Cassie's eyes light up. "That sounds great. I need to clear my head," she said, echoing his own thoughts. David nodded.

"I think I'd rather just watch at the moment," Sarah said. "I don't feel like waving a sharp and deadly piece of metal around right now."

"Understandable," William said.

He gave their answer to Caelwyn. She looked at Sarah. "Can she use a bow?" she asked.

William nodded, surprised. "How did you know that?"

She smiled slightly. "A guess. Selyf, go collect your weapons and meet me behind the house in the clearing," Caelwyn continued, looking at her son. "Would you also go get Telyn's bow, please?"

"Yes, Mother. Can you practice with me when you're done with them?" He looked at her hopefully.

"Us, too, Mother," Aeddan and Addiena said in chorus.

"Of course." Selyf immediately departed to do his mother's bidding and Caelwyn left as well, presumably to make some preparations. The teens grabbed their weapons from where they'd put them, and the Brenwyd twins led them to the clearing. It was clearly used for weapons practice, with archery targets at either end and a big area in the middle for sparring. Caelwyn was waiting for them at the edge of the clearing and they went to her. Selyf appeared several minutes later with an unstrung bow and quiver. The bow was almost as big as he was. Sarah looked at it and her expression brightened a little. Kai and Dassah had followed them out and they sat with Dragon, looking interested. Caelwyn eyed their weapons. Her gaze lingered on Cassie's knife belt, so much like her own. "How much do all of you know of swordplay?" she asked William. "You must know the basics, at least. You would not be carrying weapons around otherwise."

William thought for a few minutes. "We didn't actually meet each other until a couple of weeks ago, so we've had different training. It's actually pretty unusual in our time to know how to use these kinds of weapons at all. Cassie, David, and Sarah were taught by Cassie's father, and he did a good job, though I don't know how he learned swordplay. They can fight and defend themselves well."

"And you?" Caelwyn asked.

"I was..." He paused, thinking about the best way to word his response. He didn't want to tell her about his recent affiliations, not yet, anyway. He'd just met her and it was an uncomfortable subject to talk about, even with his friends. "My father, rather, was part of an organization that taught swordplay and other weapons to its members. The knowledge had been passed down for centuries. I've been training since I was ten."

"I see. Then you are the most experienced?"

"Yes, I think so."

Caelwyn nodded. "You should all know what you're doing then. Would you like to go first?" she asked.

"Uh, sure." He glanced at his friends. "You guys mind?"

"Not at all," David said. "That gives us a chance to think up some method of defense."

"Thanks, I think."

"You're welcome."

Caelwyn beckoned to William and he followed her. She drew her sword. William copied her motion. "You're not going to use your knives?" he asked, curious.

"Normally I would, but when I test people, I use whatever is their preferred weapon," she explained. William nodded.

They stood, facing each other. No one spoke. The combatants eyed each other warily, waiting for each other to make the first strike. William felt cold, calculated excitement start to rise in him, making his heart pound and blood surge, the way he always felt when about to start a fight. Something about swordplay excited him, woke something in him, made him feel happy and content. He had a natural talent for it, and several of the older, more experienced men of the Brotherhood, including his father and the Master himself, had commented on it. It was this natural talent that gave him an edge over many of his opponents, who had little or no natural talent and had to work extremely hard to improve. Not to say that William had ever slacked, but he'd improved at a much faster pace than other initiates his age. He balanced lightly on his feet, waiting for the first strike. He knew that this opponent could not only match him but in all likelihood could beat him quickly if she wished. In addition to the supernatural speed and agility he'd encountered with Cassie that all Brenwyds possessed, Caelwyn had been training much longer than he had, and she lived in an era where fighting and defending yourself was important for survival. He wondered if she'd fought in any of Arthur's battles against the Saxons.

He watched her eyes, knowing that was generally the first indication of any attack, yet also remained aware of what the rest of her body might be doing. Her eyes flicked ever so slightly to his left, her sword arm muscles tightened almost imperceptibly, and she lunged, quick as a cat, striking at his left side. His sword was already rising in response even as she started her lunge, and the clash of metal rang out in the otherwise silent clearing like the toll of a bell. The fight progressed, each opponent seeking for the other's open spots, no matter how slight.

William realized that Caelwyn was slowly increasing the level of difficulty she used against him, and increasing her speed as well, trying to figure out how far she could push him before he couldn't defend himself anymore. At first he could hold her off pretty easily, getting in offensive strikes of his own, twice almost succeeding in disarming her. But as the minutes wore on and sweat started to trickle down his back and into his eyes, she pushed him more and more into a defensive position, coming in faster, harder. He was amazed by her speed, agility, and dexterity with her weapon. Never had he fought someone like her before. Cassie was close, but she lacked the experience and finesse Caelwyn possessed. Even his father would have had trouble defeating Caelwyn – if he could at all.

After what seemed to William almost an eternity, the fight ended when he raised his sword to block a cut at his neck. He realized too late that it was a feint, when Caelwyn abruptly changed her angle and brought her sword down hard on his blade near the hilt and twisted it out of his grip, weakened by the shock of the blow. He was completely astonished by her strength. That she'd been able to change direction so quickly on a committed blow required a tremendous amount of strength, and the fact that she could still slam into his blade with such force after such a move was more amazing still. Well could he understand the Brotherhood's fear of Brenwyds.

She lowered her sword, looking pleased. "Very good. You have been trained very well."

"Thank you," he said, bending down to pick up his sword. They walked over to the others. They all looked impressed, including Caelwyn's children.

"That was awesome," David said. "Do we really have to go after that?"

"She did beat me," William pointed out.

"So? You held her off for, like, fifteen minutes. Probably better than I can do."

"You counted?"

"He's approximating," Sarah explained. "I can't believe neither of you wounded the other."

Cassie agreed with her. "Especially since some of those moves looked really complicated. Certainly not the hacking and blocking and hoping-I-can-get-a-lucky-strike-in thing I do."

"You do more than that," William said. "You're good. You shouldn't sell yourself short."

"Have you determined who's going next?" Caelwyn asked. William translated.

"I guess I'll go," David said. "Get it over with." He and Caelwyn walked to the middle of the practice area. The fight started, and David did a pretty good job of defending himself. He just couldn't match her speed, and the fight was over in about ten minutes.

Sarah went next and Caelwyn tested her with the bow. Sarah was a good shot, but wasn't used to the long bow and so had to adjust. Caelwyn made suggestions via William, and Sarah's aim improved until Caelwyn was satisfied. Caelwyn told her she'd test her with the sword another day when she felt more up to it.

Finally, Cassie stood facing the Brenwyd woman. Cassie had watched Caelwyn very carefully when she'd fought the boys, and had gathered a good idea of her fighting style. Caelwyn gestured for Cassie to draw her knives. She hesitated a moment, then did so, watching Caelwyn's face intently the whole time. When Caelwyn finished drawing her own knives, she glanced at the ones Cassie held, and her gaze froze on the knife in Cassie's right hand. William wondered why. Cassie's knives were actually designed in the Celtic style, and thus shouldn't draw any attention.

Beside him, he heard Caelwyn's children take in sudden breaths. "Do you see what I see?" Selyf asked.

"I think so. But how does she have it? Mother has it, look," Addiena said. She turned to William. "Why does your friend have Seren?"

William realized abruptly what was causing all the commotion. Cassie had a replica of the knife that was called Seren, but Caelwyn had the real thing. *Why did we not think of that?* he wondered. "It's not Seren, it just looks like it," he told her. She narrowed her eyes, but a flicker of movement and flash of metal attracted their attention to the practice field, where the fight had begun.

William hadn't seen the first strike, but Cassie's skill was readily apparent as she fended Caelwyn off with seeming ease. She wielded her knives with a precise and easy grace, matching the older woman blow for blow, and Caelwyn fought the same way. The fight continued, slowly escalating as the minutes ticked on. Five minutes... seven... ten. William wondered how long they could keep this up. He knew Cassie was skilled, as he had found it unexpectedly challenging to find an opening and disarm her during a practice fight back in Virginia. But he had merely been trying to beat her, not assess her skill level. Caelwyn had more technical skill, but Cassie's strength lay in being able to meet her speed, something the others had a hard time doing.

William thought the sight looked a little unearthly, and could understand all the legends that had popped up about the "Faery Folk." Watching them, the art of combat seemed to be a dance, smooth and graceful with exact, seemingly effortless movements that flowed like a stream. This, taken into account with the beauty of their features, created a majestic and pretty terrifying sight. William was glad they were on his side. Or, more accurately, he was on theirs.

Just as his watch said twelve minutes had passed, Caelwyn sneaked in several hard strikes through a small opening and disarmed Cassie. They stood, looking at each other, breathing hard. Everything was still. Sunlight streamed down from the sky and reflected off Caelwyn's dagger, the rainclouds from earlier having completely dissipated. William could've sworn the dagger caught fire, with white flames that extended around Cassie and an instant later were gone, leaving him unsure as to whether he'd seen it or not. Yet he noticed small flames remaining around the blade, and realized that they had actually been there throughout the fight. He stared, making sure his eyes weren't tricking him, and wondered how it was possible that a knife could emit flames.

Cassie's eyes were wide and wary, and even Caelwyn looked a little surprised. William heard the kids whispering, "Did you see that? Why her? Who exactly are these people?" Caelwyn sheathed her knives, and Cassie bent down and did the same. Before she sheathed her Seren replica, Caelwyn put a hand on her wrist and spoke something to her quietly. William guessed she used Latin because Cassie understood and answered her.

Sarah shook her head slowly in amazement. "Wow. I have never seen her fight quite like that before. That was so effortless, it was scary. Where did she learn all those moves?" she asked, sounding a little in awe.

"You mean, her dad didn't teach her to fight like that?" William asked.

"Not while I was around."

"She learned by watching," David said. "She does that. She'll watch someone do something new, and five minutes later does it so well you assume she's been doing it all her life. Didn't you

The dagger caught fire, with white
flames that extended around Cassie
and an instant later were gone.

notice how closely she watched me and William? She was gathering information."

"Her speed and agility also helped," William said. "How did her dad learn to fight, do you know?"

"Nope. He just said he picked it up from studying medieval fighting techniques for so long. His specialty *is* medieval history," David said.

William thought there was probably more to it than that, but seeing as Cassie's dad was currently a prisoner of the Brotherhood 1500 years in the future it wasn't like he could go ask him at the moment. Maybe Cassie would know more. She and Caelwyn walked over.

"The ones who taught you did well," Caelwyn said. "Very well. But I can teach you more... and I think it is vital that you improve."

"Why?" William looked her right in the eye, sensing a chance to get a question answered that he'd been wondering about since Camelot, something Cassie had mentioned in the garden. "There's something else going on, something you know but we don't. The reason you took us to Camelot. What is it?"

She gazed at him calmly. "You're right. It's something Merlin said before he disappeared, something I now think I'm starting to understand, which I believe applies to you four. But I don't think–"

"That you can tell us just yet," he finished for her. She nodded.

"William, what is it?" Sarah asked. William told them.

"Oh, please, not another prophecy," Cassie groaned. Dassah put her head under Cassie's hand, either giving moral support or asking for a scratch. Probably both.

"But she said Merlin said it before he disappeared... that legend about what's-her-name sealing him in a rock, maybe?" Sarah mused. "How long ago did he disappear?" William put the question to Caelwyn. At her reply, he raised his eyebrows.

"What now?" Cassie asked.

"She says that Ganieda is Merlin's daughter," he answered.

"Merlin's daughter? Since when did he have a daughter?" David asked. "I've never heard any legend about that."

"Ganieda," Cassie murmured, thinking. "I think... I've read that Merlin had a sister named Ganieda. It's possible that people remembered the name and that it was connected with Merlin, but not how exactly. That's interesting. How long ago did you say he disappeared?"

"I didn't. It was nine months ago."

"I guess that would fit with what the legends say," David said. "None mention Merlin being around at Camlann."

"And if Merlin issued some sort of prophecy, and Caelwyn thinks we're involved in it... that might be part of what we're supposed to do here," Cassie said thoughtfully. "It may even explain why we apparently will send Guinevere into the future. Especially if..."

"If what?" Sarah asked.

"She was – will be – pregnant, and if it coincides with Camlann..."

"Then the child might not even be Arthur's at all," William finished.

"Exactly. But even if it wasn't, I still don't see that as a good enough reason to hurl a sixth-century queen into twenty-first century England. There must be something else that drives us to it."

"But what could it be?" David wondered.

"Maybe it's got something to do with whatever Merlin said," William suggested. Cassie nodded absentmindedly but otherwise didn't reply. Her thoughts were clearly far away.

"Do you know of Merlin?" Caelwyn asked, curious about their prolonged discussion.

William looked at her. "Yes. The events and people of King Arthur's reign... it's a very well-known legend in our time. That's part of why we keep acting so shocked. In our time there's nothing to really confirm or deny the legend, and it's somewhat controversial."

Caelwyn's eyes widened, but Addiena burst in before her moth-er could say anything. "In your time? What do you mean? You've been saying that," she demanded.

"Ummm..." William glanced at Caelwyn. She nodded. "Well, you see, we're not really from a different country. We're from a different time period, far in the future. I was actually born and raised in Britain... about fifteen hundred years from now." The three stared at him incredulously.

Caelwyn stepped in. "Remember the stories about the *lapsus tempi?*" she asked her children. They nodded. "There's one at the Ynis Witrin church, and that's the one they came through."

"You... you are from the future?" Aeddan asked William.

"Yes," William answered.

Aeddan's face took on an air of puzzlement. "Then why do you look – hey!" This last ejaculation came as Addiena elbowed him.

William had a pretty good idea of what he'd been about to say: *Why do you look like King Arthur?* He had no idea. Cassie seemed to have one, but hadn't shared it yet. He thought of Cael-wyn's prophecy in her diary and recalled the last line: *the heir of Arthur.* Maybe that was it. He might be descended from Arthur. He was British born and bred, and Arthur did have two daugh-ters. Perhaps that's what Cassie had thought of. It actually made a lot of sense. If Cassie was the descendant of Caelwyn talked about in the prophecy, and given how he'd already helped her... yeah, that made perfect sense. If he hadn't gotten Cassie out, no way would she be able to throw down the Brotherhood, but he had, so maybe that was the extent of what the prophecy meant about him. Being a descendant of Arthur might also explain why he looked like the king and why he resembled Gwen slightly. His mind started to grow more settled as he accepted that theory. It fit with all the information he knew, and explained things pretty much perfectly.

He realized Selyf had just asked a question and was waiting for an answer. "I'm sorry, what was that?" he asked the redhead.

"I wanted to know if I was mentioned in any of the legends you talked about." He looked so hopeful William didn't want to answer, but he had to.

"No. They don't mention Brenwyds at all, just Ladies of the Lake and witches and such. That's as close as it gets."

"We're not witches! Witches are bad," Addiena declared, sounding offended.

William suppressed a smile. "Of course you're not," he said. "It's just what the legends say."

"Hmph. It figures that they would remember the rumors but not the truth," Addiena grumbled.

"Addiena!" Caelwyn said. "Not now."

Addiena huffed. "You would think people would remember correctly, especially since we're the king's cousins."

"You're related to the king?" William asked, surprised. He wondered about the girl's earlier comment as well, but decided not to ask because of Caelwyn's reaction.

"Yes, Arthur is my cousin," Caelwyn said. "He has no Brenwyd blood, and I'm only half. My mother, Anna, was Uther's sister. My father was a Brenwyd. Arthur and I actually grew up around the same area, and I saw him fairly often. I didn't know he was my cousin until my mother told me, not long before Arthur put forth his claim to the kingship."

William blinked. He was starting to think he should write an accurate book about King Arthur when he got back to the present.

"What are they saying, William?" Cassie asked.

"They're related to the king."

"What?"

"Yeah, apparently her mum was Uther's sister."

She frowned thoughtfully. "Imagine that."

"Are you going back to your time soon?" Aeddan asked.

William returned his attention to them. "I don't know." He looked at Caelwyn. "Do you have an idea of when we'll be able to go back?"

"Not anytime soon. I asked our bard while I was in the village what he knew about time slips, and he said that according to myth they can only be accessed when there is an opening, which occurs when particular melodies within the slip reach their absolute crescendo. If a person uses an opening, they have to wait for the particular opening they went through to mend and crescendo again before they can go back through. Otherwise, there's no telling when you'll end up. Apparently, they can only be traveled with a Brenwyd nearby, because we're the only ones who can hear the melodies."

"What does it mean for an opening to 'mend'?" William queried.

"From what I understand, time slips work by certain melodies growing until they're ready to be traveled through. If they're not used, the melody dies down until the next time it swells, but if it is used, it makes something like a tear in the music and that must mend and swell again before it can be used to get back to that particular time." William tried wrapping his brain around that. "I realize it's a rather abstract concept," Caelwyn went on, "but we don't really know much about them. They appear only in our oldest legends, the ones referring to our origin, and are rarely mentioned or discussed."

Cassie tapped him on the shoulder. "Now what'd she say?"

"I'm trying to figure it all out. Maybe you'll understand it better." He repeated Caelwyn's words for her as best he could.

Comprehension dawned on Cassie's face. "Of course! That's what I sensed. Remember when I mentioned how some places going up and down on the time slip seemed to have broken melodies, and others seemed very full, and one seemed like it would burst, it was so full and rich?" she asked. "I made a comparison with a bunch of thread."

"Yeah, I remember that," David said. "So that really full one must have been the one we went through. But how did Gwen know it was ready?"

"She didn't. That's why she asked me. I remember after we got here, the melody that seemed so full before had quieted to almost nothing and seemed really broken. If we have to wait for that to become full again... we might be here awhile."

"But how much time is passing at home?" Sarah asked. "Is there any way we can know that? If we're here too long, and the times are synchronized..." Her voice trailed off. William quickly asked Caelwyn if she knew.

"You'll come out close to the time you left, maybe give or take a few days. That was what the bard implied, and I believe it would make sense if it's the same melody." The others let out huge sighs of relief when William translated that.

"How long do you think it'll take for the... melody to mend?" William asked Caelwyn.

"I do not know, but you won't leave before –" They were interrupted by the clatter of hoofbeats as Ganieda appeared in the yard, apparently having used the transfer ability.

She looked around, seeming very excited, then spotted Caelwyn and called to her. "Caelwyn! Telyn and I went by Eira's on our way back and as we were leaving her labor pains started. She needs you."

"Has her water broken?" Caelwyn asked, hurrying over. The others followed.

Ganieda shook her head, her eyes bright with excitement and anticipation. "Not when I left. Telyn's with her, and I passed Bleddyn on my way out of the village. I told him and he took off at a run."

"I'll gather my medical supplies, and Wynne and I will go." Caelwyn said.

"Can we come, Mother?" Aeddan asked.

"You can walk to the village. I don't want you tiring the horses too much." Caelwyn moved like a blur and was soon gone.

Ganieda was walking her horse, who was huffing and puffing a bit. "You three wait until I get my horse cooled off and in the stable, and then we'll depart," she told Selyf and the twins. They nodded. Ganieda turned her gaze to William. "It would be best for you to stay here. I mean no offense."

William nodded. "None taken. That's alright. We should rest, anyway."

"You can do so in our rooms. They are up the stairs. Boys sleep in the first room from the stairs, and girls the second."

William nodded. "Alright. Thank you."

"You are welcome." She turned her attention to the younger three. "We should go now. Births can go quickly. Come, children." They exited the yard.

William, Cassie, David, and Sarah all looked at each other. "This has certainly been an interesting day," Sarah said. "What did she say, William?"

"She was just saying where the bedrooms are. They're upstairs, guys in the first room and girls in the second."

"Sleep is sounding like a good idea," Cassie said, stifling a yawn. "We've been up for what, over a day or something?"

"Something like that," David agreed. Cassie turned toward the house with the dogs, and the others followed.

William paused in the doorway before going into the house and looked up at the sky. "Cassie says You have a reason for us to be here," he said to God. "Please help us understand what it is soon. We really need some guidance."

"We'll get it," Sarah said from behind him. He started and turned. He hadn't realized she was there. She smiled at him. "Have you read Jeremiah 29:11?"

"No."

"It says, 'For I know the plans I have for you, declares the Lord. Plans to prosper you and not to harm you. Plans to give you hope and a future.'"

"I like the future part of that verse."

"Me too. We just need to trust. Trusting can be hard, but it's always rewarding." She stepped closer and did something that completely surprised him. She wrapped her arms around him in a hug. "You're not alone anymore, William. You have people who care for you. We'll figure out everything; it just needs time."

"Umm, yeah. I know." He felt a little uncomfortable with her arms around him, but she didn't seem to feel that way.

She looked up at him. "You know, you could return my hug. It's generally the polite thing to do. And it's what friends do. Everyone needs a hug once in a while. They're very comforting. And you, my friend, have looked to be in serious need of one since we got here. This whole time-travel thing doesn't fit very well with your logical view of the world, does it?"

"Not at all," he agreed, tentatively putting his arms around her.

"I don't suppose there's a lot of hugging that goes on in the Brotherhood, is there?" She sounded slightly amused.

"No. Definitely not." She released him. He thought she looked a little flushed. He suspected he did, too. He'd never hugged anyone before, let alone a girl.

"Get used to it. We do it a lot where I come from." She rushed through the words a bit and turned quickly into the house. He looked after her for a minute, feeling confused but oddly pleased. He followed her and they walked to the back of the house, where they discovered Cassie and David discussing which parts of the Arthurian legend were and weren't true, and how best to ask Caelwyn about them.

A Plot & a Betrothal

Two months later...

Looking at the man sitting miserably across from him, Mordred could hardly believe his own good fortune. Outwardly, however, his expression was sympathetic and when he spoke, his voice was rich with compassion. "My dear fellow, it is not an enviable situation you are in."

The man groaned. "But God knows I can't help it. I've tried staying away from court, and have avoided seeing *her* when I am there, but if I don't see her it is equally torturous." His stance, normally proud and confident, drooped dejectedly and his features, which attracted ladies all over the kingdom, were mournful. He had just confided to Mordred the source of his trouble, and Mordred's mind was working furiously to figure out how best to use it to his advantage. It was just the opening he had been waiting for, what his mother had assured him would present itself.

"Does she return your affection?" he asked, pouring the man some wine.

"I don't know. At times I think she might, but then *he* comes and she shows far more to him, as is proper." His tone was dolorous.

"Could it be a mere sham, perhaps?"

"Unlikely. He is her husband of seventeen years and she has borne him two children."

"But no sons."

"No. Although..." The man's voice trailed off. Mordred looked at him keenly.

"Although?" he prompted.

The man hesitated a moment. "Caelwyn took in four wards a couple of months ago. The story is that they're from Armorica and are staying with her to receive advanced weapons training. Apparently their parents are closely acquainted with Caelwyn."

Mordred shrugged, disinterested. "What of it? I, too, have heard of them, though I've never seen them. She's been known to do such things before. Many parents send their sons to the Brenwyds for advanced training."

"Two are girls," the man said.

Mordred frowned. "Is that so? How odd. Still, it is common enough in Brenwyd culture, and the queen has encouraged other ladies to learn the arts of war." His tone indicated disapproval.

Something like amusement at Mordred's tone flared faintly in the other man's light blue eyes. "It was one of the boys I was thinking of," he said. "They say he bears an almost uncanny resemblance to Arthur."

Mordred's interest was piqued. "Oh?"

"So they say. I have never seen the boy, so I wouldn't know. Most people also accept that his family is Roman."

"But not you, I presume." The other man made no reply. "Are you suggesting Arthur sired a son on another woman? How old is he?"

"Fifteen, I think, but Arthur would never do anything like that. It goes against the faith, and he loves... Guinevere." The last word was forced out almost torturously. "Besides, he has not made any action to recognize the boy, and now would be the time to do it, before Gwendolyn is married. Still, to have attracted so much attention... there must be something."

"True, true," Mordred agreed, putting the comment away in his mind to think about later. "Have you any idea whom Arthur has chosen for Gwendolyn?"

"Cador's eldest, I believe. Arthur will make the official announcement in three weeks' time, on her sixteenth birthday. You got the feast notice, of course?"

"Yes. Are you going?"

"I must."

"And you must also see the queen."

"Yes."

"And you came to me. Why?" Mordred wondered aloud. "There has never been great love between us."

The man was silent for a few moments. "I think you are the best able to help me," he said at last.

Mordred arched an eyebrow. "In what way?"

"You must know the rumors about you..." the man said, hesitant. "That you can help a man achieve his heart's wish, whatever it may be."

"Ah, yes, rumors. Helpful things, aren't they?"

"Are they true?"

"Anything can be true, can't it?" Mordred paused. "I will help you, Lancelot, but it will come at a price."

"I expected as much. What is the price?"

"Tell me what you want first."

"I already told you. I want her!" He slammed his fist on the table. "Even if it is only once."

"Then you are not talking of marriage."

"It is not possible."

"Is it not?" Mordred asked softly. He walked around the edge of the table to stand behind the knight. His voice became softer still, reminiscent of a serpent's hiss. "Is it not, indeed? What if Arthur died? Of an illness? Or on a hunt? Then she would be a widow. You could have her then. Quite easily."

Lancelot recoiled. "You wouldn't... he's your liege lord, too! That's treason." He sounded shaken.

"So is what you want." Mordred moved from behind the champion. "But I won't use such drastic measures, so do not fret. I was simply suggesting possibilities." He made sure to modulate his tone to be reassuring. The voice was a potent weapon, but one had to use it properly for it to be truly effective.

"No, I don't want that. If... if you could just make her receptive to me, for a night, an hour, that would be enough."

Mordred shrugged carelessly. "If that is all you want, I will do it. But you must follow my instructions to the letter and obey me implicitly in the aftermath. If you do not, there will be... unpleasant consequences."

Lancelot thought about it. "Is that all?" Mordred nodded. "Then I accept."

Mordred smiled. "Good." He started walking about the room, and hummed for several minutes, ostensibly thinking. The tune sounded meaningless, but he could sense his control over the knight strengthen. "Our opening is obvious – the feast celebrating his daughter's birthday and betrothal. He will be busy, and much drink will be circulating. I will give you a potion to put in the queen's cup that will make her sleepy and wish to retire early, but not enough to make her fall asleep. After she leaves, you follow her. She will not be able to resist you, and may even think you to be Arthur. I will stand guard and be sure to warn you in plenty of time if anyone comes. You leave, and no one is the wiser."

"Are you sure Arthur would have no knowledge of it? I wouldn't want to hurt him..."

"No, no, you may rest assured on that account. You may even do him a favor by... attending his wife."

"And, pray tell me, what would that be?"

"You might be able to give him an heir. No, hear me out," he said as Lancelot started to protest. "Arthur would think the child his, and it would boost the sub-kings' confidence in him. It would reassure the people as well. It always comforts them to have the line of succession all neat, from father to son." His voice was calm, sensible, almost melodic. He could see the knight falling prey. The wine was likely helping as well. "You would have served the kingdom in the best way possible, though few would know it. If you are to have her, you must consider the possibility of a child. The queen's not past it yet. Do you still want to go through?" A silence. Mordred could tell the man was wrestling with his sense of honor and conscience. Dratted things never let a man get anything done. Better to look past present complications to the end result. He resumed humming, a barely perceptible sound.

"I do," Lancelot said at last. Mordred clapped him on the shoulder.

"Excellent! I will meet you at the stables with the potion that night. It shouldn't be hard for you to get it to the queen. And then," he paused, "what will be, will be." Lancelot left soon after, and Mordred watched him ride out of the castle gates, a smile on his face and triumph in his mind. *At last*, he thought, *after twenty-one years since Arthur's coronation, the wait is over. This time we will not fail, and the throne will be ours.* His thoughts turned toward a cell in the castle, where a very important prisoner was being kept. "You tried your best, prophet," he murmured. "But you have failed. Arthur will fall, and the Brenwyds with him."

<hr />

Cassie jumped back, the blade of her opponent narrowly missing her chest. She had been bloodied in these matches before, nothing serious, but she much preferred to avoid injury. She blocked an overhead blow, and used her free arm to make a pass at her opponent's knuckles, hoping to hit them hard enough to loosen the girl's grip on her sword and enable Cassie to disarm her. Unfortunately, her opponent was wise to the trick and moved her hand in time to avoid the blow. Cassie gritted her teeth. This was getting tedious. By her judgment they'd been at it for about fifteen minutes, and neither showed signs of weakening. *Think, girl,* she told herself. *What else can you do?* As she deflected a blow on the left, the answer came to her. She waited for another overhand blow, and it came soon enough.

This time, instead of moving out of the way or blocking with one knife and striking with the other, she made an X with her knives and caught the blade in midair. She immediately used her leverage to force the blade to turn, sliding her X down its length as she did so. Her opponent tried to counter, but Cassie clearly had the advantage. A triumphant smile started to appear on her face. The sword fell to the ground and Cassie pressed a knife point gently at the base of the other girl's throat, signaling the end of the match. "Gotcha," she said in Brythonic, grinning.

She lowered her knife, and her opponent picked up her sword, also smiling. "I will beat you next time," she warned, her blue-green eyes sparkling.

Cassie chuckled. "We'll see."

"Very good!" a voice rang out from the side. Caelwyn had been watching the match and was pleased by the results. "Both of you did well. But Telyn," she warned, "you must watch for tricks like that. In a real fight your opponent won't be nearly as considerate as Cassie."

"I know, Mother." Telyn took the criticism good-naturedly. She knew it would only make her better, and she knew that she and Cassie were on an equal level of swordsmanship. In the two months she had been with them, this Brenwyd girl from the future had improved rapidly beyond what she already knew. The others had improved much as well, but Cassie's Brenwyd blood gave her an extra boost.

"That is all the lesson we shall have today," Caelwyn said as the girls came to the side of the field. "I must ride to Camelot. Arthur is holding a meeting with his counselors at ten hour." Cassie glanced up at the sun as she patted Kai on the head. He and Dassah always made a point to watch her training sessions. So far he hadn't said anything, but Cassie knew as soon as Caelwyn left, the dog would give his opinion. If Caelwyn was to get to Camelot in time, she had to hurry.

"What do you think it's about?" Telyn asked.

"Officially, I don't know a thing, but unofficially..." Caelwyn smiled. "I think there will be a wedding soon."

"Gwendolyn?"

Caelwyn nodded and Telyn grinned. "If that's so, I might know before you. Gwendolyn and Jenifer are coming here today."

"Ah, yes, I had forgotten. In that case, we shall compare notes when I return."

"Where'd William go?" Cassie asked. He'd been there practicing with them earlier, but had left to do something. Ganieda, Sarah, and David had gone to the Brenwyd village nearby to get supplies and check in on Eira and the baby, and Selyf and the twins were at the Ynis Witrin church for their lessons with Joseph.

"He offered to collect Selyf and the twins from Ynis Witrin," Caelwyn said. "I don't feel comfortable with them riding around the countryside by themselves, and I don't have time to get them myself. Now if you girls will excuse me, I must go see the king." She departed. Cassie picked up a bow and some arrows from the ground, intending to get some shooting practice in. Kai and Dassah started giving her their usual rundown of the session. She actually found it quite helpful, because they'd "replay" certain parts for her through their memory.

Telyn watched her for several minutes. "Are you happy here, Cassie?"

"Why do you ask?" Cassie inquired, nocking another arrow.

"Curiosity. You have all adapted very well to a society, time, and language not your own, but you must be homesick. Especially since we do not know when you'll be able to go back."

Cassie shot. "I'm not *unhappy*, if that's what you want to know. I miss my parents, and my friends. I just hope your mother's right that we'll come out about the same time we left."

Telyn examined her carefully. "What is happening at your home that makes you so anxious?" she asked. "It is something big, and important, and causes you grief. I've sensed it."

Cassie hesitated. "It's kinda complicated," she replied. She shot again. Though they had been with Caelwyn's family for two months, neither she nor the others had told them the exact circumstances that had led to their trip through the time slip. Part of it was that they had still been getting over it, and part of it was that they weren't sure just how much they could spill about the future without messing up the whole time-space continuum, or if that was even an issue.

"Whatever it is, it has to do with your parents. Whenever you think of them, I sense an overwhelming sadness and worry, beyond what I would expect. You left them in some situation, likely dangerous, that you were trying to get them out of, did you not?"

Cassie shot her a look. "Mind-reading again?" she asked dryly.

"Emotion-reading. You know I don't read minds without permission or cause."

Cassie nodded. Telyn was ever mindful of others' privacy with her mind-reading talent. "Well, you're almost spot on, as usual, but it's not all my story to tell, and I don't think I should say much about it at the moment. When are Gwendolyn and Jenifer coming?" she asked, changing the subject.

"Fairly soon, I expect," Telyn said, accepting that her friend wasn't ready to share the story yet.

Cassie drew the bowstring. "It's just so strange to think that Gwendolyn might be getting married. She's our age!"

Telyn laughed as Cassie released. Of all the things they'd had to adjust to, Cassie and the others seemed to have the hardest time with the difference in the marriage age. It was made more acute by the busybodies in the village who hinted broadly at that particular topic when they went there. "Yes, but it's completely natural to us. And she is turning sixteen soon," Telyn said, eyes twinkling.

Cassie laughed. "As if that makes a huge difference. She took Telyn's hand and squeezed it reassuringly, sensing her friend was still worried about her. "Don't worry about me, or the others for that matter, Telyn. We're fine."

Telyn nodded, but with a sad sort of smile on her face. "I know, but forgive me for not wanting you to return just yet. Once you do, we'll never see each other again." Cassie had no reply to this. Both knew it was true.

Do not focus on it, Kai said. *Too much is happening in the present to worry about the future.*

"Yes, but there's a fair amount happening in the future, too, if you'll recall," Cassie said.

Of course. But worrying about it will not do anything except make you worried.

"You know," Telyn said, "you must tell us the full story before you leave. I insist on it."

"As you wish." Cassie saw Telyn's gaze become distant suddenly, and guessed they'd have company soon. "Who is it and how many?"

"The others are almost back from the village, and they've met up with Gwendolyn and Jenifer. They'll be here soon."

"How many guards?"

"Three. Only very foolhardy bandits prowl the road this close to Camelot and, of those, only the most idiotic would attack during the day, particularly this close to a Brenwyd settlement. We... unsettle them. Especially with the rumors..." Cassie nodded her understanding. The girls hurried to the house to disarm themselves, and were standing in the door as the party rode into the yard. The air came alive with chatter and movement, with greetings being exchanged and horses being dismounted and led into the stable. The guards stayed at a respectful distance, close enough to keep watch but far enough away to give privacy.

Because Gwendolyn and Jenifer visited often, Cassie and her friends had gotten to know the princesses fairly well, though the two had no idea the four were from the future. As far as they were concerned, the visitors had traveled to Britain from Armorica at the behest of their parents to receive advanced weapons training, which wasn't too unusual in this time period. The Brenwyds were revered weapons masters, and humans often came to learn from them.

Jenifer was ten, and very cheerful and inquisitive. She suspected that there was more to the teens than they revealed, and always tried to ferret information out of them. So far she wasn't having as much luck as she'd like, but Cassie thought she might just figure it out if she kept at it. Gwendolyn was the elder, and far quieter than her sister. She accepted things without much question, but Cassie suspected she knew far more than she let on. Gwendolyn looked a good deal like her mother; the biggest difference between them was eye color, for Gwendolyn had green eyes like her father's. Her hair was the same chestnut shade as Guinevere's and her face had similar features, but they were softer and more classically beautiful.

"Where's William?" Jenifer asked. She'd taken a real liking to William in particular out of the four. Cassie thought maybe it was because he held the most in, rebuffing or rerouting many of her questions, and so she was absolutely determined to figure him out. William had been a little wary of her at first, not being comfortable around young children, but had become fond of her over time. It was hard not to. Cassie actually suspected that he now redirected Jenifer's questions as a form of teasing.

"William went to collect Selyf and the twins from Ynis Witrin," Telyn answered. "I don't know when they'll be back."

"Oh." Jenifer looked a little disappointed. She was used to going off and playing with the twins and Selyf while the others chatted.

Sarah smiled at her. "I'm sure they'll be back soon," she assured the girl in halting Brythonic. While she and David now knew enough of the language to get by, they were not quite fluent. Cassie, on the other hand, had picked it up without much trouble. "Generally those three are ready to leave by the time someone gets them," Sarah added.

Gwendolyn laughed gently. "I would imagine. Father Joseph and Father Thomas are nice, but I was always glad to get home." Cassie had been surprised to learn that Arthur was having his daughters educated, something not many women, or men for that matter, could claim in this time period, even if they had high rank. They went around back to the clearing.

"How did practice go?" David asked.

"It went well," Cassie said. "We were at it for a good while."

"Cassie won," Telyn added. "But I shall beat her next time."

"You will, will you?" Cassie asked playfully. "That's what you said last time."

"Where is Caelwyn now?" Ganieda asked.

"She went up to Camelot," Telyn answered. She threw Gwendolyn a mischievous look. "Perhaps you could shed some light on the reason?"

Gwendolyn smiled. "Perhaps I could." They waited. She stayed silent, looking up at the sky. After a pause she realized, or pretended to realize, that everyone was looking at her. "What?"

"Oh, go on, tell them," Jenifer urged, bouncing a little in excitement.

"Very well." Her eyes reflected excitement and happiness. "I'm going to be married!"

"We knew that," Ganieda said. "We want to know *who* you're marrying."

"I'm happy with it. Father let me choose from those whom he

thought best. The boy is very nice and respects my opinions. I've known him for some time." She paused.

"Come on, out with it," Telyn said impatiently. "The whole kingdom's been buzzing with speculation for months, and I will read the answer from your mind if you don't say who it is in the next two minutes." No one mentioned the main reason why – at this point, whoever married Gwendolyn would inherit the throne with her when Arthur died. And only Cassie, David, Sarah, and William had any inkling of how close that might be, after learning that Arthur had been crowned king only after the victory at Badon. They also had a good idea of who Gwendolyn's betrothed was.

"Constantine, Cador's eldest son," Gwendolyn said after a long pause, her eyes shining. Cassie, David, and Sarah shot each other knowing looks. They'd been right. Telyn and Ganieda caught the looks and surmised the meaning.

"That's great, Gwendolyn," Sarah said. "Do you know when the wedding will take place?" Gwendolyn nodded.

"Next spring. Father will make the official announcement on my birthday in two weeks."

"There's going to be a big feast that lots of people are being invited to," Jenifer broke in. "Your family is invited. Will you come?" She looked very hopeful.

"Of course we'll come," Telyn said. "I doubt we could miss it even if we wanted to, and you know we always go up to the city for your birthdays."

Gwendolyn glanced at the other three, sensing their unspoken question, and knowing they were too polite to voice it. "The invitation includes you four as well," she said. "In fact, I would very much enjoy it if you came."

"Thank you," Cassie said. She wouldn't have minded going at all, but she wasn't sure William would be so keen. He'd mentioned to her the idea of his possibly being an heir of Arthur, before she brought it up, and that had been the general consensus from the group. It explained everything, and Cassie thought it ironic that one of the people who was supposed to destroy the Brotherhood had been raised by it. However, while that conclusion settled their minds, it did nothing for the rest of the populace. Caelwyn had spread the word that her charges, except for Cassie, came from families with Roman blood, which conveniently explained William's dark hair and Roman features. Still, Cassie knew William felt uncomfortable about the attention he attracted because of the resemblance, and he stayed away from Camelot unless a trip was necessary.

"Please say you'll come," Jenifer pleaded, giving them pleading puppy dog eyes, a tactic apparently used by children in any century. "You'll like it. There's food, and people, and stories, and it's fun." Cassie and the Thompson twins met each others' eyes. They knew each other so well that they could tell what the others were thinking. They didn't feel comfortable giving a final answer without William.

David looked at Jenifer with a smile. "We'll do our best." He changed the subject. "Is there anything else important going on in Camelot?" The discussion turned to other things, and the princesses went back to Camelot still not entirely sure if the four would accompany Caelwyn and her family or not.

⁂

Caelwyn looked at them across the table. "I do not see why you should not go. I believe you would enjoy it." They were eating dinner, and the question of whether or not to go to the celebration had been broached. The table in the dining area of the house's great room was low to the floor, so everyone sat on mats instead of in chairs.

"You would be alone here if you stayed," Siarl said.

"There are the animals," Cassie pointed out.

"You wouldn't raise too many questions," Siarl continued. "You know the language and customs well enough now, and it's become fairly common knowledge that you four are here. It might raise more questions if you do *not* go."

"And suspicion," Caelwyn said. "I've heard that some people actually doubt you are here, as you don't go to the city often."

"That's not necessarily a bad thing," Sarah said. "It's not like we need everyone to know."

"And do you not already know that your visit isn't remembered?" Selyf asked.

"Sort of," Cassie answered. "My father knows almost everything there is to know about this time period, and I've certainly never heard him mention coming across a document or story about four teenagers traveling back in time. I've never heard of any time travel tales at all originating from this period. Well, unless you count Mark Twain's *A Connecticut Yankee in King Arthur's Court*, but I wouldn't if I were you." At that comment, the others exchanged amused looks. Cassie was prone to making such references to future things, and Caelwyn's family had learned not to question her too closely about them, as doing so often left them even more confused.

"There's another thing, as well," William said, ignoring Cassie's final comment. "Since our future hasn't happened yet, it's still uncertain what will be remembered and what won't. If it's possible for us to do something here that changes what we know as our history, there's no telling what could happen."

"I don't see what that has to do with going to the feast or not," Ganieda said. "It's not like any earth-shattering events are likely to happen." She eyed them keenly. "Unless you know otherwise."

"If we did, I don't think we could say," David said. "But people in our time have almost no clue exactly what was happening in Europe in this time period. From the fall of Rome until a couple of centuries later, not much is known for certain."

"You've said that," Telyn said. "But you won't tell us much about what *is* known, either."

"You know why," Cassie said.

"Well, it is your decision," Caelwyn said. "But I think it would be better for you to go. Gwendolyn and Jenifer would appreciate it." William nodded acknowledgment.

"Father, have you had any luck in finding the missing Brenwyds?" Telyn asked, moving on to a different subject.

Siarl sighed. "No. I'm starting to grow more worried. The disappearances have been escalating over the past two months. I've even heard whispers that a group has been organized and is claiming responsibility," he said. Cassie tensed, and sensed William do the same beside her.

Caelwyn frowned. "I hadn't heard that."

"I heard it just today. And Bran told me that he's been trying to contact some of his family who live in the settlement not far from Caer Lial, but hasn't heard from them. He's traveling there at the end of the week to check on them," Siarl told his wife.

"Caer Lial?" Ganieda asked. Her face had paled. Siarl nodded.

Telyn put a hand on her friend's shoulder comfortingly. "I'm sure it's nothing serious," she said.

"What's wrong with Caer Lial?" Sarah asked.

"It was in that area my father disappeared," Ganieda replied.

Sarah's eyes widened. "Oh, I'm sorry. I didn't know."

Cassie was thinking: *Caer Lial... I know that name.* "Are there any big stone buildings around there?" she asked nonchalantly.

Caelwyn looked at her curiously. "There's Arthur's stronghold in the city. It's his northern headquarters. It used to be-"

"The Roman city of Luguvalium, I know. What about outside the city?"

"I do not know." Caelwyn gave her a penetrating look. "Why the interest?"

"Oh, I visited a large stone building outside it not long before we came here and wondered if something like it existed in this time."

"Caer Lial still exists in your time?" Aeddan asked.

"Yes, but we know it as Carlisle," Cassie said.

David straightened as she said that, realizing why the name was so familiar. "You're not saying–" He stopped abruptly.

"Not saying what?" Addiena asked.

"Yes, I think it might be the same building," Cassie said. She knew David was also thinking about it being the Brotherhood headquarters, but that was not a subject to get into right now.

"Do you think there really is such a group?" Selyf asked his father.

"I'm not sure. I've heard a name in connection with it that seems to fit, but I'm not entirely convinced," Siarl said.

"What's the name?" Telyn asked.

"It's a little odd, but the connotation is evil. I've heard it's called the Reficul Brotherhood." Cassie stared down at her plate. *It's starting,* she thought. She noticed William tense further, and glimpsed Sarah and David exchanging glances. Kai and Dassah bristled as well.

Cassie noticed Telyn looking at them curiously, picking up on their heightened emotions. But Cassie shook her head, indicating she shouldn't ask. Telyn nodded slightly. *Should we tell them?* Cassie asked Kai.

Not right this moment, he replied, *but definitely soon. They need to know.*

A question from Addiena pulled her focus back to the table. "Why is the conn-o-ta-tion evil?" she asked, pronouncing the big word carefully. Siarl hesitated. Cassie didn't blame him.

"If you spell it backwards," he said at length. "It spells out Lucifer, the ancient name of the devil."

❦

William felt someone shaking him. He opened his eyes blearily. "What?" he whispered.

"Come on. We need to talk," Cassie's voice whispered back in English. William sat up. He glanced around and saw Sarah shaking a lump he assumed was David. They crept out silently, careful not to wake the others. Cassie led them to the stable, which didn't surprise William. Over the past couple of months, the stable had become their de facto meeting place when they needed to discuss things in private. They entered, and Sarah carefully latched the door behind them.

The animals were startled by their entrance, but Cassie calmed them quickly. Their own animals weren't as surprised. *I thought you would have been out here an hour ago,* Kai said.

"We had to wait for everyone to be soundly asleep." Cassie said.

"When was this meeting planned and why was I left out of it?" David asked grumpily, looking sleepy.

Cassie shot him an apologetic smile. "Sorry. I couldn't sleep well, and we need to talk without being overheard." Her expression turned serious. "These reports of Brenwyds going missing... I don't like it."

"You heard Siarl. It's the Brotherhood, and we've heard it's been going on for a while," David said, sounding more awake. He turned to William. "This is when they started, isn't it?"

William nodded. "Yes." All sleepiness was gone. "Do we tell them?"

"Not yet," Cassie said. "But soon."

Wynne stretched her neck over the stable wall. *You know who is behind the disappearances?* she asked.

"Yes, but–" Cassie broke off. "How do you know English?"

Your horses. I had to learn to understand them as they had to learn to understand me. But how do you know who is behind it?

"We've met them. In our time."

Then you should tell Caelwyn. Her tone sounded reproachful.

"It's not that simple," William said. The horse looked at him. "We can't mess up history as we know it. We have to be careful."

"Still, she's got a point." Sarah said. "If we don't tell, they'll figure out we're hiding something."

"I don't plan on hiding it forever," Cassie said. "We will tell them, when the time's right. I just don't think it is now, not yet. But that's not the only reason I dragged you guys out here." She stopped.

"And the other is?" David prompted.

She hesitated, glancing at William quickly. He wondered at it. *Go on, girl,* Twi encouraged. *It is important.* William had a weird feeling the horse was looking at him, especially as she said this.

"I've been having more dreams of Gwen in the future," Cassie confessed. "Every time I see her, she's farther along in her pregnancy."

"When have you been having these dreams?" Sarah asked.

"Off and on ever since we got here. They haven't been long like the first couple, either. Just... images, a brief glimpse of her for maybe a minute doing different things, but she shows more and more every time I see her. Earlier tonight, I had the first really coherent dream since the one at Gwen's." She stopped, troubled. Twi nudged her back and Cassie rubbed the star on her forehead absently. The others waited. She would get to it. "It was a conversation between Gwen and Eleanor, the lady who took her in. Eleanor needed to go see a friend who was dying, and asked Gwen to go with her. She said she didn't have to, and I got the impression she was pretty close to the end of her pregnancy. Gwen said she'd be happy to go with her for company. She wanted to see more of twenty-first century England. I guess she had told the woman when she was from. It was their destination that caught my attention." She stopped. William wondered what was bothering her. "They were going to Carlisle." There was a pause.

"So?" Sarah asked, breaking the silence. "It may be Brotherhood headquarters, but that doesn't necessarily mean anything. Though it's kinda weird that you're dreaming of her pregnancy. Have any idea why?"

"I don't know. Maybe..." Again her gaze turned to William.

"What?" he demanded. "Why do you keep looking at me like that?" She was about to answer, but before she could, something weird happened. William suddenly felt a burning in his chest, and he found it hard to breathe. He staggered, and David, who was standing next to him, caught him before he fell.

"What the heck?" he heard David mutter, but he couldn't answer. He felt light-headed and nauseous. His vision seemed to dim for a moment, and he could hear nothing but the blood pounding in his ears. He thought he might pass out, but as abruptly as it started, everything passed. He straightened slowly, David still supporting him.

"Are you alright?" both girls demanded, worried. Phoenix nickered from across the aisle, sending an inquiring thought, also worried.

"I... I think so," William said.

"What on earth was that?" Cassie asked. She put a hand on his forehead, as if checking his temperature. "Sit down."

"I'm fi-"

"Sit." She forced him down onto a bench in the aisle. Sarah sat down beside him, hazel eyes wide, as David looked on. Cassie placed two fingers lightly on his wrist, checking his pulse.

"Is that really-" he tried again, but she shushed him. Her eyes seemed to go a little unfocused. *What is she doing?* he wondered.

She is checking your vitals and song, Phoenix offered. *That was not normal.*

William knew Cassie thought it was pretty serious if she was doing that. She released his wrist and her eyes refocused. "Your pulse is weak, but beating regularly and gaining strength. Your temperature seems fine." She stopped.

"And the song?" he asked.

"Completely fine, as far as I can tell. What happened?" Her voice was calm, not nearly so worried as a minute earlier, having reassured herself he was okay.

He shook his head in bewilderment. "I have no idea. I got this... burning sensation, here," he pointed, realizing the place was right over his heart, "and I had a hard time breathing. I also felt lightheaded and nauseous."

"I was sure you were going to pass out," Sarah said. "Your face went totally white."

"I felt like I might. But it didn't last long. I feel fine now."

"Have you had anything like this happen before?" Cassie asked. "No," he answered.

She studied him. "I think we should go back to bed."

"Translated, I should go back to bed," William said with a grin.

That roused a weak smile from Cassie. "Well, yes. But it's sometime near midnight, and I think we've talked all we need to for now."

"But Cassie, what were you going to say?" David asked. She looked at him inquiringly. "In answer to William's question. You were about to say something."

"Oh." William couldn't read Cassie's expression, but she seemed uneasy. "Nothing. Just a theory I've started noodling." She stopped.

"So what is it?" Sarah asked.

Cassie opened her mouth, closed it, glanced at William, then opened her mouth again to speak. "I'd rather keep that to myself for the moment. What just happened... I think it plays a part in it, but I need to figure out how." Her eyes pleaded with them not to push her.

David nodded slowly. "Okay, Cass. But you can tell us when you're ready, you know. We won't laugh. Probably."

Cassie snorted. "Thanks." They headed back to the house.

"Hey, guys?" William said before they entered the house. "Could we not mention the, um, seizure thing to anyone else? I'm sure it was nothing."

Cassie shrugged. "If you want, but if something like that happens again, I'm telling. You don't fool around with things like that."

"What do you think it was?" he asked.

She shook her head, looking troubled. "Hopefully, just what you say. Nothing. But if it happens again, well, I don't know." She vanished into the house, the others following, all of them shaken by the night's events.

11

A FEAST

Cassie found herself once again in the courtyard of Arthur's hall. This time, though, she knew what was happening and could understand the conversations around her. It was the day of the feast celebrating Gwendolyn's birthday and betrothal. The feast didn't actually start for a good while, but Caelwyn had told Guinevere she would come early to help out, and Gwendolyn had asked Telyn and Ganieda to come with her, and had also requested that Cassie and Sarah tag along. Telyn told Cassie they often came early to events and, she added with a grin, it let them ride into the city in breeches and change later without worrying about getting their dresses dirty.

"You're here!" a voice called, attracting Cassie's attention. She saw Jenifer with her mother behind her making their way through the hustle and bustle of activity in the yard as preparations were being made for the feast and guests were arriving. As the queen and her daughter passed, people stopped what they were doing and bowed or lowered their heads respectfully before resuming their tasks. Cassie dismounted and gave Twi's reins to the stable boy who'd been hovering at the horse's nose, waiting for her rider to dismount. It was the same boy who'd tended Twi the other few times Cassie had traveled to the court, and Twi had developed a liking for him. Apparently he was well-stocked in apples.

"Thank you, Gavin," she said, smiling at him.

"You're welcome, Cassie."

Jenifer broke into a run and greeted her cousins enthusiastically before addressing Cassie. Her green eyes were bright with excitement. "You came! Gwendolyn will be happy to see you. She's very nervous." Because of the noise in the courtyard, Jenifer had to raise her voice to be heard.

"Jenifer!" Guinevere said in a lower voice, sounding a little vexed. "Decorum, please. You may say what you wish in private, but please, remember our rank in public and act accordingly. The world does not need to know how Gwendolyn feels."

Jenifer blushed slightly, abashed. "Sorry, Mother. I'll remember."

Caelwyn laughed. "Give the girl a little slack, Guinevere. It's an exciting day."

"And an important one." Guinevere looked at her daughter with both long-suffering and a hint of amusement. Cassie felt for her. Jenifer might be a princess, but she was also ten years old – and energetic on any normal day. A special day apparently multiplied her energy by ten. "Why don't you take them to Gwendolyn?" the queen suggested.

"Yes, Mother. Come, follow me." Jenifer led them through the crowd into the castle. There was even more activity going on inside, and Cassie felt relieved when Jenifer led them beyond the commotion to the royal family's apartments. It was quiet there, with only a few people scurrying here and there. At one point Cassie paused, examining part of the wall closely. Ganieda noticed she was lagging and turned.

"What is it?" she asked. The others stopped. Cassie turned from the wall and hurried to catch up.

"Nothing. Let's go." As they continued, Sarah cast Cassie an inquiring glance and Cassie nodded slightly. She had detected very faint seams in the stone wall, confirming her suspicions that this was the hallway she and David would tread sometime in the not-too-distant future. She'd had a strange feeling about this feast since first hearing about it, the feeling that something big and not necessarily good was going to happen. She'd tried discounting it, but it kept growing. Today it felt like a pit of dread in her stomach, with drips of some unidentifiable, mucus-like liquid slowly falling into it and accumulating on the bottom. She tried to shake the feeling once again as they entered Gwendolyn's rooms, seeing that Jenifer had been correct and Gwendolyn really was nervous. She looked relieved to see them.

"I'm glad you're here," she said. "I feel all jittery."

"Everything will be fine," Telyn assured her, embracing the other girl. "It's a good day! It's not even overcast outside."

Gwendolyn smiled nervously. "I hope you're right. I just feel like something is bound to go horribly wrong."

"Nothing will go wrong," Jenifer said brightly. "What could? It's a feast, and Father's not allowing any weapons into the hall besides knives to eat with. Besides, it's not as if he's invited barbarians." The conversation turned to the guests – saying such and such a person was here, someone else wasn't. Cassie's interest was caught by the mention of Lancelot.

"Neither he nor Mordred are here yet," Gwendolyn was saying. "I don't miss Mordred, but we're used to having Lancelot here." Cassie and Sarah exchanged glances.

"They should be here in time," Jenifer said. "I heard that Lancelot is finishing his investigation in the north and he and Mordred are traveling down together."

"Are they?" Ganieda asked. "I thought they weren't fond of each other."

"That doesn't stop people from traveling together," Jenifer said with a shrug of her shoulders, though she also looked a little puzzled.

"What's Lancelot been doing in the north? He's been there a while, has he not?" Telyn asked.

"He's investigating the reports of Brenwyds disappearing,"

Gwendolyn explained. "They've been increasing lately. And he's trying to find out about the other rumors, you know... the ones about Brenwyds and witchcraft."

Telyn looked grim. "Yes, that's what Father said. He also said some group, the Reficul Brotherhood, is claiming responsibility for the missing Brenwyds."

"But why would anyone want to do that?" Jenifer wondered.

"People hunt what they fear," Cassie said, without thinking. "They're wary of Brenwyds because of their abilities. It doesn't take much to turn wariness into fear."

Jenifer's green eyes widened. "Hunt? You mean, kill?" Her voice went a little squeaky.

Everyone turned to Cassie. She sighed. She hadn't meant to say that. "Unfortunately, yes. In fact," she added, thinking fast, "that's part of why we came here. Persecution is stepping up in... our home, and our parents wanted us out of the way until it dies down."

"I haven't heard this," Gwendolyn said.

"It's not widely known."

"But Sarah - you, Dafyd and William aren't Brenwyd," Jenifer said.

"No, but we, um, lived pretty much right next to a Brenwyd settlement and our parents thought it was a good idea to get us out of the way as well," Sarah said. Telyn and Ganieda exchanged glances with Cassie and Sarah. *Not now*, Cassie thought to Telyn.

You will tell us when we get home, Telyn said mentally in a tone that brooked no argument.

As you wish, Cassie answered.

"Let's talk about something else," Ganieda said quickly. "This isn't anything to be dwelling on during such a joyous occasion." The talk turned to other things, but Cassie couldn't shake the feeling that a shadow was just at the door, about to walk in and ruin everything. She resolved to tell Caelwyn everything when they got home. The knowledge couldn't wait any longer.

David reined Fire in, avoiding a horse uncomfortably close to him. He was making his way through Camelot with William, Siarl, Selyf, Bleddyn, and the twins. Eira had stayed home with the baby. Bleddyn didn't want to leave her alone long, and would take the twins and Selyf back home with him before it got too late. The city was in a festive mood, with people thronging the streets and laughing with friends as they made their way either to the great hall or to various inns. David thought the girls had been smart to go early with Caelwyn. He glanced over at William. He had his cowl up, shadowing his features. William hadn't been sure whether he should go or not, until the moment when they actually left. David had pointed out that they didn't exactly have great lighting in this century, so the resemblance wouldn't be easily apparent. It would also seem odd if everyone except William went, so he caved. He hadn't really been looking forward to an evening on his own, and David was glad there would be another guy he knew at this feast.

They finally got to the courtyard, where stable boys were waiting to collect the horses. Siarl was recognized, and they were led to a relatively quiet part of the castle and told to wait. Soon enough, the king entered the room and greeted Siarl. "It's good to see you. You've been away from here far too long, my friend."

"Arthur, design a quiet city with no crowds and I would visit you more often," Siarl answered with a chuckle. Arthur laughed. He was dressed in full ceremonial court dress, much fancier than what he'd been wearing the first time David had seen him. He wore a white tunic and a purple cape trimmed in a gold color. It looked like a combination of Roman and Celtic styles, which was fitting for the kind of king Arthur was. He used Roman techniques combined with Celtic traditions to rule, while encouraging a British cultural identity and pride.

"If such a thing could be managed, I would do it. Still, I'm glad to see you've braved the crowds for one night," he said. He sounded like he was in a merry mood.

"Only a very special occasion could make me do so. Congratulations on Gwendolyn's betrothal."

"Thank you. The lad is young, but he has a good heart and has already proven he can lead." The king also spoke to Bleddyn, asking about his wife and child. He spoke to Selyf and the twins. He greeted David and William last, gripping their forearms in the sixth-century version of a handshake and saying he was glad they had come, then turned back to Siarl. "Caelwyn is in the hall, greeting the ladies with Guinevere."

"Are all the knights here? I've heard Lancelot has been in the north," Siarl inquired.

"Yes, but he made it back not over an hour ago. He and Mordred traveled back south together. All the knights are here." Arthur sounded relieved and satisfied.

"As it should be," Siarl said. "If you'll excuse me, I need to go greet my wife."

"And I need to find my way to the hall as well. Guinevere won't forgive me if I'm late." The king had a fond smile on his face as he mentioned his wife. It was clear he loved her.

Siarl turned to his three youngest before leaving. "Behave yourselves, and stay with Bleddyn, Dafyd, and William. Your mother would be most upset if you got lost."

"Yes, Father," they choroused. The men left.

"So what now?" David asked.

"That's up to you," Bleddyn said. He had blond hair and piercing blue-gray eyes that reminded David of Cassie's. "What generally happens is people circulate, greeting friends and exchanging gossip and news before the feast starts. The actual feasting then goes on awhile, and lots of people end up drinking more wine than they should. After that, the bards sing and tell tales for a while."

"When does it end?" William asked.

"Officially, it ends when the king retires, but many stay in the hall past that, often well into the wee hours of morning."

"When will Arthur make the announcement?" Addiena asked. "I want to be here for that."

"I don't know. You'd have to ask him." Bleddyn looked at David and William. "Are you prepared to face the hall?" He didn't sound very enthused.

"You don't like crowds much, do you?" William asked.

"No, most Brenwyds don't. Because our hearing is very keen, we hear much more than we wish to." He grimaced. He wasn't very old, only nineteen, but acted much more mature than some nineteen-year-olds David knew back home. Then again, none of them were married with a two-month-old child.

"Oh. That must be inconvenient," William said.

"It is, extremely. Still, keen hearing is a valuable trait. Come, we should go." They left for the hall. As David had suspected, it was not well-lit, with wall torches throwing odd shadows against the walls. Several chandelier-like fixtures were also hanging low from the ceiling, made of iron with candles in little holders.

William was scanning the crowd. "I don't see the girls," he noted.

"They'll be out soon," Selyf said. "They're probably helping Gwendolyn get ready. Girls take a long time to get ready."

Addiena sniffed. "Because we care about how we look," she said. "Boys don't get it." David had decided the young girl looked somewhere between cute and pretty in her dress. It was made of fine linen material, and had more elegant and intricate stitching around the collar than usual. She used a fancy belt at her waist instead of her everyday one. Her hair was pulled back in two braids so her slightly pointed ears were visible. Bleddyn was hailed by some friends, and fell into conversation with them.

"We should find Mother," Aeddan said.

"Where is she?" Selyf asked.

"Over there," William said. They made their way over.

Caelwyn looked relieved to see them. "Good, you're here." She wore attire similar to Addiena's, and her hair was pinned up in a bun. "I have a job for you. I've already told the girls."

"What is it?" David asked.

"I need you to listen carefully to everything around you and be on the lookout for anything suspicious." She lowered her voice and drew them into an alcove partially shielded from the rest of the hall. "I have a feeling that something's hovering over us, and I need to know the extent of the rumors about Brenwyds. People won't talk with me around, but you two are unknown in Camelot. Stick to the story about being from Armorica, but don't mention you're living with me. Listen to the undercurrents of a conversation. Watch people's expressions. Come and find me if you hear something especially suspicious."

"Can we spy, too, Mother?" Aeddan asked.

Caelwyn smiled, but David noticed a deep apprehension in her eyes. "Of course you can. Just watch yourselves and stick together."

"Do we have to stay with Dafyd or William? That's what Father told us," Selyf said. "But if we do that, people will know we know them."

"Stay within sight of them."

"Okay." They drifted out of the alcove, eager to start their assignment.

Caelwyn bade David and William stay for a moment. "I'd keep an eye on the girls once they come out, if I were you. Most of the men here are honorable, but no telling what the younger ones might do once they get drunk. If something starts to happen and you have to intervene, try to do it outside the hall," she advised.

"But nothing will happen, right?" David asked, troubled by the possible scenario Caelwyn had just raised. It hadn't occurred to him before.

"Hopefully not. Generally not. But you never know. I'm giving you this warning in part because of my instructions to the girls. I asked them to flirt a little if they had to. It's amazing what men will drop to impress an attractive girl."

David snorted. "Flirt? This will be interesting. I'm sure Cassie loved that idea."

Caelwyn chuckled. "She wasn't keen on it, but I'd watch her the most closely. She doesn't know her effect on young men. Now go. They should be out soon enough," she said, shooing them away. David and William departed from the alcove, keeping an eye on the three younger ones. The two boys went into the crowd a little, while Addiena seemed content to stick close to David and William.

"I wonder what Caelwyn's so worried about," William mused, switching languages to English. "I think it's something more than the rumors. No one would dare try anything here, in the king's own home. Even talking about it in a public place like this would be dangerous."

David nodded. "I noticed that, too. She must know or suspect something we don't know about." William grunted agreement, looking around. Several long tables ran the length of the hall, and David guessed each could seat around eighty or so.

"There they are," Addiena said suddenly.

"Who?" William asked.

"The girls. They're coming out now, through that door. See?" She pointed. William and David looked. Other people were doing the same, bowing respectfully and making way for the small party entering the hall. Jenifer was in front of her sister, looking excited and wearing a small circlet on her head. Gwendolyn was behind her, and wore white. She also had a circlet on her head. Telyn and Ganieda were with them. The two princesses made their way to their parents while Telyn and Ganieda hovered beside the door. Several minutes later Sarah and Cassie appeared. The four girls scanned the hall, obviously looking for something. Cassie met David's eyes, then got the others' attention and indicated the direction of the boys.

David just stared. Cassie looked stunning. Her dress was a light blue, with the fancy embroidery around the collar that David had learned to identify as Brenwyd work. It was simple and elegant, the way all Brenwyd-made clothing was. The sleeves and skirt flared out slightly at the bottom, with embroidery at the ends of the sleeves and bottom of the skirt. It suited Cassie perfectly. The stitching was done in a deep blue and she wore a delicately worked gold necklace at her throat with her locket hanging just below. David didn't know it, but the other necklace was to disguise the strange make of the locket, since she refused to take it off. Her hair was down save for two small braids that ran gracefully along her head, drooped to cover her ear tips, and met in the back with the rest falling loose. David had known Cassie for years, and had recognized the fact that she was prettier than other girls he knew, though he had always dismissed it. Finding out she was part Brenwyd had thrust it back into his focus, but he had told himself he had gotten over it. Judging by his reaction upon seeing her now, he had a feeling he'd been fooling himself. He'd just gotten good at seeing past the fact she was remarkably pretty, because if he took the time to actually think about it...

"No wonder Caelwyn told us to keep an eye on them," William muttered, interrupting David's train of thought. He was looking at Sarah. David turned his gaze to Sarah. She also looked pretty, wearing a green dress and a gold hair clip, but there was a definite difference between seeing your sister dressed up and your best friend dressed up. He did notice that Sarah's dress was in a different style and sleeveless, though. She wore a shawl covering her arms, fastened in front by a silver pin.

"Yeah," he agreed, and heard Addiena giggle softly. He looked down at her. "What?"

"Nothing," she said. Just then the girls came up.

Cassie frowned at David. "What are you staring at?" she demanded. Still definitely Cassie.

"Uh, nothing. Caelwyn said she told you about the assignment?" David asked quickly.

"Yes," Telyn said. "I hope you boys don't get jealous. All flirting will be done purely in the interest of ferreting out information. It's amazing what men will spill to pretty young girls." She looked excited, her blue-green eyes sparkling.

"Are you actually looking forward to this?" Cassie asked.

"I've done this before. It can be fun." She smiled. "You don't really have to do anything. Flattery works pretty well." She drifted off into the crowd.

"Right," Cassie muttered. "Easy."

Ganieda smiled. "Don't trouble yourself about it. Just keep your eyes and ears open," she said. She looked over the crowd. Sadness descended over her features.

"What is it?" Sarah asked. Ganieda looked startled.

"Hmm? Oh, nothing. Just thinking... but come. We shouldn't linger together too long. When Caelwyn talked about listening for things, it was mostly aimed at you four. The rest of us are known. You are not." She moved off in the opposite direction from Telyn. Addiena also moved away, joining Aeddan, who was standing not too far off in the crowd.

"I wonder what she was thinking about," Sarah said, concerned.

"Maybe her father," William suggested. "As I understand, it was around this time last year that he disappeared."

"Understandable," Cassie said softly. She looked around.

David thought something was bothering her. "Is something wrong?" he asked in English.

"I don't know. Like Ganieda said, keep your eyes and ears open. Something's going to happen tonight. I know it. Don't ask me how, but I know it."

"What's going to happen?" David asked. "Is this one of your hunches?"

"I think so. I'm not sure what it is, but it's not good." She focused

"Something's going to happen tonight.
I know it. Don't ask me how, but I know it.
I'm not sure what it is, but it's not good."

on William. "How do you feel?"

He looked surprised. "Fine. Why?"

"Just checking."

"Cassie, it's been two weeks since... whatever that was. I'm fine, really."

"If you say so." She looked around again. "I guess we should start mingling."

"Yep," Sarah said. "William, come with me. I need a chaperone for a bit."

"Umm, okay," he said. They walked away, leaving Cassie and David. She looked after them, and David thought she looked worried.

"Hey," he said. "They'll be fine. Those are two people I know we don't have to worry about." She turned her eyes on him.

"Normally I'd agree, but William is starting to worry me. Ever since that... seizure thing, he's been... not himself exactly. Whenever I spar with him, he seems to tire more quickly than usual. He's more sluggish in the morning, more ready to go to bed early."

David had noticed those things, too, but he hadn't thought about it much. "That doesn't have to mean anything. He's probably just tired. I've been tired myself. It would be really nice to sleep in once in a while." The hours people kept in the sixth century were not at all similar to the hours American teenagers kept in the twenty-first century.

"That's not all." They pressed against the wall. Cassie lowered her voice to a whisper, and David bent down slightly to hear her clearly, very aware of how close she was to him. "I've been checking his song regularly. It's weakening. Not by much, but it's weakening. If it gets much worse, I'm telling Caelwyn. Something's going on."

David frowned. That didn't sound good. "Can you fix it?"

"That's what's so odd. Other than being weaker, there's nothing wrong with it at all. I don't think it's something I can fix. Not by just singing, anyway, and it varies. Sometimes it sounds weaker, other times stronger, but not quite as strong as it should be." She must have noticed David's confusion. "I know it's a bit hard to explain, but that's the best I can manage."

"It's fine. I get what you're saying, mostly anyway. Do you have something in mind that could explain it?" he asked.

She hesitated a moment before answering. "I might. Remember those dream snatches I told you about?"

"Yeah."

"They've been getting me thinking." She looked around, lowered her voice even further, and whispered in David's ear exactly what she was thinking.

He looked at her, disbelief in his dark brown eyes. "Are you serious?" he asked, mind whirling. Granted, he could understand her reasoning, but still... it sounded crazy. *Although*, he told himself, *no crazier than the fact that we're currently fifteen hundred years in the past.*

"Would I joke about something like that?"

"Well, no, but..."

"I know, I know, it sounds nuts. But if you take a moment to think about it, it actually makes some sense. And at Gwen's I was down in the stable talking with Twi, and Phoenix made a casual mention of a rumor circulating the Brotherhood castle concerning–"

She stopped abruptly as a small group of people moved closer to where she and David stood. Instead of continuing to talk, she smiled brightly and (in David's opinion) rather flirtatiously to dispel any ideas that they had been talking about something serious. Again, he was struck by how pretty she was. Though he knew the smile was just an act on her part, he discovered that he liked it very much. "We should probably start watching and listening now. I'll tell you the rest later." He nodded, and smiled back at her, offering his arm. She rolled her eyes and stifled giggles, but she took it. They moved out and started mingling with the crowd.

Cassie was trying her best to keep her discomfort from showing. This sort of crowded situation was exactly what she tried to avoid. The hall would be loud to a regular person, but for her it sounded like a cacophony of noise and hurt her sensitive ears. She had learned to ignore noise, but it wasn't easy here, especially since she was supposed to be listening for anything suspicious. She had also noticed the heightened attention David was giving her. It made her slightly uncomfortable, yet at the same time she was rather enjoying it. He certainly looked very fine in the fancy clothes Caelwyn had provided for him... *Oh, get off it, girl,* she scolded herself. *It's just David.*

David looked around for William and Sarah. He spotted them – or more accurately, Sarah – talking with a small group of ladies. This kind of assignment was right up her alley. She loved meeting and talking with new people. William was standing a little behind her in the shadows. He did look more tired than usual. And if Cassie was right (as she usually was)... He looked around for Guinevere. She was standing by Arthur and Gwendolyn, along with a guy David guessed was Constantine. Constantine looked older than Gwendolyn, maybe early twenties. As David watched, another man walked up to them. He had curly blond hair and was taller than the king, but beyond that David couldn't tell much about him. The king, queen, and Gwendolyn looked very pleased to see him.

David slipped his arm from Cassie's hold. "Do you mind staying here for a minute? I'll be right back," he said. She nodded, but looked at him curiously.

"What is it? Do you see something?" she asked.

He shrugged. "I don't know, but it'll probably attract less notice if you stay here." He smiled, despite feeling jittery. He had no clue how she would take his next words. "No offense, but you do stand out a little, even with the ears covered."

He thought a flush came over her face. "I knew I shouldn't have trusted Telyn to pick out a dress. I'd have preferred the dark red one," she muttered. David didn't know what she was talking about.

"Well, I think it looks nice. It suits you," he said, feeling a bit more confident since she hadn't punched his arm or anything, which he'd been half expecting.

She gave him a cautious look he couldn't interpret, but he thought the corners of her lips turned upward slightly. "Um, thank you. Now go off and investigate whatever it is you think you see. I'll be fine," she said. Cassie hoped David couldn't tell how much his compliments pleased her. She didn't want him to think her shallow. She felt surprised by how happy she felt, and decided that the sixth century's mindset on relationships was rubbing off on her. Not a good thing.

"See you later, then." David headed for the royal party. Once, glancing back, he saw that some big youth had come up to Cassie and was making conversation. Judging from her expression, she wasn't very impressed, but David figured she could handle herself for a few minutes, though the sight made him feel very much like going back there and telling the guy off. He reminded himself that Cassie would not appreciate him coming back without having gathered any information. He made his way closer to the royal group so he could do some discreet eavesdropping.

"Found anything, Lancelot?" Gwendolyn was asking. David started. *Lancelot!* An idea started forming in his mind, something that might explain why Cassie and Caelwyn felt something would happen tonight. He listened closely.

"No, not yet. But I will. Villages don't just disappear for a reason," the knight answered.

"Villages?" Arthur sounded surprised. "What do you speak of?"

"You haven't heard?" Lancelot lowered his voice, and David moved closer. Now he could see the knight's face. He had light blue eyes and handsome features, but David thought he looked a little nervous. "The Brenwyd village outside Caer Lial was found abandoned. A nearby settlement thought it odd that there had been no contact for a week and sent men to investigate. No one was there."

"Was there any clue to what happened? Signs of struggle?" Arthur asked, worry lines becoming apparent on his forehead.

"Some, but there was no blood. It was very odd. The men showed me the village. Even the animals were gone. Something strange is happening."

"Have you found any evidence of this group I've heard is claiming responsibility for these things, the Reficul Brotherhood?" Guinevere asked, her face set in a worried frown.

"No. But I go back up north tomorrow. I will make it my object to find out what I can." David thought he saw a flicker of some emotion cross the knight's face as he answered the queen. "But let's move off such gloomy topics. Caelwyn or Siarl would likely be better able to answer your questions." David sensed that was as much as he'd hear. He moved away, disquieted by what he'd heard. A whole village gone missing? That sort of thing did not just happen.

David kept his eyes trained on the group. Gwendolyn and her fiancé wandered off, and Arthur struck up a conversation with another man, though David thought that now the king's smile seemed a little forced. Guinevere and Lancelot were left talking. David watched them, interested. Guinevere smiled at the knight, but David didn't think she acted like she was in love with him at all, despite the legends. She certainly didn't look at him the way she did at Arthur. Arthur called to her, and she moved to his side. Lancelot followed her with his eyes, a strange expression on his face that David couldn't interpret. He covered it quickly, and did something which struck David as odd. The queen had left her cup on the table she and Lancelot had been standing by. The knight looked around casually enough, but David thought he seemed nervous. He took something from his pocket – a vial, maybe? – and poured the contents into the cup. He put the vial away quickly, picked up the cup, and took it over to the queen, smiling. She took it, probably saying thanks, and Lancelot moved away, but kept within sight. David had seen enough. He had to find the others.

SCANDAL AT CAMELOT

Cassie wondered where on earth David had gotten himself to. She didn't mind him going off to do investigative work, but almost as soon as he'd left, this guy had come up to her and started talking, effectively preventing her from doing any useful eavesdropping. Not that she couldn't handle it, but she was pretty sure it would have been easier to shake him with David around. She certainly wasn't learning anything of interest, and the guy was making it clear that she should be in awe that he had chosen to pay attention to her. "I, myself, serve one of Arthur's best knights," he was saying. Cassie guessed he was about seventeen or eighteen. He hadn't asked her many questions, but was very eager for her to know all about his accomplishments. Perhaps he was trying to make up for his rather plain features.

"Oh?" Cassie said, smiling pleasantly (she hoped). "Who?"

"Why, none other than Sir Mordred. He has served the king for ten years and done many valiant deeds. I have learned much from him, and he says I will be ready to be knighted before the year is out."

"Really?" Maybe this conversation would be more fruitful than she thought, considering her suspicion that Camlann would be taking place soon. "How impressive." He talked on, and Cassie discovered Mordred had a house outside Caer Lial where he lived most of the time. *Interesting,* she thought, recalling that her father had told her Mordred had founded the Brotherhood.

"Well, lad, who's this young lady?" a voice broke in. The boy straightened.

"Sir Mordred. This is Cassie." Cassie inclined her head respectfully and curtseyed slightly before looking up. Her heart was pounding. What did the knight who caused the downfall of Arthur's kingdom and started Brenwyd persecution look like? *Not bad,* was her first thought. His face was square and open, giving off a friendly aura. His eyes were light gray, and his hair light brown. Cassie didn't think he was any older than thirty. He smiled pleasantly at her, but she had an uncomfortable flash of familiarity. Where had she seen him before? She was sure that she had, or at least someone who looked a lot like him, and that it hadn't been a good meeting.

"Delighted to make the acquaintance of such a beautiful young damsel. I don't believe I've seen you at court before," he said.

Oh, give me a break, Cassie thought, though she wasn't sure if it was in response to the knight's words, or her impression that he was familiar, a sensation she was getting tired of feeling upon meeting people for the first time. Probably both. She forced herself to smile prettily. Now would be an excellent time for David to re-enter the picture. Or perhaps William. "I'm glad to meet you as well. The fame of Arthur's knights is known far and wide. It's an honor to meet one of them." She blessed the acting skills she had honed during school plays. He nodded to her and turned to his squire. He leaned over and whispered something in his ear, low enough that a normal human wouldn't have heard, but not low enough for Brenwyd ears. Cassie feigned disinterest, but could hear every word.

"Go check my horse. I might need to leave in a hurry. I want my gear where I can reach it easily, and check the other as well."

The boy nodded. He bowed to Cassie. "I hope we meet again soon," he said.

"And I as well." She smiled. He walked away briskly.

Mordred turned to her once again. "I don't believe you mentioned where you're from. I know you haven't been at court before," he said.

Cassie guessed her flattery had pleased him. "Oh, a few times, but this is my first public event. I come from Armorica."

"Is that so?"

"Yes."

"And you are unescorted in a foreign court?"

"Oh, no. My escort will be back soon. He went to speak to some friends. Personally," she lowered her voice as if confiding a secret, "I find talk of danger and politics boring."

Mordred chuckled. "Often it is." His attention was attracted to the sound of laughter nearby. Jenifer, Addiena, and Bleddyn were talking, and Addiena had laughed. Cassie watched Mordred intently, and saw an intense loathing enter his eyes as he watched her. It was gone quickly, but it put Cassie on her guard. She, or Telyn rather, had styled her hair to cover her ears, and she appreciated how much of an advantage it gave her.

"Children are adorable, are they not?" she asked with a light laugh, redirecting his attention.

"Yes, quite. Do you have Brenwyds in Armorica?"

"Oh, yes. They're a very helpful people."

He studied her. "Helpful... yes. Very odd, the way they help, isn't it?" he asked, a strange light in his gray eyes.

Cassie shrugged. "They help the best way they can. I admit, sometimes they can be unsettling, but I like them overall. They are very pretty." She thought that would be the kind of comment he'd expect her to make.

"Well, I'd watch your step around them. They can be tricky."

Cassie opened her eyes wide. "You don't say! I've never had bad dealings with a Brenwyd, and that's a fact," she stated, feeling somewhat obligated to put in a good word for her people.

He was about to answer, but William appeared suddenly and took her arm. "There you are," he said. "I've been looking for you. I told you to stay where I left you." He had a congenial smile on his face, but Cassie made out traces of alarm in his eyes. Mordred started slightly. "I hope you don't mind if I take her, sir."

"Oh, not at all," the knight said, sounding startled. "Have we met before, lad?"

"Highly unlikely, sir. Come, Cassie, there's someone who wishes to speak with you." He quickly steered her away.

Cassie noticed Mordred staring after them. She wasn't surprised by his reaction upon seeing William. It was typical. What surprised her was that William seemed to recognize *him*. "Not that I'm ungrateful, William, but what was that about?" she asked in English at the first opportunity.

He shot a look back over his shoulder. "Don't you know who that was?" he asked, sounding incredulous.

Cassie wasn't quite sure why he was so agitated. "Yeah, it was Mordred. I know what he did – will do. I can take care of myself. He didn't realize I'm Brenwyd."

"That's not what I meant." They'd reached the edge of the hall and could speak in relative privacy. "I... know him."

"What?"

"In our time."

She stared. "Excuse me?" She wasn't sure she'd heard him correctly.

"I know it sounds crazy, but it's true. He's younger here, but it's him. I'd heard rumors, but..." He shook his head. "I never suspected they were true."

"What was true?"

"Mordred. He's the Master of the Brotherhood. In our time. The one you're supposed to... you know."

"Are you serious?" she asked, gasping. "I knew he founded the Brotherhood, but he's the Master still? How?"

"Yes, and I don't know. I've certainly never heard of him going through a time slip. The rumor is that he found the secret of immortality and won't rest until all Brenwyds are dead. That's why I pulled you away."

"Oh. Thanks," Cassie said. "So that's why he looked and sounded familiar. I saw him through a window at the castle, and then we heard him in the tunnels... Do you think he recognized us? In our time?"

"I don't know. But if he did, why wasn't he more wary about me?" William wondered, mostly to himself.

"It is a long time to our time," Cassie said. "He probably forgot, especially if that little glimpse is all he sees of you. We should tell Caelwyn, though. She has to know." William nodded agreement. "Where's Sarah? Don't tell me you left her at the mercy of the wolves."

"I'm right here," Sarah's voice said. She was exiting the main throng. "Did you find out anything?"

"Plenty," Cassie said. "Have you seen David?"

"Isn't he with you?"

"He was, but then he went to investigate something."

"And good thing I did," David said, approaching from behind them. "I think I figured out what's got you so on edge, Cass."

"Oh? What?" she inquired. He told them what he'd seen.

Sarah gasped. "That's not good. Are you saying that whole debacle could happen tonight?"

"You mean whatever caused the legend that Guinevere ended up with Lancelot? I think it might," her brother said grimly. "We should keep a sharp eye on them."

"Should we tell Caelwyn?" Sarah asked. "Where is she, anyway?"

"I don't know," Cassie said, troubled. "Normally I'd say yes, but with this whole time-travel thing thrown in, I'm not sure."

"But if the scandal is what is remembered in our time, wouldn't it happen despite anything we might do to prevent it? Technically, we were part of this history," Sarah said.

"That's not very comforting," William said. "If that's the case, then we know we'll fail before we even try."

"But we should at least try," Sarah said.

Cassie nodded, her mind made up. "I agree. Where's Caelwyn?"

"I saw her somewhere over there," David said, indicating the direction. "But we can't tell her in here. There's too great a chance we'll be overheard, and we can't use English with her." They were interrupted by the announcement of dinner. Cassie glimpsed Caelwyn among the crowd, but she and Siarl went to the high table, while Cassie and the others were seated with Caelwyn's children at a different table. Cassie made sure to keep her mind blocked from Telyn. She was pretty sure the other girl would have a block up around her mind anyway as she was in such a crowded place, but Cassie didn't want to risk her accidentally picking up on her thoughts. All throughout the meal the four teens looked for an opportunity to get Caelwyn away, but none presented itself. Cassie kept an eye on Guinevere the whole time, and she noticed the queen seemed to fade over the course of the evening. She wondered why Caelwyn and Siarl didn't notice. Maybe, she reflected, they were too distracted by everyone around them to pay attention. The one time Cassie tried to use her ability to listen to the queen's song, she had a phenomenally hard time finding it. With all the other songs breaking her concentration, some of them more discordant than others, she eventually had to give up the attempt. She guessed that the liquid David had seen Lancelot pour into Guinevere's cup had been some sort of sleeping potion.

At last, the feast part of the night was over and Arthur stood to officially announce Gwendolyn's betrothal to Constantine, the oldest son of Cador, who was the lord of the area that would become modern Cornwall. Gwendolyn blushed prettily and looked down, and her fiancé took her hand. Anyone could see that both were happy. The next part of the evening would be storytelling by the bards. As the first began his story song, Cassie leaned over to Sarah and whispered in her ear. "I'm going to go tell her now. Everyone's focused on the bard. If Guinevere leaves, come and get us." Sarah nodded. Cassie shifted slightly, and as she did she saw Guinevere lean over to Arthur and speak to him. He looked concerned, but Guinevere smiled and kissed him, clearly telling him not to worry. Then she quietly got up and left the table. "Nuts," Cassie said.

"Now what?" Sarah asked. David and William, who were sitting on the girls' other side, leaned in to hear them.

"I'm going to have to follow her," Cassie said.

"Not by yourself you're not," David said.

"It would attract less notice," Cassie said. "And someone needs to tell Caelwyn."

"I'll do that," Sarah said. Cassie started to get up, and David rose with her.

"I'm going with you," he said. At that moment, Bleddyn asked David to help him with Selyf and the twins, since he was up. They were all but asleep, and he wanted to get home to Eira. David glanced at Cassie, who nodded. He figured this would be an excuse for him to get out of the hall, and he could catch up with Cassie later. He assumed Guinevere would be followed by Lancelot to her bedchamber, and he knew its general location. He agreed, picking up Addiena. Selyf, though sleepy, was walking and Bleddyn had Aeddan. Cassie rose to leave. She had also noticed Lancelot leaving the hall a few minutes earlier, and she couldn't let him get that far ahead.

✜

Mordred watched Lancelot slip out of the hall, unnoticed by most and seemingly unremarked on by all. A smile crept over his face. Everything was falling into place. Now all he had to do was make sure Arthur saw it and ensure that the right story spread. He had worked out with Lancelot where the event would take place, so he knew exactly where to lead the king. His thoughts drifted to the young maid he'd met earlier in the evening. Her beauty had been startling, but she gave him a bad feeling. She made him feel uneasy about his plan. He had to find out more about her. And the boy! Mordred recalled Lancelot's comment about Caelwyn housing a boy who resembled Arthur, but hadn't given much thought to it. Now he himself wondered if Arthur had sired a bastard son. There were four children from Armorica with Caelwyn, Lancelot had said, two boys and two girls, one of them Brenwyd. Mordred realized that the girl he'd met must have been one of the four, and was likely the Brenwyd. He berated himself for his stupidity. She'd had her ears covered, but he should have known. He thought about the boy again, in light of his mother's prediction. A worm of fear started wriggling its way through him. Unless he found solid proof of the boy's parentage that said otherwise, he would have to be eliminated.

⁂

Sarah watched worriedly as Cassie slipped out of the hall. She knew Cassie could take care of herself, but Lancelot was big, and she had a feeling he would not be pleased to be interrupted. She hoped David would catch up with her quickly. William took her hand and squeezed it reassuringly. "She'll be fine." Sarah looked at him, surprised by the physical contact. Usually he didn't initiate such things. He looked tired, and he probably felt tired, otherwise he would have volunteered to go with Cassie. "Do you want me to go with you to tell Caelwyn?" he asked.

She shook her head. "I'll do it. You might draw too much attention, going up to Arthur's table. And one of us should stay here. It could look suspicious if all four of us are gone."

"What are you talking about?" Telyn's voice asked. She was across the table and was looking at them curiously. Sarah wondered if she had picked up something from their minds. She'd been keeping hers blocked – something she'd learned to do very well over the past two and a half months – but you never knew.

"Nothing," William answered quickly. "What is this tale called?"

"It's the journey of King Bran into England," Telyn said. "It's well known, but it's a good story."

Sarah rose. "I have to use the necessary. Tell me what I missed when I get back." Telyn nodded and returned her attention to the bard. Sarah was a little sorry she couldn't stay to listen to it. It was about a king who sounded like he was a giant. He came to England and met a fair damsel who asked him to marry her. He agreed, and she said that, before he could marry her, he must combat an evil giant who had conquered the land. Sarah took a route that would lead her to the head table, but made it look like she intended to go somewhere else. She walked behind Caelwyn and tapped her shoulder.

The woman turned and looked at her in surprise. "Is something wrong?"

"I need to tell you something," Sarah said. "Now. It's very important."

"What is it?"

"I can't tell you here."

Caelwyn nodded, her brow furrowing in worry. She and Sarah exited the hall through a side door, and Sarah closed the door behind them. "What is it? Did you find something out?" Caelwyn asked.

"Yes." Sarah took a breath. "You see, in the King Arthur legend we know..." She told Caelwyn the whole story. The Brenwyd woman said nothing, but her eyes widened in incredulity.

She was silent for a few moments after Sarah finished. "Do you know where they went?"

"No."

"Thank you for telling me. I must tell Arthur. Don't worry," she added, seeing Sarah's look of alarm. "I will tell him only what is necessary." Caelwyn opened the door and they reentered the hall.

Sarah looked at the high table, and her heart sank. Arthur was no longer there. Caelwyn also saw the problem. "Go back to the others, Sarah," Caelwyn said. "I'll take care of this." Sarah nodded and went back to her place at the table. Telyn looked like she was concentrating hard on something. William looked at Sarah when she got back, raising his eyebrows in inquiry.

"I told her," Sarah said. "She'll take care of it."

"The king left several minutes ago with Mordred," William told her grimly. "I asked Telyn to tell her mother. She said she would try, but it's hard for her to concentrate–"

"It is done," Telyn said, opening her eyes. She narrowed them at William and Sarah. "Now why is that important? Mordred lives in the north. Perhaps he is going to tell Arthur some information about the missing Brenwyds."

William shook his head. "I'm sorry, Telyn, but that's not what's happening."

"We'll tell you later," Sarah said. "Here and now... too many people. But praying that Cassie and your mother intervene in time would be a good idea." Telyn's eyes narrowed further, but she nodded and looked away, worry coming over her face as she bowed her head. Sarah leaned against William. She knew he wouldn't be expecting such a thing, but she needed some human reassurance right now. The end of the King Arthur story always made her sad, and here she was living it.

After a moment, Sarah was surprised to feel William put an arm around her, warming her. It also made her heart beat faster, and lifted her spirits. She looked up at him. He was looking down at her, a little uncertainly. She thought he was blushing a little. She suspected she was, too, but she found she didn't want him to take his arm away.

Cassie was confused. She was tracing Lancelot by the sound of his footfalls, but he wasn't going to the bedchamber as she had expected. He was going in almost the opposite direction. She quickened her pace, taking care to walk silently. She couldn't afford to lose him. She hoped Sarah had gotten to Caelwyn, and that the woman would somehow realize their direction. She stopped at a fork in the hallway and strained her ears. She couldn't hear the footsteps anymore. *God, what do I do?* she cried silently. The answer came to her a moment later. *Why didn't I think of that sooner?* she thought. She extended her song-sense down each corridor, looking for Lancelot. She found him, and shuddered at the discordance. She sensed Guinevere with him.

She ran down the right corridor, slowing as she spotted a door ahead. She approached the door cautiously, her ears pricked for any noise. "What... what are you doing?" Guinevere's voice came to her. She spoke with undertones of alarm, but the words were slurred and slow.

"I'm doing you a favor," someone else said. *Lancelot.* He sounded eager. "I love you, Guinevere. I can't help myself."

"No... stop," Guinevere said. By this time Cassie was to the door. Peeking inside, she realized that they were in the same garden where she and the others had first met Arthur. How would the others find out?

Suddenly an idea came to her. *Twi!* she called.

What? the mare answered.

Tell Caelwyn and David that Guinevere and Lancelot are in the garden where we came on our first day here. It's critically important. Is David still out there?

He left a few moments ago. I will tell them. What is happening?

I'll tell you later.

Oh, girl, I think you should know – there are horses tacked up and ready for a hasty departure.

Whose? Cassie demanded. Twi showed her images of the rid-ers. Cassie felt her blood run cold. One horse was Lancelot's... and the other was Mordred's. Was he involved in this somehow? He had helped expose Lancelot in the stories, but could he have set him up as well? Jenifer had mentioned that the two had trav-eled south together.

Cassie saw Lancelot starting to pull at the sleeves of Guinev-ere's dress, and she heard fabric starting to rip. Guinevere tried to fight him, but she was too weak, though she did manage to slap his face away for a few seconds. Cassie looked at the size of the knight. He was tall, taller than Arthur, and very muscular. She swallowed. She wished David were with her, and hoped he or Caelwyn would come soon. Praying for courage, she fully opened the door. "Stop that!" she yelled. "Do you have no honor?"

Lancelot whirled around at her voice. He was obviously in the process of undressing, but Cassie was extremely grateful that he still had his pants on. His face hardened. Guinevere looked at Cassie with a pleading expression. A little hope appeared in her eyes. Cassie could tell she was struggling to resist the drug. "Who are you?" Lancelot demanded.

"I'll be keeping that to myself." Cassie gave him her best glare. She stepped toward him. She wished she were armed. There was no way she could get involved in a fist-fight with this guy and win. "What do you think you're doing?"

He stepped toward her menacingly. "It's none of your business, girl. You'll leave and say nothing if you know what's good for you."

"Fat chance." Cassie stepped closer to him. "Leave here now, before I go get the king."

"Would you really? You could try. I would stop you. And believe me, girl, you wouldn't like that."

Watching him, Cassie realized he was going against his better instincts. The meanness in his voice sounded forced, and in his eyes she saw doubt. She took another step closer and adopted a more compassionate tone. "This isn't what you're really like, is it? Is someone forcing you to do this?"

His face contorted into an expression of anger. "No! No one forces me to do anything." His eyes were wild. Cassie felt a hollow feeling inside that she recognized as fear. Neither Caelwyn nor David had shown up yet. Lancelot grabbed her arm and yanked her to him roughly. She stared up at him, struggling to free herself from his grip, but it was no use. He threw her underneath some bushes. She gasped as the wind was knocked out of her when she hit the hard ground. Lancelot had practically picked her up to throw her, and tears came to her eyes from the impact. Her head had knocked against something hard, making her feel dizzy. She cried out as she felt a hard kick to her side, pushing her farther under the bushes and causing her head to hit the hard thing again, most likely a rock. She felt immobilized, and her vision swam. *I will not pass out*, she told herself sternly. She could tell Twi had picked up on her distress and was starting a ruckus. That would rile up the other horses.

Twi, no! Cassie ordered. *That will just make it worse.* Cassie knew by Guinevere's renewed protests that Lancelot had gone back to her, but his kick had sent intense pain streaking up and down Cassie's body. Any movement exacerbated it, but she still struggled to get out from under the bushes. The atmosphere of the garden had become forbidding and the darkness was more complete. Cassie felt colder and chills danced along her spine. Something was present that she couldn't quite name, but it was definitely not good. Doubts began running through her mind. Why was she trying to get up? It didn't matter what she did. Arthur was doomed. She couldn't change anything. She was just one little girl caught up in events much too big for her to handle. Tears began to well up in her eyes.

Dimly, she became aware of footsteps echoing from the corridor. Her heart leapt with hope, fighting against the doubts. She managed to turn over so she could see who entered, but it was not David or Caelwyn. It was Mordred and Arthur. Her spirits plummeted once more. There was no way Arthur would believe the truth.

The king stared at the scene in his garden. Guinevere was underneath Lancelot, though she had her arms braced behind her on a bench, trying to keep herself from the ground as she sought to pull away. However, there was no mistaking what Lancelot was trying to do. Cassie saw Lancelot turn his head and freeze. His back was to her, so she couldn't see his expression. No one seemed to notice her. "Lancelot," the king said, sounding terribly shaken. "What is the meaning of this?"

There was a pause. Lancelot got up. "She made me do it," he accused, pointing at Guinevere. She was trying to pull herself up using the bench, though the drug was finally starting to take full effect. At his accusation she stopped, however, and stared at him in horrified shock. Cassie realized that Lancelot had succeeded in getting part of her dress off, but Guinevere had a shirt-like tunic on underneath so she was still covered. "She egged me on, drove me to it. She... she wanted a son for you."

Guinevere shook her head violently, looking toward her husband as a cry escaped her lips, probably some sort of denial. The two locked gazes for a moment, a look of absolute anguish on the king's face, and then Guinevere slumped as she succumbed to unconsciousness.

Cassie had heard uncertainty and a wildness in Lancelot's voice, like he didn't know what he was saying. She listened to him with her Brenwyd sense. His song was wildly discordant now, and it hurt her almost like a physical pain. But there was something else she sensed, and it came from Mordred. She could barely make out his song, which sounded even more messed up than Lancelot's, because there was a thin veneer of regular melody over it, almost like a covering.

Lancelot moved his accusing finger to Mordred. "And he helped me! It was his doing!"

Mordred looked at Lancelot calmly. "That is ridiculous. I would never betray my king like that."

Liar! The word exploded in Cassie's mind. More footsteps sounded down the corridor, and she felt an immense wave of relief as Caelwyn and David entered the garden. Caelwyn's mouth was pressed in a thin line. With her entrance, the garden's atmosphere seemed to grow lighter. She and David took in the scene. Lancelot looked at them and fled. Cassie noticed that David's eyes continued to rove the garden, looking for her. Arthur looked shell-shocked, and he stumbled to where his wife lay on the ground. Caelwyn put a hand on his arm. "Arthur, there's more to this than it seems," she said gently. "Don't doubt your wife. Go back to the hall. I'll take care of her. Go to your daughters."

Arthur raised his eyes to hers. They looked at each other for a long minute. "But... he must be gone after. I cannot let him get away, not with this..." His voice trailed off, but his fists were clenched. Cassie suspected his shock was turning to rage.

"Now is not the time," Caelwyn said. "Now, you must go back to the hall before the people start to wonder where you are. Justice will come in due time." Arthur said nothing. "Cousin," Caelwyn said gently, "please. Even if you went after him right now, you must not fight him with emotions clouding your judgment. For that fight you are not certain to win, and this kingdom needs you yet."

"Emotions?" He stood and wheeled on her. "He has just attempted to violate my wife, and you advise me to let him escape?" Cassie was rather glad she was hidden under the bushes, and noticed David had made himself scarce behind a column. It was an uncomfortable scene to watch.

"I know," Caelwyn said. "I would go after him with you in a heartbeat, believe me. But you must be calm when you meet him.

You have certainly told me enough times not to fight when my emotions are in control. Now you must do the same." Her face was deadly serious. "Arthur. Please. It is Gwendolyn's betrothal feast. You are the king. You cannot leave now."

He turned from her to stare at his unconscious wife. "Too often have I had to sacrifice for being a king instead of an average man," he said in a hard voice. Caelwyn watched him pensively. She knew she had strong influence with her cousin, but in a matter of honor such as this... She knew he had every right to pursue Lancelot, but she knew just as certainly that he must not satisfy his desire for vengeance right now. He closed his eyes and let out a long, slow breath. With it went his angry stance. "And now I must do so again, though it goes against all that is in me," he added softly, the anguished expression returning to his face. Caelwyn let out her own quiet sigh. Arthur knelt, kissed Guinevere on the forehead, then rose and turned abruptly back into the house. Mordred had slipped out unobtrusively sometime during the conversation.

Cassie rolled out from under the bushes, the pain having mostly faded. David spotted her immediately and went to her. "Did he hurt you?" he asked, his eyes dark with what Cassie could tell was anger.

"I'm fine," she said. "Just a little shook up." He helped her stand. They went to where Caelwyn was examining Guinevere.

Caelwyn looked up at Cassie concernedly. "Are you alright?" Cassie nodded. Caelwyn examined her, and her eyes widened. She muttered something Cassie didn't catch, but then she started singing. Cassie felt herself strengthened, and the last of the pain went away.

"Thank you," she said.

Caelwyn looked at her with unease. "There's been witchcraft in this garden tonight. That's what was causing you pain."

"Witchcraft?" Cassie and David asked simultaneously, eyes wide.

Caelwyn nodded, looking worried. "But it was not Lancelot. He was helped by someone who knows witchcraft, someone who shaped tonight's events to fit his or her own personal agenda."

"Mordred," Cassie said. "It has to be Mordred. His song sounded wrong, not discordant exactly, but just wrong. And Twi said that his and Lancelot's horses are tacked up and ready to leave at a moment's notice."

Caelwyn stared at her, her eyes veiled. "Are you certain?" Cassie nodded. Caelwyn sighed, closing her eyes. "Mordred. I should have known." She looked down at Guinevere. "He'll have to wait." She looked back up at Cassie. "Are you sure you're alright?"

Cassie realized she was trembling. "I think so. I just feel shaken up. He threw me under the bushes."

"I can tell," Caelwyn said, looking at her dress. "I'm deeply sorry, Cassie. I should have been teaching you how to recognize and combat witchcraft."

"What?" Cassie asked.

Caelwyn looked surprised. "You didn't think we just used our song-sense for healings, did you? Brenwyds help combat the evil in this world, whether it be witchcraft or something else. You might say we are like guardians of the earth. You did not know?"

"Um... sort of. My father told me something like that once, but he said that the craft was lost, or something like that."

"Considering how much time has passed, and some hints you've given about Brenwyds in your time, I'm not surprised." Caelwyn looked extremely displeased with herself. "I should have known. I must start teaching you this. It is a Brenwyd's most important skill. Usually Brenwyd children start to learn it as soon as they are old enough to understand the concept, so I assumed you had also. I apologize."

David put an arm around Cassie's waist and hugged her to him. She felt surprised, but also grateful. His warmth stilled the remainder of her trembles. His arm made her feel secure, and she needed a sense of security at the moment. "What do we do now?" David asked.

Caelwyn sighed. "This night's events will spread far and wide, I fear. Sarah told me of some of the consequences. You did well to try and stop it."

"But we failed," Cassie said miserably. "We tried, and we still failed." She felt like she might cry. Why hadn't she guessed? Why hadn't she told Caelwyn sooner? She knew the King Arthur story backwards and forwards. She could have prevented this.

"You were brave to try, in light of what you know," Caelwyn said compassionately, putting a hand on Cassie's shoulder. "And you were even braver to take on Lancelot alone and unarmed. He is quite formidable. I have only ever seen Arthur best him in sword-play." She paused, then turned Cassie's head to look her in the eyes. "Cassie. Do not blame yourself for this. This," she gestured at Guinevere, "happened because of one man's passion and another's lust for power. Even if you had told me what you know sooner, I would not have known it would happen this night. I might have been more guarded, but it would have happened sooner or later. Understand?" Cassie looked into Caelwyn's eyes several moments longer before nodding. "Good." Caelwyn looked at the two of them. "I think you should go back to the hall for now. Listen to the bards' tales. But tell Siarl to come help me. I cannot carry Guinevere back to her rooms by myself." David and Cassie nodded and headed back down the corridor. The scene between Caelwyn and the king weighed on their minds, but neither wanted to talk of it. It was not their business.

"I'm sorry I wasn't able to come sooner," David said. "By the time we got Twi's message, we were halfway to the bedrooms."

"It's alright," Cassie said, her mind calming. "Mordred and Arthur actually arrived at a good time. And I interrupted Lancelot before anything really happened."

"But you shouldn't have had to face him alone. If he had really hurt you in any way–"

Cassie stopped and faced him. "David, I'm fine. Really. I've been hurt worse in falls off my horse. Caelwyn's right. We can't blame ourselves."

He looked down at her. "But what about the witchcraft stuff Caelwyn was talking about?"

"I felt it, and I didn't know what it was. It scared me, but I didn't realize... and if Mordred really is the Brotherhood master, maybe that's why we had to come back."

"What?" David asked, totally confused. Cassie had just switched thoughts on him in the middle of a sentence. Not that it was unusual, but it was still confusing.

"William told me Mordred's the Brotherhood master. He doesn't know why he apparently survived fifteen hundred years, but he has. Did. Will. Whatever." They started walking again. David tried to wrap his mind around what Cassie had just said.

"Is William sure?" he asked.

"He sure acted like it." David thought she was going to say more, but she was silent the rest of the way to the hall.

⁓⁊⁊⁊⁊⁊⁓

He started awake, knowing something of great import had just happened. He listened. All was quiet. He looked out the window and saw nothing out of the ordinary. He bowed his head and closed his eyes, sending out his Sight. It led him to Camelot, to a small garden with four people in it. He recognized all of them. Watching, he realized what had happened. Mordred had made his move. "God, help us," he murmured. "If there was ever a time this kingdom needed You, it is now."

He was startled out of his watching by footsteps in the corridor. The door swung open, and a woman strode in. "And how is our prisoner tonight?" she asked. Her hair was flaming red and her eyes were dark, a stark contrast. She wasn't tall, but her presence intimidated many.

"I was better before you came in," he answered.

The woman laughed. "Ha. I'm glad you're in such good spirits. I have some news for you." He looked at her calmly. "The first step has been taken. All that you have worked for will fall."

"No." he said. "Not all. God has raised up warriors to oppose you and your son. They will throw down all *you* have worked for."

She sneered. "Is that all the prophecy you have for me, old man? I would expect better from you."

"It is all you deserve. You may have a small victory, it is true, but you will lose the war."

"If we do, we will drag your precious Brenwyds down with us," she snarled, her eyes seeming to burn with dark fire.

"They will drag you down, Morgan, and they will rise. We serve a bigger God than you."

"We shall see who serves the bigger god," she said. She turned and left, slamming the door behind her.

He gazed after her, shaking his head sadly at her pride. "Pride goes before a fall, Morgan," he said softly. "And as your pride is great, we shall see how big your fall will be."

$\mathcal{I}$NVESTIGATING

$\mathcal{S}$arah listened to Cassie's story incredulously. It was almost noon on the day after the feast. While it hadn't been a complete fiasco, rumors had been flying well before the last guest left, though no one knew exactly how they had started and the rumors themselves were rather vague. Guinevere had slept soundly through the night and was still sleeping, but Arthur hadn't slept at all. He had ridden out at first light alone, and no one knew when he would be back. Gwendolyn was a nervous wreck, and Jenifer not at all like her usually cheery self. The whole city was full of whispering, and people spoke in low voices. Mordred had left not long after Lancelot, and no one knew what would happen next. No one, that is, except for Cassie, David, Sarah, and William, and what they knew wasn't comforting. Siarl had immediately called a meeting of Brenwyd leaders. The feast had also revealed the depth of the suspicion humans had toward Brenwyds, as well as the disturbing information that a whole Brenwyd village had vanished in the north. Cassie and William had told Caelwyn what they knew of the Brotherhood in the twenty-first century, and Caelwyn had said she would tell Siarl to help him in his investigations.

Caelwyn was still at the castle trying to keep things running smoothly, and so the others were there as well. The loyal knights –

Gawain, Galahad, Bedivere, Bors, and the rest – had gone out looking for Mordred, Lancelot, and the king. They knew what had really occurred. Currently, all the young people were in the round room, exchanging information.

"I do not understand how you were able to realize what was going to happen, given what you saw," Gwendolyn said. "It's as if you already knew what he was planning and what you saw merely confirmed it." She blinked, realizing what that statement sounded like. "Not that I am implying you were complicit with Lancelot, of course," she added hastily.

The four glanced at each other. They had debated the night before about what to say and what not to say. They'd already planned on telling Caelwyn's family the whole story, and had decided that it wouldn't hurt for Gwendolyn and Jenifer to know as well.

"And if there was witchcraft like Caelwyn said," Jenifer added. "Why didn't you battle it, Cassie?"

"Ah... I didn't know that's what I was sensing, and I don't know how to, um, battle it, " Cassie answered.

"You didn't know? Why not? Do not all Brenwyds know?"

"I've never learned. Caelwyn told me about it just last night. Where I'm from... I thought Brenwyds could only use the songs to heal."

Telyn was frowning. "But even given where you come from, why wouldn't you know? It is a skill all Brenwyds learn. I cannot believe such an important skill would cease to be taught."

"It's a long story," William said.

"I like stories," Jenifer said. "And I could use a good one right now."

"You told me yesterday you would tell us the whole story," Telyn said to Cassie. "I think knowing it is important. Please, tell us."

She is right, girl, Kai's voice declared, startling everyone. *It is time.* He and Dassah walked into the room and sat by Cassie's chair.

"Where on earth did you two come from?" Cassie asked.

The hallway.

"Thank you, Captain Obvious. Did you walk all the way here from Caelwyn's?"

How else do you think we got here? A horse? We thought you might need help.

"Help is certainly welcome," William said.

"Tell us the story," Jenifer said impatiently. The four looked at each other. *Where to start?*

"Jenifer," Sarah said. "Remember how we said we were from Armorica?"

"Yes."

"Well... we're not. We're from *America*, except for William, and we are from the twenty-first century, not the sixth," Sarah said bluntly.

Jenifer stared at her. "What?" she asked.

"This is not our time period. We are from about fifteen hundred years in the future. Is that good enough for you?" Both princesses stared at them incredulously.

"What?" Gwendolyn asked. "That's... that's not possible. You're jesting."

"I wish," Cassie said. "Believe me, I wouldn't have thought it possible either, but bear with us, please. About three months ago, in mid-June, Sarah, David, and I were on a camping trip. We live near mountains and had gone up on our horses to spend the night." She narrated from there, spilling the whole story save for the prophecy. Except for some exclamations here and there, the audience stayed silent. Cassie concluded by saying, "So we've been here, waiting for the time slip to mend and trying to figure out just what we're supposed to do here." There was a long silence.

"That is a... a rather fantastic story," Gwendolyn said at last.

"Then this Reficul Brotherhood isn't just rumors," Telyn said softly.

"No," William said. "I'm afraid not. This is when it started."

She narrowed her blue-green eyes at him. "And you worked with them. That's why you're so skilled with the sword. You'd been trained to hunt us." She sounded reproachful and accusing.

William winced. "Yes. Brotherhood members are experts at lying and perverting the truth. I was told that Brenwyds were children of the devil who existed to enslave all humanity. When it's what you're taught since you were a baby, you can't help but believe it."

Telyn scowled. "That's absolutely ridiculous," she huffed.

"I know that now," William said.

Telyn softened her gaze. "You shouldn't blame yourself for believing their lies. You saw the truth and got out. Do not worry about it anymore. The Brotherhood is behind you."

"We keep trying to tell him that," Sarah said.

"And Mordred leads it," Ganieda mused, her brow furrowed. "It makes sense, I suppose. He's never loved Brenwyds. And he lives in the north where they have been disappearing." Cassie thought she looked as if she wanted to say something else, but stopped herself.

"Why does he hate Brenwyds so?" Sarah asked.

"I've heard it's because he had a younger sister named Morgause," Telyn answered. "She got very sick, and he took her to a Brenwyd healer, but it was too late. The healer did all he could, but she still died. He blames us for her death." She hesitated. "And then there is his mother."

"His mother?" Cassie asked. "What's she got to do with it?" She hadn't heard anyone in this era mention Mordred's mother yet, but if the legends were right, she could have very much to do with recent events.

Gwendolyn answered. "She is a witch, and she hates Brenwyds as well. She... tried to lead a rebellion against Father ten years ago and nearly succeeded, but he defeated her, with Mordred's help. That's why he was accepted as a knight. Instead of executing her, as most thought he should, Father decided to exile her to the Orkneys, a very inhospitable, isolated island chain off the north of

Caledonia. Mordred commands a garrison of guards that keep an eye on her. According to all reports, even those from Father's own people that he sent to investigate, she is still there."

"But that does not mean she has not been influencing her son," Telyn remarked darkly.

Before Cassie could ask who exactly Mordred's mother was, Ganieda got up and started pacing. "Father knew this time was coming. He warned us of it. We need to act quickly," she said.

"And do what?" David asked.

"I'm not sure. His last prophecy, before he disappeared, I'm sure it's about you four, but I'm not quite sure beyond that."

"What does this prophecy say?" Cassie asked warily.

Ganieda hesitated, pausing her pacing. Just then, Caelwyn entered the room. Her face was grave. "Is Mother alright?" Jenifer asked her anxiously.

"As well as can be expected," Caelwyn replied. "She's awake now. Is your father back yet?"

"Not that I know of," Gwendolyn said. "What were you saying about this prophecy, Ganieda?"

"Umm," Ganieda sounded uncomfortable, glancing over at Caelwyn.

Caelwyn looked at her. "Go on. I was going to tell them myself," she encouraged her.

"Very well." Ganieda took a breath. "Father said that two boys and two girls would appear to help the kingdom in its weakest hour and make sure its legacy survives."

"Hmm. That's good, I guess," Cassie pondered. "Although... there's probably more to it than just that, since..." It sounded like she was unaware she was speaking aloud.

Sarah looked at her. "Don't tell me you know what it means," she exclaimed.

"Hmm?" Cassie looked at her. "Oh, sorry, did I say that out loud?"

"Do you have an idea?" William asked.

"Sarah just told me not to tell you if I knew."

"She does," the Thompson twins said together.

"Okay, so I have part of an idea," Cassie said. "But I don't have all of an idea. I need to think more."

"But what's the start of your idea?" Jenifer asked. "How can you only have part of an idea?"

"Well," Cassie said, "'legacy' can mean a couple of different things. It can refer to an inheritance, to a bloodline or ancestry, or, in historical terms, it can mean the big-picture significance of something, like the overall significance of the Roman empire or something like that, which by the way was pretty darn huge."

"And which meaning do you believe this prophecy refers to?"

"All of them, most likely." Cassie could tell Jenifer was settling into a questioning mode, so she switched the subject. "But the big question at the moment is, what happens now?" She looked at Caelwyn.

Caelwyn sighed. "That is indeed the question. This... event was completely unexpected. There were no real hints or warnings of rebellion. Magic, yes, but not treachery. We need to discover where and when Mordred plans to strike next." She looked around at them all. "This information is not to leave this room. Though we heard no whisper of Mordred's plans, he appears to have turned many of the knights to his cause, how or why I know not, but it is likely that witchcraft was involved. Instead of slowly escalating, this rebellion has seemingly exploded out of thin air."

Gwendolyn paled. "The knights? Are you sure?"

"Yes," Caelwyn said grimly. "I have tried to See what is to come to the best of my ability, but the future... it is murky. I do know that war is coming, and soon." Sarah wondered what that meant, but knew from stories that Caelwyn did have a prophetic ability.

Gwendolyn took a breath. "Then we must learn more. Father always says that wars are won or lost based on knowledge."

"Quite right," Caelwyn agreed. "The next logical step would be to send out spies to learn Mordred's plans, perhaps infiltrate his ranks. But we do not know where he is headquartered in the north, exactly, and whoever goes must be on guard against magic."

"Wouldn't Brenwyds make the most sense?" Jenifer put in.

"Yes, but Mordred would recognize one in a heartbeat. It must be someone else." Caelwyn turned to the window. "Siarl has already sent out Brenwyd riders to alert other communities, but we cannot make any definite moves until Arthur returns. Mordred was canny in aiming his first blow to destroy Arthur's morale."

"But... but Father should go fight him for Mother," Jenifer cried. "Mordred's just made him mad."

"Yes, but that in itself is a danger, Jenifer," Caelwyn answered, frowning. "If you fight and react out of anger, mistakes can be made – bad choices that could have been avoided had you waited for your head to clear. The balance between anger and calm in this sort of situation is most important for a king, since the choices he makes, good or bad, can affect so many."

"Send us," Cassie said suddenly. While Caelwyn had been talking, she, William, Sarah, and David had been having a quiet conversation in English.

The others turned to look at them. "Send you where?" Caelwyn asked, brows furrowed.

Telyn frowned too. "You wish to go north? But you have never been there, and Cassie–"

"No, we have been there," William said. "I was raised in Mordred's castle up north. Yes, it's different in this time, but I know my way around, and so do they." He nodded toward Cassie and the twins. "There's an underground tunnel system we can use to get in, which I know exists already. I doubt Mordred would be looking for intruders so soon after last night."

Caelwyn appraised them. "Those things do not dismiss the dangers. And infiltrating his dwelling is very, very risky."

"But we could do it," Cassie said. "You said yourself that we need information, and the best way to get it is to go into the dragon's den, so to speak."

"Hmm." Caelwyn thought for a moment. "I will consider it. And I will propose it to Arthur."

⁘⁘⁘

Cassie stared at the castle standing clearly against the night sky. "Wow. It doesn't change much," she observed.

David looked at her. "What do you mean? It's way smaller." That was true. Instead of resembling a Norman-designed castle, it had more Roman lines and looked more like a mansion or villa, but was still imposing and made completely of stone.

"True," Cassie agreed. "But it wouldn't take much to adapt it to a classic medieval castle design. See, this building here is clearly the front of the castle as it is in our time. All Mordred would need to do is add wings to enclose a central courtyard, and add a couple more towers. He's already got one on the far side." She examined the building critically. "I highly suspect he took the stone from Hadrian's Wall. It's not far from here. In fact, that tower looks almost exactly like one of the milecastles on the Wall."

"Well, let's hope that the tunnels lead to the same places, or we're sunk," William said. The plan was to sneak into the castle and find anything they could about Mordred's next move and/or the missing Brenwyds. Then they were to sneak out without getting caught, hopefully. Caelwyn had been reluctant to let them go, but they had convinced her that they stood the best chance of anyone. William had made a special trip north to see if the castle, and more importantly the tunnels, existed in this century, and had come back to report its current design and confirm that the tunnels were, indeed, there. He'd drawn out a map, recognizing as well as Cassie that the main layout was still basically the same, and the others had memorized it. The plan had been presented to Arthur, who approved, but was curious as to how they knew so much. However, he was busy assembling the army, because reports had reached him that Mordred and Lancelot were raising an army to attack Camelot, and therefore he didn't question the teens too closely. Reports had also come in confirming that other knights and even a few sub-kings had decided to cast their lots in with Mordred, and Arthur's spies were busy figuring out who had turned and who remained loyal.

Brenwyd scouts traveled throughout the kingdom to gather whatever information they could on Mordred's influence and his movements. Brenwyds and their horses made a very effective intelligence force, which was what made it possible to accomplish so much so quickly. It had been two days since the feast, and while Arthur and his loyal knights knew the real story about Lancelot and Guinevere, the false one was circulating widely, and Arthur was being pressured by some of his kings to execute Guinevere for adultery. Caelwyn speculated that Mordred had planted Brotherhood members in key towns and cities to spread the tale as quickly as possible and increase the pressure on Arthur, which would distract him from the approaching war.

Before the teens left, Cassie had told Caelwyn to present the plan about the time slip to Guinevere, because she knew the time was drawing close. More importantly, she had figured out why it was absolutely necessary that Guinevere go to the future.

"How do you feel, William?" Sarah whispered as they cautiously made their way to the entrance they would use. William's tiredness had started becoming more apparent in the last two days, which they'd spent in Arthur's hall, though he insisted he was fit enough for the mission.

"Fine. I'll tell you if I get too tired," he said. The others all met each others' eyes and silently agreed to keep a close eye on him. William would never admit something like that on such an important mission. It worried Cassie, but she knew she couldn't do anything about it just yet. They arrived at the entrance and all but Sarah dismounted. They'd agreed someone should stay behind in case something went wrong, and Sarah had volunteered. Her preferred weapon, the bow, worked best in open spaces, and she knew the others had to go. William knew the layout, Cassie could sense people coming, and David was far less squeamish than Sarah, though her squeamishness had lessened in the last two and a half months. She watched them disappear into the passage, then backed into the trees to hide. She bowed her head in prayer, asking God to give them all protection.

Cassie led the way in the tunnels, with William giving directions when needed. She could see in the dark just fine, and they didn't want to risk a light. The tunnels had been practically unused for centuries the last time they'd been down here, but there was no telling if that was true or not in this time. The tunnels looked like they were much better maintained in this century, indicating use, but they saw and heard no one. Cassie paused as they reached the exit door, extending her song-sense to see if anyone was around, but sensed nothing. "I think we're good," she whispered. The boys nodded.

"Everyone remembers their assignment?" William asked. The other two nodded. Because he knew his way around better, William had volunteered to creep around alone looking for any Brenwyd prisoners, while Cassie and David would go to the library – or what they hoped was the library – to look for anything that might give them a clue as to Mordred's immediate plans for the future. William opened the door and all three exited cautiously. No one else was in sight.

They separated, knowing they had exactly two hours to meet back at the rendezvous point. Cassie and David walked softly around the corridors, relying on the map William had drawn. They did not speak, and Cassie kept her radar up constantly to locate anyone who might be about the castle at this time of night. They met no one, but the atmosphere of the castle gave Cassie the creeps. It felt stifling and hard to breathe in, and she had the uncanny feeling of being watched. She recognized the sensation, having felt it when she'd been here before: evil. She felt relieved when they reached the library. She put a hand on the latch and pressed an ear to the door, listening. Her senses told her no one was inside. She unlatched the door, and they entered.

They knew immediately that they were in the right place. In the middle of the room was a table with pieces of parchment spread out on it and several candles still burning. Various scrolls and leather-bound books adorned the shelves. They examined the pages on the table. They were maps. One showed the whole Isle of Britain. Another, which drew Cassie's attention, was a more detailed map. Studying the lines, she realized it was a drawing of a battle. "David, look." He peered over her shoulder. "Did we just get as lucky as I think we did?" He moved another parchment partially covering the one they were examining, revealing a name. He smiled.

"I do believe we did." The map showed Mordred's battle plans, and the location he intended to use: Camboglanna. Although Cassie knew what it was, she couldn't interpret the map.

"Can you read a battle map?" she asked David.

"I was going to ask you that."

"Oh." She slung her bag from her back, unzipping it to pull out her notebook. "I'll just copy it. I'm sure Caelwyn will know how to read it."

"Don't take too long," David advised. "Those candles mean someone was in here not too long ago, and they probably mean to come back."

"See if you can find anything on the Brenwyds while I'm working." She copied as fast as she could, but was slowed by the unfamiliar symbols. Abruptly she stopped and looked toward the door, dropping a hand to her side where her knife hung. David picked up on her body language and put a hand on his sword hilt, waiting for

Cassie to say who was coming, and if they would enter the library. Somewhat subconsciously, he drifted closer to and slightly in front of Cassie, so anyone bursting into the room suddenly would have to deal with him before getting to her. Cassie hastily closed her notebook and grabbed her bag. "Curtains!" she whispered. "It's our only chance. Whoever is coming down that hall is someone I do *not* want to meet."

No sooner had they ensconced themselves in the curtains and the fabric stopped moving than the door opened and two people entered. Cassie peeked out through a slit between the fabric and the wall. One person she immediately recognized as Mordred. The other was a short, red-headed woman who looked to be in her late forties. Listening to them on a deeper level, Cassie trembled. Their songs were beyond discordance and confusion; they represented a full embrace of evil. The shield-like melody Mordred had had around himself in the garden was gone.

"You have done well," the woman was saying. "The whole kingdom is in confusion and Arthur is having a hard time rallying his kings. You must force him to battle before he can gather his full strength. Once Arthur is dead, the rest of the kingdom will fall to us easily. No one will dare to stand against us when they know of our power, and they cannot deny your claim to the throne."

"I am collecting our forces as quickly as I can. I do have some incentive in mind that would help immensely to drive Arthur swiftly into battle," Mordred said.

"Oh? What?"

"His wife and daughters."

"A good notion," the woman said. "But that venture will be difficult. Camelot is well guarded."

"I can get around that issue. Don't worry."

"And what of Lancelot? Can he be trusted?"

"I'm sure of it. I explained things to him and he proved most understanding."

No sooner had they ensconced themselves in the curtains than two people entered. One she immediately recognized as Mordred. The other was a short, red-headed woman.

"Excellent. We cannot fail."

"Perhaps." Mordred didn't sound too sure, piquing Cassie's interest. Was Mordred having doubts?

"Don't tell me the old man is getting to you with his mutterings," the woman said scornfully.

"Of course not!" Mordred snapped. "But I would be a fool to ignore them, and you yourself have foretold my death." He glared at the woman with a mix of bitterness and fear.

"But we have now made sure that cannot happen," the woman said silkily. "There is no reason for you to worry." She was standing close to him and put a hand on one side of his face.

"We prevented sons by Guinevere, but what if Arthur sired a brat on another woman?" Mordred said, countenance dark.

"Preposterous. It would go completely against his beliefs."

"Then explain to me why a boy almost the very image of Arthur has appeared in Camelot. I saw him at the feast."

The woman sighed. "Is it really important? The Romans spread their seed far and wide during their empire," she said, turning away from him, her voice indicating disinterest.

"Normally I would pay no attention, but... I felt like I was looking at my death." Cassie and David held their breaths. They knew who he was talking about.

"Hmm. That could be of concern. Those feelings don't lie," the woman said. There was a short pause before she spoke again. When she did, her voice was matter-of-fact. "The solution is simple. Kill him. Better to kill him and be safe than let him live as a potential threat."

"He's staying with Caelwyn. He's one of her wards."

"Oh, he's that one, is he? I, too, have heard the rumors. That does complicate things." The woman was silent as she appeared to be thinking. Cassie hardly dared to breathe, though she would have found it hard enough to do so in the presence of such evil anyway. "You shall have to kill that Brenwyd witch, too."

"I would like nothing better. With Merlin out of the way, she remains the main obstacle to conquering Arthur. He relies on her greatly. If not for her, he would have pursued Lancelot immediately and would have fallen into our trap and already be dead. But how is such a thing to be done?"

"Caelwyn guards an object," the woman said slowly, tapping a fingernail on the table. "An object I would dearly like to possess. You know of what I speak."

"Yes."

"I have Seen that she will try to hide it, not long from now. When she does, it will be at night, with no one else. You must watch her, and close in at the appropriate time. It cannot slip from our grasp again."

"I understand. I will set a watch on her immediately."

"Good." A pause. "You went and saw the old man. What did he say?"

"Nothing of import."

"Mordred. Don't lie to me." Cassie thought the woman must be either his mother or his lover.

Mordred sighed. "Only a meaningless rambling. He said to 'fear the son newly conceived but already grown.'" Cassie stifled a gasp. Who was the old man who had spoken these words?

"What?" the woman asked, sounding startled.

"I told you, it is meaningless."

"Nothing that man says is meaningless. In vain, yes, but not meaningless. Did you question him as to the meaning?"

"Of course not, Mother. I stopped paying attention to him long ago. I'm surprised you still want him alive." So the woman was his mother. Clearly, she was no longer in exile on a bunch of isolated islands. But that meant the woman must be...

"He knows our Enemy, and he has helped me make guesses about how to move next. This boy you mentioned. I have heard there are others with him?"

"Yes, three. Another boy and two girls. One of the girls is a Brenwyd. They are from Armorica."

"Hmm... Four, two boys and two girls. I have Seen such a group, and they could prove most dangerous to our goals. Kill them, too. We can't risk any mistakes at this point," the woman said in an emotionless tone.

Cassie couldn't believe the woman sounded so calm about ordering people killed. Then she fully realized that it was their own deaths she had just ordered, and the world seemed to tilt. *Seriously not good*, she thought.

There was the sound of crackling parchment. "Very well. I must go meet with my Commander. There is much to be done," Mordred said.

"Yes," the woman said. "But the prize is all worth it." She spoke in a gloating, satisfied tone. The two left.

Cassie waited until she could no longer hear their songs before signaling to David that it was alright to emerge from the curtains. "I'm thinking your theory from the feast is right, Cass," he said, his eyes wide.

"Me too. Now we just have to convince him."

"Do you think she knows Merlin's prophecy about us?" David asked.

"It sounded like it. I wonder who their prisoner is." Cassie looked into David's eyes. "You do realize she just issued death warrants for us?"

He nodded, worried, looking paler than usual. "And Caelwyn's. This is not sounding good at all."

"I know." Cassie looked at the table. "They took the map!"

"You got most of it."

"But not all of it," she sighed. "I don't think it will change anything in the long run, but I get the feeling I missed something important." As she spoke, David went to a shelf and moved a couple of scrolls. "What are you doing?"

"I glimpsed something that looked interesting right before... here it is." He took a thick, hide-bound book from the shelf.

"What is it?"

He handed it to her. "See for yourself." She opened the cover and read the elegant script written on the parchment. Goose bumps appeared on her arms and her shakes returned as she read: *The Diary of Morgan le Fay.*

"Oh, my," she whispered. She flipped it open carefully. "This... could be useful. Though why a person would leave a personal journal in a library is beyond me."

"That's what I thought." He looked at her with concern. "Are you okay?"

"Yeah... it's just, Morgan le Fay? The most infamous witch in Arthurian lore? David, she has to be Mordred's mother. And she just ordered Mordred to kill us," Cassie repeated. "How on earth did we become so important?"

David shook his head slowly, the full reality of that statement sinking in. The past couple of months had alternately seemed like either a very realistic dream or a vacation to him. Those illusions vanished at the thought that an ancient witch wanted him dead. He looked down at Cassie. She looked scared, but at the same time grimly resolved. He couldn't help thinking that while she had looked lovely in the dress at the feast, this Cassie – fully armed in a tunic and breeches – was more natural, and for some reason, much less intimidating. He took a breath. "Well, I'm not exactly sure on that one, Cass, but I do think that leaving now would be a very good idea."

William pressed himself against the wall. He was entering the dungeon level, and there were people here, unlike in the other low areas of the building. It indicated that there were prisoners being kept in the cells. He would have to be careful. He slipped through the door, avoiding two guards doing their rounds. The dim light helped him, and he'd borrowed a dark cloak from Caelwyn, knowing it would help him blend into the shadows further.

All seemed quiet for now. Very cautiously, he opened the door, his sword partway out of its sheath. He looked through. No guards were to be seen, but he heard low moans and a few whimpers. *Mordred must be very confident that his prisoners can't escape,* William thought. He stopped dead as he realized why. *Devil's iron!* He'd seen what it had done to Cassie. She still bore scars from her brief encounter with it. He didn't even want to think about the effect it would have on full-blooded Brenwyds. He stopped outside the first door and peered in its window cautiously. A man knelt praying beside a bed. William frowned. The man didn't have pointed ears. If he wasn't a Brenwyd, what was he doing here?

William started when the man spoke. "So, you came. I wondered when you would." He stood and turned, and William studied him curiously. He had dark gray hair and warm brown eyes, but they held a weary look, as if tired of the world. At first glance William thought he must be in his late sixties, maybe even early seventies, but then realized that it was only the deep lines and wrinkles etched in his face that made him seem so. He was probably more like mid-fifties. He smiled kindly. "How do you like the sixth century?"

"Uh, fine." William wondered how the man knew he wasn't from this century. "Who are you?"

"I am called Merlin."

William stared. "You're Merlin?! But you disappeared a year ago!" As soon as he said it, he realized how dumb that sounded. It was obvious how Merlin had "disappeared."

"Yes, and now you know why. But we can't waste time with idle chatter. You are on a stricter timeline than you know, William Douglas."

"How do you know my name?"

"God told me of your coming, with your friends. I have watched you over the past months."

"Oh. Oookay."

Merlin chuckled at his guarded tone. "You should be more used to the knowledge God deigns to give certain of His followers, especially having lived with Caelwyn for the past two months. It will prove vital if you are to succeed."

"Succeed in what?"

"Shh, not so loud. We don't want the guards to overhear us. And I think you know what I mean."

William nodded slowly. "I think I do. The prophecy Ganieda mentioned."

"Yes. Now, about this coming battle. I do not know if you can change what you know as the outcome, or even if you would want to. I do not know what will happen, but I have Seen that Mordred will survive. You can set the stage to bring him and the one he worships down in the years to come. In fact, you must – if you yourself are to survive."

"What do you mean?" William asked warily. It sounded like Merlin was suggesting William had a good chance of dying in the near future. He didn't like that thought.

Merlin looked at him compassionately. "You have been feeling weaker than normal as of late, have you not?"

"Umm... yes." William wondered just how much this man knew about him. It was creepy.

"The reason is one you must realize and accept soon. It is not for me to tell you what it is, but your friend Cassie knows."

"She does?"

"Yes, and deep down you know it as well. You have tried to deny it these past months, but taking a firm grip of it is necessary if you are to throw Mordred and his organization down."

William stayed quiet, thinking, but deciding not to dwell on Merlin's cryptic remarks for now. He could worry about them later. He had a more pressing concern. "What do we do to succeed? I know that Mordred wields great power. I've seen the effects. How can even Cassie destroy it? We're not strong enough to beat him," he said at last, voicing the doubt that had long been on his mind. He felt surprised to be admitting this to Merlin, especially since he'd just met him, but he knew the man could be trusted. He was also probably the best person to ask about such a thing, according to the legends.

"It is because you know that that you are not strong enough to beat him that you stand a chance of succeeding. When you admit your own weakness and give yourself to God, He more than makes up for what you lack. Mordred is strong, yes, but he cannot stand against the living God. You have been pulled from darkness, William, and now you must make a stand against it. The Brenwyds are vital to our world. They fight actively against our enemy to keep the darkness at bay. Mordred knows this, and he thinks he cannot grasp all the dark power that he wants until the last Brenwyd is killed. That is why he has made it his mission to hunt them down. But there is a deeper truth that Mordred does not realize, or discounts as false if he does. God blessed the Brenwyds because they stayed loyal when almost no one else on this Earth did. But now many believe and turn to Him because of Jesus' sacrifice. They also have the power to keep the darkness at bay. What Mordred doesn't realize is that even if he kills every last person with Brenwyd blood, he still cannot grasp what he seeks as long as there is a Christian in the world, no matter how weak they may be. God is made perfect in our weakness, and He uses the weak to bring down the strong. Do you understand what I am telling you?" William nodded slowly, turning the information over in his mind.

"But then what's the difference between Brenwyds and Christians, if they can do the same things? I mean, besides the obvious," he asked.

"The difference is that Brenwyds have a greater connection to the unseen, are more aware of the influence it holds on the earth.

They can bring the demons down with song, and call out the better side of people the same way. They heal what evil has made wrong. As I told Caelwyn once, they are a bit like Earth's guardians against evil. The world can survive without them, but it would be a darker world, harder for Christians to live in." His tone became brisk. "Now, tell Caelwyn what is going on. It is indeed Mordred behind the Brenwyd disappearances, but he's not by himself. His mother is helping him."

"His mother? Isn't she supposed to be in exile?"

"Yes, but Mordred brought her back down secretly several months ago. Her name is Morgan le Fay. Watch your step around her, lad. She's a powerful witch, and supports her son in everything. She motivates him in all that he has done and will do. She's even more dangerous than he is."

Well, that's just great, William thought. Suddenly he caught the sound of footsteps.

Merlin apparently heard them as well. "You must go now, before the guard comes. If you're caught, we are all doomed." That sounded melodramatic to William, but Merlin sounded completely serious about it, and he decided to take him at his word.

"But what about the Brenwyds?"

"Mordred isn't planning on harming them until after his imagined victory. He wants to capture as many of the strong ones as he can, to show them that resistance is futile, and then execute them himself in a big exhibition. You still have time to deal with it." The footsteps grew louder. "Go! Remember what I said. But William, don't tell anyone we have talked. At most, you may tell your friends and Caelwyn, but only if necessary. Arthur must face this test alone, and it is better that the others not know yet."

"What about Ganieda?"

"She will understand. Now go." William quickly slipped back through the door he'd entered by, latching it behind him. He looked at his watch. Ten minutes to get to the rendezvous point.

He made his way as quickly as he could back through the castle, slipping in and out of shadows. At one point, he nearly bumped into a party of several men and a red-haired woman, but hid down a hallway in a doorway just in time.

The woman stopped and looked around, perhaps sensing someone was there. William hardly dared to breathe. She wasn't very tall, barely reaching five feet, but she exuded an intimidating atmosphere that seemed to give her another two feet in height. "What is it, my lady?" one of the men asked.

"I thought I heard something," the woman said. William prayed they would move off soon. If they decided to investigate the hallway, he was toast. "Must have been a mouse," she said at last. "Come." William waited a good five minutes after they'd left before daring to creep from his hiding place. That lady scared him. He wondered if she was Morgan le Fay.

He hurried on, arriving at the door exactly as his watch said two hours had passed. Cassie and David were already there, and they looked very much relieved to see him. "Cutting it close there," David said.

"I arrived exactly on time, for your information. I would have been here sooner, but some creepy lady and her entourage almost ran into me," he explained.

Cassie and David exchanged glances. "Did she have red hair?" Cassie asked.

"Yes. Did you meet her?"

"Sort of." She looked at him very strangely. "We have a lot of talking to do."

"That we have," he agreed, wondering about what Merlin had said, that Cassie knew some secret about him. "But let's do it in friendly territory." He opened the door, and they descended into darkness.

Sarah was starting to feel antsy. Not that she hadn't been so since the others left, but it had been over two hours and they still weren't back. How long did it take to go through the tunnels? Dreamer nudged her. *Do not worry. They can handle themselves.*

"I know, but I think I got the hardest job. Waiting without any clue of what's going on in there."

I sense Cassie, Twi said. *They will be here soon. They are fine.*

Sarah let out a sigh of relief. "Oh, thank God," she breathed. She started going about tightening girths and replacing bridles, but just as she finished with Fire, the last, all the horses tensed.

Quiet, Twi said. *Someone is there. Girl, stay in the tunnels for a few minutes. We have unwelcome company.* Sarah guessed the second warning was aimed at Cassie. Quietly, she picked up her bow from her saddle pommel and put an arrow on the string. She listened, and presently heard slight sounds of someone walking in the woods. Two someones.

"I'm telling you, I saw something," a man's voice said. Sarah and the horses stayed stone still. More rustling.

"Bah, there's nothing here. Who would be out here at this time of night?" another man said.

"Mischief makers. Maybe some Brenwyd has caught wind of what the Master's doing," the first said.

"So what? The rumors have been circulating the kingdom for months. If someone wanted to do something about it, it would have been done already. You're seeing things. Let's go back. It's going to rain." As he spoke the words, rain started to fall lightly. "See? We won't find anything once it opens up. Let's go before we get too wet. So what if it's a Brenwyd? None of those unnatural people will be around for much longer after our victory." They departed, making a great deal of noise as they went. Sarah was not impressed with their forestry skills. A deaf old woman would have been able to hear them coming. *A distraction, maybe?*

"Twi, tell Cassie and the others to hurry up. I want to get home.

Those men aren't the only ones who dislike getting soaked." Twi relayed her request and the others appeared within a few minutes. "How'd it go?" Sarah asked.

"Well enough," her brother replied, but he looked grim. "We found out a lot of stuff. Let's get back to Camelot. We'll talk there." They mounted and rode off quickly. The rain turned from a light sprinkle to a steady stream. Once they reached an open space beyond the trees, they urged their horses into a gallop as the weather continued to deteriorate. Just as it became a full-out downpour, they vanished.

Gathering the Pieces

Fortunately, it was not raining at Camelot. They came out in the field surrounding the city and slowed their horses to a walk. "Glad to be out of there," Cassie said with a slight shudder.

"Agreed," William said.

Cassie thought he looked troubled. "Are you feeling alright?" she asked.

"I'm *fine*, Cassie. Don't worry so much," he said in a somewhat heated tone. Cassie wasn't so sure, but she knew now was not the time to push it.

"So what did y'all find?" Sarah asked.

"Cassie and I found a battle map, and a book that could prove pretty interesting," David answered.

"A map for Camlann?" William asked.

"Yeah, but it actually happens at Camboglanna. That's what the map said, anyway," David corrected.

"And the book?" Sarah queried. "Did you take it?"

"It's in my bag," Cassie said. She couldn't wait to get the thing *out* of her bag. It made her skin crawl. She knew it would probably be useful, but after feeling the evil of its author, she wasn't too keen on reading it. She wondered if she was overreacting, but she'd felt a little on edge since Caelwyn had revealed the deeper role Brenwyds played in the world. The idea made her feel a little daunted. If she was supposed to defeat Mordred, she'd have to learn how to battle witchcraft and wizardry. Could she learn what she needed in time? Would she be strong enough to defeat him?

"What's in it?" Sarah asked.

"Apparently," David said, "it's the diary of Morgan le Fay."

"Morgan le Fay?" Sarah exclaimed. William looked over at David in alarm.

"Yes, and she's Mordred's mother," Cassie said.

Sarah frowned. "Really?" she asked.

"Yeah. She and Mordred almost caught us in the library," Cassie said. "By the way, she gave Mordred permission to kill us."

"What?!" William and Sarah said, halting their horses to look at the other two.

"Why on earth?" Sarah asked. "What have we ever done to her?"

"It's not what we *have* done," David said. "It's something she thinks we're *going* to do. And don't ask me what that something is, but apparently she thinks it will mess up her plans." He glanced over at Cassie, wondering if he should mention the other reason. Cassie had a good idea of what he was thinking, and shook her head slightly.

"Well, that might not be too far off, according to Merlin's prophecy," William said. "She's helping Mordred develop a plan to take over the kingdom."

"We gathered that, but how do you know that?" Cassie asked, curious. They were almost to the gates.

William hesitated. "I'll tell you later. I don't want anyone to overhear. I promised my source I wouldn't go noising his name around just yet." Cassie looked straight into William's eyes. He thought she might already have an idea of who he'd met. They stopped talking. The guards at the gate let them in, having been told by the king to expect them. They rode silently through Camelot, with only the sound of their horses' hooves hitting the cobblestone path.

Glewlwyd was waiting for them at the gate to the hall compound. He'd been expecting them. "You're to go to the hall leading to the king's private quarters," he told them. "The mission went well?"

"It did," Cassie replied. They cared for their horses hurriedly, anxious to report their findings.

Kai and Dassah entered the stable just as they were ready to leave. *You are back, you are alright,* Dassah said, sounding relieved.

Cassie stroked her head. "Of course we are. Mordred never even knew we were there."

It is good you are back. Your father will want your account of what happens in the big house tonight.

"Oh? What's going to happen?"

You will see, Dassah said mysteriously. *Come.*

Did you find what you were looking for? Kai asked as they walked toward the castle.

"Yes." Cassie told him what they'd found.

He bristled at the mention of Morgan's book. *Get rid of that soon, girl. No telling what evil it is tainted with.*

"I don't want to keep it, believe me," Cassie assured him. In the castle, all was quiet. At least, all was quiet in the main areas of the castle. As they approached the family quarters, Cassie heard sounds of activity. Curious, she quickened her pace until she was several yards ahead of the others. She rounded a sharp corner and nearly ran into Jenifer, who was carrying a chest that looked far too heavy for the small ten-year-old to be lifting.

"Oh!" the girl exclaimed, losing her grip on the chest. Cassie grabbed it before it hit the floor and grunted at the weight. "You're back. Did it go well? Where are the others? Why are you wet? What's Mordred–"

"Whoa!" Cassie interjected. "One question at a time, please. Yes, they're behind me, and it was raining in the north. What on earth is in here? Bricks?"

"I'm not sure actually. We're moving lots of things to the chamber to keep them hidden from Mordred in case he attacks here." By this time the others had rounded the corner. Jenifer released a breath that sounded like a sigh of relief upon seeing them. "Good, you're all okay."

"Where are your father and Caelwyn?" William asked. "We need to speak with them."

"They are down in the chamber," a voice said. It belonged to a man about Arthur's age who was coming down the corridor. He was also carrying a chest, but was doing so with much less strain than Jenifer. "You're Caelwyn's wards, I assume?"

"Yes," Cassie said. She noticed how his eyes rested on William and saw the surprise that entered them as he studied him. William gave no indication of noticing. Maybe he'd gotten used to it.

"My name is Gawain. A pleasure to meet you."

Cassie would have started had she not been holding the chest. *I really need to get used to meeting legendary people in this century,* she told herself. "Likewise, sir," she said.

"Follow me," the knight said. "Arthur wanted to meet with you as soon as you returned, and four extra pairs of hands would be very welcome."

"What is going on, exactly, sir?" David asked. He offered to take the chest from Cassie, but she shook her head.

"We are securing the kingdom's treasure so Mordred can't get his dirty hands on it," Gawain answered.

"Where?" Cassie asked.

"You'll see," the knight said. He led them down the hall in the direction of Arthur and Guinevere's room, meeting Telyn, Ganieda, and Gwendolyn on the way. Each expressed her relief at seeing the four back from Mordred's castle unharmed. Cassie had a feeling she knew where they were going, and wasn't surprised when she spotted an open door in the wall that hadn't been there the last time she'd walked down this hallway.

"The treasure chamber is underneath Camelot?" Sarah asked, glancing at Cassie.

"Yes," Gawain replied. "There used to be a Brenwyd settlement on this site and they constructed tunnels running all underneath the hill, for an advantage when fighting invaders. It let them get into and out of the village even when under siege. They construct-ed a large chamber to house the settlement's valuables and serve as a refuge during times of war. The settlement is long gone, de-stroyed by the Romans, but the tunnels are still there. It was part of the reason Arthur picked this spot as his southern headquarters. He commissioned some Brenwyd workers to incorporate the tun-nels into the fortress, and to extend them beyond the city walls." They descended a staircase into the darkness, which wasn't totally dark because there were torches at regular intervals. The knight led them through the maze, and Cassie took note of the way he went. She suspected it would be important later.

After about ten minutes, they emerged into a large chamber. Cassie paused to take it in, as did the others. It wasn't spectacu-larly large, but was still plenty big. She saw a lot of chests, weap-ons, armor (such as it was during this period), and some cubby-hole-looking things with scrolls and a few books. It wasn't visually overflowing with gold and jewels as most people pictured when they thought of a treasure chamber, but it was very impressive. She suspected the treasure lay in the numerous, tightly locked chests. "Looks like your dad was spot-on, Cass," David said in English, looking around. "This is a lot of stuff."

She nodded. "Dad's generally right about things," she said.

"Him, too?" William asked. "Is it some sort of family trait?" Cassie chuckled, but didn't reply. She became aware of several more men making their way toward the entrance where they were standing, and moved out of the way. Ganieda, Telyn, and Gwendolyn had already gone past and were setting down what they had carried.

"Caelwyn and the king are over there," Sarah said, spotting them on the other side of the chamber. "Let's go."

Caelwyn looked up as they approached, relief visible on her face. "Well?" she asked, attracting Arthur's attention. He'd been helping Guinevere move a large chest into a better position.

"We found out something about his plans, alright," Cassie said. "Is there any place in particular I should set this down?" She was still carrying the chest she'd taken from Jenifer. She inclined her head respectfully to the king and queen, but suspected that if she bowed, the weight of the chest would cause her to fall over.

"I'll take it," Arthur said. "Being drafted into the work force already, are you?" He smiled at her, but she could see the tiredness and worry in his eyes.

"Jenifer was carrying it and I almost ran her down. I thought I might as well take it," Cassie answered.

"She shouldn't have been lifting something so heavy," Guinevere remarked, walking around the chest to join her husband. Cassie noticed out of the corner of her eye that William seemed to stagger for a brief moment, but recovered quickly, though he still looked paler than he had a few moments earlier.

"What is all this stuff, Sire?" Sarah asked shyly. She was in awe of Arthur, and wasn't quite sure the proper way to address a king. She'd noticed Arthur was pretty relaxed about formality in private settings, but wasn't sure about just how casual it was.

"The treasure of the kingdom. Gold, plunder from barbarian invaders, and tithes. The church needs a safe place to keep all their offerings, so I offered this place. Very few people know about it, and you all must not tell anyone. Understood?" he said sternly.

"Yes, Sire," they responded. He turned, beckoning to them.

"Come; I want to hear what you discovered. Did he know you were there?"

"No, Sire," William answered.

"Good." They withdrew to a smaller chamber off the bigger one. Caelwyn and Guinevere followed and listened as the teens related what they had learned. William abstained from mentioning his meeting with Merlin, saying merely that he'd talked to a man who was imprisoned, and Cassie and David hid some of the particulars of the conversation they'd overheard between Mordred and Morgan. The adults listened attentively, worry growing on their faces. As they finished, Cassie produced the book and the partial copy she'd made of the map from her bag.

Caelwyn took the book, holding it as if it might burn her, and Arthur studied the map. "What is this you used to copy it on?" he asked. "I have never seen the like."

Belatedly, Cassie remembered paper hadn't been invented in this period, hence why the few books and maps she had seen were made with parchment. Oops. "Oh, uh, it's something I brought from home."

He looked at her keenly with his piercing green eyes for a moment, then went back to studying the map. "I'd like to have more of it," he murmured, then continued in a louder voice. "Do you remember anything beyond what you have here?"

"A little." She drew it for him.

"Hmm. Mordred may have shown himself to be a traitor, but he's clever. Very clever." The king was frowning deeply. He tapped the paper. "I must start moving the army immediately if we're to reach Camboglanna before weather starts becoming an issue. I'd rather go up and surprise him than have him force my hand. Also, this plan is contingent on Mordred and his army having the defensive position. If we get there before he realizes we're moving, it will upset his plans very nicely."

"Um, Sire?" David said. "That wasn't all we heard. He *wants* to force your hand. He said, um..." David felt very uncomfortable. Reporting to a king wasn't something school had prepared him for.

"Yes? Did he say how he planned to do it?" Arthur asked, waiting patiently.

"He said he'd try to give you 'some incentive,'" Cassie explained. "He implied he would try to do it by, er, kidnapping the queen and princesses, Sire."

Arthur scowled angrily. "I'm not surprised. It's an effective way to start a war – or force a surrender." He looked at Guinevere. "I want you and the girls to stay in the castle. No riding out for any reason, not until after Mordred is dealt with."

She nodded. "Then you do not wish me to come with you," she said. He sighed and put an arm around her waist, drew her to him, and gazed at her tenderly. He had obviously been completely assured of his wife's fidelity.

"I would like nothing better, but I think you should stay home this time. Especially considering…" He stopped speaking abruptly, looking as if he'd said more than he ought. Guinevere gave him a warning glance, clearly understanding what he alluded to. Cassie wondered what it was.

"Very well. I can stand it. But I must come to the next battle," Guinevere said, smiling back.

"But of course," Arthur assured her, giving her a quick kiss. He looked at Caelwyn, who had remained silent and was paging through Morgan's book. "What do you think?"

She looked up, troubled. "You should take strong Brenwyds with you. If Morgan rides with Mordred, you'll need them. She will uphold him with her foul spells, and they must be dispelled if you are to have a chance of defeating him."

"You are coming, are you not?" he asked. "With Mordred out to kill you, it would be best for you to ride with us." Cassie and David had relayed that piece of information to the king, but had decided to wait and tell Caelwyn alone that the four of them were on Mordred's hit list as well.

Caelwyn hesitated. "Later. I still have some business to attend to, preparations to make. Siarl will go with you." She turned to the teens. "You're sure they didn't know you were there?" They nodded. She still looked worried. "I wish I'd known Morgan le Fay would be there. All the reports said she was still in exile... but that's that. I'm sure you all are tired. You should go rest." She frowned at William. "You, in particular, appear weary."

"I'm fine. Really. Do you need any help moving things?" William asked. He was getting irritated by people asking how he felt and commenting on his appearance. Truthfully, he did feel tired, and he also felt a little dizzy, a feeling that had begun since coming over to report to Caelwyn, Arthur, and Guinevere. But he was fit enough to move a few things before going to bed, and he didn't appreciate being treated, to his mind, like an invalid.

"Extra hands would be welcome," Arthur said. "Many things were down here already, but I'd prefer to bring the rest down as well. Some of it could prove very interesting to Mordred." He paused. "Merely follow the others around, and tell no one yet what you have just told us. It must stay secret for now." They nodded.

Cassie looked around, examining the room they were in more closely. "What's this room used for?" she asked.

"It's a crypt. Several Brenwyd leaders are buried here," Caelwyn answered. The group exited the crypt, and the teens were quickly integrated into the moving process. Besides Arthur's and Caelwyn's families, several knights joined in the effort – Gawain, Tristram, Galahad, Bors, Bedivere, and Kay. They were Arthur's most loyal and trusted knights, and they handled the really heavy stuff. Kai and Dassah also helped as much as they could by dragging chests into position with their jaws and relaying messages via Cassie or Caelwyn as to who needed help with what.

Cassie and David took the opportunity to talk about what they had overheard between Mordred and Morgan. "I'm not quite sure what to make of it," David said, gathering various things as instructed and placing them carefully in a chest. "I mean, if what you think is true *is* true, it makes a little more sense, but it still sounds pretty fantastic."

"David, our whole situation is pretty fantastic, if you hadn't noticed yet," she replied, helping him. "What I want to know is if there's enough evidence for me to tell him and convince him. What do you think?"

"You have enough. You should tell him as soon as possible, even if you didn't have enough. Did you notice how he acted around Guinevere?"

"He staggered a bit when she first came into close proximity, but I didn't really notice anything after that."

"He was pretty pale all throughout that conference, and was breathing a little heavy. But he seems to have rebounded some since we left. I've been watching him."

"So have I. I'll tell him when we get back to Caelwyn's." David hoisted the chest up. "Do you want me to take an end?" Cassie asked.

"Nah, it's okay. It's not that heavy. You know, maybe you should look through that diary to see if you can find the prophecy Mordred was referring to. She might have written it down in there, and it might make things clearer."

"Maybe, but are you sure that would be a good idea? Considering the source, I don't know if I want to just go rifling through the book. And besides, how would we know it was true or not? I doubt she was getting her prophecies from God."

David thought about that for a moment. "Probably not, but isn't it a source of information to use against the enemy? In that light, it wouldn't so much matter if it was true or not. All that would matter would be if Morgan and Mordred think it's true, because then we might be able to use it against them."

"Hmm, good point," Cassie agreed. She opened the door for him. "I feel like I've got all these various puzzle pieces of information floating around in my head. They only seem to fit together one way, and it forms a pretty hard-to-believe picture. But I feel like I'm missing the most important piece, the one that says it is what it is without a doubt."

David chuckled. "Cassie, I've felt like that almost ever since that camping trip. Has not knowing everything stopped us so far?"

"No."

"Then don't worry about it. Only God sees the big picture while we're trying to figure it out. He can do some pretty impossible things, you know. What's that one verse say? 'With man this is impossible, but with God all things are possible,' or something like that?"

"Yeah, I know. God practically shouted that one in my face when we were at Gwen's."

"Then why don't you start believing it?" He stopped and looked down into her eyes. He used to be only a little taller than her, but now he stood nearly a full head above her. Cassie wasn't quite sure if she liked it or not. "Not everything has to be backed up by hard fact, historical or otherwise. Think about what we've been through."

"I know, I know. I just keep having these really annoying reality checks. William is also a very factual kind of person, if you haven't noticed."

"Yes, but I think you have enough evidence to convince him. Not to mention that time travel has probably adjusted his mindset." He smiled. "As long as you tell him before we go back home in time, I won't bug you about it."

She smiled wryly, looking up into his eyes. "You can rest assured of *that*. And I've got to check the time slip. We can't afford to mess this up."

"No, we can't," he said, serious. It struck Cassie just then how much David had matured and grown in the last two and a half months, and not just in height. He had really developed into a warrior, looked at things more spiritually, and didn't act silly as much, though he still joked around often enough. She decided she definitely liked that change. "What is it?" His voice intruded on her thoughts.

She realized she was still looking up at him, a small smile on her face. She flushed and hoped he didn't notice. "Oh, nothing. You've gotten too tall."

He laughed at her statement, glad for the chance to pass the look off. He had been thinking it was entirely possible to get lost in Cassie's twain-colored eyes. The blue and gray swirled together and led you further into them. "Yeah, I really have to look down for you now. Look at eye level and I might miss you."

She swatted him playfully. "Hey, I'm not *that* short." They headed down the hallway. They were just getting ready to round the last corner on their way to the door when Dassah's frantic thoughts reached Cassie.

Hurry, girl. He has fallen. I do not know how. Come! The Border collie was almost yelling in panic.

Who? Cassie queried.

William. He was helping Gwendolyn set a chest down when he collapsed suddenly. We do not know why. Hurry!

Cassie grabbed David's arm. "Drop the chest. We'll get it later. William's collapsed."

Sarah felt bewildered and extremely worried. Everything had been running smoothly, and they were nearly done, just waiting for Cassie, David, Tristram, and Gwendolyn to come back from wherever they were. William had been going back up to see if they needed help when Gwendolyn entered, carrying a large chest she obviously couldn't wait to put down. Sarah had noticed William's energy level flagging, and he'd taken several rests in between trips, but she'd kept him from lifting the really heavy objects, and had been comforted by the knowledge that they would all soon head off to bed. Everyone else was feeling tired as well, so Sarah had chalked up William's lethargy to the mission they'd just gotten back from. Guinevere came over to ask her daughter a question just as Gwendolyn and William were setting down the chest, and William just collapsed. Kai had been standing close behind him (Sarah suspected the dog had been shadowing him per Cassie's orders) and broke his fall so he didn't injure himself, but he was still out cold.

Caelwyn took Guinevere aside and had a conversation with her that Sarah couldn't hear. Guinevere then left, and Sarah assumed it was to get water or something. Caelwyn examined William and seemed perplexed, as they all were. He wasn't injured, and where he'd been standing was level ground. There was no reason for him to have fallen and certainly no reason for him to have passed out.

"I don't sense anything wrong with him physically. He shouldn't have fainted," Caelwyn said. "He seemed pale earlier, but he said he was fine."

"Perhaps he was more tired than he let on after the mission," Kay suggested. Sarah noticed how all the knights had been sneaking sideways glances at William, and now she thought they were too obviously trying not to stare, especially as Arthur crouched near Caelwyn with a concerned expression.

"Did he seem particularly tired after you got back?" the king asked Sarah.

She shrugged. "He was tired, but I think it's safe to say we all were, so I didn't think much of it, Sire. I have no idea why he would fall."

Sarah heard rapid footsteps and looked up with relief to see Cassie and David enter the room. "What happened?" Cassie demanded, frowning.

"He just collapsed," Gwendolyn said. "He was helping me set down the chest, and as it touched the ground he went down." She sounded very distressed, as if she considered it her fault.

Cassie knelt on the ground next to William with David behind her. Dassah and Kai came to either side of her, and Sarah guessed they were giving her a visual of what had happened. Her frown deepened. "The idiot," she muttered. "Why didn't he tell us he was feeling that bad? And why didn't we keep a closer eye on him?" She said this in English, so the king, knights, Gwendolyn, and Jenifer all looked confused. Caelwyn, Telyn, and Ganieda had picked up a pretty good understanding of English while Cassie, David, and Sarah were learning Brythonic, and caught what she said.

"You can't blame yourself," Telyn said in Brythonic. "He should have mentioned it."

"No excuse," Cassie said. She looked really worried.

"Cassie, is there something else going on?" Sarah asked in English. "Do you think he could have had another, uh, attack like he had in the stable two weeks ago?"

"Maybe. I guess I've waited too long," Cassie answered.

Sarah frowned. *Waited too long for what?*

"No, you haven't," David said. He seemed to be the only one who knew what she was talking about, which Sarah found odd. Generally Cassie shared her ideas with Sarah first. "You waited until you were sure. We still have time."

"Pray it's enough."

"What's this?" Caelwyn asked. She hadn't understood everything perfectly, but had caught the importance of the words.

An uneasiness entered Cassie's eyes and she glanced at the king, who had absolutely no clue what they were talking about. "I'll explain later. Now, too many people." Caelwyn nodded.

"Will he be okay?" Jenifer asked, tired of all this talk in a language she couldn't understand.

"For now," Cassie replied. "He just exhausted himself, that's all. He'll be fine once he sleeps it off." She stood as Guinevere re-entered. Cassie looked at her oddly, a confused expression on her face. She looked between Guinevere and William, and suddenly her eyebrows shot up as she made some sort of connection. Sarah thought she looked pretty shocked, but there was also a triumphant look, like something had just been confirmed. Cassie whispered something to David, and he nodded. Sarah wondered about this new secret Cassie and David seemed to share. She suspected it was important, and thought she should know, as David's twin.

"There is a room ready for him," Guinevere announced. "I don't think you should move him farther than that."

"No," Caelwyn agreed. "Not tonight. We should all go to bed."

"How are we going to get him up to the room?" Sarah asked. "He's heavy."

Everyone was surprised by what happened next. Arthur got closer, slid his arms under the unconscious boy, and stood, bearing him easily. "I'll take him. I know what room Guinevere has prepared." He walked after her. Everyone except Caelwyn looked suitably shocked, but Cassie and David got over their surprise quickly and looked knowingly at each other. *I have got to find out what's with those two,* Sarah thought. Jenifer was the first to follow her parents, and the dogs were the last to leave the chamber. Galahad, the last person, shut the chamber door behind them.

Caelwyn cornered Cassie and David before they went to bed. "You've figured it out, haven't you?" she asked.

"Cassie figured it out, and she told me," David said. Cassie nodded.

"How long have *you* known?" Caelwyn asked her.

"I wouldn't say known, exactly. I've strongly suspected since the day Gwendolyn invited us to her betrothal feast, but I wasn't completely, absolutely, one hundred percent sure until a few minutes ago. That's why I haven't said anything. But now I think he should be told when he wakes up. We can't wait any longer. Time is against us," Cassie said. Caelwyn nodded agreement. "How long have you known?"

Caelwyn smiled as she answered. "Since your first day."

Cassie's jaw dropped, and David gasped. "Why didn't you say anything?" the girl asked.

"Because I knew you had to figure it out for yourselves. Would you have believed me if I'd told you?" They slowly shook their heads. "Also, I thought you'd had enough shocks that day."

David chuckled. "That's for sure." His expression turned more serious. "But why did he collapse like that?"

"Kai said Guinevere had approached right before he collapsed," Cassie said. "Remember?"

"Yeah, but... oh." An odd look crossed his face.

"Oh, indeed," Caelwyn said. She looked at Cassie. "You sensed it, didn't you? I saw your expression."

"Yes," Cassie said. "That's what confirmed it for me. How far along... ?"

"Just enough for her to know. She told me she already suspected before the feast and now she's certain, but it would be a bad time for that news to get out," Caelwyn said.

"And with Mordred after her and Arthur going to war," Cassie added, "she *must* go."

"Yes. I will broach the subject with her, but I think Arthur should know as well. Do you agree?"

"He should know she'll be safe," Cassie said.

Caelwyn nodded. She looked past the two, suddenly feeling weary. Her Sight pushed itself to the forefront of her mind and she started to speak. Cassie and David listened in confusion and some alarm. "I See a darkness stealing over the land like a snake, winding its way around every valley, every hilltop, every village. It has been slowly creeping, slowly advancing, though the light has stopped it from overtaking the land completely. But the light is fading in Britain and the darkness is growing. Is there any hope? Ah, I see there is. A faint light, but growing stronger. It will cast down the darkness and shatter it. A son of kings and daughter of Brenwyds will throw it down. Though that day is far in the future, it will happen. God has spoken. The darkness will not triumph. The light will overcome it." She stopped. Cassie and David looked at each other with wide eyes. Caelwyn's eyes had almost seemed to glow as she spoke, green and gray mixing like the colors of a turbulent sea. She looked at them. "This prophecy is for you. You knew of it before, didn't you?"

"The gist of it, yeah," Cassie said. "It wasn't written that fancy, though."

"How did you know of it?"

"I have your diary," Cassie confessed. "It's been handed down in my family since, well, *now* I guess. I'm, uh, descended from you."

Caelwyn, instead of acting surprised, actually laughed. "Are you? I might have guessed it. You remind me of myself when I was your age. You will do well. But now, I think, we should go to bed. There is much to do." They parted.

Secrets Revealed

William pried his eyes open, feeling groggy, and stared at the ceiling. He was lying in a strange bed in a strange room. Where was he? This wasn't his room at his house in Carlisle... Abruptly he remembered when he was in time, but this wasn't his room at Caelwyn's, either. He tried to remember how he'd gotten here. The last thing he recalled clearly was helping Gwendolyn set down the chest she'd been carrying. Then it got fuzzy. He thought he remembered Guinevere coming over to ask Gwendolyn a question, but beyond that, absolutely nothing. Had he passed out? Considering how his energy level had been lately, it wouldn't surprise him too much, but if he had, it would be just plain embarrassing. He wasn't a fainter. He'd never passed out in his life. Then again, he'd never felt as tired as he had the last few days, either. Had he come down with some strange sickness? He'd heard of diseases that caused extreme lethargy, but did they exist in sixth-century England? He didn't know. What he did know was that his head hurt and his back felt a little sore. He sat up and stretched cautiously, then swung his legs over the side of the bed. He wondered what time it was.

He heard the patter of feet in the corridor, and the door opened slightly. Jenifer poked her head in. Her expression brightened upon seeing him awake. "Good, you're awake! How do you feel?"

"I feel alright," he responded. She came and sat by him on the bed. "What happened?" he asked her. Her eyes grew worried.

"You collapsed after helping Gwendolyn with that chest. Cael-wyn couldn't figure out why, and she's one of the best Brenwyd healers. Father carried you here to sleep. The treasure chamber wouldn't have been very comfortable." So he *had* fainted. In front of Arthur's knights. And King Arthur. Seriously embarrassing. "We were hoping you could tell us why you fell down," Jenifer continued.

"Well, I'm not really sure. I guess I was just a whole lot more tired than I thought."

"You're not ill, are you?" She twisted a lock of her hair around a finger.

"I don't think so. Where are the others?" he asked.

Her expression turned glum. "Busy. Father's gathering troops. The knights are helping him. Mother and Gwendolyn are organiz-ing supplies. Caelwyn took Cassie somewhere after we broke fast, and they're still not back. David and Sarah are helping Mother and Gwendolyn. I was helping, but I got bored. No one has time to play. Telyn and Ganieda went back home. They're watching the younger ones and probably doing other things Caelwyn asked them to do. I wanted to go with them, but Mother said I had to stay here. She said Cassie and David heard Mordred wants to capture Gwendo-lyn, Mother, and me, so that Father will do what he wants. So I have to stay here, where I can be properly protected." She sounded scornful of the danger and depressed about the solution.

"She's right, you know. You don't want to fall into Mordred's hands, believe me," he said.

She looked at him curiously. "How would you know that?"

"Well... like I said a few days ago, I used to be part of the organi-zation that he founded. They're not nice people, and Mordred set the standard for that."

"Hmm." She sighed. "It's too bad. He can be nice when he wants to."

How I know, William thought. Many times, the Master – Mordred – had helped him with his sword work, or offered an encouraging word when the Commander was unusually brusque. After making the decision to break with the organization, William had slowly realized that the Master hadn't really been interested in him as a person, only in his potential. Thinking back on their encounters, he saw clearly the man's hatred for Brenwyds. And he could never forget the blatant example of cruelty he had seen when he was eight...

"I suppose you'll have to go back to the future," Jenifer said, interrupting his musings, for which William was grateful.

"Yeah. It's where we belong."

"When do you go back?"

"Whenever the time slip's ready."

She looked at the floor. "Is Britain very different in the future?"

"Different enough. There are all sorts of new things that make life much easier and it's a very different culture, but I think you'd still know places. And King Arthur is a part of British culture, you know. People love stories about your father."

"Am I in them?" She sounded more like her usual perky self in that question.

"No, which is strange. According to what I was taught, Arthur didn't have any children. And now I know he had two. I can't imagine how people forgot."

"Will you remember me when you go back?" She sounded very small, like she might cry.

"Of course I will." He shifted a bit uncomfortably. He didn't want her bursting into tears on him. He had no clue how to deal with crying children. "Don't think about it right now. We've still got stuff to do first."

"Like what?" she asked, her green eyes full of curiosity. "Do you know what that prophecy talks about?"

William hesitated. What should he tell her? He assumed the

prophecy had something to do with sending Guinevere to the future (though why they should do that he still didn't know), but he didn't want to tell the young girl that. Cassie hadn't shared her idea yet.

Jenifer took his hesitation as refusal to tell her. "You can't tell me, can you?"

"It's probably best to wait," he agreed.

She nodded. "I'll miss you when you go back." She looked so forlorn that he took her hand in his and squeezed it.

"I'll miss you, too. I don't have any younger siblings. Actually, I don't have any siblings at all."

She looked at him thoughtfully. "You know, I thought you might be my sibling when you first came."

Her candid admission took him a little aback. "Um, I can see why you'd think that." He paused. "Want to know something?"

"What?" she asked eagerly.

"Cassie and I think the reason I look like your father is because I'm descended from him."

She blinked. "You mean, you think he's like your grandfather?"

"Sort of. A lot of times removed, of course, but close," William said.

"So we're related?"

"I guess you could say that." He hadn't really thought about that aspect of his being Arthur's descendant. That meant this little ten-year-old in front of him was either his many times removed great-aunt, or his many times removed grandmother. Seriously weird. It was like Cassie with Caelwyn's family. *Oh,* he thought, *I guess that means I'm distantly related to Cassie too. Now there's a really scary thought.*

Jenifer distracted him before he could decide how he felt about that. She grinned and clapped her hands together. "I knew it! But you don't want me telling anyone, do you?"

"I'd prefer not."

"I won't, I promise," she said. William smiled.

At that moment, Dassah entered the room. She trotted up to William and stood on her hind legs, putting her front ones in his lap. "Hey, Dassah," he said, patting her head. "How are you?" She bobbed her head, which he guessed meant good. She sniffed his face, maybe doing a dog checkup. She licked the tip of his nose and dropped back to all four legs. "Am I supposed to follow you somewhere?" She shook her head. "Should I stay here?" She nodded and lay down on the floor.

"Would that mean stay here?" Jenifer guessed.

"It would," said a voice from the hallway. Cassie walked in, followed by David and Sarah. "Well, look who's up. I told you he wouldn't miss noonmeal," she said, smiling.

"It's lunchtime?" William asked, alarmed at the idea he'd slept in that late.

"Not quite," Cassie said. She sat down on his other side. "How do you feel? And don't you dare lie to me." She glared at him.

"I don't intend to," he assured her. "I feel okay. I have a slight headache and my back hurts a bit."

That would be from where you slammed into me, Kai grumbled, entering. He moved a little stiffly. *You weigh a lot.*

"Oh. Uh, sorry. When did I do that?"

"He broke your fall," Sarah said. "Otherwise, you probably would have hit your head really hard, and would have more than a slight headache."

"Oh. Thanks, Kai."

You are welcome. But do not do that again anytime soon. Once a week is all I can do. He cocked his head, and William realized he was making a joke.

"I'll try not to. It wasn't intentional, believe me."

"Whether it was or not, we need to talk," Cassie said. She looked at Jenifer. "Jenifer, I think your mother wants you to go and help her organize supplies."

"Translated, you want to talk in private. It's alright. You can just say so." She hopped off the bed. "See you later." She left.

"Was she in here long?" David asked.

"Not too long. I only woke up a few minutes ago," William said. He stood up, and swayed as the room seemed to spin.

Cassie steadied him. "Easy there. I wouldn't get up so quick if I were you. It wasn't exactly a normal collapse you had last night. And I'd sit back down. We'll be talking awhile."

He did as she said. "Are any collapses normal?" he asked. She didn't smile. David closed the door. Sarah sat where Jenifer had been sitting. "Is something wrong?"

"No and yes, and sort of at the same time," Sarah said. "It's a little complicated. Actually, not really, it's just... it just sounds strange."

"What does?"

"The reason you collapsed," Cassie said. "The reason you're tired. The reason you almost fainted in the barn a few weeks ago."

William frowned. "You think that's all connected? Why?"

"I *know* it's all connected." She stood up and began pacing. "I told you I've been having more dreams about Gwen."

"Yeah." They'd slipped back into English.

"And that she was going to Carlisle?"

"Yeah."

"And that she was heavily pregnant when she went to Carlisle?"

"You implied that." He wondered what she was getting at.

"When's your birthday?" she asked – abruptly, in William's opinion.

He blinked. "What?"

"When's your birthday?" She was looking at him with a completely serious expression.

"Why?"

"I'd like to know."

"The twenty-fifth of May, but what does that have to do with anything?" William felt completely baffled. He'd grown used to how Cassie sometimes related completely different topics, but he couldn't imagine how his birthday and Gwen going to Carlisle in the twenty-first century possibly related. Or could he? He frowned as a vague idea began to form.

"May," she murmured. "It's September now, so... that'd be right."

"Right for what? What are you trying to tell me?"

She stopped pacing and stared directly into his eyes with not even a hint of mirth in her expression. "Guinevere is Gwen. You know that. Guinevere is currently pregnant. She got pregnant before the feast, by Arthur. It was several weeks ago. Gwen said she got to Glastonbury in October about sixteen years before we get there. Late May is nine months from early September. The reason you're feeling weak, the reason you almost fainted in the stable a couple of weeks ago, the reason you collapsed last night after Guinevere walked over to ask Gwendolyn a question, is because she is pregnant with *you*." She pointed, putting the tip of her finger right on his chest. William felt so shocked he didn't know what to say. "The Commander is *not* your father. That's why you don't look like him. Your father is... King... Arthur." William stared at her, mouth half open. He'd guessed about halfway into her speech what she was leading up to, but...

"That's... that's..." He tried to form some sort of answer.

"Entirely possible," David said. "Believe me, we've looked at this forwards, sideways, and upside-down. It completely checks out."

"Listen," Cassie said, jumping back in. "Just bear with us here for five minutes, okay? I had a dream last night that explains everything. Gwen and Eleanor went up north to visit Eleanor's dying friend. While there, Gwen wandered around seeing how everything had changed, and ended up on Brotherhood property, where she actually saw the Commander and another guy burying a couple of bodies. They caught sight of her and captured her, throwing her in a cell so she couldn't go to the police. Fortunately, it was a better room than I got. Not surprisingly, the stress caused her to go into labor, a little premature but nothing serious. By some miracle she delivered safely and the baby – a.k.a. you – was okay. Take a detour to the Commander and his wife. She also goes into labor, but hers doesn't go so well. She labored too fast, was too early, and the baby – which was a boy – was stillborn. I'm not done yet," she said, putting up a hand as William tried to insert his thoughts. "Three more minutes. So anyway, the Commander's wife is dying because of blood loss, and she keeps repeating that she wants to see her baby. The Commander can't bear to tell her that the baby is stillborn, but he remembers that Gwen gave birth to a boy earlier, so he goes to her cell and takes the baby – you. He didn't intend to keep you, I think, but he gives you to his wife to hold as she's dying and she makes him swear to take care of you. I think she knew you weren't hers, because she never says 'our son' in reference to you. After the Commander agrees, she dies. The Commander couldn't bear to break his promise to her. I think he felt like he'd be taking away his last link to her. He knows that the Master will order Gwen and you killed. So he goes back to Gwen's cell – and she's been frantic this whole time, mind you – and offers her a deal: he'll raise her baby, give him a chance at life, and she'll claim his own stillborn son as hers. I don't think anyone really knew about the switch. That's why the secret kept so well. Gwen takes the deal – she doesn't have much of a choice – and the rest is history. Make sense?"

William's brain was scrambling. He could hardly believe what she was telling him, but he knew she wouldn't make it all up, and he *wanted* to believe it. It explained everything about his life, why the Commander had been so stand-offish, why he didn't look like him, why he did look like Arthur. "You're sure?" he asked.

"I'm sure. You think I could make all that up? If you don't believe me, ask your horse."

"Phoenix? Why?"

"He's the one who first mentioned the possibility to me, though I didn't think much of it at the time. He told me then that it was only rumors, but actually he knew it was true. I checked it with him this morning."

"And he knew because?"

"You're not the only one with really old parents. Wynne is – will be – his dam."

"What?" William wasn't the only one asking that question. David and Sarah also looked surprised.

"That's what he said. But he also said that she got pregnant by a runaway stallion in Glastonbury, not by any stallion in this time. She told him about Gwen's lost child, so he decided the best thing to do was find you. And he did."

"And I thought I knew my horse," William muttered. "Anything else you want to spring on me?" he asked in a louder voice, not really expecting a serious answer, but he got one anyway.

"Well, yes, actually, but I'll give you a minute first."

"Oh. Thanks." He sat there, trying to take it all in. "Wow. That's... not something you hear every day."

"That's for sure," Sarah said. "I'm still getting over it, and she told me fairly early this morning." William bent forward, putting his elbows on his knees and his chin in his hands. "You okay?" Sarah asked.

"Yeah. Just taking it in. It's definitely not the worst thing I've ever heard. It's just a bit... wild," he answered.

"Well, I definitely prefer Arthur to the Commander," David said.

"Does... Arthur know? Or Guinevere?" William asked.

"No. I wasn't about to drop that bombshell on him or her. Caelwyn agreed," Cassie said.

"You told Caelwyn?"

"She'd already guessed. Has it sunk in enough yet?"

He looked up at her. "No, but you may as well tell me the rest now," he said resignedly. Cassie and David chuckled at his answer.

"Oh, come on, that wasn't that bad," David said. "The rest is interesting and pretty optimistic, if you ask me." He paused and frowned. "Well, there is the fact that you made it onto Mordred's hit list because of it, but it is for a good reason." William gave him a dubious look.

"What?" Sarah asked. She sounded wary. "You guys did not tell me this."

"We don't know quite what to think of it ourselves," Cassie said. "And I learned something new this morning which makes it more interesting."

"What were you and Caelwyn doing?" Sarah asked.

"She was teaching me how Brenwyds go about disabling spells and fighting witches and wizards." Cassie's eyes lit up. "It was really interesting, actually. Remember what I told you back home about my dad saying something about using counter-melodies? It turns out that's exactly what you do. So Caelwyn just made up completely random melodies that I had to figure out the counter for. They weren't spells, just random melodies, and–"

"Okay, Cass," David said. "I think we have established that you are excited about this. What did you learn this morning that makes things more interesting? We are leaving for Caelwyn's soon, and we need to get everything said," he reminded her. "You can finish telling us about the melodies later."

Cassie blushed a little. "Sorry. I didn't mean to ramble. I just found it so fascinating. I didn't know I could do so many things. But anyway, Caelwyn said that she went through Morgan's book last night, and she showed me a particular prophecy that's very important." She paused, frowning. "The only problem is that the sword it mentions has been missing for years."

"Sword? Cassie, you haven't even told us what this prophecy says. Are you sure it involves us? I rather think we've got enough already," Sarah said.

Cassie looked at her, amusement lurking in her gray-blue eyes.

"Oh, it's not us. Not all of us, anyway. It concerns one son of Arthur whom we all know."

William groaned. His whole life was starting to feel like it was defined by prophecies. How many were there now, three? "For heaven's sake, Cassie, I'm still adjusting to the idea that... that I *am* his son. Now you're saying there's a prophecy about it?"

"I didn't say it. Morgan did, technically. But I get ya, and yes. It goes along with the prophecy we found in Caelwyn's diary and actually gives a little more detail on how you're gonna help me defeat Mordred."

"Didn't I do that already by getting you guys out?"

"Yeah, but that's not all you'll do, according to Morgan. Mordred is actually pretty terrified of you because his mother made this prophecy about how a son of Arthur would be the one who kills him."

"Wait, what?" William felt like he was reliving their first day in the sixth century with all the shocks he was getting. "I thought that was going to be you."

"So did I, but you're welcome to it," she said, chuckling. "But part of what Caelwyn explained to me today is that one way Brenwyds fight is with music and song, not weapons. God blessed Brenwyds with the ability to hear the songs in nature and use a person's song to heal them and whatnot, you guys know that. But the main reason God gave Brenwyds that ability is because Brenwyds are extremely important in fighting Satan. You know that verse in Ephesians that says, 'For our struggle is not against flesh and blood, but against the rulers, against the authorities, against the powers of this dark world and against the spiritual forces of evil in the heavenly realms'?" David and Sarah nodded. William decided to look it up in Cassie's Bible later. "That's exactly what Brenwyds do. They fight invisible battles for humanity, and they do it with song. The dark forces use the song in Creation against itself by twisting it and making it completely serve their purpose. Brenwyds can straighten it back out again. Mordred's learned magic from Morgan, twisting songs to manipulate things for his own purposes. Caelwyn thinks he uses it as a kind of shield against harm, because that's what Morgan did. She thinks my big job will be tearing down whatever shield he's got protecting himself, so that he can be killed. Tearing down something like that is really exhausting, so it would make sense that I tear down the shield and you actually do the deed. Remember that conversation we heard between the Commander and Mordred? Apparently Morgan, and therefore probably Mordred, think that if all the Brenwyds are removed from the earth, God somehow won't be able to work on Earth like He does now, which would greatly further whatever evil purposes they've dreamed up. Of course, even if they succeeded in wiping out Brenwyds, they don't realize that Christians can still stymie them, but, well, that's just their logic."

There was a silence as the other three absorbed what Cassie had just said. Cassie realized that they might not understand it fully, but she found it intensely interesting. At home, though she didn't like to admit it, she had seen her abilities as a bit of a nuisance, as they set her apart and made her a target. Now, however, she learned that there was a very specific purpose to those abilities, and it excited her.

Her words were almost exactly what Merlin had told William. "But it's you who would really defeat him," he concluded.

Cassie shrugged. "If you like."

"Cass, did you say something about a sword being missing?" David asked.

"Mmm, yeah. That could prove to be problematic."

"How?" William asked warily, not sure he wanted the answer.

"Well, it's an older entry in the diary, soon after she had Mordred, and it goes that she tried to See his future – apparently, she has that gift – and she Saw that he would be killed by a son of Arthur and the Sword of Kings," Cassie explained. "Caelwyn said that she usually wouldn't put faith in a prophecy from a person like

Morgan, but it does dovetail with her own prophecy that we found in that diary in the library, and she actually prophesied the same thing aloud to me and David last night. The sword really is missing, and David and I heard that Mordred's worried about it – apparently it disappeared strangely – so Caelwyn says it would be good to keep all that in mind while battling him and Morgan."

"Okay," William said. "So what's this Sword of Kings and how did it disappear strangely?"

"Haven't you ever heard of the Sword in the Stone?" Cassie asked, sounding amused.

"That story's true?" Sarah sputtered.

"Yep. Caelwyn says that the Sword in the Stone is the Sword of Kings. Very few kings have ever used it, but those who did reigned for a while, and there was always peace during their reigns. Actually, it was forged from the same meteorite as Seren, and was made for the leader of the Brenwyds at the time. When he knew he was about to die, he called his people together to a large rock and said that the way they would know to follow a human king would be if he could pull the sword from the rock. It wasn't called the Sword of Kings at the time; that came later. He then plunged the sword down into the rock, binding it with song and praying that God would only allow the sword to be drawn by those He chose to lead. So the sword stayed there for several centuries and many kings tried to draw it, but very few succeeded, and it was always put back into the rock. Then twenty-seven years ago King Uther died, apparently childless, without naming an heir. There were rumors of a hidden son, but no one knew who he might be. So Merlin called all the nobles and their sons to the rock, saying that God had revealed to him that the next king would be the one who pulled the sword from the stone. So everyone tried, and no one succeeded. Ector's household was running late because of weather and arrived as the last nobles were departing. So he and Kay try but the sword's still stuck there and Merlin says to Arthur, who'd traveled with them, why don't you try it? Arthur tried protesting that he'd been dropped at Ector's when only a few days old and raised with Kay but wasn't really noble, but Merlin kept insisting he try and Ector said go ahead, so he did, and the rest is history."

"Huh," David said thoughtfully. "Interesting. So that part of the story was remembered pretty well."

"But who dropped Arthur at Ector's court?" Sarah asked. "The legends say Merlin, don't they?"

"Yes, but that's not true," Cassie answered. "It was Caelwyn's mom, Anna. When Igraine had Arthur, the political situation in Britain was pretty dicey, so she and Uther decided it would be best for him to grow up somewhere without him or anyone else knowing who he really was. They thought it was his best chance of survival. They asked Anna to find a safe place for him to be raised, and she took him to Ector, a good and honorable man who lived near their Brenwyd village. But the problem was, by the time Uther died, no one knew where Arthur was – ergo the sword in the stone contest."

William whistled. "No wonder he became such a legend. That's the kind of stuff people remember." *And he's my father*, he thought to himself. *Guinevere is my mother. That's just weird. Gwendolyn and Jenifer are my sisters. That part actually feels right. And it's not as weird us them being my long-removed grandmother and great-aunt.*

"So what happened to the Sword of Kings?" David pressed.

"It broke," Sarah said. "I remember this story. Arthur fought against some knight and won, but the sword broke. It was after that he got Excalibur. Did he really get it from the Lady of the Lake?"

"That's something I didn't ask. Caelwyn was telling me the story while explaining how to do things, so I wasn't really thinking about questions," Cassie explained. "But the rest of it is right, except Arthur's opponent was a Saxon war leader. Caelwyn said everyone was shocked because there was no way that sword should have broken. The fragments vanished a year later and no one knows where they went."

"I might," Sarah muttered darkly. "And his name is Mordred."

"Morgan, more likely," Cassie said. "Mordred wasn't old enough, but she would know the prophecy about the sword being the one that would kill him, so it would make sense."

"So would the sword be in Mordred's castle?" David wondered. "Or would she have completely destroyed it?"

"Hopefully not," William said. "That wouldn't be good."

She would not be able to, Kai said, startling all of them. He and Dassah were lying on the floor, watching the proceedings with interest but not saying anything, apparently satisfied by the way the conversation had been running. The four had forgotten he was there. *Brenwyds made things so they could not be destroyed easily and certainly not by evil.*

"How do you know this?" Cassie asked.

You are not the only one who has learned things in the last three months. Dragon knows much, and he has told us.

"So we also need to find the pieces of this sword and get it reforged before we go home," Sarah said. "How much longer do we have, d'ya think?"

"I checked that, too, and the slip won't open for a bit longer. Hopefully it will be enough time." Cassie said.

A knock at the door attracted their attention. Jenifer peeked in. "I know I'm not supposed to be here," she said, "but Caelwyn wants to go back to her house so Mother sent me with some fresh clothes for William. Those things are damp from the rain earlier, and slept-in and dirty." She came in and plopped the clothes on the bed. "Are you done talking?"

"For now," Cassie said. "Perfect timing." The girl nodded and left the room.

"You should get changed," Sarah said, standing. "We'll leave you alone." They left. William stayed seated for a few minutes, still absorbing the information. He felt as if a huge weight had been taken off his shoulders. Even while he'd been with the Brotherhood, he hadn't felt entirely comfortable about the Commander being his father. That feeling had grown since meeting Cassie, especially since he'd turned against the Brotherhood and his father. But to find out he wasn't! William felt a sense of relief. He was grateful he'd had the chance to meet his real family, even if they had no idea he belonged to them. He grabbed the clothes Jenifer had left and started to change.

❧⑤⚵⑤❧

Cassie kept an eye on William as they bade farewell to the royal family. He seemed none the worse for wear after his collapse the night before and the information they'd told him this morning, but she detected a longing in his eyes when he looked at them – *his* family – knowing that they didn't know. He acted pretty well recovered, but Cassie noticed that around Guinevere he was a little wary and his face tightened with fatigue. The sooner he got back to Caelwyn's, the better. She noticed Guinevere seemed distracted, and guessed Caelwyn had told her the plan. She wondered how Arthur had taken it, and how much Caelwyn had told them. They departed, hurrying to Caelwyn's house.

Cassie lingered in the stable after the others left, and David stayed with her. "You didn't tell him everything," he said. She was standing by Twi, rubbing her down with a cloth. David was behind her. She wasn't sure if his tone was accusing or not.

"I didn't need to. Some things are better left unsaid." She rubbed Twi harder. The mare leaned into the rubbing, thoroughly enjoying it. "I don't want to focus on it myself."

"How long?" David asked.

She paused in her rubbing. Twi swung her head around and butted her shoulder gently in protest. "The time slip won't be ready for Guinevere for a little bit longer. He's got to make it 'til then."

David stepped closer to her, putting a hand on Twi's neck. "That wasn't my question."

She didn't turn around. "I'm not sure. At the rate he's been tiring, I wouldn't worry about it, but as the deadline gets closer, who knows?"

"Cassie." He turned her around. "There's something worrying you. Don't try to fool me. What is it? You can tell me."

She looked up. Her eyes were suspiciously bright and she blinked rapidly. "In the dream, it was just you and me helping Guinevere. No William. No Sarah. Why?" She paused. He didn't answer. "The most logical thing I can think of is he's too weak to move by that point and she stayed with him. Or... we were too late." Undeniable tears rose in her eyes and he instinctively hugged her to him. She didn't resist. He felt her tears wetting his tunic and her arms slip around his back. "I don't want to lose anyone else."

"And we won't," he said firmly, trying to reassure her. "We'll get it done in time. Remember the prophecies. He's got to stick around to get those done. Have faith."

"I'm trying. In my heart I know the truth, but my head tells me all the bad things that can happen."

"It's your heart that matters. Don't pay attention to your head. God's in your heart and He sees the big picture." She looked up, tears streaking her face, and smiled weakly.

"Don't pay attention to my head, huh? Dangerous advice," she said.

"You know what I mean." She dropped her face back against him. He felt her relax, but she didn't pull away. His heart started beating faster.

Twi looked at them. *If you are going to be like that, could you go somewhere else? I would like to eat my hay in air clear of human emotions.* Cassie and David quickly backed away from each other, each flushed. Twi nuzzled her rider and spoke so only she could hear. *You should listen to him. He speaks sense.* Cassie could think of no appropriate reply and simply patted her neck. She had a sudden pang of homesickness, not just for home, but for the time before these things started happening, when she was just a normal girl in Virginia doing normal things. *Except I never was normal,* she thought. *I was always different.*

That is not a bad thing, girl, Kai said, coming into the stable. *Sometimes being normal does not cut it. People who are different are always needed.* She sighed.

David was watching her. "You know what, Cass?" he said.

"What?"

"When we get back home, once this is all over, we are going to finish that camping trip."

She looked into his eyes. "Really?"

"You bet."

"You think we'll succeed?"

"Of course. We've got to. Our God is way bigger than Mordred," he pointed out.

She smiled, albeit hesitantly. "Well, that's true. Jeremiah 29:11. I'll just keep reminding myself."

He nodded. "Good. We'd better get up to the house. Come on." They left.

Kai, what were they talking about? Dreamer asked.

It is William, Kai answered. *He is the king's son, and his mother is pregnant with him, but she must have him in the future for everything to turn out as it should. If they miss the opening...* He let the sentence hang.

It is why he has been so tired, Phoenix said. *They must get her forward.*

But they did that already, did they not? Twi asked. *We saw her. She sent us back.*

Then everything will be okay, Dreamer said.

But she has not gone forward yet, Kai said. *She must go forward to send us back.*

And that is not certain in this time, I think, Phoenix said. *It is hard to explain. Humans understand it better.*

Humans are complicated, Twi said. *They think complicated thoughts. That is fine with me. Humans seem confused more than half the time because they think complicated thoughts.*

But when they figure out the thoughts, they understand everything, Dassah said, entering the stable. *They have figured it out. Now they must act.*

What will happen if they do not send her back in time? Fire asked.

None of this will have happened, Kai said. *Everything will be messed up. I do not want to think beyond that.* A silence fell.

That will not happen, Wynne said. She'd been listening to the conversation with interest. *The One will make sure all happens as it should. Did not the girl have a vision telling her so?*

She did, Dassah said. *But it only showed herself and David helping. And it started badly.*

I know, Wynne said. *I heard her and my woman talking.* Sadness had crept into her voice.

Kai, we should go to the house as well, Dassah said. The dogs left, and the horses returned to their hay.

FINAL PREPARATIONS

Cassie looked in on William, her brow creased in worry. It had been about two weeks since his collapse, and he was losing strength quickly, as she had feared. He hadn't gone out of the house since yesterday, and had rested most of the day. It had been four days since he'd really had enough energy to practice swordplay, though that didn't stop him from trying. He'd tried to go out yesterday, but Caelwyn had restricted him to the house and he hadn't raised much of a protest, which worried Cassie further. This morning it had been a visible effort for him to get to the kitchen for breakfast and Caelwyn had sent him straight back to bed before he collapsed again. He went without protest. Now he was sleeping, but uneasily. "I can feel you worrying from here, Cassie," William's voice broke into her thoughts.

She started. "I'm sorry, I didn't mean to wake you."

"You didn't." He sat up and leaned against the wall. Cassie could see the bags under his eyes. "I don't feel sleepy, exactly, I just feel... extremely lethargic." Cassie wasn't quite sure what to say. They knew why – they were running up against the deadline to send Guinevere to the future, and at the moment William was essentially existing in two places at the same time, which sapped his energy. Not to mention only one of his existences could ultimately survive in this time. "You shouldn't be so worried," he said after a moment.

"Shouldn't I?"

"No. I'll be fine. We already know it works out, right?"

"I guess, but it's still not –"

"No buts," William cut her off. "Your problem is that you think too much and too hard. You've probably got the clearest idea out of any of us about all the ways this... time paradox thing could work out, which is making you worried, so just stop thinking and reasoning about it. It's not helping you any."

"*I* need to stop reasoning? I thought you would *prefer* it if I used clearer logic."

"Most of the time, yes, that would be nice, so the rest of us can follow your train of thought. But this is not exactly a logical situation." He paused. "You told me once that I should practice having more faith in things I can't know for sure. Maybe now you should take your own advice and have faith that everything will work out how it's supposed to."

Cassie stared at him. "I can't believe I just heard you say that."

William smiled slightly. "Well, you could say the last few months have made me re-evaluate my worldview. And... I don't think any of us are the same people we were."

Cassie nodded. William watched her try to conceal her worry. He was worried, too, but it was a distant sensation, as if his inner self was watching his outer self worry through a window. It was a curious sensation, and it was coupled with a splitting migraine that severely disrupted his ability to concentrate on anything. He closed his eyes, welcoming the soft blackness the action produced that meant he didn't have to concentrate on seeing. It was ridiculous to have to concentrate on such a thing, but he did, and he hated the feeling. He also couldn't stand the intense lethargy that held his body and mind captive. He'd been fighting it off for the past few days – the last couple of weeks, really, since waking up with a headache after the mission to Mordred's castle – and had been mostly winning, but today it was overwhelming. He hated the feeling of helplessness it produced, the way it fogged his mind and made him waste the day away. Without realizing it, he fell asleep.

Cassie heard William's breathing change, becoming slower and heavier, and knew he'd drifted into sleep. The sound of small footsteps padding on the floor came from behind her. "Is he better?" Addiena's worried tones broke in on her thoughts.

Cassie turned to her. "He's sleeping. Let's leave him like that." They retreated to the kitchen, where the others were gathered. Cassie looked at Caelwyn. "We can't wait any longer. It has to be today or tonight. The melody we need is getting toward a crescendo point, but would it be possible to make the slip open sooner if we need to?" She had traveled to the Tor every day for the past two weeks to see if the melody they needed was approaching readiness. Fortunately, she knew which one to use because of both her dreams and the day she'd sat on the Tor and first discovered the time slip. Two days ago she had thought the melody they needed seemed louder than the others. Yesterday it had definitely been louder, and this morning its volume and intensity had reminded her of the melody she and the others had traveled through on the Tor in the twenty-first century.

"Perhaps," Caelwyn said. "If it is close enough, you could likely sing it open."

Telyn looked up from her lap, where she was embroidering a tunic's neckline. "What is going on?" she demanded. "You've never explained why he collapsed and he's gotten weaker. Are you going home? Could they help him in your time?" Her voice took on a slight tremble as she posed the last two questions.

"No, *we're* not going back, not yet," Cassie said, hesitating to tell her the rest.

"Then what?" Ganieda asked. "You've all been acting strangely for the last two weeks. I know all the war preparations have been going on, but Arthur and the army departed days ago. What is going on that you haven't told us?" Selyf and the twins stayed silent, but watched the scene intently. Sarah, David, and Cassie exchanged glances.

"Tell them," Caelwyn said. She headed for the door. "I must go tell Guinevere." She turned back, looking each of her children and Ganieda in the eye. "What you are about to hear, you must tell no one. Understood?"

"Yes, ma'am," they all said. Caelwyn left, followed by Dragon.

"So what is it?" Selyf asked.

"Well," Cassie said, thinking how best to approach the subject. "You know that woman I told you about who helped us get to this time?"

"Yes." Telyn said.

"The woman is Guinevere." She explained everything from there, helped by David and Sarah. The others stared at them, incredulous, when they were done.

"You mean William is our cousin?" Aeddan asked. Cassie blinked, the thought not having occurred to her before. She supposed that would also make William related to her, albeit rather distantly.

Sarah answered him. "Yes, I suppose it does. I doubt he's realized that, though."

Telyn shook her head slowly. "So he'll just keep getting worse until you get Guinevere to your time?"

"Yes," Cassie said. "But it's not our time, exactly. It's about sixteen years before we come here. During those years he'll grow to the age you know him at now."

"And you're going to send Guinevere forward tonight?" Ganieda asked.

"We have no choice," David said.

"Does Arthur know?"

"Sort of, I think," Cassie answered. "Caelwyn didn't tell me exactly what she told him."

"But she's not coming back, is she?" Addiena asked. "What will you tell him then?" They stayed silent.

Telyn examined each of their faces keenly, and probably picked up something from their thoughts. "He won't survive, will he?" she asked softly. Cassie slowly shook her head. A heavy, almost palpable silence fell. Cassie felt like it might choke her.

"What about Gwendolyn and Jenifer?" Selyf asked.

"We don't know," Sarah said. "Nothing we've ever heard mentions Arthur having any children with Guinevere."

"If Arthur is going to die," Telyn murmured. "Then Mordred will... no, it can't be." She sounded on the brink of despair.

Cassie moved over to her. "Telyn, I don't know why everything is happening this way. But there is hope. There's always hope."

"Telyn," David said, "does your mother... guard something? Something Mordred would want?"

She looked up at him, eyebrows raised in surprise. "How did you know?"

"Morgan mentioned it when Cassie and I overheard her and Mordred talking. She wants him to get it for her."

Telyn scowled. "She would, but she doesn't understand the nature of its power at all. Yes, Mother does guard something, and I don't think she would mind you knowing. One of the tasks of the Brenwyd race is to guard objects, powerful objects, to keep evildoers from getting their hands on them. Sometimes the objects are lost, but they always find their way back to a Brenwyd. Ten years ago, this particular object's caretaker died and evil men got their hands on it and began to wreak havoc. The king ordered a search for the object and sent only the knights the Brenwyds chose to regain it. Morgan was also looking for it. When it was found, only

Mother, Galahad, Bors, and Percival were there to take it back. Galahad would have died in the battle for it, but Mother healed him at the last possible moment."

"The Holy Grail," Cassie said in disbelief. "Your mother guards the Holy Grail."

"How did you know?" Telyn asked, surprised.

Cassie released a short burst of laughter. "Arthur's reign may not be remembered with much accuracy, but the search for the Grail is one of its keystones. No wonder Morgan wants her hands on it."

"Yes, but her perception of the Grail's power is wrong." Ganieda said. "The Grail works according to the faith of whoever is using it. If the person has no faith in God, it's just another cup with nothing special about it. But if a person has faith in God, well, that has a lot of power."

"So it wouldn't work for Morgan," David surmised.

"Not really, and certainly not with the power she thinks it has," Telyn said. "She knows and believes God exists, but she hates Him and does not choose to put her faith in Him. It wouldn't help her any to have it, but if she gets it and realizes it won't work for her–"

"She'll destroy it," Cassie finished for her. Telyn nodded.

"And that would be bad," Selyf put in. "Things like the Grail aren't destroyed easily and if they are, it doesn't happen quietly."

"What does the Grail do?" Sarah asked.

Telyn hesitated. "People have been healed while using it," she said. "Some people also believe it can serve as a direct link between whoever has it and God. Jesus used it and it caught His blood. So it has become a reminder of His power on Earth, a symbol to help people to connect with Him."

"And that's why Mordred wants it," Cassie said slowly, realizing the full extent of what Telyn was saying. "He would see something like that as something that ties God to this Earth, sort of like Brenwyds. He probably thinks that if he can destroy all objects like that, it will further remove God from the Earth." She was more thinking aloud than saying it to elicit a response.

David raised his eyebrows. "That actually makes a lot of sense."

Selyf scowled fiercely. "Does Mordred honestly think that?"

"It's probable," Telyn said. "Mother did tell me his reasoning behind wanting to kill Brenwyds. She found it in Morgan's book."

Cassie fingered the locket clasped at her throat. "So that's what I saw," she murmured. "The Grail Quest. That has to be what Mordred's after. That's why he wanted Dad."

"What do you mean, what you saw?" Aeddan asked.

"Well," Cassie began, "awhile ago now, I had a dream with your mother, Arthur, Galahad, and Bors in it. I didn't know who they were or what it was really about at the time, but I did see Caelwyn getting Galahad to drink from the Grail."

David looked at her. "I remember you mentioning that. Then the Grail must be what's in the treasure chamber that the Brotherhood wants so badly. The reason your dad kept the project secret."

"Exactly," Cassie said. "I actually wondered if the Grail was what's in there after that dream, but I wasn't really sure and it seemed pretty far-fetched to me at the time, so I didn't mention it."

"What are you talking about?" Addiena asked.

"My dad works as a... person who digs up things from the past to figure out how people from years ago – such as in this time period – lived. When the Brotherhood kidnapped him, he was working on finding Arthur's treasure chamber. There's no real, hard evidence for where Camelot is in our time, so the tunnels and chamber are unknown. My dad kept the project very secret, so I think he knows the Grail is in Arthur's treasure chamber and didn't want Mordred to find it."

"But it's not," Telyn said. "I don't know exactly where it is, but I know it's not there."

"It might not be there right now," Cassie said, "but it might get moved there in the future." Telyn nodded thoughtfully.

"Well, wherever it is, you can ask Mother and then tell your father when you go back," Selyf said. "It is good to know that even with Mordred's intentions, the Grail is still not in his possession in your time."

Cassie smiled. "Yes, but there is the slight problem of getting my father and mother out of Brotherhood hands first."

Caelwyn held Guinevere's hands. "I know you don't want to do this, but you must. It's very important. Vitally important."

Guinevere's blue eyes searched Caelwyn's green-gray ones. "You haven't explained exactly why," she said. "That's not like you, Caelwyn. Why do you not tell me?"

Caelwyn sighed. "Some things I simply cannot tell you, Guinevere, as much as I'd like – long – to."

"But going forward in time? That seems rather drastic." Guinevere stood rigid and turned her back to Caelwyn, crossing her arms. "If you were not the one talking to me, I would assume it was the insane fantasies of a deluded mind! I have my family, my life, here. Things may be bad right now, but I will endure it. I will not be called a coward who ran away. I will not abandon Arthur." Her voice was hard, with fierce undertones. Caelwyn sighed inwardly. Guinevere was at her most obstinate when she used that particular tone of voice.

"Oh, Guinevere, it's not cowardly, far from it. If you didn't have to, I wouldn't insist on it. It's for your child's sake, Guinevere."

Guinevere whirled back to her. "And what about Arthur? I know you didn't tell him exactly what you're planning, not in the detail you told me. I gathered that from our discussion afterward. He told me to do as you said, but what will you tell him after the battle? I don't suppose I'll be able to come back."

"Don't worry about Arthur. He will understand." Caelwyn tried to soothe her. She stood and put a comforting hand on Guinevere's arm. "Remember that language I've been teaching you? It's the language you'll need to know, and Wynne knows it, too. She'll help you."

"You'd let me take your horse? Caelwyn, I can't let you do that. You'll need her."

"Not as much as you will." She sat again, and pulled Guinevere with her. "Guinevere, listen. I won't be here much longer. I'm trying to make sure this kingdom survives the storm, and part of that involves you going forward."

"But... you mean, you're going to die? Caelwyn, you can't! Your children need you. Your husband needs you. Arthur needs you. Especially if I–"

"He can make his own decisions. What will happen, will happen. I'm not afraid. And though the future is not set in stone, we must make sure what is supposed to happen, does happen. And for it to happen, you *must* go forward," Caelwyn insisted.

Guinevere looked at her, tears starting to form in her eyes. "What about my children? I cannot just leave them. Gwendolyn is to be married, and Jenifer is still a child. You're asking me to leave my family – forever – for a place and time I know nothing of!" One of her hands moved to hover over her belly as she took a deep breath. "You know me well enough to know that I would go to great lengths to protect any of my children, even unborn, but this... how can you be so sure it's necessary?"

Caelwyn gripped Guinevere's hands tightly. "I cannot tell you right now, Guinevere, and for that I am deeply sorry. Believe me, I know it's a lot to ask. The girls will be taken care of. My family will watch them and take care of them, I promise." Guinevere stared out over the garden, where a gentle rain watered the plants. The last week had been very rainy around Camelot, adding an air of gloom to the landscape. Caelwyn continued. "Tonight, I'm going to move the Grail. Mordred cannot be allowed to get it. His men are in the area. My forest friends are watching them. I'll send

Cassie and Dafyd to get you. It has to be tonight."

Guinevere shifted her gaze back to her friend. "Tonight? Why tonight? And why won't you come yourself? You're not saying... Caelwyn, no!"

"What will happen, will happen," Caelwyn repeated gently. "Things may go better than I expect. I do know how to defend myself, you know. Cassie and Dafyd will help you. You can trust them. Please, Guinevere. You must do this. It is vital if Mordred is to be thrown down. Remember Merlin's prophecy?"

Guinevere looked at her, but she didn't say what was on her mind. She stood again. "Of course, I remember. Cassie, Dafyd, Sarah, and William are the ones, I assume?" Caelwyn nodded. "How do they know of this time slip, exactly?"

"You will find that out. I can say no more."

Guinevere eyed Caelwyn keenly, then turned her gaze back to the garden "How is William?"

Caelwyn thought for a minute. "He's not very well, but we hope he'll be better soon."

"Who is his father, Caelwyn? Tell me, please. I want – and need – to know." She paused. "That is – I know Arthur would never..."

"No, I understand." Caelwyn stood slowly. "I can't answer that question fully right now," she said, putting a hand on Guinevere's still-flat stomach. "But I can tell you that Arthur has never been unfaithful to you. You are correct to trust him." She paused and looked into her friend's deep blue eyes. "This child will be born healthy. You will endure much sorrow before you hear him call you Mother, but you will. Never doubt that you will. He will find you."

Guinevere's eyes widened, taking in what Caelwyn had and hadn't said. "It is a boy?" she asked in a whisper. "How do you know? A Seeing?"

"No. I cannot tell you how I know. But I have been perusing Morgan's diary. Carefully, but I have been able to glean how she thinks. In it, I found a prophecy. A prophecy that foretells Mordred's doom at the hand of yours and Arthur's son. What I am asking you to do... it is deeply connected with that prophecy. How much truth it ultimately contains is unclear, but Morgan and Mordred both fear it. It can be used against them... perhaps even to win this war."

Guinevere raised her eyebrows. "To win this war? Caelwyn, the child will not be born for months, no matter what time..." Her voice trailed off, and Caelwyn could tell she was starting to put some of the pieces together. After several minutes she nodded slowly and put her hand over Caelwyn's. "Thank you for telling me. I think... I think I understand, at least a little, now, why I must go. But what... what do I tell the girls?"

"Tell them you must go far away for a long time for safety. They won't question you much more than that, I think."

A half-smile flitted across Guinevere's face. "Gwendolyn, no, but Jenifer? She has an inquisitive mind, that one. She'll want to know all the particulars."

"Tell her when she's in bed and sleepy. She won't feel much like questioning then," Caelwyn said. She put a comforting hand on Guinevere's arm. "They will be fine. Explanations will come later." She looked up at the sky. The rain started falling with more force. "I should get home. I have things to do before tonight."

She started to turn away, but Guinevere caught her arm. "Please, come see the girls first. They would be happy to see you."

Caelwyn knew why Guinevere suggested it. It would likely be the last time she would see them. "Very well. But I cannot linger long." Together, the two women walked into the house.

~✶~

Sarah watched Caelwyn examining William anxiously. He'd only woken a few times since morning and never for long. Cassie had checked the time slip again and reported with relief that it would definitely be ready that night. It was now late afternoon.

Sarah felt like it was the calm before the storm of events to occur that night. Caelwyn sighed and stood. "The only thing to be done is to get Guinevere forward. Nothing else can help him now."

"Will he bounce right back, or will he need a few days to recover?" Sarah asked.

"I'm not sure, but seeing how he is now, I would keep him in bed or at least in the house for a day, no matter how energetic he feels. And you enforce that, too." Sarah nodded. Caelwyn put a comforting hand on her shoulder. "He'll be alright, Sarah."

"But what if they miss the opening?" Sarah asked.

"Thanks to Cassie's dreams, she has an idea of when the slip will open. And if they arrive too late, she will sing it open again."

"Can she do that?"

"Yes. Your friend is very powerful. I've been pouring the knowledge she needs into her for the past fortnight. She learns quickly."

Sarah's lips quirked up in a half-smile. "I know. It drives a couple of our teachers a little crazy because she learns so fast. Occasionally, she actually lets herself get behind a little. She hates doing it, but she doesn't want to attract attention."

Caelwyn chuckled. "When someone has Brenwyd blood, it's hard not to. You've known her a long time, haven't you?"

"Yes. She moved into our valley when we were five. She was shy at first, but David and I kept bugging her, so she learned to like having us around."

"She's lucky to have you as friends."

"We're lucky to have her, more like. I wouldn't change anything. Well, the whole Brotherhood situation, but..." Sarah looked down at William, "maybe not all of it."

Caelwyn gathered the girl into a hug. "Do not worry, Sarah. Everything will turn out alright. God knows what He's doing."

"I know," the girl said, her voice muffled. "I feel like that's the only thing keeping me sane at the moment."

Caelwyn laughed. "That's good." She released her. "Do you know where Cassie is?"

"I think she's in the barn. She likes thinking in barns. She says animals help her think because they're not complicated like people."

"That's true enough," Caelwyn said and headed for the barn, where she found Cassie sitting on the fence that defined the end of the loose box and the beginning of the aisle.

The girl looked up as Caelwyn came in. "Any change?" she asked.

"No." Caelwyn sat beside her. "I'm going to Camelot tonight. Telyn tells me you know of the Grail." Cassie nodded. "Then you probably know what I'm going to do."

"Mordred's waiting for you."

"If he's busy with me, he won't worry so much about Guinevere. That's your chance. Dafyd will go with you. Do not trouble yourself about me."

Cassie nodded again. "How did she take it?" she asked.

"She wasn't happy, but she'll do it."

"How much did you tell her?"

"No more than I had to, but she likely guessed much from what I didn't say." Twi stuck her head by Cassie and the girl started scratching around the base of her ears.

"What time tonight, do you think?" Cassie asked.

"Late. I will not use the transfer ability, so Mordred will be drawn to me. I'll send Wynne to get you if anything happens," Caelwyn answered her. Both of them knew something would.

Cassie frowned. "But can't you use it anyway? Is it that important for you to draw him to you?"

Caelwyn gazed at her. Yes, she learned quickly, but she was still young, too young to fully understand that for a major victory over evil, there must also be sacrifice. "Yes. His men will come with him, and I am sure I can incapacitate enough to prevent them from going to Camelot and capturing Guinevere. If you get tied down fighting, you will likely miss the opening." She could tell Cassie was about to protest, and held up a hand. "Hear me, Cassie. God ordains all things to unfold in a particular manner. Why, I do not know, but I know that for everything to correctly work out tonight, and in your time, I must go alone to Camelot and travel without transferring." She smiled slightly. "Also, I must deliver a prophecy to Mordred, and knowing him, it will haunt him."

"What... oh." Cassie looked at her. "You mean... the prophecy about me?"

"Exactly." Caelwyn held a hand out to Cassie. "Come, I still have a few things to show you." Cassie hopped down and took her hand. They went to a practice area Caelwyn had found, about a mile from her house near a stream. There she and Cassie spent the rest of the afternoon. Cassie didn't realize it, but Caelwyn, instead of actually teaching her more, was testing what she had learned. As the sun drew low to the western horizon, Caelwyn called a halt. "You have learned all you need to."

Cassie looked surprised. "But there must be more I don't know," she protested.

"There are always things you don't know," Caelwyn said. "And you will constantly learn as you use your abilities. But I am satisfied that you know enough. You passed all the tests."

"What tests?"

Caelwyn laughed. "I've been testing you all afternoon, dear. You passed all of them flawlessly."

"Oh." They sat near the stream, teacher and student highlighted by the sun's late afternoon rays. "Caelwyn?"

"Yes?"

Cassie played with the blades of grass. "There's something I've been meaning to ask you about. Sometimes I get... feelings, hunches about things. Like I should go left instead of right, or trust this person but not that person. The thing is, I find out later that they're always right. Is that a Brenwyd trait?"

Caelwyn nodded. "I had a suspicion you have that one. Not just anyone has dreams as you do. It's called Second Sight. To use it properly, you must focus on a specific person or place. Your Sight will then show you what that person is doing or what is happening in that place. Some people gaze into the fire as they search, but I personally do not think it makes a difference whether you do or not."

Cassie frowned. "I thought that was something people had that made them give prophecies."

"It does do that. I have it myself. It is, as you say, feelings and hunches about things. From those hunches can come prophecies, such as the one I told you a fortnight ago. But Sight is not merely a Brenwyd trait. Many of our gifts are simply amplifications of traits and abilities normal humans have. Second Sight is such a one. Most of the time it lies dormant in regular humans, only manifesting itself as unconscious feelings and hunches. Occasionally, though, it is more pronounced and humans have the Sight. Merlin is an example. Morgan is another."

"Morgan? But she's evil."

"She was not always so. Her father's name was Aurelius. He was descended from a patrician Roman family that stayed in Britain when the legions left. He united the tribes for a time, but he was not a leader like Arthur. He was hard, and many saw his actions as cruel. Morgan grew up constantly vying for her father's attention, and the only way she thought she could gain it was with magic. So she started learning the dark arts, and they transformed her into what she is now. The Sight was one of her natural gifts, but she has used it much for evil purposes."

Cassie frowned. "Aurelius? Wasn't he related to Uther?"

Caelwyn eyed her keenly. "Yes, they were brothers, but not much alike. Uther was more like Arthur. Aurelius died on a boar hunt, and Uther tried to regain his kingdom, though it was mostly in shambles at that time and the kings were very suspicious of anyone trying to be High King. It was into that situation Arthur was born."

"So Arthur and Morgan are cousins? And wouldn't you be related to her, too?"

Caelwyn grimaced. "Unfortunately. It is a reason Morgan always opposes us. She feels that she should be the one to rule Britain. If Mordred were to succeed and claim the throne, he would likely be a puppet of his mother."

Cassie recalled the comment Morgan had made about Mordred's claim to the throne. That made sense now. "Who was Mordred's father?"

"Lot of Lothian, Morgan's husband. He died in the rebellion ten years ago."

Cassie was quiet, turning the information over in her head. She sighed. "I guess I just don't understand why I have all these Brenwyd talents since I'm so far removed from a full-blooded Brenwyd. It doesn't make sense, and to be honest, it's not all that helpful at home." She paused. "My father said it's because God chose to make the Brenwyd blood strong in me."

Caelwyn put a hand on the girl's shoulder. "Your father is correct. Whether you think your traits are helpful or not, God knows you need them. Have you not discovered that?" Cassie nodded. "I know it is difficult for you in your own time, but rest assured that they were not given in vain. You have already become more comfortable with them, I think?"

Cassie nodded again. "But here they're normal. Brenwyds are normal. It's been nice not having to hide. But when I go home, I'll have to hide again."

Caelwyn thought for several minutes. "I do not have all the answers you want, but do not let your own culture discourage you. Use your gifts. They're meant to be used. Do not fear them or wish you did not have them."

Cassie looked up at her and smiled. "No, I don't wish I didn't have them. Not anymore."

"Good." Caelwyn paused. "Now, I will give you a word of caution. I have taught you how to combat magic, but be careful not to let yourself get caught up in its practice. There is a fine line we Brenwyds must walk, and you must be careful not to stray from it. Never sing anything that goes against what you know to be right. If you are in doubt, listen for Creation's song. It will set you right, and if you sing it, the effects may be greater than you could imagine. It breaks any spell a witch or wizard could possibly come up with, for it is still as pure as the day it was created."

Cassie nodded. "I'll remember that."

Caelwyn smiled at the girl. She had grown fond of her over the past months. Caelwyn drew Seren and handed the hilt to Cassie. Cassie raised her eyebrows, but Caelwyn encouraged her with a nod. Cassie took the knife. Gentle white flames rippled to life up and down the blade. "Yes, I knew she was for you," Caelwyn said. "She chose you that first day, you know."

"The flame thing?" Cassie asked. She recalled how the knife had seemed to extend its flames over her completely at the end of her first duel with Caelwyn. It had warmed her with a soothing warmth, and she had almost thought she sensed joy in them, though she knew flames were an inanimate substance.

Caelwyn nodded. "Yes. Each bearer is chosen in that manner. I already knew the next one would not be one of my daughters, but she did surprise me when she chose you. It confirms that you are of my blood. I am descended from her first bearer, and it will light only for women of our bloodline. I know not why or how, but the smith who forged it was a little unusual, even by Brenwyd standards. He likely imbued the metal with a song to make sure the flames could not be used for ill."

"How do you control the flames?"

"It responds to your thoughts. If you don't want a lot of flames, concentrate on little flames. If you want a lot of flames, concentrate on a lot. Try it." Caelwyn backed away a little.

Cassie looked at the knife. *Big flames,* she thought, imagining fire leaping from the metal. The knife responded. Flames flared up, reaching in front of Cassie about two feet. She started. *Small flames!* she thought hastily. The flames subsided. "I see," Cassie said. "Was it really forged from a shooting star?"

"Yes," Caelwyn answered, moving back to her previous spot. "I do not know how the smith captured the fire in the metal, but we call it flamestone. The Sword of Kings also has this ability, so you may want to share with William what I have told you." Cassie nodded, and offered the knife back to Caelwyn. She didn't take it. "You should keep it," she said.

"You'll need it more than I will," Cassie said. "Please."

Caelwyn searched her face. "Very well." She took the knife and re-sheathed it. "We should go back now. 'Tis nearly suppertime, and there are hungry people at home to feed."

17

Déjà Vu

Cassie slept fitfully that night and so heard Caelwyn creep out of the house a little after the midnight hour. Dragon accompanied her. "God, please help her," Cassie whispered. "Your will be done." She knew Caelwyn wouldn't send Wynne for some time and tried to sleep. She succeeded in achieving a sort of semi-conscious sleep state, and her mind followed Caelwyn's journey to Camelot. She saw her approach the city and leave Wynne just outside the wall. She watched as Caelwyn hid the Grail in the chamber and noted its exact location. And she watched as her mentor was ambushed by Mordred's men and killed. She jerked fully awake, tears spilling from her eyes, chest heaving in silent sobs. Wynne's frantic thoughts reached her. *I'm coming, I'm coming,* she told the mare. She quickly extricated herself from between Addiena and Telyn and went to wake David, grabbing her knife belt, bow, and quiver on the way.

David woke immediately, and she suspected he'd slept as badly as she had. "Time?" he asked in a low voice. She nodded. As he grabbed his sword belt and buckled it on, she checked on William. He slept uneasily, his face revealing discomfort. His breathing was shallow. He was running out of time. She hummed his song, hoping it would revive him a little.

Footsteps alerted her before Sarah appeared, Dassah and Kai behind her. Her eyes looked moist. "How is he?" she whispered.

"Not good," Cassie answered. "We've got to move."

Sarah nodded. She sat down by him. "I'll keep him here if he gets a sudden energy rush," she said. "Be careful, please." She gave each a hug.

"We will be," her brother said, his arms holding his sister close before releasing her. "Cassie, let's go." They left the house as a piercing, mournful howl split the air. It sent chills down Cassie's spine. She knew who it was: Dragon, mourning his mistress. It gave her an increased sense of urgency.

"We've got to get out of here before the others wake up," she said. Wynne cannoned into the yard, snorting loudly and eyes rolled so that they showed white. Cassie quieted her, not wanting to wake the others just yet. They tacked up in record time.

"I'll go on ahead to Camelot," David said. "You should go make sure all the men are dead." Cassie nodded. There was the chance that Mordred would come attack the house to kill them. Alone, he would be immensely foolish to do so, but if some of his men had somehow survived with only minor wounds, he could chance it. If that was the case, the others would need to be wakened, and quickly.

We must hurry, Wynne said. She sounded absolutely grief-stricken, but remained focused on the task ahead. *Mordred said he was sending men to capture Guinevere. We have to get there first.*

"I won't be long. Do you want to come with me?" Cassie asked her.

Yes.

We will stay, Kai said. *We will lead the others.*

Be careful, Dassah said. *We cannot lose you.*

"We'll be okay," Cassie said, giving each a quick scratch on the head before vaulting onto Twi's back. Once mounted, the two spurred their horses in opposite directions.

Cassie, Twi, and Wynne hurried to the clearing where Dragon sat howling. They hadn't run into anyone, so Cassie had a feeling there was no danger from Mordred toward the others for tonight. The dog stopped howling as they emerged from the trees. *What are you doing here? You need to be getting the queen away,* he said.

"We came to make sure all the men were dead," Cassie said.

They are. That evil traitor escaped, he growled. *If I ever get my teeth in him again...*

Cassie knelt by Caelwyn's body, wondering at the peaceful expression on her face. She put two fingers at Caelwyn's throat, looking for a pulse she knew she wouldn't find. Cassie's throat constricted, her shoulders started to shake, and tears began to fall. She felt like she was losing her parents all over again, though at least she knew there was hope to be with them again. This was worse because Caelwyn's children would not see her again until they got to heaven.

Cassie sobbed, feeling as if her heart was being clawed by lions. The rest of the world blurred. The night seemed to grow darker and press in on her, as if trying to crush her. It was in that moment that she fully accepted the task God had placed in front of her, latching onto it in the desperate hope that it would keep her from becoming completely nonfunctional. Somehow, she would get it done.

Approaching hoofbeats sounded through the forest, and she hastily remounted Twi and moved her and Wynne from the clearing. She turned once they were completely ensconced in the trees and watched as the others came into view.

From that moment on, she felt she had entered her dream, except now she knew what was going on. She almost felt she could sense herself watching. It was a creepy feeling. She urged the horses to Camelot and met up with David. They entered the city using the secret underground tunnels. They arrived at the hall complex using the way Caelwyn had shown Cassie earlier that week. Guinevere opened the door at their knock. "She's dead?" she asked.

Cassie nodded, unable to speak. Pain crossed Guinevere's face and tears made their way from under her eyelids. "It's time to go, my lady," Cassie managed after a few minutes. "She killed all the men Mordred had with him, but he might come back with more. And we have to be there at the slip when it opens."

"I prayed it wouldn't come to this," Guinevere said in a low voice. "What of my daughters?"

"We'll come back to check on them," David told her. "They'll be safe enough here. We need to go now."

The queen nodded. "Let me get changed and gather some things." She did so quickly and they retraced their path to the door. Guinevere hesitated before entering the passage. "Could I just go check on them?" she asked. Cassie gazed into her eyes, so like William's, and folded.

"Be quick." She left.

"I don't recall you mentioning this in your dream," David said.

"Caelwyn told me a few days ago that just because you see yourself doing something in a dream doesn't mean it will happen exactly as you saw it. It follows the general course of events, but not always the details, like conversation."

"Oh."

Guinevere returned in ten minutes. It looked like more tears had traveled down her face, but her countenance was composed and her voice was steady. "I'm ready. Let us go." They hurried through the passage to the horses. They mounted and traveled to the Tor. They approached the time slip. Just as Cassie recalled from her dream, heavy mist rose off the water and created a forbidding, eerie atmosphere. She listened for the melody they needed. It was full and rich and loud, but wasn't quite ready yet.

"Do I go now?" Guinevere said. "And how exactly do I go through this... slip?"

"Not quite yet. And you just ride through the spot. I marked it earlier. See?" Cassie pointed to a stick stuck upright in the ground.

"I see."

Cassie kept listening, wondering if she should try singing to make it open quicker, but remembered the men from her dream. It was possible they could avoid them since she knew they would be coming, and she didn't want to give them any help in locating them. They waited silently as the minutes ticked by. Cassie kept listening... listening... listening... and heard it reach full crescendo. There was no mistaking it, with the volume and intensity. "Now. You've got to go now," she told Guinevere.

Guinevere nodded. "Very well," she said. She turned Wynne, but hesitated a minute, looking back at the two teens. "You two be careful. Tell my daughters that I never wanted to leave them and that I love them with all my heart. Tell Arthur the same and say... say that I will never forsake him, no matter how far away I am." A glistening rose in her eyes, and her voice broke slightly upon uttering Arthur's name.

"We will," Cassie said. Suddenly, she tensed as the horses went on full alert. She snatched her bow up from her pommel, grabbing an arrow and putting it on the string. She sensed the minds of strange horses on the plains beyond the bridge, and she knew they sensed her. There was a strange fogginess in their minds, but they called to her eagerly – no, desperately, she decided a minute later. The only clear thought she could sense from them was a cry for help. She also could tell they were beginning to act up on their riders. *Rats*, she thought. *I hope the men don't suspect anything from that.*

"What is it?" the queen asked, putting a hand to where she'd strapped a dagger to her side.

"Nothing good," Cassie said. "You really need to go. And by the way, next time you see us, do *not* tell us anything, just push us on through at about nine-thirty that night." Guinevere looked puzzled, but David moved Fire closer to her and slapped Wynne's flank before she could question.

Hey! the mare protested, starting into a canter. *That was uncalled for.*

"Sorry," David said. The mare continued forward, and Cassie both saw and sensed the horse and rider disappear through the time slip.

She knew it had been successful and let out a huge sigh of relief, replacing her bow and arrow. "We did it," she said. "But did you really need to do that?"

"Hey, you gave me the idea!"

Stop talking, Fire said. *The enemy is closing in. Transfer?*

"Yes," Cassie said. "But we have to have enough space to get up to speed. We'll have to get across the bridge."

"We can't let them get to the monks," David said.

"They won't harm the monks. It would make no sense. But after hearing Morgan and Mordred's conversation, they'd love to kill us. Come on." They urged Twi and Fire into a canter, keeping a wary eye out. Cassie still sensed the horses, and they seemed to be getting closer. She hoped it was just because she and David were approaching the bridge. They crossed the bridge, and Cassie cringed inwardly at the sound of the horses' hooves on the wooden boards.

Just as they were about to spur their horses to transfer speed and Cassie began to relax, she saw movement out of the corner of her eye and abruptly realized the strange horses had gotten much, much closer. *How on earth did that happen without my noticing?* she wondered briefly before Twi darted forward into a gallop. "Duck!" Cassie screamed at David as she sensed Fire copying Twi's move. David tried, but he'd been caught by surprise when Fire suddenly accelerated to keep pace with Twi, and had gotten a little unbalanced. Normally it wouldn't have been a big deal, but tonight it made all the difference as an arrow streaking through the air buried itself in his upper right arm. He cried out in pain and Cassie pulled back severely on Twi's reins, causing the mare to rear as she spun her on her haunches to go to David's aid. She ducked under another arrow she heard coming toward her and sent her own in the direction from which it came. The loud thump that occurred several seconds later told her she'd found her mark.

"Don't pull it out," she warned David. "It'll just make it worse."

He nodded, jaws clenched together in pain. "What... was it you said about... all the details not... necessarily being the same?" he forced out through gritted teeth.

She smiled faintly at his attempt at a joke. "Sorry. Just try not to move it." She snapped off the end so it wasn't such a danger.

"It's my sword arm," he said. "Is... help coming?" Cassie searched for the horses back at Caelwyn's with her mind. She guessed her aim had made whoever was out there more wary, buying them some precious time. Or maybe she'd shot their only archer. She felt Dreamer and informed her of the circumstances. She also took the time to investigate the enemies' horses more closely. To her surprise, the horses' minds were even more clouded than before and it was hard to sense them. The harder she probed for them, the more elusive their thoughts became until she couldn't sense them at all. She listened with her Brenwyd sense and sure enough, there was a spell at work. *Nuts.*

Before she could even begin to do anything about the problem, the horses appeared from the mist with their riders, completely surrounding her and David. Twi snorted and reared in defiance, and Fire pawed the ground. Several of the enemy horses neighed in response, sounding angry and confused.

One the men walked forward on his horse, who was actually behaving himself. "Well, men, look at our luck. Here are two of Caelwyn's wards, if I'm not mistaken. The Master will be pleased we captured them." Cassie shivered as she recognized the voice. It

The horses appeared from the
mist with their riders, completely
surrounding Cassie and David.

was Mordred's squire. He grinned at her. She glared back. "How nice to see you again. Why don't you tell us where the third member of your party went and who it was?"

"Who says we had someone else with us?" Cassie asked. "That seems a rather illogical jump to conclusions." She sent out another mental call for help, hoping Telyn or the horses would sense her distress.

"There are three different sets of hoof prints leading to the island, and I can tell they were made just tonight. I happen to be an excellent tracker." Cassie actually remembered him mentioning that at the feast. "So, who was it?" he asked. "One of your friends?"

"We'll be keeping that to ourselves, if you don't mind," Cassie said. "Even if we told you, you can't get to her now, anyway."

"A her, was it? Hmm." He examined Cassie carefully. She considered starting to undermine the spell on the horses, but getting herself and David out of this predicament alive seemed more important at the moment. She had a feeling that if she started singing, they would only be more motivated to close in and capture them quickly, and David couldn't defend himself with a wounded arm. "Well, even if you don't tell us now, you'll have to tell us eventually. I've learned how to question Brenwyds very effectively in Sir Mordred's service."

"Well, that's great, but we really need to be going," Cassie told him, trying to buy time. She knew the others would show up eventually, but they had to tack up and gather their weapons first. "So how about you let us go our way and we let you go your way, and we part ways without shedding blood?"

He laughed. "I'm afraid that isn't an option, little witch." Cassie was about to make an angry rebuttal, but he turned his attention to David. "Is it a custom in Armorica to let the women handle things? If so, it is no surprise you need our help to defend your kingdom. Or are you a mute?"

"No," David said, forcing the words out. The pain in his arm was like hot iron, and it throbbed sharply. "But you shouldn't... underestimate girls. They can be pretty formidable when roused."

"Truly?" The squire drew his sword. "Then I think I shall test your words. You have thirty seconds to lay down your weapons and surrender to us. Otherwise, we shall attack and you will die. You would not want to be responsible for your girl's death, would you?" Cassie and David looked at each other, each seeing desperation in the other's eyes. The odds were definitely not in their favor, but they couldn't surrender. They had no choice.

Cassie turned back to the squire. She searched again for Dreamer, found her, and thought all of her alarm in her direction. She felt the horse respond with agitation. "Here's our answer," she said, and shot an arrow straight into the squire's chest. He fell from the horse with a surprised expression and the others attacked after a moment of stunned immobility, during which Cassie shot another man. One of them raised his sword into the air and yelled, "Kill them!" David gritted his teeth and drew his sword with his injured arm, switching it to his left quickly. He couldn't help uttering a hoarse cry as stabs of pain shot through his body like lightning, almost causing him to drop his sword before he had it secured in his good hand.

Everything seemed to start moving in slow motion for Cassie, her body moving mechanically as she fought for her life, employing the techniques and movements that had become automatic for her over the past few months. Five men headed for her and three for David. This was what she hadn't seen in her dream: the outcome. She knew they'd try to separate them, and pressed Twi up against Fire's right side, guarding David's weak side. The gelding knew better than to kick at her, but the close quarters made it harder to maneuver. Cassie shot two more men before she had to draw her knives. The remaining six closed in. She sent a quick message to their horses, attempting to break through the spell barrier and get them to dump their riders. The message got through, perhaps spurred by the strength of total desperation, and Cassie and David gained a few precious minutes. Cassie worried about the horses, trying to call to them so she could break the spell later, but they ran off into the night, her calls unheeded. She and David used the time they had gotten to break free of the ring surrounding them, but were forced to pull up after a thrown spear almost killed Twi. *I hate spears*, Cassie thought. Her quick maneuver had saved Twi's life, but the halt gave the men the opportunity to close back around the two teens. Cassie kept an eye on David out of the corner of her eye. He was doing well enough, but the pain from the arrow had to be taking its toll. The fight could not last long. At least now they had the advantage of horses, and it didn't look like there were any other spears, thank God. It struck Cassie that this was a fairly silent battle, save for the clash of metal, rasp of breath, and grunts of effort from the combatants. The lack of noise pressed heavily on her, causing the metallic clangs to make her ears ring all the more.

As she stabbed one of the men attacking her, the man's dead weight wrenched the knife out of her hand, leaving her left side completely open. Busy with a man attacking her on the right, she couldn't do anything as she glimpsed another man rushing to take advantage of her opening and slashing at her unprotected side. She made it under the guard of the man on her right, but knew she would be too late to block the blow coming in on her left, even with her fast reflexes. She was just about to vault off Twi when a sword intercepted the enemy's weapon, stopping it in midair. David had switched his sword to his weak right arm and blocked the slash using both hands on the hilt, but he screamed in pain at the impact and the man quickly slapped David's blade aside to go for his heart. Cassie threw her knife and it was a bullseye. The man slumped over, dead. Cassie vaulted to the ground to collect one or preferably both knives – *never throw your weapons away in battle, girl,* she chided herself – but another man grabbed her from behind and held her in a stranglehold. She struggled, but the man was very strong and she quickly started to feel lightheaded.

Twi! she shrieked mentally. The mare responded by kicking the man in the head. He fell and Cassie slipped out from under him, gasping for breath, just before he would have pinned her to the ground. His sword scraped her arm, but it was nothing drastic. She snatched up her knives.

Girl! It was Fire. Cassie turned to see the remaining men besieging David. Fire reared, kicking out at the men with his forelegs, but he was only buying his rider time. Twi cantered up to Cassie and she vaulted on the run. She threw one of her knives, downing a man, but didn't dare throw the other. She could tell David couldn't hold out any longer. The pain was too great. She grabbed her bow and an arrow, but before she could shoot, someone else did.

A man about to thrust his sword into David's unprotected side fell without warning, and Cassie glimpsed an arrow in his back. She heard the whistling of other arrows in the air, and the remaining men – how many were left? – slumped to the ground. She and David both looked at each other in surprise and confusion, but their unspoken question was answered by the appearance of Telyn, Ganieda, and Sarah from the mist. "Oh, thank God," Cassie said feelingly, relief rushing through her in a flood. "You three have the best sense of timing ever."

"You are welcome," Telyn said simply, dismounting her stallion to check if any of the men remained alive.

"I told you two to be careful," Sarah exclaimed as she rode up to her brother and looked at the arrow embedded in his arm.

"We tried," David said. "Honest."

"You two did not fare badly," Ganieda commented. "But why did you attack them?"

"They were about to kill us," Cassie said. "We had no choice." She retrieved the knife she'd thrown. She glanced at Sarah, who was obviously trying hard not to look closely at the scene surrounding her, but didn't look like she'd throw up. The dim lighting probably helped. Cassie was feeling a little sick herself. Killing was just plain *wrong*, no matter the reasons. "Feel okay, Sarah?"

"Yeah. Just don't make me help dispose of them," she responded.

"We won't." Cassie heard footsteps, and looked up to see the three monks from the church approaching. Apparently, the battle hadn't been as quiet as she'd thought.

"What happened here?" Joseph exclaimed, looking at the carnage on the plain. The others stared in disbelief, looking sickened.

"My apologies, Father Joseph," Telyn said. "They attacked Dafyd and Cassie. We just got here. Do you have medical supplies? Dafyd's hurt." She nodded toward several lumps on the ground, and Cassie just began to register movement and low groans from them. "These as well."

"It's not that–" David tried to protest.

"Don't even think about it, David Thompson," Cassie warned him. He subsided. She went over to Telyn. "How bad are they?"

"Bad enough," Telyn said. "That one there is breathing his last, but the others would likely pull through with treatment." She sighed. "The question is whether to treat them or not. They are in rebellion."

"Right now they're wounded, hurting human beings," Cassie said. One of them rolled over and his groans grew louder. She had caused that. She or David. "We have to help them." She knelt by his side. He was bleeding badly from a side wound. In the background, she heard Sarah and Joseph tending to David, bandaging his wound after removing the arrowhead. Cassie tore off part of her tunic to try and stem the bleeding of the man beside her. The pressure caused him to look at her, but she could tell he was delirious.

"Cassie," Telyn said uncertainly. "I know you have noble intentions, but–"

"But what?" Cassie asked a bit heatedly, looking up at her. "If we ever expect men like this to stop being our enemies, we need to help, to show them we aren't a threat. It's worked before." Telyn didn't reply, and Cassie focused on healing the wound, singing in a low voice. The man's side stopped bleeding, and he relaxed into a peaceful sleep. It didn't worry her, as Caelwyn had told her that healed patients often slept afterwards. The healing sped up the natural processes of the body, which tired the person out, though not as much as the healer. Cassie closed her eyes and swayed a little as fatigue washed over, creeping into her limbs and settling in them like lead. Stubbornly, she rose and went to the next wounded survivor. His wounds she healed to the point they were no longer mortal, but didn't expend the energy to fully heal them. David's wound could wait, too, she decided, as it wasn't life-threatening.

"We can tend to them in the church," Joseph's voice drifted into her ears. "If you would be so kind as to help us transport them." Cassie nodded wearily and turned to see how David was. His arm had been bandaged, though the blood on his tunic looked bad. She looked down at herself. She didn't look much better. From the corner of her eye, she glimpsed Telyn rise to her feet and guessed she had seen to other survivors – however many there were. Cassie didn't know, and didn't feel like counting, but it made her feel better to know not all of them had been killed. She instructed the horses to let the monks put the wounded and recovering men on their backs, and they obliged willingly.

Suddenly she recalled the reason they were at the hill in the middle of the night and turned to Sarah, who was closest to her. "How's William?" she asked her. "Better?" Sarah nodded, a relieved smile on her face.

"He wanted to come with us, actually," Telyn said. "But we talked him out of it easily enough. You got her through, I assume?"

"Yes. It was after that Mordred's men came. We tried to transfer, but they surrounded us before we could." Cassie took Telyn's hand in her own and looked into her blue-green eyes. "I'm sorry," she said quietly.

Telyn lowered her eyes and blinked rapidly. "She knew what she was doing," she said in a tremulous voice. "She got the Grail to safety. Dragon told us. Mordred doesn't have it. She would have killed him, but there was a loose rock... one little loose rock..."

Cassie hugged her tight. "It's okay to cry," she whispered in Telyn's ear. "Believe me, I know." Telyn took her advice, sobbing on her shoulder. Cassie saw Sarah speaking in a low voice to Joseph, probably delivering the news of Caelwyn's death. The other two had gone back to the church with two of the horses, each carrying one of the injured. Fresh tears pricked her own eyes and they all stopped what they were doing to mourn. At length, Cassie released Telyn. "How are the little ones?"

"Not... well," Telyn said, taking in deep breaths of air and trying to recompose herself. "William's watching them. We... we must determine what to do next." Siarl had left with Arthur, taking many men from the village with him, including Bleddyn.

"Someone should go check on Gwendolyn and Jenifer," David said. He and Ganieda had returned in time to hear Telyn. "Maybe we should move them. They're practically sitting ducks."

"I agree," Ganieda said. "They... they need to be told." Her voice cracked. She held a piece of parchment in her hand and was scanning it curiously.

"What's that?" Telyn asked.

Ganieda shrugged, a puzzled expression on her face. "I know not. I found it on one of them." She indicated the dead men. "I cannot make any sense of it. Look." She handed it to her. Telyn's face also took on a confused expression.

"What does it say?" Cassie asked.

"Nothing," Telyn said. "It doesn't say anything. It's merely a collection of jumbled letters and numbers, and this strange symbol in the corner. See?" She showed it to them.

The crude symbol reminded Cassie of a swastika, except the points were going the wrong way. And it seemed to be broken in the middle... she inhaled sharply. It was a broken cross. "It's the Brotherhood," she said. "That's their symbol. And I bet I know someone who could read this."

"William," David and Sarah said simultaneously. Cassie nodded.

Telyn turned to Joseph. "Could you take care of this?" she asked, gesturing to the bodies strewn on the grass.

He nodded. "Of course. We could take care of your mother, too, if you'd like."

Telyn shook her head, blinking rapidly. "We can do it. Thank you, though." She whistled for her stallion, Lleu. He trotted over. "Who wants to come with me to Camelot?"

"What of Guinevere?" Joseph queried. "You act as if neither parent is at home."

"Guinevere went to safety," Cassie said. "That's why those men were after us. They wanted to know where she is."

"Why did you not take the princesses?"

"It wasn't for them to go," Cassie answered simply. He nodded. "Very well. God be with you, my children." He turned and started heading back toward the church.

"I'll go with you to Camelot, Telyn," Ganieda volunteered. "But we will have to wait for the fathers to return Bryn. I think Cassie and Dafyd should get back to the house." Bryn was her mare, and she and Dreamer were being used for ambulance duty.

"I won't argue with that," David said. "Don't want to hog all the excitement."

"Excitement?" Cassie said, shaking her head. "If you're calling this excitement, you and I have very different definitions of that word." She vaulted onto Twi's back. David grabbed the pommel of his saddle with his left hand and pulled himself aboard with difficulty, though Sarah helped him with a leg-up. As with most other saddles in this time period, there were no stirrups to help with mounting, and Fire was 15 hands and 3 inches.

Fire snorted and swished his tail in annoyance as David ungracefully hauled himself up. *Have you never heard of a mounting block?* he grumbled.

"Of course, but I haven't seen any around in this time. Have you?" David asked him.

No, but you should make one.

"If we're not back within an hour, start worrying," Telyn said. Cassie nodded, and then she and David took off for Caelwyn's.

On Their Own

William strained his ears to hear the sound of returning horses. It was driving him crazy not knowing what was happening. *Twitching like a nervous rabbit will not make them get back any faster,* Kai remarked from his post by the door.

"I am not twitching like a nervous rabbit. I'm just antsy," William said.

Which is another word for nervous. And you are twitching, Dragon said from his spot by the fire. William was surprised to hear him speak. The dog had collapsed after getting back and hadn't moved. William got the feeling he was deeply depressed, and he was also in pain from cracked ribs. He didn't blame him. He felt pretty depressed himself. Caelwyn was dead, and he had been completely out of it on her last day. Her last few days, really. He had been able to tell when Cassie and David sent Guinevere through the time slip, because the drain on his energy had stopped immediately, and more noticeably, the splitting headache had disappeared. It had happened so unexpectedly that it had woken him up. He was still tired, but it was a manageable tiredness, and he could focus on things again.

The twins wandered into the kitchen, red-eyed and distraught. "Are they back yet?" Aeddan asked. William shook his head.

Addiena deposited herself in his lap and cuddled against him, sobbing. "Mother's dead! And nothing can bring her back," she cried.

He didn't know what to say. He hoped the others would be back soon. He wasn't very good at this comforting business, as he'd always been taught to not show his emotions. "You'll see her one day in heaven," he offered hesitantly.

"But that's so far away. And Father's away with Arthur. What if he gets killed? What will happen to us then?" She looked up at him with wide, worried eyes, tears dripping down her cheeks. Her gaze tore at his heart and raised tears in his own eyes. No eight-year-old should have this kind of thing happen to them, especially not in the way it had. He impulsively held her tighter to him.

"I'm sure that won't happen," he told her. Suddenly they snapped to attention as hoofbeats sounded from the yard. Selyf came running from the bedroom, and all of them burst into the yard.

"... your arm, David," Cassie was saying. She looked up and smiled as she saw them, but it was a weary and sad smile. "Well, what d'ya know. The zombie lives." She dismounted and gave William a hug.

"Thanks to you," William said, hugging her back. "What happened?"

"Ran into some of Mordred's men who were passing by," David said as he dismounted. "Good to see you up. You had us seriously worried there for a while." William did a double take as he caught sight of the bandage on David's upper right arm and the blood staining his tunic.

"Are you alright?" Selyf asked, also seeing the bandage.

"I'm fine. Just a scratch," David said, waving off his concern.

Cassie gave him a hard look. "A mere scratch would not account for the amount of blood on your tunic. And I know most of it's yours."

"Okay, maybe it's a little more than a scratch," David admitted. "It's not life-threatening." They led their horses into the stable.

"Where are Telyn, Ganieda, and Sarah?" Aeddan asked.

"They're going to check on Jenifer and Gwendolyn," Cassie said. "They'll be back soon." She unfastened Twi's girth. "William, could you untack Fire? David is not to move that arm."

"Sure." William did as she asked.

David shot Cassie an irritated look. "I've untacked one-handed before," he said.

"Not with a great gaping arrow wound in your arm, you haven't," she retorted.

"Arrow?" Addiena asked, sniffling. "Was... was it a big fight? How many men? You did get Guinevere there safely, didn't you?"

"Sort of, about ten, and yes," David answered. "Well, one more if you count the guy Cassie shot in the trees, but I wouldn't. And she shot a few more before they got within sword's reach."

"How did they know where you would be?" Selyf asked.

"Their horses, I think," Cassie said, taking the saddle off Twi's back. "I sensed their horses and their horses sensed me, and they started getting agitated, which alerted their riders. I'm pretty sure there was some sort of spell involved. Anyway, we had to wait for the slip to open completely. That gave them more time to find us. Fortunately we got Guinevere through before they attacked. We managed to get most of the men, but it's a good thing Sarah, Telyn, and Ganieda showed up when they did."

"And you were down an arm," Aeddan noted, "so you did very well. How many were left by the time the others got there?"

"Um... two or three?" David guessed.

Addiena climbed up the fence that separated the stall from the aisle, trying to get a better look at David's wound. "How badly does it hurt?" she asked him.

"It's better now that the arrow's out. Kind of a dull, throbbing pain," he answered.

She nodded, looking relieved. "Good. That means the arrowhead probably wasn't poisoned."

"Poisoned?" David asked.

"Mordred's mother, Morgan, makes very bad poisons," Aeddan said. "The king fought and defeated her years ago when she led some kings in rebellion, but lots of the enemy arrows and blades had poison on them. Many men died because of it."

"There wasn't any poison on the arrowhead," Cassie said. She had finished untacking, but Twi was pretty sweaty so she was taking more time to rub her down. "I checked." David grabbed a handful of straw and started rubbing Fire down with his good arm.

The humans stopped talking and Cassie tuned in to the animal conversation. Kai growled. *I wish I had been able to come with you.*

You could have ridden, Cassie said.

I have no wish to get back on a horse like that again, Kai grumbled.

Regardless of what we would wish, Dragon said, *I think it will be necessary in the near future. You must go to the battle. You can help. And the king should know about... Caelwyn. Siarl too.*

But right before a battle? Is that wise? Cassie asked.

There is more to it than that, Dragon said, looking up at her. *You found a slip of paper on one of the men, did you not? It likely contains important information.*

How did you know about that?

I told him, Fire said. *It is important. I could tell.*

We'll see, Cassie responded. *William's got to make sense out of it first. Oh! I should probably mention that to him.*

What is this paper? Dassah asked.

It's a paper we found on the body of one of the men. We can't make heads or tails out of it, but it's got the Brotherhood symbol in the corner.

How could you make heads or tails out of a paper? It has no head or tail, Dassah wondered.

It's just an expression, Cassie explained.

Oh, right. I knew that.

Cassie suppressed a chuckle at the dog's abashed tone. "Hey, William?" she said.

"Yes?" He looked over at her.

She took the piece of parchment from her bag. "Take a look at this, would you?"

He took it, examining it curiously. His eyebrows rose and his expression turned serious as he realized what it was. "Was it on one of the bodies?" he asked. She nodded. He frowned, taking the paper closer to the torch that lit the stable.

"Can you decipher it?" David asked

"Yes, I think so. Cassie, do you have some paper I could work on?"

"Yeah." She fished out her notebook and a pen. "Here. Let's go to the house." The words had barely left her mouth when hoof-beats sounded in the yard, announcing the arrival of Telyn, Sarah, and Ganieda. Selyf, Aeddan, and Addiena ran out to greet them. Cassie heard them talking, and was surprised to hear Gwendolyn's and Jenifer's voices.

As they entered the stable, Ganieda spied William with the piece of paper. "Can you decipher it?" she asked.

"Yes, it's the same code system I know. I'm working on it," he answered.

"What what says? What is going on?" Jenifer demanded. "Where's Mother?"

"You didn't tell them?" Cassie asked. "And what are they doing here? They're much better guarded in Camelot."

"No, and even the castle isn't safe from treachery. A couple of the guards were in Mordred's pay and were in the process of kid-napping them when we got there. They were most upset when I informed them their allies were dead," Telyn answered, unsaddling Lleu. "We decided coming here was safer at the moment." The others exchanged alarmed glances.

"Is anywhere safe?" Cassie exclaimed.

"During an uprising? Not really," Ganieda said. "You never know whom to trust."

"But what if Mordred comes here?" Selyf asked. "He has to know there aren't..." he paused, gulping back tears, "aren't any adults."

"I doubt he would come," Telyn said. "He's lost too many men tonight. He has bigger things to worry about."

"Would someone please explain what is going on?" Gwendolyn cut in, raising her voice. That attracted everyone's attention. Gwendolyn never raised her voice. Her face was pale, but her cheeks were flushed and her green eyes sparked with emotion. Cassie couldn't tell which. "All I know is Mordred's done something, Mother's gone somewhere, and where is Caelwyn? We deserve answers." She crossed her arms, waiting.

"And where's Wynne?" Jenifer asked, looking around. "Did Caelwyn go to join Father? With Mother?" The others all looked at each other.

"It's a little difficult to explain," Ganieda said gently. "But we will tell you everything. Your mother is safe. She had to go... go to where she would be safe, but she's there now. She rode Wynne there. Caelwyn..." She heaved a breath that might have been holding back a sob. "Caelwyn is dead. Mordred... killed her about an hour ago." The two princesses' faces took on expressions of shock and horror.

"What?" Gwendolyn asked softly. "You speak truly?"

I saw the black-hearted traitor do it, Dragon said. *He fled after he did the deed.* Silence descended on the stable like a cloak, thick and stifling, making the air hard to breathe. Gwendolyn closed her eyes and bowed her head, tears creeping out from under her eyelids to make trails down her face. Jenifer looked from one solemn face to another, her wide eyes begging for someone to contradict the statement. Tears rose in her eyes and her shoulders started to quake. Ganieda took her in a tight hug.

Cassie turned to Twi, unable to keep watching. *God, why did this have to happen now?* she thought. *Why?* A bark from Dragon attracted everyone's attention. *We cannot break down now*, he said. *It is exactly what the traitor needs, what he expects. Caelwyn would not want it. She warned you this was coming. You*, he said, indicating Cassie, *Saw it. We can mourn properly later. We must move on, for now. The kingdom depends on it.*

"He's right," Ganieda said, wiping tears from her face and Jenifer's. "We can't stop fighting."

"Fighting? What do you mean? We haven't been fighting," Gwendolyn said.

"Begging your pardon, Gwendolyn, but I disagree," David said.

She looked at him, and her eyes went wide as she saw the bloody bandage on his arm. "What happened?" she asked.

"Ran into some of Mordred's men at Ynis Witrin." He glanced at Cassie. She nodded slightly. "Cassie and I were getting your mother to where she needed to go."

"Where?" Jenifer asked.

"Geographically, to the same place where we were," Cassie said. "We'll explain more later. Now, I think..." her voice choked, "we should go... take care of Caelwyn." The group walked to where she lay, all signs of life gone. Dragon insisted on leading the way, despite his cracked ribs. He walked steadily on, ignoring the pain, and laid himself down beside her. The clouds had cleared some for the past few hours, but now they gathered again and rain poured from the sky, appropriate for the tragic ceremony they were about to perform. Telyn and Ganieda had brought a large blanket from the house that they wrapped Caelwyn in. They buried her where she had fallen, in Brenwyd fashion, marking the place with a crudely-fashioned cross the twins had made so they could find the place again to make a more appropriate marker later. Then they all went quietly back to the house. It was in the wee hours of the morning and pitch black. They entered the kitchen and gathered around the low table. Dragon collapsed on the hearth, the pain overcoming him at last. Selyf threw some logs in the fireplace and lit them while Telyn saw to the dog, healing him.

Cassie unwound the bandage carefully from David's arm. The white gauze underneath was almost completely black with dried blood, and it was still bleeding a little. She peeled the gauze back carefully, keeping the pressure on the exit hole of the wound. David winced. "Sorry."

"It's okay," he grunted.

Cassie eyed the ugly hole in her friend's arm with a frown. "I might have to stitch this."

"You could heal it," Telyn said. "It would be better. I could help you. It would go faster."

Cassie nodded, thinking, *Duh.* "Or we could do that." She blinked, trying to focus her tired eyes. "Are two people really necessary?"

"No. I could do it, if you want." Telyn could sense Cassie felt uncomfortable about using her talent in front of everyone, not to mention she was exhausted. David darted a quick look at Cassie. It didn't matter to him, but he, too, knew Cassie was a little self-conscious about her talents.

Cassie nodded. "Sure."

"How long will this take?" David asked.

"A few minutes," Telyn said, eyeing the wound. Her face took on a look of concentration and half a minute later she started singing. The others watched as David's arm seemingly healed itself as Telyn sang, and Cassie felt goose bumps rise on her arms.

David slowly moved his arm around, his eyes wide in astonishment. "That's a whole lot better. Thanks," he said in an admiring tone.

"You're welcome," Telyn said. "So William, what does the paper say? I know you've finished translating it." William had an inscrutable look on his face, but Cassie detected a slight wariness in his eyes. She figured the healing had spooked him a little. He was still struggling with the rhetoric that had been pounded into him for years, even though he knew it was lies.

He put the piece of paper on the table and cleared his throat. "I couldn't make an exact word-for-word translation, but I got the gist of the message." He paused, looking extremely troubled. "Telyn, how many Brenwyds rode with the king?"

"More than usual, since they're fighting Mordred and Morgan. Morgan's been a known witch for years, and Mordred has been under suspicion for just as long. The king made him one of his knights because when Mordred wished to join him ten years ago, it was in the middle of a huge conflict with Morgan over the Grail and he was the one who brought her to the king for punishment and publicly denounced her," Telyn answered.

"Nice son," Sarah commented. "Was it an act?"

"Apparently, but it convinced many people that Mordred was different from his mother. Looking back, I think Morgan knew she wouldn't win against Arthur at the time, so she started planning long-term to bring him down." Telyn glanced at William. "One of the things Morgan said to Arthur before she was led away to her exile was, 'You have won for now, but one day your kingdom will come crashing down and you will have no son to save it.' Most people dismissed it at the time as spite, but as the years went by with no son, or even another daughter after Jenifer was born, rumors spread that Morgan had cursed the queen's womb to barrenness. Mother thought that perhaps Morgan had made some sort of potion that would prevent Guinevere from having any more children, period. Guinevere had just had Jenifer when that happened, so it would make sense."

"So that's what he meant," Cassie murmured.

"What who meant?" Jenifer asked.

"Mordred. When we snuck into Mordred's castle, David and I overheard a conversation between Morgan and Mordred. He said something about having prevented Guinevere from having sons."

"Really?" Ganieda said. "Why were they talking about that?"

Cassie glanced at William. "Because William spooked him at the feast. Mordred was thinking, uh, that Arthur had, um, well, you know," she said, stumbling over actually saying the last part.

"Father would never," Gwendolyn said. "I know why Mordred would think so, but why would it concern him?"

"Well, you see, Gwendolyn," David said, glancing at Cassie, who nodded, "Morgan made a prophecy that Mordred would be killed by a son of Arthur."

"Really?" Jenifer asked. "Are you sure it wasn't a daughter?"

"Jenifer!" her elder sister scolded. "Don't say such things." Her brow furrowed. "A son, not Father himself? Then this battle they're going to... it won't end well. Father has no son." She looked down at the floor.

"I wouldn't be so sure about that last part," Cassie said. Gwendolyn looked back up at her, inquiring. Cassie looked at William. "William, why don't you explain?"

"Um... are you sure?" he asked, sounding a little nervous.

"Well, it helps explain why we sent Guinevere forward, doesn't it?"

"Sent forward?" Jenifer asked, her eyes narrowing. "What does that mean? To where?... Or..." Her eyebrows shot up. "You sent my mother forward in time?" Her voice rose and went a little squeaky. Gwendolyn gasped, her eyes wide.

"Yes, but only because we had to," David said.

Jenifer drew breath to ask more questions, but William stopped her. "Jenifer, remember when I collapsed?" he asked her.

"Yes," she answered. "But what–"

"I'll get to it," he assured her. "And remember the talk we had the next morning?"

"Yes."

"And what I told you that I asked you not to tell anyone in answer to what you told me you thought about me when we first met?" Her eyes started to narrow again. Cassie could practically see the wheels turning in her brain.

"Yeeesss," she said, drawing out the word. Gwendolyn looked puzzled, but waited to see where William was going. The others also felt puzzled as to his method, but they knew where he was headed.

William took a deep breath, as if preparing himself to dive into deep water. "Well, it turns out that I was wrong, and you... you were right. Are right."

At first Jenifer just kept looking puzzled, but then Cassie saw memory and comprehension rise from the depths of her eyes and become evident as absolute and complete bewilderment on her face. She stared at William, unblinking, mouth slightly open, not saying anything. "I've never seen that before," Addiena said, smiling a little for the first time that night. "Jenifer stunned beyond words."

"What's this?" Gwendolyn asked warily. "What is it you all know that I do not?"

"But how?" Jenifer said, recovering her voice. "You were... you said... you're from... Father wouldn't... Telyn said... but then Cassie and David sent..." She paused, and her eyes widened even further (a feat, in Cassie's opinion). "Mother... she was pregnant, wasn't she? That's why she felt sick in the mornings. And you sent her..." She continued staring at William.

"Pregnant?" Gwendolyn asked, sounding shocked.

"Yes," Sarah said, "by Arthur." Gwendolyn looked from her to William, her eyes slowly widening as the implications dawned on her.

"She lands almost sixteen years before we go through the time slip," Cassie began quietly. "She's only about a month pregnant right now. Right before she's due, she travels to Carlisle – Caer Lial – with the lady who takes her in, to visit a friend. While your mother is exploring the area, she accidentally strays onto Mordred's castle, which is Brotherhood headquarters, and is imprisoned. While there, she goes into labor and gives birth... to a healthy baby boy. Another woman, the wife of a high-ranking Commander, also gives birth on the same day, but it is early and stillborn and the wife dies as a result. Grief-stricken, the husband goes to Guinevere's cell, not realizing who she is, – how could he? – having heard a pregnant prisoner was taken and she birthed a boy. He takes the live baby boy to his dying wife, swearing to her to take care of him. After his wife dies, he goes back to Guinevere's cell and tells her he is taking her child. She has no choice in the matter. When ordered to kill her, the man takes her to the road and stabs her, making it look like an accident, but before he can finish the job, the lady she was staying with comes up and he runs, figuring she will die of her wounds anyway, but he is wrong. She survives. Fifteen years later, said son travels with adopted father to Virginia to capture a certain Brenwyd family, and the rest you know," she finished. William shot her a thankful look. He couldn't have explained it half so well.

Gwendolyn looked at him wonderingly, as if seeing him for the first time. "You... that's why you look like Father. You... you're our *brother*. Our full brother." She said the words softly, almost vacantly, like her mouth was saying the words without notifying her brain.

William met her eyes squarely. "Yes," he answered, just as quietly.

"Are you alright, Gwendolyn?" Ganieda asked, concerned. Her eyes had lost their focus and seemed to just stare blankly.

Gwendolyn shook her head and her eyes refocused. A smile bloomed on her face. "Oh, yes. It's just... that's a shock I was *not* expecting," she said.

Jenifer rose from her place and went to William, flinging her arms around his neck in a fierce hug. He looked startled, but returned the hug after a moment. "So I *was* right," Jenifer said, sounding smug. She pulled back to look into William's face, frowning thoughtfully. "But are you younger or older than I am? I've always wanted a younger sibling. Then Gwendolyn wouldn't boss me around so much." Her usual forcefulness returned to her words.

"Uh, well, you know Jenifer, that's a good question," William said, blinking at the idea that the ten-year-old might technically be considered older than he was.

"I do not boss you," Gwendolyn objected. "You simply don't behave as you should all the time."

"Both," Aeddan said thoughtfully, "I think both. He's lived longer, but was born way after you."

"So younger older?" Jenifer mused, settling down close beside her new-found brother. "I think that makes sense. And you do boss me, Gwendolyn. I *do* try to behave."

"Try harder," Gwendolyn said. "But Telyn, I thought you said Caelwyn thought–?"

"I talked with Caelwyn about that, actually," Cassie said. "She said Morgan could try all the potions she likes but it won't change a prophecy, and God is certainly not hindered by a mere herb mixture."

"That sounds like Caelwyn," Gwendolyn said. "And if you put it in those words…"

"So William, getting back to the mysterious paper?" David prompted. "I'm all for family reunions, but you still haven't said what the paper says."

"Right," William said, refocusing. "So how many Brenwyds went exactly, Telyn?"

"I'm not sure, but all are very powerful. It's because of Morgan and Mordred. Their magic has to be countered. And when we go to war we send only our best," Telyn said proudly.

William winced. "That's what I was afraid of," he said gravely.

"Why?" Selyf asked.

"They're walking into a trap," William declared. "From what this paper says, I think the main goal of this battle isn't necessarily to break the king's power; it's to draw the strongest Brenwyds into one place so Mordred can get them out of the way. It'll be easier to conquer Britain if the Brenwyds are gone, so he's starting with the most powerful. In the note, he's instructed his men to round up as many as they can and take them to his castle as part of a larger operation. Beyond that, it doesn't say, but based on what Merlin told me–" He got no further, for a general outcry arose. Ganieda alone remained silent, but her face paled and her knuckles turned white as she grasped her tunic hem. Even the dogs expressed surprise.

And when did you see Merlin? Dragon won out over the uproar. William colored.

"Ah, well, actually I wasn't supposed to tell anyone I'd seen him." *Oops*, he thought.

"He's alive?" Telyn asked.

"Yes, but imprisoned in Mordred's castle." He sighed. "I guess it doesn't matter if you know or not now."

"He told you not to tell anyone, did he not? Typical," Ganieda said. "What has he Seen?"

William shrugged. "He didn't tell me much of his thoughts, but he explained more about why Mordred is so bent on wiping out Brenwyds, which matches up with what you said the next day, Cassie. Mordred thinks he can't get the power he wants until all the Brenwyds are gone."

"Which is why he wants to draw all the most powerful together in one place," Sarah said. William nodded.

"It's amazing the evil people will commit to get their own wants," Telyn said, frowning. "But we cannot merely sit here with this information. We must go warn the Brenwyds and the king."

"Would they be at Camboglanna yet?" David asked.

"Likely," Gwendolyn said. "Most of the war bands are mounted, and the infantry is trained to march hard and fast."

"But would they start fighting right away?" Cassie asked.

"If both armies are there, it's possible," Ganieda said. "The king will try to sue for peace, but I do not think Mordred would accept."

"No, he won't," William said. He looked outside. It was still fully dark, though dawn was approaching and the rain had ceased. "But they won't fight in the dark, will they?"

"I don't believe so," Gwendolyn said. "But seeing as it is Mordred..." She shrugged.

Jenifer's brow furrowed and she looked up at the ceiling. "Dragon, did not you say that... Mordred killed Caelwyn?" she asked.

He did, the dog answered.

"Then he's still nearby, and couldn't possibly get back to the north for at least a week. We have time. Lots of it." New hope appeared on her face.

Or we might not, Dragon said. *The horse he rode tonight – it smelled like a Brenwyd horse. If he has been capturing Brenwyds, he may be taking their horses as well, knowing of their special ability.*

"And if that's the case," David said. "That battle may very well start tomo– this morning, rather." He shook his head. "Can we know for sure?"

"Mother... Mother would have been able to," Telyn said, choking up a little. "She had the Sight. I don't."

"But I do," Cassie said.

Telyn looked at her in surprise. "You do? You have not mentioned it before."

"Because I didn't know what it was until this afternoon when I asked your mother."

"How could you not know?" Addiena asked.

"A lot of knowledge about Brenwyd abilities has been lost by the time we are from," Cassie said. "I noticed it, but didn't know what it was."

"Your hunches," Sarah said. Cassie nodded.

"Can I ask what this Sight thing is?" William asked.

"It's the ability to look for people far away, or see what's happening at a faraway place, and it'll even guide you when you don't ask it to," Telyn said. "It's always right."

"Do you trust my instincts now, William?" Cassie asked mischievously.

He put his hands up in surrender. "Pardon me for not realizing you had Second Sight when you didn't even know you had it," he said dryly.

"I still trusted my instincts," Cassie retorted.

He smiled ruefully. "I will trust your feelings from now on. And I've been doing that, just so you know."

"Do you know how to focus it?" Telyn asked.

Cassie nodded. "Your mother explained it. Should I focus on Mordred, then?"

"Yes, but don't be surprised if it takes a few minutes to get to him, or shows you other places and people. The Sight has a will of its own." She sighed. "And sometimes it will show nothing at all."

"Wonderful." Cassie closed her eyes and focused. *Okay,* she told herself, *I want to know what Mordred's up to.* Her mind's eye produced an image of him. The image appeared in a room with another man she recognized as Lancelot and a woman she recognized as Morgan. They were talking. At first she couldn't hear them, but the volume increased until she could have sworn they were right next to her. She listened to all they said, a hollow sense of fear rising within her. Her vision abruptly veered from Mordred to men she liked far better. The king stood with Siarl, looking out from what she knew was a fort. Lights from below moved around, representing soldiers, and somehow she knew they were setting up defenses. She heard the king say, "The battle will come today," and the vision dissolved.

She blinked, coming back to Caelwyn's kitchen. "What did you See?" she heard Ganieda ask.

"Mordred's back in the north. Lancelot's with him. The battle will come today." Cassie looked around at the others, worry evident on her face. "Mordred knows Arthur beat them to the fort, and he's changed tactics. They're planning a double attack. One to draw the king and his troops from the fort onto open ground, and another, smaller force led by Lancelot to come in from behind and take the fort. If they do that, their victory is certain. They plan to take the Brenwyds as Lancelot is taking the fort."

You have no time to lose, Dragon said. *You must leave at once.*

Telyn nodded and stood. "Who's going besides me?" she asked.

"I'll go," Cassie said.

"I'm coming," David said. "My arm's good as new, thanks to Telyn."

"I'll go," William said. "I feel fine. I slept enough yesterday. You can't convince me to stay at home for this one." He crossed his arms and looked at them defiantly. The others exchanged glances at that announcement, questioning who wanted to argue with him.

"Are you sure?" Cassie asked. He nodded firmly. She listened to his song. It was strong and energetic, more so than she expected. *Besides,* she thought, *we could always keep him in the back if we need to fight. And he might throw Mordred off balance.* She shrugged. "Okay." He looked surprised by her easy acquiescence, but didn't question it.

"I'll come with you," Ganieda said. "Perhaps there will be a chance to free my father with Mordred busy."

"I want to go," Jenifer said.

"Oh, no you don't," Gwendolyn said. "You're too young for battle."

"I could simply watch."

"There's no simply watching on a battlefield."

"It's my father, too!" she appealed to William, green eyes wide in a pleading expression. "Please?"

He shook his head. "I'm agreeing with Gwendolyn on this," he told her.

She glowered at him. "Brothers are no fun," she decided.

Sarah laughed. "They can be, believe me. When we get back, why don't you and I have a talk about brothers?" she asked her.

Jenifer brightened slightly. "I think I'd like that," she said.

William groaned. "Oh, no. That doesn't sound good."

David grinned and clapped him on the shoulder. "Don't worry, my friend. I know a thing or two about dealing with sisters," he told him.

"Now that that's settled," Cassie said. "We need to get moving if we're going to get up north in time."

"I'll come with you guys, too," Sarah said.

"Are you sure, Sarah? Battlefields can be pretty nasty," her brother said.

She knew that this time he wasn't teasing her about her squeamishness, but was genuinely concerned. "I'm sure. We've come this far together and we can go a little farther," she said. David saw a determined light enter his sister's hazel eyes and realized she was not the squeamish girl she had been. She would be alright.

"If you do not mind, I'd like to accompany you as well," Gwendolyn said, casting a look at Jenifer. "I can wield a sword well enough, even if it's not my preferred activity. I wish to see how it unfolds for myself." Her eyes fell to the floor, and Cassie wondered how much of the truth she had guessed as to the outcome of the battle. She was very good at guessing what wasn't said.

Telyn put a comforting hand on Gwendolyn's arm. "Of course you can," she said. "Selyf, you'll be in charge. I would go to Eira's once we're gone."

He nodded seriously. "Very well."

"So seven of us are going?" Telyn mused. "Good. There's enough."

"Enough what?" Sarah asked.

Telyn turned and started to walk out. "You will see," she answered Sarah. "Selyf, Aeddan, come help me, please." They were back within five minutes carrying chain mail shirts and sleeveless, stiff leather tunics.

"Ah, a good thought, Telyn," Ganieda said. "I forgot about these." They dropped their burdens on the table.

Telyn picked up a mail shirt. "A Brenwyd smith made these shirts. It would take a very sharp sword indeed to pierce one. There are shields, as well, that we should take on the way out."

They flew into a flurry of preparations, gathering weapons and packing saddlebags. They dressed for battle, putting the chain mail on over their tunics and the stiff leather tunics over that. A grim mood settled over them. This was no mere skirmish they were preparing for; it was a battle that would determine the fate of a kingdom, a fate four of them knew was basically sealed. It was during this preparation that they realized Seren was missing. Cassie asked Dragon where he'd put it, as it had not been with Caelwyn's body. Dragon replied that he had not touched it and had assumed one of them had taken it. Telyn said that she hadn't seen it. It didn't take a genius to figure out where it was: Mordred had snatched it. Dragon lamented that he had not seen him do it, but the others assured him he couldn't have helped it. Cassie resolved to get it back before she had to leave the sixth century. There was no way she'd be able to find it after returning to the future.

Jenifer followed the four from the future around, asking questions about what their time was like and how it was different from hers. She'd done the same thing at Camelot after learning they were from the future. The answers seemed to wake something in her, a longing for things that she would never see but that sounded wondrous.

At last, they were ready. All wore cloaks over their armor, as there was an autumnal chill in the air. Telyn, Cassie, and Sarah had bows and quivers with arrows on their backs in addition to their swords, or knives in Cassie's case. Cassie fastened her emergency bag to her saddle. The boys had their swords, with shields slung on their backs. Gwendolyn had a Celtic sword and spear, as did Ganieda. They also had shields. The sun was rising and the sky in the east was blood-red. The horses snorted and pawed the ground. The only one not displaying excitement was Lleu. The gray had been to war before, having originally belonged to Telyn's uncle, but had lost him in a battle. He held a dim view of war. The younger ones gave farewell hugs and everyone held back tears. "You take care of yourselves," Telyn instructed, hugging each of her siblings. "Stay on guard, and pray."

Jenifer hugged Gwendolyn farewell and turned to William. He bent to her level and she hugged him tight. "Please come back. I wish to know what it's like to have a brother," she whispered in his ear.

"I'll do my best, I promise," he answered. They released each other. Cassie was busy getting the dogs situated on the horses. Dragon had decided to stay and guard the young ones. Kai was on Lleu and Dassah was on Twi. Kai still disliked this travel method, but refused to let Cassie go into a battle situation without him.

Since none of them had been to Camboglanna before, they had determined the closest they could transfer to the battleground was a plain outside Caer Lial. They would have to ride from there after getting directions. The riders looked down at the ones on the ground. The ones on the ground looked back.

Farewell, Dragon said. *Be careful and come home in one piece. Remember there is safety in numbers and the One is always there for you.*

"We'll remember," Telyn said, glancing eastward. The sun was just peeking over the horizon. "We should go before the sun rises any higher." She looked at her siblings one last time, then urged Lleu into a gallop, vanishing from sight just before the trees. The others followed her. Cassie was last. She paused, holding Twi back with difficulty, and looked around the place she had called home for the last three months. She wondered how her parents were, how time was progressing at home. She pressed a hand against her locket.

"What are you waiting for?" Addiena asked her.

"I'm waiting to go home," Cassie replied without thinking.

Twi snorted. *We will certainly not get home any faster for lingering here. Let us go. We have things to do. We will get home in good time,* she said impatiently.

Dragon stood on his hind legs, putting his front paws on Twi's shoulder. *Caelwyn spoke a prophecy before she left this world. It is intended for you and William. Will you hear it?*

"I know it," she said softly. "It says that one day a female descendant of Caelwyn will bring Mordred and his followers down, aided by Arthur's heir – and so start to heal the rift between humans and Brenwyds."

Very good, but it is Arthur's son.

"Where I read it, it said 'the heir of Arthur.'"

Where was this?

"In Caelwyn's journal. Perhaps that part was changed on purpose, as she did say 'son of kings' when she actually said it to me. Anyway, we found it on a piece of parchment hidden between two pages that had been pasted together to conceal it." Cassie looked at the young ones thoughtfully. "Perhaps you could get the journal ready while we're away. I do have to find the thing fifteen hundred years in the future."

"We can do that," Selyf said. "But Mother has several journals. Which one was it?"

Cassie smiled at him. "I'll leave that up to you. I will tell you that it didn't mention the events of the last three months."

He nodded. "We'll get it done."

Twi pawed and wrestled with Cassie for her head. *Let us go, let us go, let us go,* she chanted. Cassie gave Twi her head, the black Anglo-Arab exploded like a racehorse from the gate, and their surroundings blurred.

THE BATTLE OF CAMBOGLANNA

Telyn, Cassie, and the animals heard the battle first: the clash of weapons, the battle cries of men, the screams of horses, and the shrieking of carrion birds. They pulled up when the others could also hear it clearly. Telyn wrinkled her nose, being able to smell the stench of blood that rose above the field in a thick, invisible cloud. The dogs raised their hackles and the horses pranced nervously, smelling it as well. "What, exactly, do we do when we get there?" Sarah asked, pulling her bow from her quiver and dismounting to string it. Telyn and Cassie did the same.

"We should see how it is going," Gwendolyn said. "If it is going well, we should find one of the knights and tell them about the rear attack. If it is going poorly, we must get to the fort and stop Lancelot." Cassie felt no small amazement as she looked at her friend, whom she knew to be not at all given to violence, dressed in full battle attire with sword at side, spear in hand, and shield on back. She looked the very image of a Celtic warrior maid.

"With just us seven?" David asked. "Plus horses and dogs," he added hastily.

"I will be able to rally some men to help," Gwendolyn said. "But I know not how many."

"What about your father?" Cassie asked. "Aren't you going to tell him Mordred's plan?"

Gwendolyn actually smiled slightly, though it was strained. "Cassie, in battle my father is on the front line and fairly unreachable. We should avoid the main part of the fray and concentrate on stopping Lancelot and warning the Brenwyds."

"Agreed," Ganieda said. "Telyn, why don't you take care of that?"

"I'll try," she responded, looking in the direction of the battle. "But I don't know if Father will hear me in the midst of a battle."

"Speaking of that," David said, digging around in his saddlebag. "Cassie, I think you and Telyn should wear these." He tossed her some cloth strips.

She caught them and frowned. "Is this really necessary, David?" she asked.

"It could help prevent Mordred's men from snatching you two if they do get the Brenwyds. That's the idea, anyway. You're the one who says to prepare for everything." Cassie shrugged and gave a piece of material to Telyn.

Telyn looked at it. "And this will help how?"

"By putting it around your head so it covers your ears," Cassie said, tying the cloth around her head. "I've worn one covering my ears for four years with no one the wiser. And he's got a point. I've been in Mordred's cells once and I do not want to go back there as a prisoner ever again." She rubbed her wrists, where the crisscross scars were still faintly visible from her time in devil's iron cuffs. Telyn rolled her eyes, but recognized the sense of the suggestion and went about putting the makeshift headband on. Cassie helped her.

Telyn shook her head at the unaccustomed covering. "You've worn one of these for four years?" she asked Cassie, sounding impressed.

"Yep. Not fun, but necessary." Twi pranced underneath Cassie, impatient to be off.

Lleu spoke instructions to all the horses, unheard by all the riders save Cassie. *Battle is no place for antics. Your main goal is to see your rider through unharmed. Do what you have to do to make that happen. Do not lose your head, whatever you do, and* listen to your rider. *You must be steady. Be on constant watch for weapons. If your rider dismounts, keep a sharp eye on them. Understand?* The other horses indicated their comprehension.

"Let us pray before we go," Ganieda said. They closed their eyes and bowed their heads. "Father, we thank You for seeing us safely thus far, and we pray You extend Your protection as we ride into battle. Guard our hearts and minds, for the enemy always seeks to destroy us from the inside. This is not a normal foe we fight today, but our own countrymen led astray and given over to evil. Help us to remember that and extend Your mercy when we can. Put Your defending angels around us and the Brenwyds, so that evil will not triumph. But even if it does this time, Lord, we know that it is all in Your plan and You already have another in motion to bring it down. Evil might triumph for a day, but soon enough the sweet taste of victory turns to bitter gall in their mouths and they are punished for their misdeeds in the Lake of Fire. We go forth in Your name to fight the Darkness and bring the Light. We fight for our kingdom, and we fight for our friends and loved ones, but above all we fight for You. Show Your glory this day on the battlefield, that the lost may see and believe. Amen."

"Amen," the rest echoed, including the animals. Cassie felt new strength flow into her limbs, her fatigue draining away. The others, too, looked reenergized.

Telyn gathered her reins and turned Lleu toward the battlefield. "Come. We have not a moment to waste."

❧❦❧

Cassie was not at all prepared for the sight that met her eyes as they crested the last ridge and looked down over the battlefield. It was a deep valley that looked like a gorge, with a sharp turn a mile from where they stood. Fighting was everywhere she looked and the noise was almost deafening. She wasn't sure which side was which, until she noticed a fort built into a hill to her right. After seeing that, she could pick out Arthur's forces defending and Mordred's attacking. She found the king and, sure enough, he was on the front line. She recognized Siarl's horse beside him. She looked for Mordred but didn't see him. Listening with her song-sense, she sensed him vaguely, but he wasn't on the battlefield. Morgan was with him. She gathered that at the moment both sides were even, but Arthur's force was gaining ground. They were pushing Mordred's forces back. She extended her sense toward the fort and didn't feel any force coming up behind. She frowned and sent out a query to the birds circling overhead to find out if they could see the men from their position.

"Those are Picti warriors," Gwendolyn said, pointing at the enemy forces. Many of them wore blue war paint and little or no armor (little of any kind of garments, really). "Mordred must be mad to use them. They could easily turn on him."

"Still, it appears to be going well for us," Ganieda said.

Cassie caught Telyn's eye and sent a questioning thought her direction. Telyn nodded slightly, indicating she sensed it as well. "Too well," Telyn said. "Let's make for the fort." They turned and headed up the ridgeline. Cassie felt like they were sitting ducks, but no one below noticed them, too busy fighting to look up. She didn't blame them. Real battle had no heroic music playing, and there was no camera tactfully cropping out the worst of the gore. Real battle was just men grimly fighting for survival, and it wasn't pretty to look at or listen to. The screams of the wounded and dying cut Cassie to the core and brought tears to her eyes. The colors of the battlefield were red, black, and white – red the color of fresh blood, black the color of dried blood, and white the color of corpses.

Kai and Dassah went in front of them. The teens each held their reins in one hand, keeping a firm grip on their weapons with the other. They descended a steep trail they discovered that led to the base of the fort. The horses picked their way carefully, avoiding the rocks and leaning back on their haunches to keep from slipping.

The sounds of battle were much more pronounced at the bottom, and Cassie winced. The heavy metallic scent of blood was so strong she could taste it in the back of her mouth, and her stomach churned. Gwendolyn took the lead. The path ended by the side of the fort and they followed the base of it to come out before the entrance. At the moment, the area immediately before the fort was the safest on the field because the main fighting was happening further up the valley. They rounded the side of the fort and halted, taking in the scene before them. Men lay on the ground, either dead or wounded. Others moved among them, picking up the wounded and taking them into the fort for care.

"There!" Gwendolyn said, sounding relieved. "There is Bedivere. We can tell him." She dismounted.

"I will accompany you," Telyn said. Bedivere seemed to be directing the efforts to help the wounded. A bloody bandage covered his left thigh. His back was to Telyn and Gwendolyn. Another man caught sight of the girls approaching and pointed. Bedivere turned around. Cassie saw his eyebrows go up and surprise enter his expression as he saw the girls. He walked toward them, limping.

They were close enough that Cassie could hear what passed between them, but far enough away that the knight didn't notice the others in the hill-fort's shadow. "What in heaven's name are you doing here, Gwendolyn?" he said, frowning.

"We have information you must know," Gwendolyn answered. "We must reach the Brenwyds. This whole battle – it's a trap to lure them into Mordred's clutches. He wants all the strongest out of the way to make it easier to conquer the kingdom. He's planning a double attack. He's drawing the main force out into the valley, but another force will come from the rear to take the fort. Our army will be sandwiched between hostile forces."

Bedivere scowled. "The devil! Just the kind of thing he would do." He sighed. "There's no reaching your father at the moment, and I have mainly injured men under my care. The healers are doing their best, but they cannot heal every injury without draining themselves. How many men are coming behind?"

Telyn glanced back at Cassie. *I don't know*, Cassie thought to her, disgusted with herself for not thinking to find that out.

"We don't know," Telyn told the knight.

His expression darkened. "Hmm. Well, we have fifty able men holding the fort, and you can add about fifteen more if you count those who are only lightly wounded. That gives us sixty-five, perhaps a few more if the Brenwyds can heal others." He looked at Gwendolyn curiously. "How did you find out about a double attack?"

Gwendolyn gestured behind her. "Cassie Saw it."

Bedivere looked behind her in surprise, finally noticing the others. "Truly? Well, seeing as Caelwyn trained her, I shan't doubt it. Where is Caelwyn? We could use her."

"She's dead," Telyn said in a low, monotone voice. "Mordred... killed her this morning."

Bedivere's eyes widened in shock and sorrow. "What? Dead?" he whispered. No answer was needed. Bedivere put a hand on Telyn's shoulder. "I'm sorry, lass. She'll be missed by many." He sighed heavily with head bowed.

Kai growled deep in his throat. Cassie looked at him. *What is it?* she asked.

Trouble, he answered, sniffing the air. The wind had picked up, blowing toward them from behind the fort. *We must move quickly.*

Is this what you seek? a raven circling above asked Cassie. A picture of a group of men waiting by a faint trail formed in her mind. About half were painted with blue paint; the others looked to be Britons.

Yes, thank you. "We've got to move now. They're about to attack," she called out.

"Where?" Bedivere asked. Cassie felt surprised that he didn't doubt her.

"There's a trail leading from behind the fort down the hill. They're waiting at the base."

"I know what you speak of. It hasn't been used in years." He scowled. "We should have known it wouldn't be so easy. There's still no sign of Mordred, or his witch mother." He paused, thinking. "I can bring about thirty men down the trail, leaving the rest to defend the fort. Wait here for me. Telyn, tell your father what's going on. He'll tell the king." He turned and headed to the fort. The teens remained where they were, waiting anxiously.

Abruptly, Cassie sensed... something. She couldn't say what, but something had shifted, and it wasn't good. She heard Telyn gasp. "Did you feel that?" Cassie asked her.

Telyn nodded, tight-lipped. "Mordred's making his move." She and Gwendolyn remounted. "We cannot wait for Bedivere."

"What?" David asked. "What happened? I didn't feel anything."

"It wasn't in the physical realms," Telyn said. "Morgan... she's doing something. Turning the tide." She closed her eyes, an intense, concentrated look crossing her face.

Cassie searched for Mordred with her Sight. She found him, and saw Telyn was right. He was making his move, and he had a lot of men with him. He had drawn Arthur's forces out into the valley so Lancelot could take the fort easily. Once his ally had done that, Mordred would truly move in to try and crush Arthur's army.

"It's up to us," William said. He had a hard, determined look on his face. "We have to stop Lancelot. If he succeeds, Arthur's doomed for sure." He turned Phoenix back toward the path, the others following. The climb back up the steep hill tired the horses, but there was no help for it. They hurried to the back trail, traveling through trees that provided cover, but ahead of them the trees stopped abruptly. They reined in, looking down. The hill wasn't nearly as steep here as it was in front of the fort. Lancelot and his men were starting to make their way up the path. There were no archers, but each held a nasty-looking spear, and there were various daggers, knives, and swords. *We have to be nuts*, Cassie thought, gulping as she took in the large company. She estimated that there were sixty to seventy.

"So how are we going to do this?" Sarah asked nervously, twisting Dreamer's mane in her fingers.

William studied the scene intently, taking in the landscape, the weaponry, and where they might have weak spots. "Telyn, Cassie, Sarah, you start off shooting from here," he ordered. "Even the odds as much as you can. Spread out to make it harder for them to pinpoint where the arrows are coming from. They can't shoot back at you. David, Gwendolyn, Ganieda, and I will spread out with you and wait until you've gotten the numbers down enough, and then we'll charge them. Kai and Dassah, you come with us when we charge. Once you three run out of arrows, join us and pray Bedivere comes soon. Oh, try to chop their spears in half. That'll take out their long-distance weapons." He looked around at them. "Sound alright?" They nodded, amazed by his confident tone. "Then let's get moving. Don't start shooting until you hear me give the go-ahead through your horses. We need them in the most vulnerable position possible." The teens spread out.

Cassie rode up toward the fort under the tree cover, David following her. They stopped when they were a ways in front of the enemy. Cassie took an arrow from her quiver and placed it on the bowstring. "Cassie?" she heard David say softly. "What happens if we die here?"

"We go to heaven," she said, just as quietly.

He nodded. "Yeah, but what about the people in our time? What will they think?"

Cassie blinked. *What indeed?* She hadn't thought about it. "I don't think we'll die," she said at length. "I don't think God is done with us yet."

"Mmm, me neither. And you are generally right." He smiled at her and she smiled back. Their smiles slowly faded as they stared at each other, trying to read what was in the other's face. Cassie looked away, feeling embarrassed. David nudged Fire closer to Twi, wanting to say something that had been on his mind since earlier that morning. "Cassie, you do know I really don't care what shape your ears are, right?" She looked back at him, questioning. "I've been thinking. Back at Caelwyn's, when Telyn did the healing instead of you. I don't mind, but I don't think you should feel uncomfortable using your talents in front of us. We are your friends, after all." He took a deep breath. "You are a pretty darn amazing person, Cassandra Pennington, and I am glad to be your friend. Sarah feels the same, and so does William. Your talents make you unique, and that's a good thing, so don't be afraid to use them."

She stared at him, a fierce blush coming to her cheeks. How had he known she had been hesitant? He echoed what Caelwyn had said in their last training session. "David... I don't know what to say. You... you mean that?"

"Absolutely. I just thought you should know that, you know... just in case." She tore her gaze from him and stared at Twi's withers. Twi snorted, and Cassie felt she was amused.

Now. Start now, Phoenix's voice entered her head. Cassie raised her bow and aimed, her thoughts and emotions all in a whirl. She decided to save pondering David's words until she had more time. The first men of the company were now parallel with Cassie's position. She couldn't see Lancelot. A good thing for him, as this first arrow would have been for him, otherwise. The arrow hit home, and Telyn's and Sarah's did as well. The men fell into confusion, trying to figure who was attacking them and from where. Cassie kept firing, hitting a man each time. Those who weren't killed were wounded enough to take them out of the fight (she hoped). As the men began organizing themselves to charge up the hill, she heard Phoenix say, *Attack*. David spurred Fire forward. Cassie held her fire so he could get to the company without her accidentally harming him. The surprising charge of four people yelling on horseback from the trees drove the men back into the valley. Cassie ran out of arrows and prepared to enter the fray.

About half the company was dead from the arrows, but the rest were rallying, having realized the attacking force was ridiculously small. Lancelot, somehow having escaped the arrows, shouted orders. Kai and Dassah jumped on men, biting wherever they could and nimbly avoiding the weapons thrusting to and fro. Cassie saw Telyn coming up behind them on Lleu, and the stallion released a loud bugle. Twi answered, rising in a rear, and Cassie let her go when she landed, drawing her knives. They had the advantage of surprise, but the men they were fighting were well trained. Many had fought in real battles before, more than likely, and they were shaking off their surprise. They also had a huge numerical advantage. Several headed for Cassie and she concentrated on fighting. She caught glimpses of her friends from the corners of her eyes: Gwendolyn and Ganieda wreaking havoc with their spears; David, William, and Telyn slashing and hacking with their swords. Sarah still shot arrows into the fray, having fastened an extra quiver to her saddle at Caelwyn's.

Cassie completely dropped Twi's reins and guided her on leg, seat, and mental commands alone. She had worked hard on this with the mare, and the training proved its worth now. Twi responded to Cassie instantly without argument, girl and horse completely in sync with each other. Twi deftly avoided spears and swords, getting her rider into the best possible positions to disable the wielders without being injured, though one time Cassie didn't move soon enough and a sword came down on her leg. A cry of pain tore from her lips, but she was able to fight off her assailant. Quickly examining her leg afterwards, she determined the wound wasn't deep, but wrapped a hasty bandage around it anyway to stem the bleeding.

Suddenly Cassie became aware of Dreamer calling to her. *Help!* The blue roan mare showed her an image of several men closing in around her and Sarah. Sarah had run out of arrows, and Cassie knew her friend couldn't take on that many men at once with the sword. She wheeled Twi around and they rushed to Sarah. Sarah was doing alright and one man lay unmoving on the ground, but three more were besieging her.

"Hey!" Cassie yelled. "Haven't you ever heard three against one isn't fair?" The men whirled around in surprise. Sarah looked extremely relieved to see her. Two men moved to attack Cassie while the other turned back to Sarah. Cassie cued Twi to rear, causing the men to cower away from her deadly hooves. One ducked away to within Cassie's reach and she slashed toward him, catching him off guard. A few minutes later all the men were down.

Sarah averted her eyes. "Thanks. I was panicking for a minute there," she said to Cassie. Her face was several shades paler than normal.

"No problem. Nice shooting."

"I did what I could," Sarah said, looking out at the battle. Cassie looked as well, grateful for a breather, and took the opportunity to heal the gash in her leg and several small wounds the horses had received. It looked like about twenty men or so were left. But they fought with everything they had, and the girls' friends were hard pressed to defend themselves. Cassie also noticed some wounded struggling up off the ground with their spears, trying to rejoin the skirmish. She was amazed at how well they were doing. Seven teenagers cutting a group of nearly seventy grown men down to twenty? Not bad. But Cassie and Sarah saw the tables turning. Lancelot was still alive and he and his men were slowly forcing the other five teens and two dogs back.

"Oh, where is Bedivere?" Sarah asked in a slightly despairing voice.

Movement at the top of the path caught Cassie's eye. "There!" she said, pointing. She recognized Bedivere's profile, but only ten men were with him. *Hmm. Well, that would probably be enough,* she hoped. She wondered what had taken so long. Or maybe it hadn't been as long as she thought.

"Thank God," Sarah said as they headed back down to the valley. They had barely exited the trees when something went terribly wrong. Cassie heard a faint buzzing sound, but dismissed it. Abruptly the buzzing became a high-pitched screech, well out of normal human hearing but just within hers. She clapped her hands over her ears, dropping her knives and screaming as the sound tore at her eardrums. It was like fingernails across a chalkboard but a thousand times worse. It felt like a bear was clawing at her eardrums, trying to rip them into oblivion. She saw Sarah looking at her, saying – no, shouting – something, but she couldn't hear her. She felt Twi acting up beneath her, also affected by the sound, but could do nothing about it. She felt herself losing her grip with reality. There was nothing, nothing – nothing but the awful sound. "Dear God, help me! Make it stop!" she screamed. Or she thought she did. She was no longer sure of anything.

✦

Sarah had no idea what to think. She had never seen Cassie like this, had never heard anyone scream like this before. Cassie had her hands clapped tight over her ears, like she was blocking them from a sound, but Sarah couldn't hear anything to warrant such a reaction. "Cassie! What's wrong? Talk to me!" she yelled frantically at her friend, but Cassie seemed not to hear. She tried to get closer, but Dreamer was acting up, crow hopping, kicking out, her ears pinned flat against her head. Sarah tried to calm her. "Dreamer! Steady, girl. Easy. What's wrong?"

I do not know, I do not know! The sound... it is too high, the mare answered, distressed. *Evil. The Bad One. It is wrong, it is wrong, all wrong.* Twi was also acting up, which wasn't unusual, but her rider was slumped on her back. Sarah grabbed Cassie before she could slip off, struggling to keep her own seat. She'd stopped screaming and was now quiet. Sarah looked at the others. They, too, were having trouble with their horses, and she saw Telyn slumped in the same position as Cassie. Ganieda maneuvered her out of harm's way, a feat considering how Bryn and Lleu were acting. William was having the least trouble. Phoenix looked jumpy, but he was obviously trying to cooperate with his rider, and Gwendolyn's mare seemed to be trying to do the same. In fact, William and Gwendolyn were the only reasons Lancelot's force wasn't completely overwhelming them at the moment. Bedivere and his men hurried down the hill and joined the battle.

As suddenly as it had begun, the fit passed. The horses settled. Sarah nudged Dreamer over to Twi. "Cassie? You okay?" she asked. Cassie moaned in reply, not opening her eyes or taking her hands from her ears. Gently, but with extreme trepidation of what she might find, Sarah pried her friend's hand away from her ear. She breathed a sigh of relief. There was no blood, of which Sarah had been half-afraid. Sarah shook Cassie's shoulders. "Cassie! Cassie, can you hear me?" Her friend opened her eyes slowly, blinking. "Cassie, go back to the trees, you hear?" Cassie just stared at her blankly. Sarah felt her heart leap into her throat. "Twi! Take her back."

I will, Twi said in a very worried tone. *Girl, hang on.* The black mare turned back. Sarah didn't stay to watch her, but spurred Dreamer to where Ganieda was guarding Telyn against several men. Sarah already had her sword drawn and helped Ganieda with her chore. They fought the men off so Sarah could examine Telyn. She again found nothing visibly wrong, but knew that there could be internal damage.

"What happened?" Ganieda asked.

"I don't know," Sarah said. "Lleu, take her to Cassie." She saw Kai nearby. "Kai, go with Telyn and guard her and Cassie."

Evil work has been done here. We will find the full extent before this day is over, he said grimly. Lleu and Kai headed for the trees. Ganieda and Sarah guarded their backs.

David made his way to his sister's side. "What happened, Sarah? Is Cassie alright?" he asked as he fended off an enemy soldier.

"I don't know, and I hope so."

The soldier David was fighting sneered. "Only those with the devil's blood in them are affected. It will help us cleanse the earth of their kind."

David scowled at him. "You, my friend, are sadly misinformed." He stabbed under the man's guard, and he quit talking. Bedivere and his men gave the teens a respite, and Lancelot's force was retreating a bit.

"I told you to wait," Bedivere said, coming level with the three.

"Our apologies, Sir Bedivere," Ganieda said. "But we had to come."

The knight nodded wearily. "What devilry caused the horses to act up?"

"No idea," David said, looking up toward the tree line where Cassie and Telyn could be seen outlined. "But you can bet we're going to find out."

"David, duck!" William yelled. David looked and ducked at the same time, barely avoiding a spear that sliced through the air right where his head had been. Dassah jumped on the man's arm, biting down on it. David rode up and helped her. He heard Bedivere mutter something that would have caused his mother to bring out the soap.

"What is it?" David asked.

"They have reinforcements," Bedivere said grimly. "Mordred must be getting nervous."

"What?" David looked where the knight indicated and saw a force of about forty men coming their way. "You sure they're not ours?" he asked. The knight nodded.

Sarah looked around. Only ten or so of the original enemy force, including Lancelot, were still capable of fighting. "What happened to the other twenty men?" she asked Bedivere bluntly.

"We needed reinforcements at the front. The battle began changing as I went to get them. Mordred brought out a whole fresh army he's leading himself. The king began getting pressed back to the fort and we had to help. It was hard for me to get ten," he answered. Sarah saw William cut down the man he'd been fighting. He looked up at the approaching men and knew they were the enemy. He looked around at the friendly forces, knowing they couldn't keep going long even with the addition of ten men. Sarah saw a decision snap in his face and he reined Phoenix over to Gwendolyn, Lancelot's forces having withdrawn for the moment.

William and Gwendolyn appeared to be having an argument, and were frowning intensely at each other. Sarah was struck just then by how much the siblings were alike. Gwendolyn acted submissive and gentle most of the time, but she could also be stubborn and determined, just like William. William apparently won the argument, as Gwendolyn finally nodded. William turned Phoenix toward Lancelot's forces. Gwendolyn stayed where she was for a moment, then turned and rode toward the others. Bedivere's men followed her, looking confused.

"What's he doing?" David asked her when she rode up.

"Watch," Gwendolyn said, her face impassive.

"Lancelot!" William called. "If you have any honor left, come and speak with me. I give my word you will not be harmed." He and Phoenix kept absolutely still. Several minutes passed in total silence. Then a tall man made his way from the rest of the enemy host and stood before them warily, hand on his sword hilt.

"What do you want?" the man asked cautiously. His expression was pained. Sarah recognized him as Arthur's former champion by his curly golden hair.

"For you to surrender," William answered firmly. David, Sarah, and Ganieda shot each other startled looks. What was he up to? Some men in Lancelot's force laughed.

The knight looked at William almost incredulously. "Do you now? I'm afraid I can't do that, boy."

"Yes, you can," he said. "But I am willing to offer you a deal." William gestured behind him. "My forces are small. You have lost almost all your original force. The deal is this: We fight in single combat. If you win, we will surrender and let you pass without further interference. If I win, you and your men, including those who just arrived, will surrender to us and lay down your weapons. What say you?" A long pause followed. Sarah held her breath, shocked by William's audacity. It was something she would expect more of Cassie.

Bedivere frowned. "He can't do that. He doesn't have the authority."

"Yes, he does," Gwendolyn said. "I am the daughter of the king, and I gave it to him."

Bedivere looked at her, surprised. "You did? Then why are you not offering the challenge for him? And what makes you think he can defeat Lancelot? You, of all people, know his skill."

Gwendolyn looked at the knight with a pained expression. "After what he did... I just can't face him directly." She looked back at William. "As for defeating Lancelot... well, I'm hoping and praying that he's inherited... his father's skill." Bedivere looked at her curiously, but Lancelot spoke at that moment.

He laughed humorlessly. "You, a stripling boy, would fight *me*? Very noble of you, but I'm the best swordsman in the kingdom, boy. You can't best me. And on what authority do you make this offer?"

"On the authority of the Princess Gwendolyn, firstborn of King Arthur, and the next queen of Britain," William replied without batting an eye. Lancelot looked at Gwendolyn, who nodded, then back to William, who continued speaking. "What do you have to lose by fighting me? Unless you're afraid I really will beat you and want to save face with your men by telling me off."

Lancelot scowled. "Pride goes before a fall, boy. You don't want to test me."

"It's not out of pride I wish to fight you. But there is another option. You could declare surrender now and ask the king for mercy. This has to go against your grain, fighting the king you've served for so long. You don't really want to do this, do you? Can't you see that Mordred's using you? Did he defend you when the king caught you with the queen? Who led the king to the garden that night? What's in it for you if you go along with Mordred? The queen is beyond your reach. If you have any honor or morals left at all, stop this senseless rebellion. You're undoing years of peace that you fought to gain. Will you really throw it away so needlessly?" Another long silence.

Sarah could tell Lancelot struggled with William's speech. She thought he was on the verge of giving way, but a sudden strong wind picked up, blowing dust into everyone's eyes. Sarah wasn't sure, but she thought she glimpsed a dark shadow behind Lancelot, coming close to his ear, and she felt a sudden chill, like the kind that comes from plunging into freezing water. The sensation passed quickly, but she shuddered. Something unnatural had just happened. She looked up at the treeline. Cassie was sitting up straight now, leaning over to Telyn. Sarah returned her attention to William. He sat still on Phoenix, unmoved by the wind.

Lancelot drew his sword. "If it's a duel you want, boy, it's a duel you'll get. But dismount and let us fight on equal ground."

"Then you agree to the terms?" William asked.

"Yes."

"What of your men? Do they agree? Complete surrender if I win?"

Lancelot glanced behind him. A man stepped forward whom Sarah assumed was second-in-command. "We agree to the terms," he said. "What of your forces?"

Bedivere stepped forward. "We also agree to the terms. But if you dishonor the rules of combat, Lancelot, it's my sword you'll be feeling in your gut."

Lancelot nodded curtly. "As you wish, Bedivere." William dismounted and Phoenix stood off to the side, but kept close to his rider.

"Dreamer, ask Phoenix if William really knows what he's doing," Sarah requested anxiously.

The answer came quickly. *He says not to worry. He always knows what he is doing.* That reassured Sarah a little, but her heart was in her mouth as she watched the opponents face off. She breathed a prayer, asking God to help her friend do this.

⚜

Cassie watched William and Lancelot face off. She wondered what on earth had possessed William to challenge the kingdom's best fighter. She knew William was exceptionally skilled, but would it be enough to win this duel? That she didn't know.

"He's mad," Telyn said. "No one would challenge Lancelot like this, except the king."

"Like father, like son," Cassie said. "He might just do it."

"Perhaps." Telyn sounded dubious. "But I did not like that wind."

"Could you sense anything about it?" Cassie asked.

Telyn shook her head. "It's as if something is stifling me. You?"

"The same. Maybe that shriek affected us more than we think. But whatever that wind was, it's gone now." Thankfully, both girls still had their hearing, though it was dampened somewhat. They had regained their wits quickly and their hearing was slowly strengthening, but they had discovered a strange inability to sense the songs they should. When the wind had blown up so mysteriously, Cassie had tried to listen to it in preparation for possibly having to make a counter-melody, but she couldn't focus her sense. Her ears still rang slightly from the noise. Maybe her ability to concentrate and use her Brenwyd traits would return when the ringing ceased. Whatever that sound had been, she was sure it was some form of witchcraft. She devoted her attention to the scene below them. Both fighters stood, waiting for someone to make the first move. Cassie knew from experience that William could wait quite awhile for his opponent to move. Lancelot was not so patient. He slashed at William's side. William blocked, and the fight commenced.

For the first few minutes, neither opponent appeared to have an advantage over the other. Most fights were determined within the first few strikes, but not so with this one. William fought well, making Lancelot go on the defensive. Lancelot did not like this. He'd expected this fight to be over quickly, but had severely underestimated his young opponent's skill. He started raining in harder, faster blows and William concentrated on defense. Cassie saw the advantage. Playing offense was as a rule more tiring than playing defense, no matter what you were doing. William could wear the older man down, and then slip under his guard and surprise him. He'd used the tactic on her many times over the last few months and had a lot of stamina. But would it be enough?

Suddenly, the scene changed. She was still watching two people duel, but they were different. The one closest to her she thought was William, but as she watched she realized he did not move in exactly the same way, though it was similar, and he was slightly taller. She moved her gaze to his opponent. It was Mordred. That meant the man was Arthur. Watching, she deduced the king was the better swordsman. But Mordred moved with uncanny quickness and countered each strike the king made. With a chill, Cassie realized both duels were occurring at the same time. As William fought

For the first few minutes, neither opponent appeared to have an advantage over the other. Most fights were determined within the first few strikes, but not so with this one.

to keep the fort from being taken from behind, his father fought to preserve the kingdom. Watching Mordred, Cassie glimpsed something dark behind him. The king slashed toward Mordred's right side and Mordred swung to block it, but just as he committed to the strike the king snapped his blade up higher in a blow that should have severely wounded Mordred, if not killed him. But it did not. Cassie saw the dark thing cover where Arthur's sword should have struck and the blade rebounded. The king, surprised, had no time to block the thrust Mordred put toward his chest, and could only deflect it...

And she found herself looking again on William and Lancelot. Lancelot pressed William hard, making him back up. "How long has it been?" Cassie asked Telyn.

"A little over five minutes, I think. It shan't last much longer. Lancelot dislikes long fights."

"Come on, William," Cassie urged. "You can do this."

"He's doing well," Telyn remarked. "Lancelot beats almost all his opponents in the first few strikes. Oh!" Cassie gasped as well. Lancelot had come down hard in an overhead strike and William had barely managed to deflect it, doing so at the last possible instant. For a few agonizing seconds Cassie thought he may have been stabbed. The atmosphere of tension on the battlefield tightened, constricting the air into little balls that were hard to breathe. Everything was completely still except for the combatants.

"You may as well surrender now, boy, and save yourself!" Lancelot said, loud enough for everyone to hear. William answered by slashing at Lancelot's legs, which the knight leapt over easily. The two backed away from each other and circled, each looking for a weak spot...

And Cassie's vision changed again. She knew it was her Sight showing her the other duel. It showed her a frontal view of Arthur, and she gasped. "What?" she heard Telyn ask, but she didn't reply.

Blood flowed freely from a wound at the top of the king's left arm. He'd thrown his shield away, but was having a harder time than ever deflecting Mordred's attacks. They were coming faster, no, harder. She could sense Morgan nearby, chanting something to help her son. Where was Siarl? Where were any of the Brenwyds, for that matter? She didn't See any around to counter Morgan's magic. Even if Cassie's ability hadn't been stifled, she couldn't do anything from this distance. The king was failing. She could see it, and Mordred certainly did. He pressed him, forcing him to give ground...

And it was William she was watching once again. He, too, was hard pressed. *Oh, please God,* Cassie prayed. *Help William win. Help Arthur.* As she watched her friend, he seemed to rally – slowly, almost imperceptibly, he was gaining his second wind. He was still tired, but he was steadier, better able to counter Lancelot's attacks. He gave no more ground. Lancelot, believing he had the fight all but won, was completely oblivious. He slashed at William's right, but as William turned his sword to block the strike Lancelot changed his angle and raised his sword above his head, bringing it down with astonishing speed and putting all his strength and power behind the blow with the intent to slash his young opponent from head to toe. Telyn covered her eyes. Cassie couldn't see any way William could possibly recover with the necessary strength to stop the blow in time. The tension rose to new heights, the air seeming to quiver like an arrow newly embedded in its target. Cassie couldn't tear herself away. She watched, a feeling of horror working its way through her like a slow, fat worm... and then the impossible happened. William brought his sword up with both hands on the hilt, and in a great clash of metal that caused Telyn to snap her eyes open, he stopped Lancelot's blade in midair. Lancelot looked shocked, but quickly turned to take advantage of his position, pressing downward on William's blade with all his great strength, sliding the blades against each other until the hilts locked. William gave way slowly, inch by inch.

Everyone knew the fight was all but over now. Lancelot would force William to release his sword, and then the enemy forces would take the fort from the back, assuring Mordred's victory. But Cassie could tell that William wasn't about to give up. His jaw was set, determined, and she wondered what trick he could possibly have up his sleeve. All at once she recalled a tactic he'd used against her a few times when they were locked in exactly this position. A small but vibrant hope started to rise within her and she watched intently. If William was going to pull this trick, he had to do it soon, and he had absolutely no margin for error. Lancelot continued to press down on William's blade, and William kept giving way slowly... slowly... slowly... and suddenly, in the blink of an eye, he whipped his blade out from underneath Lancelot's.

The knight staggered, losing his balance, and though he started to regain it quickly, he wasn't fast enough. Even as William whipped his sword out from Lancelot's blade, his body was turning. He turned 360 degrees and brought his sword down on Lancelot's knuckles during those brief seconds of imbalance. The sudden, unexpected pain caused the knight to loosen his hold, giving a cry of pain, and William twisted the sword from his grip. The sword clanged to the ground, and William flicked his sword point up to Lancelot's throat, where it rested. Everything was dead quiet, everyone looking on in shock, the release of tension rising in waves from the field. Cassie could see William's shoulders heaving as he drew in air.

"By all that is holy," Telyn breathed, incredulous. "He did it. He actually did it."

"No," Cassie said, equally stunned. "*God* did it."

⚬⚬⚬

Sarah felt ready to cry with happiness and relief. It was over, and William was safe. *Thank you, Lord,* she thought fervently. William kept the tip of his blade resting in the hollow of Lancelot's throat.

The former champion looked stunned. Never had he thought this boy could actually beat him. Sarah could hear both breathing hard.

"What are you waiting for?" Lancelot said in a tired, rasping voice. "Go on. Finish it." Sarah noticed blood dripping from Lancelot's knuckles and realized William's blow had broken several of his fingers. William didn't answer. "Come on. You'd be doing me a favor."

Slowly, William lowered his sword. He bent down and picked up Lancelot's sword. "No," he said. "I won't kill you. That's for God to decide. But I beat you, so order your men to disarm themselves."

Lancelot studied him for several moments before turning to his men. "You heard him. Disarm yourselves," he ordered. Sarah thought he sounded almost relieved. The men all looked at each other, but one by one they drew their weapons and laid them in a pile by William's feet. Lancelot stuck out his forearm. After hesitating a moment, William took it. "You're a better man than I," the knight said. "Do me and yourself a favor, and don't do what I've done."

"You can still turn yourself over to Arthur," William said.

Lancelot shook his head. "No... no, it's too late for me. Go to him now. I won't trouble you anymore." He turned and with a curt word to his men, they marched off the way they had come. William stood watching them. Phoenix went up to him. William put a hand up and stroked his cheek, then turned and headed back toward the others. Sarah heard the men behind her murmuring, sounding awestruck. As William approached, Sarah realized just how exhausted he was. He leaned heavily on Phoenix's shoulder for support as he made his way to them.

Gwendolyn dismounted, her arms crossed. "Do not scare me like that again," she said.

"I'll try not to," he said, extreme fatigue evident in his tone. Gwendolyn nodded, then cautiously gave him a hug, smiling. David and Sarah dismounted. William smiled weakly. "Hey."

David clapped him on the shoulder. "Great job. I remember that little trick. You've pulled it on Cassie a few times."

"Yeah," William said. "Not recently, though."

Bedivere looked at William with new respect. "I confess I am astonished. Only one other man has ever beaten Lancelot, and that is the king. Caelwyn trained you well. Well done."

"Thank you, sir," William said simply. They turned at the sound of approaching hoofbeats. Telyn and Cassie were approaching at a fast canter, looking recovered.

"Are you okay? What happened?" David asked as they halted.

"Well enough, and later," Cassie said. "The day's not over yet."

Telyn looked at William in awe. "That was amazing."

William shrugged. Cassie knew he was exhausted. "You can't collapse yet," she said. "We've got to get to the main battlefield. Now."

"Why?" Sarah asked. Cassie looked at Telyn, fear and resignation in her eyes.

"Arthur's fighting Mordred, and it's not going well."

FATHER AND SON

David helped William mount Phoenix. The guy was so exhausted, David thought he might fall asleep on the horse. David was tired, too. He hadn't gotten enough sleep the night before for this kind of activity. Was it really just last night that he and Cassie had pushed Guinevere forward in time? It seemed like so long ago, yet he knew by looking at the sun that it was only mid-morning. He hoped he would be able to sleep soon. He got back on Fire after finding a mounting rock. The horse was worn out, too. David patted his neck affectionately. The girls and Bedivere had gone ahead of them to see what was going on, but William was clearly not ready to rush into another battle so David had volunteered to stay with him.

"I'm really alright, you know. I'm just tired," William said, stifling a yawn. "Even though I've basically slept for over a day, I don't think my body was really resting."

"Believe me, I understand you," David said. "But we'd better go see what all the fuss is about." They urged their horses into a walk. "What do you think happens next?" David asked William.

He shrugged. "According to legend, Arthur and Mordred both wound each other so severely they each die. I guess that happens." His expression tightened. David noted he didn't refer to Arthur as

"Father." He had a feeling William was still in shock over the fact.

"You're forgetting the faeries who take Arthur to Avalon," David responded.

William snorted. "Seeing how far we are from Ynis Witrin, I doubt it, though I guess the Brenwyds are the faeries talked about."

"And speaking of Brenwyds, I don't like what Cassie and Telyn said about not sensing any."

"Me neither. And that sound they said they heard, and how it seems to have stifled their abilities..."

"And considering what we know of that message you translated, maybe the sound was supposed to disable the Brenwyds so the Brotherhood could snatch them."

William nodded agreement. "But what caused it? They don't have sonar technology in this century."

"I don't know," David said. "But there's something that keeps creeping me out about this battle. Like that wind that kicked up before you started the duel. I thought for sure Lancelot would give in without fighting, but then..." David shrugged. "It was weird."

"I noticed it, too. Maybe Cassie or Telyn know more." William paused, and his brow furrowed. "David?"

"Yeah?"

"You know what Cassie said about Brenwyds fighting invisible battles?"

"Yeah..." David looked at him. "You don't think..."

"Just putting it out there." They fell silent. Just as they reached the bottom of the path leading to the fort, they heard familiar voices raised in song. Then, about twenty seconds later, a horrible scream that sounded almost unearthly rent the air. David thought he could almost see the air molecules being divided by the scream. It was extremely high-pitched and sounded like a combination of male and female voices. David winced and heard William mutter something under his breath. The horses shied violently. Fire tried to rear in fright.

"Hey, now. Easy there, boy," David tried to soothe his horse. The scream ended. David's ears were ringing. He and William looked at each other with wide eyes. By tacit consent they urged their horses faster, knowing something of import must have happened. Faint cheering reached their ears.

"Is that us or them?" William wondered. They rounded the corner... and reined in hard as they saw the scene before them. As Cassie had said, Arthur and Mordred were facing each other in a duel. The king had his back to the boys, but they could see Mordred stumbling back from him and the reason was clear: there was a long, ugly gash across his thigh, and it was bleeding freely. Mordred looked at Arthur in shock. Clearly he had not expected the king to actually be able to wound him.

"I guess it was us," David answered William.

He nodded, frowning as he studied the king. "Something's wrong with him," he said.

David shot his friend an inquisitive glance. "How do you know?"

"The way he's holding his left arm. He's acting like it pains him." David looked, and he thought he could see what he was talking about.

"Where are the girls?" David wondered.

"There," William said, pointing. "Let's go." They dismounted and led their horses to where a small crowd was standing outside the fort. Ganieda spotted them approaching and alerted the others. "What happened? And what was that scream?" William asked.

"The king has a large wound at the top of his left arm that is severely hampering him," Ganieda said. "It's bleeding badly and he can't use his shield, but Telyn said she thinks it is just a surface wound. Her main concern is blood loss. Morgan is protecting Mordred, and since no Brenwyd was around to counter her, Mordred had all but won. It's amazing the king was able to hold him off for so long with that wound. Fortunately, Telyn and Cassie neutralized her enough for Arthur to get through Mordred's guard and wound him.

They say the stifling effect of the shriek they heard earlier is wearing off. As for the scream just now... we're not sure. Part of it was Mordred, but we think Morgan also contributed... and something else. They were not expecting him to be wounded." She stopped, looking back at the duel. The men were simply looking at each other, swords raised, waiting for someone to move.

David scanned the field. "Where is Morgan?" he asked.

"We don't know," Sarah said. "We've been trying to figure that out." At that moment, Mordred attacked, pure hate streaming from his eyes. Despite the wound in his leg, he was moving around well enough, though his face revealed his pain.

Arthur defended himself. "Mordred!" he called to his opponent. "Let us cease this fight and call a truce. Stop this senseless rebellion, for many more will die if you continue."

"What do I care? It matters not to me how many peasants die. All the better for them, I say, for then they go to heaven and leave their miserable life down here," Mordred snarled in reply. He thrust at Arthur's side and the king sidestepped his blade. "No, I will not stop this fight. Once you are dead, I will conquer the rest of this island in a week and who can stop me? Your army? Most of it, including your knights, lie dead on this battlefield. The Brenwyds? I have made sure they will no longer be an issue. Without the guidance of their leaders, they are like sheep, undefended and easily destroyed by the wolves."

"You're wrong," Arthur answered. "The Brenwyds will pose your biggest challenge, and they will not let you have this kingdom easily. Caelwyn will–"

Mordred interrupted him with a sneer. "Caelwyn will what? Rally them? Lead them? Ha! That would be an impressive feat for a dead woman." David heard the men around him start to mutter worriedly.

Arthur paled. "What do you speak of?" he asked tersely.

"Do you not find it odd she has not joined you here? I'll tell you why she hasn't. She went to meet her Maker this morning."

Arthur struck with renewed force. "You lie!" he accused.

Mordred laughed. "It's true, I often lie to get what I want, but why would I lie about that? I was the one who sent her." He lurched away from the reach of Arthur's sword, fumbling for something in his cloak. He brought out a knife that David recognized all too well, as did everyone else there. "See? Is this not her famed knife? Why would I have it were she not dead?" Arthur gazed at it, sorrow suffusing his expression. He bowed his head for a brief moment, closing his eyes. Mordred stuck the knife back in his cloak.

"We need to get that," Telyn muttered. Arthur raised his head, his eyes snapping open. He struck at Mordred and the fight reached new levels of ferocity. David suddenly realized Cassie and Telyn were singing softly, eyes trained on the king, and he guessed they were healing the wound as best they could from a distance. It was their voices he and William had heard singing before the scream. The aftereffects of the earlier sound were clearly wearing off. Their singing seemed to be working, because the king fought with new strength, and the wound slowed its bleeding and appeared to diminish in size. Telyn started a new, harder, higher melody, and there seemed to be a distortion in the air around Mordred, though David wasn't sure if he was really seeing it or if his eyes were tricking him. Something wet fell on his cheek, and he looked up. The sky had grown dark, nearly black, and thunder rumbled. Rain started falling, making it hard to see the combatants. Just as lightning flashed, David felt some of the dread that had been clinging to him melt away, as if washed off by the rain. He saw Mordred start to collapse on his weak leg, and Arthur drove his sword into his stomach. Mordred stared up at his former liege-lord, face pale. Arthur jerked his sword out and stared down at him inscrutably. Mordred tried to say something, but he coughed up blood and collapsed.

A grief-filled, high-pitched wail rose on the wind, making David wince and the hairs stand up on the back of his neck. The dogs whimpered and growled, and the horses neighed in distress. He heard hoofbeats, and saw a woman with flame-colored hair ride up on a pure black horse. Morgan. She dismounted and ran to her son, throwing her arms around him. The rain started falling harder and David pulled the hood of his cloak up, squinting through the downpour. Morgan looked at the king with such hate and loathing that David could feel her malevolence from where he stood. "You have killed my son," she snarled. "You will pay for this, Arthur Pendragon, and you will pay dearly."

The king remained unmoved, looking down at her. "He brought it on himself," he answered calmly, though he seemed sad.

Morgan stood, her figure dwarfed by the king, but her intimidation factor making up for the height difference. She shook her fist in the king's face. "He will not remain dead, Arthur Pendragon. He will rise again and throw your heirs down and destroy your line and legacy. None will remember you. History will forget you, just another king in a time of many. You cannot destroy my son forever, and the one who can has never been born and never will be." She said the last sentence with complete confidence, but David felt amused by it. She had no clue. Morgan stepped closer to Arthur.

David saw Cassie tense. "No," she muttered, almost dazedly. "She can't get that close."

"You may have won today," Morgan continued, "But the price has come dear to you. You cannot hold us off forever. We will crush this land. You will die knowing you have failed."

"This kingdom is in God's hands," Arthur replied. "He might allow you triumph for a little while, but He will raise up a champion to bring you down. Evil never wins for long."

She snarled. "So you say." Her hand moved to the side of her dress.

David barely registered the movement before Cassie cried, "Look out! She's armed!" Arthur started, but it was too late. Morgan whipped out a dagger and plunged it deep into his side. David heard Gwendolyn cry out and the crowd let out a collective gasp.

Gwendolyn fought free of Bedivere and ran out to her father. William edged past David.

"Where are you going?" David asked.

William glanced back at him. "Just thought I'd scare her a little." He followed his sister. Gwendolyn pushed Morgan away, and the witch slipped in the mud and fell. The dagger jerked from Arthur's body and he staggered, but William reached him in time to keep him from collapsing. David heard the men murmur around him, "Who is that lad? Where did he come from? What's he doing out there?"

"He defeated Lancelot in single combat," some of Bedivere's men informed their fellow soldiers.

"What? Lancelot? Impossible. None but the king has ever beaten him." The murmuring went on, but David paid it no heed. Morgan stood again, glaring at Gwendolyn. Gwendolyn whirled on Morgan and threw her spear with all her strength at the witch. The spear should have impaled Morgan, but instead it shattered several inches from her as it apparently hit an invisible barrier.

Morgan smiled at Gwendolyn condescendingly. "A noble attempt, princess, and fitting, but I am not killed so easily. You should stay home with your mother and be an obedient daughter. The battlefield suits you ill." Gwendolyn was trembling with rage. William had torn part of his tunic to staunch Arthur's wound, and Bedivere had gone to help him.

William walked up behind Gwendolyn and put an arm around her shoulders. "I would go now if I were you, Morgan," he said. His hood was down and he stared at the witch coolly. Morgan focused on him, and even through the downpour David saw something like fear cross her face. "And who are you, boy?" she asked, an edge to her voice.

"That's for me to keep." He nodded toward Mordred's still body. "Linger any longer than five minutes and I will find a way kill you if it means strangling you," he said calmly but coldly, with no hint of leniency.

David heard Cassie chuckle. "Nice move, William. Make her nervous," she said softly.

"Telyn, can you take down her shield?" Ganieda asked.

Telyn shook her head, scowling. "No. It is too strong. I don't think Cassie and I combined could disable that at the moment. That... shriek is still affecting us a little, and we're tired. More than we should be."

"But how is Mordred dead now? What about the prophecy?" Cassie wondered. "Not that I'm objecting, but William said he's the Brotherhood master in our time."

"Morgan said he would rise again," Ganieda said darkly. "I shudder to think of what that means, but she is rumored to practice the foulest arts of all." She did not deign to say what they were.

Morgan hauled her son onto the horse – no small feat, considering her size – and mounted behind him. She surveyed the field. "You have not seen the last of me," she said vehemently as she wheeled her horse away. The remnants of Mordred's army followed her.

Bedivere helped Arthur back to his men. Gwendolyn and William followed. William drew his hood up so it completely shadowed his face. "Thank you, my good fellow," Arthur said to Bedivere, wincing, his hand pressed against the wound. "I should have known that... she had one more trick up her sleeve." Telyn went up and carefully moved the king's hand to examine the wound, brows furrowed in concentration. The king looked at her. "Telyn." He hesitated. "What he said about your mother... is it true?"

Telyn sighed. "Unfortunately, Sire."

He put a hand on her hair. "I am sorry."

"Thank you." Telyn frowned at the wound. "I think we should go inside, out of the rain. The battle is over." Arthur nodded. Gwendolyn was looking on anxiously.

Arthur looked at his daughter. "And what... might you be doing here, young lady?" His tone was stern, but David didn't think he was angry.

"Mordred was sending a force up behind the fort to take it and put you between two enemy fronts," she answered. "We came to warn you."

Arthur's eyebrows rose. "Truly? I should have expected... something like that. And it was neutralized?"

"Yes, Father." She smiled half-heartedly. "It was not easy."

Arthur returned her smile and put a hand on her shoulder. "I would imagine not. At least tell me Jenifer is not here."

"That I can assure you of." The company started to move toward the fort. The king gave orders to number and name the dead. Above, thunder rumbled and lightning flashed. Bedivere helped the king to a private chamber. David, Sarah, and William cared for the horses. Telyn and Gwendolyn stayed with the king. Ganieda and Cassie made rounds among the wounded. Most of the Brenwyds that had been with the king had disappeared. Upon inquiry, they discovered that abruptly and without warning the Brenwyds had collapsed, screaming, with their hands over their ears. It sounded exactly like what had happened to Cassie and Telyn. Some people said they'd seen men hauling the Brenwyds away in their helpless state, killing any who tried to prevent them.

"That's got the Brotherhood written all over it," David said to Cassie after he heard it. "But how could they have made that sound?" He used English so no one would overhear them.

"That wasn't an earthly sound," she stated, cleaning a man's head wound. He was unconscious, but moaned as she washed his injury. "Telyn and I talked about it. This wasn't just an earthly battle. There were supernatural forces involved as well. I think Morgan called on some demons to help. She wanted to be sure nothing stopped her from winning. Another motive to get the Brenwyds out of the way." She hummed as she worked, apparently tuning in to the wounded man's song. Those who had survived the battle were doing their best to tend to the wounded, but with the Brenwyds gone, the ones with severe wounds didn't stand much of a chance.

"Wha– demons?" David asked, startled. "Are you sure?"

She shrugged. "Not entirely, but I know for sure this battle wasn't just on an earthly plane. Brenwyds battle the supernatural, and Morgan works for the devil. And that sound," she shuddered. "It sounded demonic. I can't really think of anything else it could have been. And that wind that kicked up as Lancelot was on the verge of giving in? Completely unnatural. Though I wonder why Lancelot had no... uh, guardian demon, I guess you'd say."

"A *what?*" David asked.

A corner of Cassie's mouth tugged upward at his tone. "A guardian demon. That's how Mordred was able to hold the king off and almost win. I Saw... something dark behind him, helping him. It even protected him from a blow that should have cut his head off. When Telyn and I got there, we put all the energy we had into neutralizing the thing. Thank God, the stifling effects of the sound were wearing off. It's what made that scream sound so unnatural and unearthly. *It* was those things, not to mention it and Morgan were heavily invested in putting up shielding around Mordred. She knew the king is the better swordsman. One more reason they had to get all the Brenwyds out of the way, but," her lips turned upward in a definite smile, "they missed two."

David shook his head, astonished at the calm way she explained the information. He could hardly believe it, but he didn't doubt her. He sighed. "What happened to the days when all we worried about was getting school assignments done on time?" he asked rhetorically.

Cassie let out a short laugh. "Summer vacation started." She moved on to the next man, still humming, though the tune changed. Healing the serious wounds had weakened her, and so she decided not to fully heal wounds unless it was necessary for the man's survival, as she was already approaching total exhaustion. David still wondered where their uncomplicated lives as teenagers living in the shadow of the Appalachian Mountains of Virginia had gone. Who could have guessed that the night Penny ran to their campsite in panic would result in them traveling fifteen hundred years into the past during the time of one of the most legendary figures in popular imagination? Not him. David was glad God had this all worked out. If he himself was in charge, David was sure he would have messed something up. He shifted his gaze to watch Sarah helping Ganieda across the room.

Telyn entered and looked around. "Where is William?" she asked.

"He was in the stable last I saw," Sarah offered. "Why?"

"The king wishes to see him."

"Did you tell him about... ?" Cassie asked, pausing in her ministrations.

Telyn shook her head. "No, that's for William to tell, and Gwendolyn and I both think the king should know. After all, he knew Guinevere was pregnant."

"How is he?" Ganieda asked.

Telyn hesitated. "He won't die, not yet, anyway, but Morgan had poison on her blade. I don't have the strength to heal a wound like that right now. I cleaned and bandaged it, and that's the most I can do at the moment. I was able to heal the internal injuries and the bleeding's under control, so I think he'll be alright until I have the energy for a full healing. The dagger actually missed many of his vital organs, I believe, so we can thank the Lord for that."

"I'll come help you," Cassie said.

"You're just as tired as I am," Telyn said. "He is not in immediate danger. Arthur insisted that we not try to finish healing the wound until we are rested. Who am I to disobey the king?" At that moment, William entered the room. "Ah, there you are," Telyn said.

He glanced at her. "Were you looking for me?" he asked.

"Yes. The king wishes to see you."

His eyes went wide. "You didn't tell him–"

"I'm leaving that to you. Go. Gwendolyn's there." He didn't move. "What is it?"

"It's just... that would be a little awkward, don't you think?"

"William," Sarah said, walking over to him and tilting her head back slightly to look him in the eye. "This is your chance to talk to your father as your father, and it might be your only chance. Don't be nervous. He'll understand, and Gwendolyn's there to back you up. Everything will be fine. Go." She put a reassuring hand on his arm.

He nodded slowly. "Well... see you later." He walked out of the room.

Telyn looked at Sarah, amused. "You're certainly convincing."

Sarah shrugged. "I just said what he needed to hear."

"Then why do I get the feeling that if I'd said that it would have taken more argument?" Telyn asked.

Sarah turned to hide a blush, going back to the man she was tending. "I don't know what you're talking about," she said. Cassie and David each made muffled sounds that sounded suspiciously like laughter. She glared at them. "What's so funny?"

"Nothing, sister dear," David said teasingly. "But I will tell you something. I don't hold any objections to him anymore."

"David!" She gave him a withering look and threw a bandage at him. Cassie, Telyn, and Ganieda laughed.

⚜

William's palms felt sweaty and he had butterflies in his stomach, big time. *Just how do you go about telling anyone, let alone a legendary king, that you're their son from the future? Especially when you yourself are still getting used to the notion?* He stopped before the door. He took a steadying breath and knocked. Gwendolyn came immediately. At least he wouldn't be completely alone. She smiled encouragingly as she opened the door. Arthur was sitting propped up against the wall. His skin was pale, but he smiled at William and his eyes were alert. William bowed. The king beckoned to him. "No need for that here, William. How are you feeling?"

"Fine, Sire."

"Tired?"

"Well, yes, Sire. How are you?"

"Ah, I've been better." The king shrugged and sighed, deep sadness entering his eyes. "Today has been something of a draw. We beat Mordred and his army back, but we have lost many, including some of my best knights and friends. Gawain, Kay, Galahad..." He closed his eyes.

"I'm sorry, Sire," William said.

The king nodded. Thunder boomed outside. "And Caelwyn. She knew. That's why she didn't confirm that she would come. I should have suspected. And now the Brenwyds with me." He shook his head, opening his eyes, great sorrow in his expression.

"They may not be dead, Sire," William said. The king – his father – raised his eyebrows.

"Oh?"

"When we infiltrated Mordred's castle, I spoke with... a male prisoner. He said that Mordred wasn't planning to kill his Brenwyd prisoners until after this battle. With Mordred, um, dead, I'm not sure how those plans will change, but perhaps a rescue mission could be sent."

"You truly think so?" Gwendolyn asked.

William nodded. "There's not much time, but I think... I think it could be done." A memory stirred in his mind. He had once read a report in the Brotherhood records of a large group of Brenwyds being rescued at about this time in history. He made a note to think more on it later.

"That would be worth investigating," Arthur said. "Siarl and Bleddyn were among those taken. Caelwyn's children should not lose another parent." He studied William. "I suppose you and your friends would take part in a rescue mission, since you have been to his stronghold."

"Oh, yes, Sire," William assured him.

"Good. I'll leave the details to you." He paused. "You're probably wondering why I wanted to see you specifically."

"The thought had crossed my mind, Sire," William admitted.

Arthur glanced at Gwendolyn. "Gwendolyn has told me of... where, or rather, when, you and your friends are from. Is this true?"

"It is."

"Hmm." His keen green eyes studied William intently. "Caelwyn mentioned something of this when she told me about the... safe haven she wished Guinevere to go to. I assume she has gone there?"

"Yes, Sire." William hesitated. "We wouldn't have done it were it not absolutely necessary, Sire."

"I believe that. But there is something else." He paused. William looked at the floor. "Guinevere was pregnant when she left." William nodded acknowledgment. "Gwendolyn told me she goes to a time... before you and your friends go through the slip."

William nodded. "Yes. She's the one who pushed us through it."

"So I assume that you would... that you would have.. met the child." William wasn't quite sure what to say, but nodded. "How many years before you go through the slip did she land?"

"Almost sixteen," William answered. "She... she ended up in October – this month – almost sixteen years before we... went through."

"I see." Arthur paused. William watched him intently, feeling a deep longing for him to figure it out. The intensity of the feeling surprised him. "Given that Guinevere would have delivered next May, and you say that she ended up in the same month we are in, I assume that she delivered that next May. So... the child... would be fifteen when you go through the time slip." William noticed that Gwendolyn seemed to be hardly breathing as she watched the two of them. He had a feeling she was waiting as much as he was for their father to verbalize the connection. "You're fifteen, are you not, William?" he asked.

"Yes, Sire," William answered. "And... I was born on the twenty-fifth of May."

Arthur took a deep breath, his eyes fixed on William. "Then would I be correct in assuming that... you are... my son?" He asked softly, hesitantly, as if afraid to ask the question. William nodded slowly, unable to speak. Arthur's eyes shone. Slowly, painfully, he moved from his position against the wall, swinging his legs over the side of the bed. Gwendolyn looked like she might say something, but changed her mind, watching with a smile. Tears were coming to her eyes, and she wasn't the only one. William blinked hastily. Arthur stood slowly and came to him, enfolding him in a big bear hug, something the Commander had never done. William hugged back tightly, tears leaking slowly from his eyes. What was it he'd been nervous about? "Oh, God, You are wonderful. Thank You for this chance to meet my fine son, and please let my dear Guinevere know how much I love her," Arthur said over his head.

"Amen," Gwendolyn said. "Now, Father, you should really lie back down. Telyn will have a fit if she finds out you got up." Her tone held no reprimand.

Arthur laughed. "Then don't tell Telyn. I think the situation merited the disobedience." He released William and got back into bed. "Come sit by me, William." William did. "How was your mother the last time you saw her?"

"Fine. She's the one who pushed us through the time slip." He paused, and felt his stomach clench in nervousness all over again. "Um, I didn't... I didn't know that she was... my mother. The, um, circumstances of my birth were... not good."

Arthur frowned. "How do you mean?" he asked. William heaved a breath, thinking how best to explain. "It's alright, William. I won't reprimand you. I don't think you've had an easy life."

"No." William launched into his tale, starting with what Cassie had seen of Guinevere in her dreams before going into exactly how he'd met Cassie. His father listened intently, with no interruption. William finished by telling him what had occurred that morning. A long silence followed. William looked at the floor. He was sitting facing his father, not far from the wall. He felt a hand squeeze his shoulder gently, compassionately. Comforting warmth spread through him. It was a nice feeling to have a caring father.

"My dear boy," Arthur said softly. "I'm so sorry. You shouldn't have had to go through that."

"No, I did have to," William said, looking at Arthur. "If I hadn't, Cassie, David, and Sarah wouldn't have gotten out, and we wouldn't have gone to Glastonbury and met... Mother, and then she wouldn't have pushed us through the time slip, and if that hadn't happened–"

"She would never have gone through and had you there and you wouldn't have been there to get your friends out and things would be very different," Arthur finished. "Yes, it's amazing how the Lord works. But all that is behind you now. You're no longer a part of that... organization, and you can't feel guilt for what they do. It is no longer part of you and never truly was, I think." He paused, and a grin crept across his face. "And from what I've heard of your duel with Lancelot, how could I hold you accountable for the things you've repented of? Be easy."

William smiled back. "Thank you... Father," he said, trying the word out cautiously.

Arthur's eyes twinkled. "I wish I could have seen that fight."

"You were busy," William answered, content spreading through him.

"Mmm, that I was. But very well done." Arthur looked at him seriously. "I'm glad you didn't kill him. He... we have been friends for many years and have been through great trials together." He sighed.

A tentative knock came at the door. "Who is it?" Gwendolyn called.

"Cassie," Cassie's voice called. "I'm terribly sorry to interrupt, something's going on outside. May I come in?"

Gwendolyn looked at her father. He nodded. "Yes," she called.

Cassie opened the door quickly and shut it behind her. She

bowed respectfully to the king. "I hope you're feeling better, Sire."

"I don't think I'm dying, but I'll feel better once that poison's out." He winced slightly. William noticed Cassie's eyes go out of focus a little, and when they refocused worry and alarm filled them. He frowned slightly. That couldn't be good.

"I hope... I hope I didn't interrupt anything, Sire," she said, embarrassed, aware that she had indeed interrupted something.

"Do not trouble yourself," Arthur smiled kindly at her. "What is it?"

"The storm outside. There's something wrong about it."

Arthur frowned. "What do mean?"

Cassie looked at him frankly. "It started out normal enough, but if it's natural now, I'm no Brenwyd. There is much evil in it. Something big and very wrong is happening that's adding fury to it. Telyn and I have tried to do healings on some serious wounds, but... it's harder than usual for some reason."

"You think the storm's dampening your healing ability? Or is it still just the aftereffects of that shriek?" William asked.

"Both, I think. The animals don't like the storm, either. They say something smells wrong about it. I think–" she was interrupted by a huge boom of thunder that made the walls shake from the force of it. Gwendolyn and William started. Cassie's eyes went wide and she froze.

"Cassie?" Gwendolyn asked. "What is it? Cassie?" Cassie gave no response. She seemed to stare vacantly, like her mind was literally a million miles away.

William shook her by her shoulders. "Cassie!" She blinked, refocusing. "What is it?"

"Something bad," she whispered, voice trembling. "I Saw... Morgan... Morgan is doing something. And Mordred. He's involved too."

"He's dead," Gwendolyn said. Cassie stared at her, the blood draining from her face. "What?" Gwendolyn asked, alarmed.

"Morgan... she said... she would... oh, no." Arthur cried out in pain and fell back against the wall, gasping for breath.

"Father!" Gwendolyn cried. Cassie went to him and undid the bandage on his side wound. A foul stench filled the room. Gwendolyn and William gagged. The wound looked awful, all pussy and green.

"God, help me," Cassie muttered and immediately launched into song, collapsing to her knees. William watched her, praying silently. He half-fancied he saw darkness creeping into the room like a snake, and a chill came over him. Cassie sang no words, but the melody she created alternated between being hard and strong and soft and desperate, and filled the whole room powerfully. It sounded like she was trying to sing two different melodies at once. William had never really thought of music as being something tangible, but that was how Cassie made it. He felt like he could reach out and touch the notes. The darkness seemed to stop advancing as she sang. William heard running footsteps from the hall and Telyn burst into the room, eyes wide. She said nothing but dropped beside Cassie, joining her. She took up the hard and strong melody and Cassie sang the softer one. The melody Telyn sang seemed to have a hard beat and meter to it, sounding like a war song. The one Cassie sang was gentler, seemingly flowing around the room like a stream, but it was still strong and firm. William heard Gwendolyn praying aloud desperately. He prayed mentally.

After what seemed an eternity, William heard the melodies become slower, less frantic, and the darkness completely retreated from the room. Telyn left off singing her melody and joined Cassie. After a few more minutes they stopped, completely spent. Arthur breathed slowly, shallowly, but regularly. He remained unconscious and his skin was pale, contrasting starkly to his black hair. "Is... is he alright?" William asked.

"He'll live, for now," Telyn rasped. She had dark circles under her eyes. "But he can't... he can't stay here. Cassie and I... don't have the strength to completely heal this. There... there's a convent near here,

I think, where we can take him. They're skilled in healing; there may... even be a Brenwyd or two there. Cassie and I can't do any more. We're all burned out at the moment."

"What happened?" Gwendolyn asked.

"Morgan," Cassie said, her voice also hoarse. "She said Mordred would rise again, right?" Gwendolyn nodded. "He just did. Morgan somehow brought him back, and she was trying to use Arthur's life in exchange. A life for a life."

Gwendolyn gasped in horror. "That's the worst kind of sorcery a person can do! Morgan is foul indeed."

Cassie nodded agreement. "But she didn't succeed completely. Her goal was to use Arthur's life force to raise and heal Mordred. The storm was supposed to dampen Telyn's and my healing abilities, I think, but she underestimated us, and God. She raised Mordred, yes, but he's not conscious yet." She looked down at the king. "The exchange was not completed, and he'll need a fair bit of recovery time. His mother can do no more."

William released a breath. "You two are brilliant. This is just what we needed." They all blinked.

"It is?" Gwendolyn asked. "For what?"

"For rescuing the Brenwyds. They'll have to wait for Mordred to recover before he can do it himself. I know they'll wait. They won't dare risk his wrath, and Merlin told me he would do it himself. We have time."

Cassie's eyes widened. "You're sure?" she asked.

"Positive. Remember what I told you at home, about the Brenwyds who escaped at the beginning of the Brotherhood?"

She nodded, her eyes beginning to sparkle with hope. "I believe we'll have some days before anything happens with Mordred," she said. "I could sense it. We can do this."

"You truly think we can?" Telyn cried desperately, tears in her eyes. "Father and Bleddyn... we can save them?"

"We'll try our hardest," William said. "I promise."

Epilogue

Cassie watched the king being placed carefully into the cart. Bedivere and Bors, who had also survived, would take the king to the convent. Cassie just had to laugh when she found out the name of the place: Avalana. It was called so because of all the apple trees, but she just found it funny that the legend said Arthur was taken to Avalon for healing by faery women when he was actually being taken by two of his knights who, while certainly not hideous, were certainly no faery women, either. *The truth can get so bent out of shape,* she thought, *even if the basic incident is remembered. Maybe Telyn and I are supposed to be the faery women. Ha.* Bedivere and Bors would disguise themselves as farmers, and they would place several baskets around the king and drape a blanket over him to hide him. For the sake of the disguise, no other men-at-arms would accompany them, but the convent wasn't very far, and as best as they could tell, Mordred's army had completely cleared out. "You young ones take care of yourselves," Bedivere told them. "You in particular, Gwendolyn. All hope for the kingdom is on you at the moment."

"Do not trouble yourself about me, Bedivere," she answered bravely. She leaned over the cart and kissed her father's forehead. Cassie could tell she was holding tears back. "I'll be fine." They hadn't told the knights that they were planning a visit to Mordred's castle to rescue the Brenwyds. They needed to go with the king. The rest of the uninjured men would help them, though they didn't know it yet. The king might be badly wounded, but they would obey Gwendolyn and Constantine, her betrothed, who had survived the battle and was staying at the fort. The storm had cleared up quickly, and Cassie was thankful it was gone. Bedivere climbed up into the cart and he and Bors departed. They watched the cart until it passed from view, everyone breathing a private prayer. The king's situation was very grave. Cassie realized abruptly just how tired and hungry she was. She swayed.

David, standing behind her, put an arm out to steady her. "I think we all feel the same way," he said exhaustedly. "I want food and bed. Or maybe bed and food. I really don't care."

"I do," Cassie said in a fatigued voice. "I want food and then bed. Anyone know where I can get those things?"

"The provisions are in the stable," Ganieda said. She went to get them.

"I have a sleeping room staked out," Telyn said. "Dassah and Kai are in it already. We can eat on our way there." William stood with his arms crossed, still looking after the cart. Cassie wondered what he was thinking. He hadn't said much about the time he'd spent with his father.

"Are you alright, William?" she asked him.

"Yes," he said, still looking ahead. "I think I'll walk around some before going to bed."

Sarah stared at him dully. "How do you, of all people, still have the energy?" she asked. "I'd lie down and sleep right here if I could."

William's lips twitched slightly like he might smile, but it took too much effort. "I'm thinking too hard to sleep right now, but I'm tired enough, believe me. I'm trying to remember something I read in the Brotherhood records that might help us." Ganieda reappeared with the food bag.

"Well, good luck," Sarah said. "We'll see you later." He walked off. Cassie noticed the few men he passed stopped and looked at him with respect. She doubted he noticed, but it intrigued her. William had won influence among the men because of his duel with Lancelot, and she noticed he wasn't wearing his hood up anymore, either. They followed Telyn to the room. Cassie could hear Kai snoring. No one had the energy to talk much.

"Cassie?" David said at one point.

"Yes?" she responded.

"When did you say the slip would be ready for us to go back?"

She frowned, thinking. "I don't know. I should probably check on that. Not for a bit, yet, I think."

"Are you really so eager to go back?" Ganieda asked.

David shrugged. "Yes and no. I want to see my parents and house again and finish up the, ah, business we have with the Brotherhood, but I don't want to leave all of you just yet. You guys have grown on me."

Telyn smiled wearily. "Seeing as we've lived in the same house for three months, I can't imagine why," she said wryly.

"Three months," Sarah mused. "Has it really been that long?"

They fell into a companionable silence. They finished their food and made ready to sleep, at long last. Before they did so, however, Gwendolyn turned abruptly to Cassie. "Cassie, about that prophecy Caelwyn found in Morgan's book. Telyn told me some more about it. Are you sure it said 'The Sword of Kings' and not just 'Excalibur'?"

Cassie nodded. "Yes, why?"

Gwendolyn looked slightly disappointed. "I was just thinking that if it merely said Excalibur, it could mean Father's current sword and not the Sword of Kings," she said.

Telyn had already lain down, but she sat up at Gwendolyn's statement. "You know, I hadn't thought of that. Where is Excalibur?" she asked.

"Bedivere took it with Father, but at least we would know for sure where it was." Gwendolyn said.

Cassie looked at them, puzzled. "What on earth do you mean? Why would the name Excalibur refer to the Sword-" She stopped abruptly. "The sketches! Are there *two* swords named Excalibur?"

"What?" The Thompson twins asked in tandem.

"Yes," Gwendolyn answered. She looked puzzled. "You didn't know?"

"No," Cassie said.

"I think those legends of yours leave out a lot," Ganieda remarked. "Though, 'tis true, not many people in *this* time know the two swords have the same name. What sketches are you referring to?"

"Back home, my father has... a diary of Caelwyn's. In it are a number of sketches. When I was looking through it, I noticed that some of the sketches labeled 'Excalibur' were actually of two different swords. I wondered about it, but forgot about it with the other stuff I was doing. It didn't seem very important."

Telyn raised her eyebrows. "You have a diary of Mother's?"

It was passed down to her father, Kai said groggily, having been woken by their chatter. *She is descended from your line. I do not believe she brought it with her.*

"No I didn't," Cassie said. "But I don't think it had any mention of us." She gestured to herself and the twins.

No, it did not, Kai affirmed, still half asleep.

Telyn looked at her. "You're descended from us? My family?" Cassie nodded. Telyn blinked. "So that's why Seren chose you. I should have guessed it."

"Please explain how there are two Excaliburs," Sarah said. "I've only ever heard of one, but I do know there are several names associated with the same sword, depending on what language you're using."

"That is true," Gwendolyn said. "Excalibur, or Caliburn, or Caledfwlch, whatever you wish to call it, was originally the name given to the Sword of Kings because of its ability to cut through solid rock. When it broke in that duel - which it shouldn't have - Caelwyn took Father to a Brenwyd smith located on an island in an isolated lake. He had another sword there that was almost the exact twin of the Sword of Kings, made by the same man in the same mold at about the same time, but it was forged of normal, hard iron instead of flamestone metal."

"Flamestone metal? What's that?" David asked.

"It is metal made from flaming stone that falls from the sky. Seren is made of this metal, as is the Sword of Kings," Ganieda explained.

"Come on, guys, don't you remember my father's story about how Seren was forged?" Cassie said. "It's made from a meteorite, and it actually does give off flames when used by the right person."

"That is correct," Telyn said.

"So Arthur's second sword was not made with this metal?" David clarified.

"Correct," Gwendolyn said. "But since it was Brenwyd crafted, the metal is very hard and durable, able to take more than swords made by humans. Since it looked extremely like the Sword of Kings and had many of the same properties, Father gave it the same name."

"Interesting," Cassie said, looking thoughtful.

"So I guess that debate is a draw," Sarah said. Cassie looked at her. "What debate?"

Sarah smiled. "If I recall correctly, I listened to about a half an hour of you and William debating about whether Excalibur was the sword in the stone or if it really was given to him by the Lady of the Lake."

"Oh, right. I remember that."

"What?" Telyn asked.

"Oh, in the legends we know, it's said Arthur got Excalibur when Merlin took him to this lake, and the Lady of this lake gave him Excalibur. Or," Cassie continued, "it was being held in the middle by a hand and he took it from the hand."

"That second part sounds absolutely preposterous," Ganieda said. "Are there really people who believe that?"

"It's just a story. In the same vein, supposedly Bedivere throws Excalibur back into the lake on Arthur's orders after Camlann, but I don't recall any lakes around here."

"Perhaps you should let people know what really happened when you go back," Gwendolyn suggested.

"They probably wouldn't accept it as truth," David said. "The traditional version is too well known."

Telyn lay back down. "Traditional version," she said, somewhat scornfully. "Sometimes people rely too much on tradition, if you ask me."

"Probably true," Cassie agreed. "But people do generally try their best to remember the truth." The rest of them followed Telyn's example and lay down for a long overdue sleep. Cassie lay by Kai and Dassah, wondering what dreams, if any, would visit her in sleep. She finally allowed the tears she had been holding in all day to come, though silently, as she now had the time to truly grieve over the day's loss. After a time, her thoughts turned naturally from sorrow to prayer. She sent up a prayer for Arthur's healing, and guidance for them as they tried to rescue the prisoners. She gave a lot of thanks for the victory they'd had that day. She lay there for several minutes after she said amen, simply enjoying the presence of God, peace washing over her. Then she rolled over, and was sound asleep within the blink of an eye.

Glossary of Horse Terms

Bay: One of the most common horse colors, a bay horse has a brown body with a black mane and tail. The lower legs are also black, unless there is a white leg marking.

Bit: The mouthpiece of a bridle, with fittings at each end to which the reins are fastened. Used by the rider to control the horse.

Blaze: White facial marking on a horse, resembling a wide stripe running up and down the horse's face between the eyes.

Blue roan: A very rare horse color, with many white hairs mixed into a black coat, making it lighter.

Bridle: Piece of equipment placed on a horse's head for riding, containing the bit and reins that a rider uses to direct the horse.

Canter: A horse's second fastest gait. Each stride is three beats.

Chestnut: Another very common horse color. Brown all over, generally with some reddish tones.

Dam: A horse's mother.

Gallop: A horse's fastest gait. Each stride is four beats.

Gelding: Male horse who cannot make foals.

Girth: Long strap that is fastened around a horse's belly to keep the saddle on.

Halter: Resembling a bridle in basic structure, but with no bit or reins. Used to lead horses when they are not being ridden.

Hand: A unit of measurement used for horses, equal to four inches.

Lipping: When a horse takes a bit of a person's hair with their lips and plays with it.

Mare: Mature, female horse.

Star: Diamond-shaped facial feature between a horse's eyes.

Tack: The equipment used on horses when ridden, including the saddle, girth, and bridle.

Trot: A two-beat gait. Faster and more bouncy than a walk.

Whicker: A soft sound made by a horse, used when calling another horse or a person in close quarters, or used in anticipation of something (generally a treat).

COMING SOON: BOOK 3

FINDING FREEDOM

Cassie's parents remain trapped at the Brother-hood's castle in the present day, but she and her friends are stuck fifteen hundred years in the past – and they now seek to free hundreds of Brenwyd prisoners from that very same ancient castle.

An epic battle ensues in the final book of the *Brenwyd Legacy* trilogy, going beyond the physical with spiritual forces at work on both sides. Much is at stake: the vast treasure store of King Arthur, the personal safety of Cassie and those she holds dear, and the future of all Brenwyds to exist peacefully among other humans.

Cassie has not forgotten the prophecy foretelling her role in the conflict between Brenwyds and their enemies. But with each new challenge that arises, she wonders... Can an ordinary girl like her live up to such an extraordinary destiny?